Praise for SUCKING SHRIMP

'As vivid as a Baz Luhrmann move – *Sucking Shrimp* is trippy without the boring acid flashbacks, just plenty of weird food in aspic' – *The Face*

'Theobald's racy style allied to an invigorating intelligence is entirely seductive ... Glowing descriptions of food, sex and drugs make this almost as good as a trip to Barcelona' – *Marie Claire*

'Stephanie Theobald is a natural storyteller and *Sucking Shrimp* is a perfect meaty read' – *Vogue*

'A vivid tale reminiscent of the cult comedy *Abigail's Party*, this book is a must-read' – *Woman's Journal*

Praise for SUCKING SHRIMP

'Scarily addictive . . . completely mad . . . extravagantly eccentric' – *Express*

'A framework straight out of Tennessee Williams . . . Theobald writes well about the attractions and disappointments teenagers find in Bohemia' – *I-D*

'Stephanie Theobald's prose is clever, elaborate and evocative . . . a writer with a lot of talent' – *Independent on Sunday*

'A refreshing addition to the coming of age genre' – *Attitude*

'Wonderfully readable' – *The List*

Praise for BICHE

'Too intelligent to be a romp, too cynical to be a romance, too funny to be a moral tale ... it's *great fun!*' – Marian Keyes, *Independent*

'Anyone who thinks sex and humour do not mix should read this orgasmic adventure ... Comic, tender and with lashings of rude bits' – *The Times*

'Genuinely evocative and amusing naughty stuff ... A witty, mucky, authentic book, which puts a new and most welcome spin on this Looking-For-The-One genre' – *Evening Standard*

'Fast, sharp and funny' – *Elle*

'Very funny and spectacularly sordid ... *Biche* is like a delicious soufflé sprinkled with minutely observed details ... Highly entertaining' – *Time Out*

Also by Stephanie Theobald

BICHE

About the author

Former fashion editor of *The European,* Stephanie Theobald now lives in London and Spain and writes full-time. Her first novel, *Biche,* was published by Flame in 2000.

SUCKING SHRIMP

Stephanie Theobald

FLAME
Hodder & Stoughton

Grateful acknowledgement is made for permission to reprint excerpts from the following copyrighted material:

Something's Burning, an autobiography by Fanny Cradock (1960); *The Fanny and Johnnie Cradock Cookery Programme* magazine No.54 (1971) and No.7 (1970); *The Cook Hostess' Book* by Fanny Cradock and Johnnie Cradock (1970) by kind permission of the Rosemary Bromley Literary Agency.

Sociable Cook's Book, copyright the *Daily Telegraph*, 1967.

Thanks to Alan Brodie Representation on behalf of the Estate of Noël Coward.

'Ariel' lyrics used by permission of Sweet City Songs Limited and PKM Music.

'Nobody Does It Better'. Words by Carole Bayer Sager. Music by Marvin Hamlisch © 1997 EMI Catalogue Partnership, EMI U Catalog Inc. and EMI United Partnership Ltd, USA. Worldwide print rights controlled by Warner Bros Publications Inc./IMP Ltd. Reproduced by permission of International Music Publications Ltd. All Rights Reserved.

Copyright © 2001 by Stephanie Theobald

First published in Great Britain in 2001 by Hodder and Stoughton
A division of Hodder Headline

The right of Stephanie Theobald to be identified as the Author of the Work has been asserted by her in accordance with the Copyright, Designs and Patents Act 1988.

A Flame Paperback

3 5 7 9 10 8 6 4 2

All rights reserved. No part of this publication may be reproduced, stored in a retrieval system, or transmitted, in any form or by any means without the prior written permission of the publisher, nor be otherwise circulated in any form of binding or cover other than that in which it is published and without a similar condition being imposed on the subsequent purchaser.

All characters in this publication are fictitious and any resemblance to real persons, living or dead, is purely coincidental.

A CIP catalogue record for this title is available from the British Library

ISBN 0 340 76844 4

Typeset in Centaur by Palimpsest Book Production Limited,
Polmont, Stirlingshire
Printed and bound in Great Britain by
Mackays of Chatham plc, Chatham, Kent

Hodder and Stoughton
A division of Hodder Headline
338 Euston Road
London NW1 3BH

For my parents, with love

ACKNOWLEDGEMENTS

Thanks to the following:
To Emma and Mark for giving me a place to finish this book when my horrible landlord chucked me out of my garret at 26 Red Lion Street to convert it into yuppie flats (by the way, does anybody want to sell me a cheap house?), to Robert Ward for the loft space, to Louise France with love always, to Adam Jones for his glass collection, to Alison McNaught for tales of being a hard nut from the Elephant and Castle, to Shireen Jilla for research materials, to Sam Lewis for the enthusiasm, to Frances Farrow, the biggest bloody socialist of all, to Bronwyn Cosgrave for helping her friends out, to Elisabet Quiroga for showing me Spain, to Toni Ollé for being an optimist and a rapscallion, to the fish women at the Boquería market, to the boys at the Hotel Liberty in Sitges, to Peter Rook for the mythology, to Christopher and Nicholas for surviving me, to Elaine Copas for being a precocious 11 year old, to Mary Pachnos my special agent, to Phil Pride my editor for her words and her enigmatic silences.

A few final points: no Ma, this mother is not you. Also, regarding references to things like *The Big Time* TV programme and the existence of beaches in Barcelona in 1983, time lines might be slightly wonky but it reads better that way.

Thanks to fantastic Fanny Cradock (and guess what, she left her estate to Help A Child To See, a charity for blind children, so she wasn't so bad after all).

Special thanks to K who kept me going when the Mediterranean wasn't enough. xxxx

'I have taken to cooking and listening to Wagner, both of which frighten me to death'

Noël Coward, 1956

Chapter One

The Sanchez family lives by the sea. Who is the father? The father is called Paco and the mother is Carmen. Paco is on the beach where he paints his boat. Carmen is in the kitchen where she prepares soup, potatoes, tomatoes and fruit. The son of Paco is called Miguel and the daughter is Maria. Miguel is in the garden where he studies a book. Maria works with her mother in the kitchen.

My name is Rosa Barge. I am fourteen years old. My mother is called Brenda. She hates the kitchen. Her idea of a special meal is boiled brisket in tinned oxtail soup gravy. She hates abroad. When she was a child and she went out in the sun without wearing a hat, her mother would confine her to a dark room for three days with strips of raw beef all over her face.

A shadow falls over my desk and there is the smell of hot Christmas cake. A man with a moist mouth puts a pale hand on my exercise book and fills it with a row of neat red ticks. Ten out of ten for the *familia* Sanchez translation and only a little less for my own autobiography. The man makes a giblety smile and says, 'Nice one, Rosa.' Mr Jones, our Spanish teacher with lips like open-heart surgery and a body soaked in Old Spice, has just graduated from Reading University. He wants to be our friend.

It seems to be working. Most of the girls feel completely at ease about spending the lesson applying mascara while Nikki Kilroy, who recently went on a package holiday to Spain with his parents, entertains his friends with English translations of the Spanish he picked up there: 'What the cunt do you think you're doing? I shit on God, do you understand? I shit on the mother who gave birth to you, you son of a prostitute, I shit in the milk.'

It is so noisy in the classroom that nobody can even hear Mr Jones read out my near-perfect autobiography. 'Now, this is very interesting,' he says, picking up my book and trying to get the attention of the class. 'Interesting!' he shouts towards the Kilroy corner. Spit flies off his lips and lands on my desk. He gives up.

'Lively lot, aren't they, *Rosa*?' He shrugs shyly, bringing a chair to the side of my desk. Sometimes Mr Jones pronounces my name in the Spanish fashion: *Rrrrosa,* which means 'rose' in Spanish. It sounds like he is crushing the air with a lash of the tongue on a palate made hard by vibrations of steel, and for those few seconds he is no longer a damp English weed called Mr Jones and I am no longer a stupid English rose in dolly-mixture colours.

He is a gravelly Mexican bandit and I am a machine-gun rose called *Rrrrrrrrrrosssssa.*

He grips my exercise book in his hands and launches into a live translation of my Spanish composition.

'*Mi madre se llama Brenda,*' he begins, in deep, rich tones, and already I hear the drumming of hoofs coming from somewhere far off. I stare at the page until my eyes go funny and the words start breaking up and flying around on the paper like a red hall of mirrors. The soft gentility of 'days' and 'meat' and 'abroad' get tossed up in the air as a stampede of red Spanish horses gallops through the middle of them, thrashing them into '*días*' and '*carne*' and '*extranjero*' as Mr Jones mouths them. He cracks open hot juicy husks of sound and releases molten spurts of double Rs and hissing Ss and, best of all, pickaxe Js that sound like live hearts torn from ribcages: '*No quiere ir al extranjero. Si salía al sol, su madre la encerraba en su habitación durante tres días . . .*' More bloody-tendrilled vowels claw their way out of the wet tonsil cave and twist their red, tangled roots round the white, clumsy blob of 'Brenda'. The hoofs are getting louder, the horses are pounding in my throat, coming closer and closer and closer, and there is dust and drums and glittering metal, and when Mr Jones says, '*Muy bien, hija,*' with the throat-scraping, kettle-descaling, death rattle J of '*hija*' – *eeeee-hhhhhhhha* – I jig in my seat, I pick up my compass and I stab Jack in the kidneys.

Jack makes a puppy yelp. Mr Jones stands up and is on the verge of saying something about the small red clot he can see oozing through the back of Jack's white shirt. Then he sees what Jack has written in his homework exercise book: 'Sir, you have lips like a freshly cut peach.'

Mr Jones puts his hand in front of his mouth, pretends to cough and then decides that the shark pool of Nikki Kilroy and his friends is more tempting than Jack Flowers in fullest courtship mode. You can't blame him really. When Mr Jones joined St Dougal's at the beginning of term, he entered the room to the fanfare of Jack Flowers shouting, 'Backs to the wall, boys! Backs to the wall!' in his best John Inman from *Are You Being Served?* voice. Then, when he asked Jack what his name was, Jack said he was called Fanny Nancy Plum Caramel Dolores Ramona Shirley Whisky Norwood.

As the weeks pass Mr Jones has been getting redder and redder, damper and damper. Not that this deters Jack. He usually gives Mr Jones a Shirley Bassey wink every time he addresses him, although his best efforts are saved for Nikki Kilroy. Nikki Kilroy is the best-looking boy in the class. He often has a tan from the package holidays his parents take him on. A package holiday means a holiday with a plane ride, a hotel, a swimming-pool and rings of squid in batter for your meals, all included. Sometimes on the way home from school I look in the window of Broad Horizons, the travel agent's. Alongside the posters advertising shopping excursions to Plymouth and Away Day trips on the Portsmouth–Le Havre ferry, there are brochures advertising foreign destinations for summer '79 such as the Costa del Sol and the Costa Brava. These are advertised with pictures on the front such as sunsets and palm trees and men who look like Nikki Kilroy spreading suntan oil on girls in bikinis who look like Fiona P.

Jack says that Nikki Kilroy really likes him but Jack is lying. Jack usually has to make do with Connor, a fat boy with a bulging eye.

'Where have you been?' I say.

'Behind the rifle range,' he goes.

'What did you do?' I say.

'Be better if he had a bath once in a while,' he says with a smirk. Jack is famous for his smirks.

I prod Jack again with the compass and get him to pass over Fiona P's autobiography while she's over in the other side of the classroom, giggling in the Kilroy corner. I note with satisfaction that she's written her usual drivel:

My name is Fiona P and I am really popular. My favourite things are: my black corduroy knickerbockers, my eyes cos they look flirty, chocolate, my diary of course, 'We Don't Talk Any More' by Cliff Richard, Nikki Kilroy – the boy who dumped me but then agreed to go out with me again and I love him – and the gold cross necklace my nan gave me.

She has illustrated this sad piece of writing with practice signings of her new autograph: 'Fiona Kilroy'. It is written in neat handwriting because she is shallow. I never practise neat handwriting. I practise putting accents over my name. Sometimes I am Rosá Barge and sometimes I am Roça Bargé but my favourite is being ¡Rosé Barcaza! because rosé is a type of French wine that Jack's mother Mrs Flowers likes and *barcaza* is Spanish for 'barge' and because in Spain you need two exclamation marks and one of them has to spin round and stand on its head.

Fiona P is always predictable. She's just got one line – 'You've got a mouth bigger than the river Tamar, Rosa Barge' – that she uses whenever she feels bad about being a dummy. 'You've got a mouth bigger than the river Tamar, Rosa Barge,' she'll say after the Spanish class, when yet again I've answered all the questions right. 'You've got a mouth bigger than the river Tamar, Rosa Barge,' she'll huff, when I outwit her in the changing room.

'You're not "mature",' she says after netball one day.

'What do you mean, I'm "not mature"?' I say.

'*I*'m mature,' she says, tossing her blonde hair back in that pathetic way. 'Sally's mature, Christine's mature. But you're not. You're not mature in the slightest.'

She is flanked by Sally and Christine, her two henchmen. They are pretty rough pieces of work. Sally is seeing a fireman (so she says) and Christine claims to be seeing someone who used to be in prison. She boasts about going to visit him in his squat at weekends and every Monday morning she turns up at school with a necklace of love bites just below her ears. Jack's mother, Mrs Flowers, lent me *Valley of the Dolls* by Jacqueline Susann so I know exactly what 'mature' means. It's all about grinding bones and bloodbaths and pieces of membrane falling out into the sheets.

'Plus,' Fiona P says, adjusting her flick, 'you haven't even got the five holes.' She pulls her gym skirt up and starts turning round and round in a slow circle – like a fancy revolving cake in a glass cabinet – pointing out the five holes as she goes. 'One between the ankles, one by the calves, one by the knees . . .' It's like she's reciting her two times table '. . . one in the middle of the thigh and one . . . one up here.'

She points to the tiny dark triangle between her regulation blue nylon knickers and the very tops of her thighs. 'These are the legs you're supposed to have. Not elephant's trunks like yours.'

I can feel myself blushing at the sight of Fiona P's dark triangle (I hate it when I blush) but I save myself in the nick of time. 'There are more important things in life than boyfriends,' I go.

'At least I've got one,' she goes. 'What sort of girl are you? A lezee?'

'What sort of girl are you? A thickee?'

'My mother said that Winston Churchill was a dud at school and look where he ended up.'

'Your mother was trying to make you feel better for being a thickee.'

'Winston Churchill was better than you!'

'Winston Churchill was a bloody fascist!'

'You've got a mouth bigger than the river Tamar, Rosa Barge!'

I am actually a bit nervous of the changing rooms. Being plump with red hair and a brace is not the ideal appearance

I would have chosen for myself (although Mrs Flowers tells me that my hair isn't red. It's auburn leaf, she says). Plus I have a thin network of blue veins over my breasts ever since they started to grow and I have stretch-marks on my hips, even though I haven't given birth to any children. I think maybe this is because my weight goes up and down a lot. Sometimes I eat nothing for about two weeks and then I get hungry and have to eat a lot. Sometimes I can do my Wrangler jeans up at the top quite easily and sometimes I have to lie down on the bed with a coat-hanger in the zip to pull them up. Sometimes I have to wear my horrible Laura Ashley skirt with an elasticated waist.

The other thing that gets noticed in the changing room is the fact that I have a few red marks on my neck and they are not love bites. They are flea bites and I get them because I live above my father's pasty shop and fishermen and the men from the lifeboat bring them in on their clothes. Personally I don't mind the fleas too much because it means you get to have flea baths on a regular basis. For a flea bath, you pour Dettol into the bathtub instead of bubble bath and then you lie in the water with all your clothes on until the flea drowns. Lying in water with all your clothes on is almost as good as being a cabin-boy at sea. I have always liked the idea of being Tom the cabin-boy from *Captain Pugwash* because you would be sailing into the horizon as a full-time job. You would scrub the decks every morning in bare feet; cut-off jeans and a stripy top, and sometimes you would try to escape by diving into the deep blue sea with all your clothes still on. (I already have the stripy top.

Mrs Flowers gave it to me. It comes from St Tropez in the South of France, which is where the French actress Brigitte Bardot lives.)

Being in water with clothes on is an unusual situation. It means that something is going to happen. In water with your clothes on you are on alert at all times. It's like the chairs game in kindergarten. Red, purple, orange, green, twenty chairs in total placed in a circle in the middle of the room. Then the words, 'Everyone on a purple chair,' or 'Everyone on a red chair,' and then the lucky few gathering in the middle of the room for the dance to match the seat. It seemed like anything could happen. It seemed like the possibility of endless possibilities. You could try pinching someone or pushing them off their purple chair because you wanted it, but then the purple chairs might be called up to do the sailor song ('Three sailors went to sea, sea, sea to see what they could see, see, see . . .'), complete with silly looking-out-to-the-horizon hand gestures. You'd realise that you couldn't cheat it. You had to wait and see what cards were dealt to you. The purple chair and the white-horse song were the best destinies. A bunch of lucky four-year-olds, cantering round in a circle singing:

'I want to be a cowboy, a cowboy, a cowboy,
I want to be a cowboy and ride a white horse,
I'd trot and I'd gallop all over the prairie,
I want to be a cowboy and ride a white horse.'

Hot and roused, you'd go back to thump down in your

chair, waiting for the next shuffle, waiting for the next thing to happen – dreaming of cowboys, cattle rustlers, prowlers, highway bandits.

I like being different. Once on TV I saw a film where an impostor chef found his way into the kitchen. He drank lots of sherry and ended up making a cake by pouring lots of ridiculous ingredients into a pot, including spaghetti and sugar and bananas, chilli powder, chocolate biscuits, sardines, cold tea, grated cheese, snails, curry and the rest of the bottle of sherry. The first person to try a piece of the cake didn't explode with disgust or have chilli fire streaming out of his ears. He just licked his lips a few times and pulled a string of spaghetti from between his teeth with a puzzled, interested look on his face.

I'm not at all scared of being the odd one out. In fact, the only bad thing about about living above Oggies is that my school uniform smells of pasties while, as Fiona P likes to point out, Nikki Kilroy's smells of chlorine. Nikki Kilroy is rich because his parents own a chain of knackers' yards and they have a swimming-pool in their house. 'They're called abattoirs, actually,' Fiona P always says. Most of the time I don't care about Fiona P. The river Tamar is as far as she is going to get. Fiona P believes that her true parents are rich, good-looking people who will come forward one day to reclaim her and reveal to her that she is, in fact, a fairytale princess. I don't believe I have the wrong parents. I believe that I was born in the wrong country.

I dream of escape all the time. My favourite thing is to sit on the top of my bunk bed with my atlas on my knees and the brim of a jungle hat – the one my father used in the National Service in Malaya – pulled over my head like blinkers so you can't see my face. My hair gets flattened and I'm just a huge head, one big octopus brain, just me and the world. The atlas has smooth, shiny pages like blue glacé cherries. I run my hands over the large, cool maps, over the lands and the seas, and I sniff the air like a wolf. But then, if the window is open, all I can smell is the extractor pipe from downstairs mixing with wafts of rancid oil from the Chinese restaurant next door. Or seagulls the size of toddlers will land on my window-sill and start screeching – like they're rubbing my nose in it about how they can fly around wherever they want – and I look down in despair only to see sacks of flour and catering packs of baked beans stacked nearly to the ceiling (my bedroom doubles as the Oggies' store room). So I think of rafts and Tom the cabin-boy and escape – until my fantasy is interrupted by the clatter of the staff downstairs:

''ansum piece of skirt, Lil!'

'Young bugger, I'll tan your ass!'

'Nice juicy bit of skirt!'

'Young bugger, I'll tan your ass!'

'I'll let ee touch me oggies!'

'You'll bloody feel the back of me 'and!'

I try to keep optimistic by remembering people who have managed to break out. Like the children in the book called *Flowers in the Attic* by Virginia Andrews. They made an imprint of the attic key in a bar of soap and then carved a new one from wood so they could get out whenever they wanted. Or like Steve McQueen in *The Great Escape* who wore American trousers called chinos to get away from the camp on his motorbike. Or Steve McQueen in *Papillon*, jumping off the cliff fully clothed with a lilo made of floatable coconut shells because he was so desperate to flee. Or Clint Eastwood in *Escape from Alcatraz*, catching beetles and cockroaches in his cell, squeezing their blood into a cup and drinking it to keep his strength up in preparation for the big day.

When I come back home after school I have to walk though Oggies and hear the kitchen-boys snigger as I go past, and the older women coo, 'Had a good day at school, my bird?' (the stupidest question in the world), and my father giving pasty information to some tourist customer. 'The corners of a proper Cornish pasty are traditionally crimped tight so the devil can't get in,' he'll be saying over the counter, in his embarrassing yokel accent. I climb the stairs, heading for my bedroom like a prisoner in striped pyjamas in *Escape from Alcatraz* marching back to his cell after slop-out. Or like Tom the cabin-boy coming up from the hold after my lunch of maggoty biscuits and dried pork and a squeeze of lime on my gums. Back up the slippery wooden steps to do deck-scrubbing duties as a man with rotten teeth and a rum-fattened stomach towers over me, shouting, 'Put your back into it, lad!' And then finally, when I'm exhausted, I keel over on deck under the burning sun with my stripy arms above me and my tanned legs with tiny hairs called cilia splayed out on the side and I lift my head up to utter my final words on earth, 'I'm . . . dead.'

My contempt (scorn) for pasties has been good for the development of my mind. I know that a catering-pack-of-beans raft is never going to get me anywhere. Strange food, on the other hand, is a perfect substitute for foreign travel.

I started off with crabs and pomegranates and rice paper, progressed on to pancakes with maple syrup (from the Little Chef on the way to Bournemouth) and then stumbled across chocolate spread and peanut butter (at Mrs Flowers' house). I tried experiments, eating dog biscuits and baby food (Rhubarb and Cream Summer Dessert sounded more promising than it was), and human blood. One day, my tooth came out during a mouthful of Brenda's Cadbury's Smash cottage pie. It was the first time her food had tasted of anything interesting. Sort of chickeny. A chickeny, frightening flavour.

Fanny Cradock is the most frightening of all. She makes green-coloured brandy butter and mauve mashed potatoes and whole boned salmons covered with individual cucumber scales and piped-in eyes and fins. I have collected her complete works – all her magazines, all her books, and I have tracked all the events of her life in my Fanny Cradock scrap book.

Once, for the Ideal Home exhibition at the Olympia in London she made the Taj Mahal in Italian meringue and in one of the issues of her magazine she showed you how to make a velvet-lined box for the ideal storage of Melba toast.

She used to do cooking performances at the Royal Albert Hall wearing ballgowns and diamond bracelets and white fur capes. Cooking is a cleanly and creative art, she says, not a grubby chore. The apron is therefore a sign of shame and she advises cooks to stand in the third ballet position when they are at the oven. In this pose you are concave instead of convex when you bend over the hotplates and there should be no dirt on you at the end of your session. I like cooking because if you cook you get to eat more food than you normally would be allowed, which is good. But the main thing about Fanny Cradock is that she is beyond cooking. Fanny Cradock's cookery books are as spiky and bloody as Spanish. She uses words like 'tragedy' ('It is a tragedy that in England pigeon breasts are so little appreciated') and makes references to death ('If you are faced with a whole pineapple, your hostess should be shot') and torture ('Lobsters should not be dismembered while still alive since this causes involuntary muscle contraction and toughens the flesh'). She tells you that the Romans liked to watch carp roasted live over hot coals so that they could first extract sexual pleasure from its death agonies before eating its flesh. When you see her on TV she speaks in a deep, raspy voice, like she smokes a lot of cigarettes. Just like Mrs Flowers.

I told Mrs Flowers that Fanny Cradock says sex is like watching a fish die slowly. She said it depended.

At school during lunch-break I usually walk alone to the furthest end of the hockey pitch (walking like John Travolta in *Saturday Night Fever*), with my unfinished novel under my arm. It is called *A Star in Faded Jeans*. It is about a girl called Jade who is born into poverty and who travels the world having adventures. It is not easy to write as I haven't been anywhere or done anything. My weekly magazine, *The Joy of Knowledge*, is hopeless on local colour. (Rome: city of many beautiful churches and the great religious centre of the Roman Catholic Church. Ireland: population of Dublin 568,772, capital of the republic of Ireland. Denmark: rain every season. Good for the dairying industry. West Germany: the river Rhine is a corridor through Europe. Amsterdam: the world centre of the diamond cutting and polishing industry with important banking, insurance and ship-owning interests.)

Because of my lack of experience abroad, most of Jade's adventures are based on Fanny Cradock's writings. Jade is always being given warm baguettes fresh out of the oven. She is often taken aside by rustic old men in the Dordogne and hotel *patrons* in Paris and the Duc de Rothschild's cook and given secret information about truffle omelettes, chocolate gâteaux and rare quiches. She went to the Caribbean and gathered armfuls of coconuts from the beach. Then she went to Greece and met a man called Socrates who watered his lettuces with wine. In Rome she learnt how the Italians used to grow rose-flavoured melons by planting the seeds in tubs of decomposed rose petals. In France she once made a steamed chocolate pudding – it was English but that was all right because it was for a writer called Somerset Maugham and it was in his villa in a place by the sea called the Côte d'Azur. In Ibiza, an island off the eastern coast of Spain, she was 'presented with a huge pile of transparently thin dried ham which looked like a dish of autumn leaves'. Jade also eats Spanish prawns – called *gambas* – as well as octopus, which I make her find as exciting as eating the Loch Ness monster.

Sometimes, to give me inspiration for *A Star in Faded Jeans*, I write out the lyrics of Dean Friedman songs in the back of my file. Nobody else in the class has even heard of him. I like Dean Friedman because he's the antithesis (the opposite) of Cliff Richard. Dean Friedman is an American and his words are completely different from English. The words in 'Ariel' go, 'I started foolin' around with the vertical hold, we got the munchies and we made some spaghetti.' Fooling around is an American way of saying sexual intercourse. Munchies is when you are hungry after you have smoked a cigarette with a green plant called marijuana sprinkled in it. Smoking these cigarettes makes you feel 'high', which means happy. They also make you feel hungry and like fooling around. All of these things I have learnt from Mrs Flowers, who is the only person who understands me. Fanny Cradock and Mrs Flowers both fill me with knowledge of human experience (an acquired taste which I imagine to be similar to the dangerous flavour of olives or blue cheese or milk-tooth blood).

* * *

Nikki Kilroy puts his hand up and asks if class is over yet. Mr Jones smiles his sticky smile. '*Ojalá*,' he says, loosening his tie.

'*Ojalá!*' There it is again. The J sound. The deepest glottal gasp of all. *Oh-hhhhhhhhhha-lá. Modern Day Spanish* says that '*ojalá*' survives from the time when the Moors ruled Spain. *Oh-ha-lá* means 'to Allah' but now it means anything from 'would that you would' to 'would that it were', and 'I would that you weren't' to 'someday maybe'.

Oh-hhhhhhhhhha-lá is quite a dreamy thing to say. You can say it when you are looking into the distance – at a beautiful sunset over the sea, for instance – and you are thinking of all the beautiful things that might have been or that still might be. Funny, then, that the sound is so violent – a sound that hacks and butchers – like a cattle-rustler tightening a rope around the neck of a baby calf, or a body-snatcher smashing a jar to get at the deformed foetus inside or a Moor in the Alhambra slicing the head off an infidel with a glittering scimitar and the severed egg falling into a golden fountain and turning dark as steak.

Some day I will eat octopus.

Chapter Two

The English lady says, 'For heaven's sake, don't make a scene. Just pay the bill and we'll go.'

The French woman makes a scene and enjoys it. The French man naturally enjoys it too. He is delighted. What good is a woman for making love if she lacks the temperament for even one small scene?

Something's Burning, an autobiography by Fanny Cradock

It is Jack's fourteenth birthday party and I am being sucked alive into the cakey oesophagus of a dead old lady.

Oesophagus. Sarcophagus. Lobster Pot.

The waitress doesn't even know how to pronounce *mille-feuille*. I think I might suffocate. 'Meal-phew-ee?' She clatters at the helm of a hostess trolley set about with Eccles cakes, fruit scones, sherry trifle and a funeral slab of puff pastry daubed with white icing. The trifle makes an eggy burp as she digs out the first portion and when that stops all you can hear in the tea-room tomb is an uneasy silence punctuated by the sound of ripping saliva and cakey chewing in sticky old mouths.

'Sounds some fancy, my lover,' a ruddy man with a thick Cornish accent whispers to the waitress with the face of a squashed currant bun. 'All the same,' he winks to the three other people sitting round the table, 'reckon it'll be four cream teas and a pint of shrimps.'

A gooey, buttercream smile slurps over her face and the grubby white cap on her head flaps slightly as she sinks the cake slice into a moist Victoria sponge.

Moist Victoria sponge! Clotted-cream tea! Cake slice! I am going to turn green and huge and burst out of my clothes and kill everyone. Burst through my horrible English skin – skin as heavy as the dead air in the Lobster Pot, dead as skin that's been dredged up months later from the bottom of a lake, ancient as the woman sitting next to me with the loo-brush hair and the face of a tough old carrot.

'Gracious!' the woman exclaims (she is so tough that white shoots are sprouting out of the side of her cheek. She has literally gone to seed). 'Gracious!' she exclaims. 'Frangipane flan. Just the ticket!'

The fruit scone lodges in my throat like a fur ball and I am buried deep down at the bottom of the lake, trapped in an airtight Quality Street cake tin smelling of stale frangipane flan. How this is like a slow death to sit here eating cream tea on a stuffy June afternoon. Splitting scones with a silver knife, spreading with butter from a pat, strawberry jam from a white china pot with a china bee on the lid and finally the dollop of clotted cream on top for the final nail in the coffin. No chance of anything exotic in the Lobster Pot. Just the chance of being buried alive by a ton of Battenburgs, butterfly buns, oatmeal parkins, fruited cobblestones, coconut pyramids, ginger sponges, lemon tarts, cream horns and more frangipane flan.

I want to hurt somebody.

'I want some devil's food cake!'

The waitress doesn't often come across bad behaviour in the tea room. You can tell because she starts rocking the hostess trolley back and forth like a nervous nanny. 'Dear life,' she stutters, 'devil's food cake? Don't have that here, my bird. Bit fancy reelly.' And she tries to catch the eye of the Cornishman – my father – for some support.

Only the bristly-faced woman – my mother – gets in there first: 'No need for fancy food!' she blusters, with such energy that her carrot whiskers shudder from side to side. She turns to my father and says, 'Now, you'll agree with me when I say this: there's nothing wrong with good plain cooking!'

My mother knows all about plain cooking. Her favourite meal is a slice of ham, a tomato and some lettuce leaves followed by a tin of pineapple chunks and some evaporated milk. Evap, she calls it. 'Nothing better than a bit of evap,' she'll say, and I'll get that exploding feeling again and shout something like '*Hija de puta!*' *Eee-ha day poo-tar* – which means 'daughter of a prostitute' in Spanish. She won't know what it means so she'll just follow it up with something like 'Bravo, Rosa. *Ira furor brevis est,*' and I'll sulk because she never wants to fight with me. When things are getting tense she'll just say something in Latin. Not even banquet Latin, not gaming-and-drinking Latin or dancing-girls-from-Cádiz Latin. She speaks Latin with that brisk, cold-shower Edinburgh accent, which is miles away from Fall-of-Rome Latin, Caligula Latin, reaching-out-for-lumps-of-meat-and-gorging-on-spitted-calf's-head-and-baked-dormouse Latin.

My mother, or Brenda as I call her, puts good food in the same category as Winston Churchill, the Royal Family and what she calls 'crêpe de Chine accents'. She thinks it is the fault of the Catholics that I have been taken over by the evil spirit of *cuisine*, although of course she is wrong. (She deeply regrets that there are no Presbyterian options on the Mousehole schooling front.) When I bring my Fanny Cradock food back from the domestic science class she goes off into waste-not-want-not overdrive or she relates the caul story for the umpteenth time. The one about how her grandmother from Dumfriesshire sold the bit of skin that was growing over her father's face at birth to a sea captain for five pounds because they were so poor. 'Granny G, she sold it for five pounds – a lot of money in those days. Every captain wanted a caul because it meant that the ship would never sink. Rare is the child who has a caul growing on his face at birth.'

I never met my grandfather but whenever I think of him it is always with a thin sliver of membrane over his face like an alien from *Star Trek*. Another monster in the family.

The waitress asks me if there's anything else I'd like apart from devil's food cake, and I say, 'Just a vomit bucket.'

Brenda lets me get away with a lot because she calls herself a free-thinker. 'Redder than the blood I am,' she is always saying, in her dark and stormy voice. She even likes me calling her Brenda (although I only do so because I'm embarrassed about anyone thinking she might be my mother).

A free-thinker means that up until the age of forty-seven she tried to convert the world to 'universal socialism'. John Knox is at the top of her list of interests. ('Education over religion. He was a believer but he said it; "education over religion".') John Knox is an excuse for everything. When I ask her why she feels it necessary to wear trousers made of fabric like the texture of cold, overcooked cabbage she brings in John Knox. 'He didn't dress up,' she intones. 'He turned down the Catholic ministerial robes. Christ didn't dress up so why should a minister?'

When Brenda failed to convert the world to universal socialism she gave in to the advances of my father – a regular customer at the Lyons' Corner House in London where she worked as a waitress – and when she failed to convert him she had me.

She is now fifty-nine years old – not exactly a vibrant age for a sparky fourteen-year-old like myself.

'Devil's food cake is American,' I inform the waitress. 'In

America they have frosting and brownies. They call biscuits "cookies".'

'Americans!' Brenda is off. 'Fat lot of good they did for us during the war! Lloyd George called Britain a country fit for heroes. More like a country fit for down-and-outs!'

The cakey munches of the other customers grind to a halt but my mother is forging ahead. She thinks the waitress is really interested in her views on Winston Churchill, 'The biggest bloody fascist of all!' and Nye Bevan, 'The Welsh! Never trust a druid!' and how the only worthwhile nationality apart from the Scots are the Russians.

'You know where I'd like to go to die?' she fumes at the waitress (who hopes my mother will die on her chair, right here in the Lobster Pot). 'Nishnakov! The most habitable place in central Siberia. It was so cold there that they had to . . .' She jogs her arms up and down to show how things were in central Siberia in the 1920s. 'It's how they developed the Russian ballet,' she says. 'Best in the world, isn't it, the Russian ballet? The Russians, they had to fight in blood for revolution. Your generation,' she wags her finger at the waitress, 'your generation must have evolution for revolution.'

The waitress squints at my mother through two frightened little currants before turning to my father. He is trying to pretend everything is normal by staring at the slice of Victoria sponge in the middle of the table like he's having a telepathic conversation with it. It is only when Jack picks up a handful of shrimps and puts them down the front of his trousers, saying, 'You are awful but I like you,' in his best Dick Emery impersonation voice, that my mother is stunned into silence.

The fact that Jack's mind is starting to hurtle out of control is fine by me. Actually, it is exciting and embarrassing by turns but the point is I am offering it up for Mrs Flowers. Both she and Mr Flowers have gone off to Spain for a holiday and I have agreed to look after Jack for his fourteenth birthday. I am only too pleased to be helping Mrs Flowers and I think I am helping her because as far as I can make out she too is embarrassed by her son and likes to be away from him as much as she can. I don't blame her for preferring Spain to him.

I don't mind too much about babysitting Jack because there are some good things about him. One of the good things is that he makes my parents uneasy. His trick is that he appears normal-ish and then he says or does something really odd, which makes you do a double-take or blush or cringe or want to snort with laughter. You can tell that my mother is not happy with the idea of a boy who colours his eyebrows blue with felt-tip pen. Nothing in her books on universal socialism and 'The Common Man' has prepared her for someone like Jack. Her strategy is to be impeccably polite with him.

'So, Jack,' she says, dabbing the cream from the corner of her mouth as if she hasn't seen what Jack has done, 'how's school coming along?'

'How are my lips coming along more like, Mrs Barge.'

He picks up a shrimp from the shrimp plate, pulls off the head and dabs yellow and brown brain juice all over his mouth.

It is at this point that my father starts to look a bit concerned. Not for Jack's sanity but for his own Lobster Pot tea. He is worried that his sandwich filling is going to end up down Jack's trousers rather than on the buttered slice of Mother's Pride he has been ploughing with columns of carefully peeled shrimps. He still needs a couple more rows.

At least my father takes more interest in his food than my mother. Unfortunately his interest is limited to Cornish crabs, shrimps and, above all, pasties. The first time I remember him ever addressing me, it was to point out interesting facts about the Cornish pasty. 'Miners took 'em down the tin mines, Rosa. Meat in one end, jam in t'other. Fishermen, mind, no more take one to sea than they'd mention rabbits or go fishing after meeting a clergyman on their way to the boat.'

I know all there is to know about pasties: the pastry must be one half fat to flour, the meat must come from a part of the cow's diaphragm known as the 'skirt', the skirt must be cut and never minced, the vegetables must be sliced and never cubed and the swede – or turnip, as it is known in Cornwall – is an optional ingredient. The only time my father ever comments about world events is to look over the top of the *Western Morning News* of an evening and fill me in on the front-page splash. 'I don't know, Rosa,' he'll say, taking off his reading glasses. 'First prize in some Best Cornish Pasty competition awarded to something with carrots and peas in!' He'll put his glasses back on, shake his head with a smile and say, 'What's the world coming to, eh, Rosa?'

Six days a week my father is down at Oggies at six in the morning, chopping up skirt, slicing turnip, crimping pastry, and only comes upstairs at midnight when the last wooden work surface has been scrubbed, the last floor tile bleached and the final testosterone-charged lifeboatman been sent on his way. Only infrequently will he allow himself a day off when Brenda drags him out for a 'special occasion', like for my fourteenth-birthday party three months ago or like today, June 10, for Jack's. Under such circumstances we always come to the Lobster Pot and my father always immerses himself in shrimps or crab. He never normally says anything apart from something like, 'Good news, Rosa. I've discovered a new place for white meat!' as he pokes a skewer into a jagged shard of crab shell with the expert eyes of a watch-mender.

Right now, though, I wonder what he's going to say about Jack's lipstick. What he says finally is, 'Dear life, Jack, you're gonna get some fishy down there, boy,' and he subtly ups his stripped-shrimp production before it's too late – pinching off heads, nipping off tails, pulling legs from underbellies, levering pink armour from backs – at a new rate of five seconds for each shrimp.

Jack sends his hand back down into his trousers, rubs

around in his crotch for a while, brings up his hand again, sniffs it and thrusts it in front of Brenda's nose. 'Kentucky Fried Chicken! Bargain Bucket! Baked beans included!'

Brenda drops the clotted-cream spoon on the floor. 'Jam tarts!' she exclaims, jumping in her seat. She is trying to pretend that everything is normal.

I don't see why everyone is getting so worked up. Traumatic mealtimes are nothing new to us. At home, they either take place in silence, with Brenda occasionally making comments to my father prefaced by 'Now, you'll agree with me when I say this . . .' or my father and I will have Brydie and Mary inflicted on us.

Brydie and Mary are the two waitresses my mother used to work with in the Lyons' Corner House. By day she would work with Brydie and Mary, and by night she would attend meetings thrown by the Socialism Society at Conway Hall where members would get basic instruction on becoming a free-thinker.

You'd have thought that having a redder-than-the-blood mother would have been an interesting asset. That at least it would be something if Brenda had an interesting line on the world as it is today in 1979. If she had something to say about Margaret Thatcher, Britain's first woman prime minister who was elected last month. Or it would be good if she forbade me to go to Spain because, four years after his death, she continued to bear a grudge against a fascist dictator called Generalíssimo Francisco Franco. But her low opinion of Spain is prompted more by the attitude of the washer-upper in the kitchen at the Lyons' Corner House during the war. 'Shambles, the Spaniard. Washed the plates in one sink, rinsed them in the next. Run out of hot water by lunch-time!'

Brenda's grasp on world politics is not good. She does occasionally refer to our new Prime Minister as 'Margaret Thatcher, milk snatcher', because she remembers the time when, as Minister for Education, Margaret Thatcher stopped free milk for children. But all that happened ages ago. What's more, she only recently learnt that Franco wasn't some Latino matinée idol. She never went for the Che Guevara/No Pasarán/May 1968/feminist invasion of the Miss World contest end of left-wing politics. Apart from the vaguely radical step of naming me after a German political activist called Rosa Luxemburg (she nearly called me Joan – of d'Arc fame), we never had any intense Frenchmen with wispy ponytails and espadrilles popping in to discuss the nature of liberty, or any women with unconventional haircuts ordering us to take off our bras. We got Mary and Brydie. To them my mother was Che Guevara, Jean-Paul Sartre and Val Doonican rolled into one because both of them followed Brenda down from London to Mousehole in Cornwall a couple of years back.

They are both Irish, which makes them emmits. An emmit is a foreigner – a Spaniard, a Russian, a Scot, a Londoner, a Bristolian, anyone who's not from Cornwall. Even though I was born in Cornwall I am still an emmit because of Brenda.

'If I'm a foreigner, why am I still stuck here, then?' I want to shout at anyone who'll listen.

I don't know why anyone would want to be Cornish anyway. Most of the people in Mousehole (pronounced Mao-zol as in the Chairman) look like they came out of a Charles Dickens novel. They look like pieces of gristle from my father's pasties. They have hunched shoulders and limps, as if they've been eating rat poison all their lives. I go round saying, 'The horror, the horror,' which is a line from a book called *Heart of Darkness* by Joseph Conrad – which most people don't read until they get to the sixth form – about a man in the jungle who goes mad because life is so shallow.

What happens when Mary and Brydie come round to our house is that Mary's cheeks go flushed after one glass of Harvey's Bristol Cream and she's off, whispering about her pig husband through her rabbit teeth. 'He's a great man – intelligent and all,' she mumbles into her stone-cold chipped bowl filled with prunes clogged in warm tinned custard, 'but his moods . . . it can ruin your day, isn't it, Brenda?'

Brenda's face will turn granite and her eyes – normally like grey jelly with tinned fruit cocktail sunk to the bottom – will cloud over like a loch on a cold day and she will boom, 'Mary! If you don't mind me saying, you're a very submissive woman!' Mary, who smells of soggy digestives, will nod rapidly in agreement and suck her rabbit teeth and try to change the subject by going back to the tea-house: 'J. Lyon and Co. – we couldn't have had a better employer, could we, Brenda?'

But Brenda's face will remain stony, which is a cue for Brydie to start talking about her latest bridge outing. 'You should follow my lead, Mary. Since John died I've done what they call, thingummy, "go out again in society".'

In her prime Brydie was a real beauty, according to my mother. Now, she likes to use Brydie as an illustration of what a waste of time bodies are and how, at the end of the day, you're better off looking like an old carrot. 'Could have had any man she wanted,' she hisses, in her dark-and-stormy-night voice. 'Then, one day, she met an Englishman. Michael. Came in for the two-shilling bacon-and-egg breakfast. Came from a toffee-nosed English family. Took her back to meet his parents. Disapproved, of course. Crêpe de Chine, you see. Broken she was. Took to the drink after that.'

Brydie can certainly handle her Harvey's Bristol Cream better than Mary. 'Course, that's not to say we don't, thingummy, gamble at bridge,' she says, pouring herself a quick top-up. 'It's more exciting when you gamble, isn't it?' She downs a big sip then turns to Brenda, tops her up, then all three raise their glasses while my mother intones: 'To friend and foe, foe and friend: let us be friends.'

Before three or four of these toasts are through you can bet your bottom dollar that Brydie will give me a dippy smile and say, 'So, courting yet, then, are you?' When I grunt, 'No,' Brydie will say, 'Ah! You're better off, so you are!' as my mother's eyes cloud over and she booms out her favourite John Knox quote: '"Education over religion!"'

When they finally get up from the table to leave, my mother will insist on giving them a pasty each to take home.

Mary will look like she's about to cry: 'No. No, Brenda,' she says, 'don't give me a pasty!'

'Take your pasty!'

'No, Brenda, don't give me a pasty,' and she turns to me and wails, 'Tell her not to give me a pasty!'

'Take your pasty!'

Brenda gets up and takes a pasty from the metal cupboard under the sink (we don't have a fridge because Brenda is convinced they give you stomach cancer) and thrusts it into Mary's bag. There will be a glow in her cheeks as if she's just handed a pound of sirloin to a woman living under the Great Ukrainian Famine of 1932/3.

Back in the Lobster Pot, Brenda is still trying to thrust food down people's throats. 'Jack!' she exclaims. 'Jack, it's time for you to eat something!'

'Not Jack, actually,' he smirks, glancing at me. 'Fanny Nancy Plum Caramel Dolores Ramona Shirley Whisky Norwood.' He wriggles around in his seat and turns to me, saying, 'Guess what! Mr Jones dresses up in skirts and puts biro tops up his bottom.'

'Jack!' Brenda exclaims again, sounding more alarmed this time. 'It's time for you to eat something. *Mens sana in corpore sano!*'

The hand dives down the trousers once more, rubs around a little and surfaces again *en route* for the nose. Jack takes a long, deep breath then exhales, saying, 'Pork chops and cabbage!'

'Waste not want not, Jack!'

'Roast topside and all the trimmings!'

'Barley sugars for those who eat their tea, Jack!'

'Plum duff with blue peppermint creams!'

I watch Jack watching my father compile his sandwich (ever quicker) and I know there is no stopping him now. 'I wonder,' Jack says, folding his arms, 'where shrimps' bottoms are.'

My father's hands freeze momentarily (poor him – taking an afternoon off in the middle of the season for this) and Brenda tries to pretend everything is normal by picking up the two paper napkins filled with leftover jam and clotted cream that she has been hiding on her lap for the past thirty minutes. She stuffs them surreptitiously into her leatherette shopping bag, saying hurriedly, 'Cornish clotted cream! Nothing quite like Cornish clotted cream!' forgetting that there is also nothing quite like squid boiled in its own ink or octopus, thrashed against the rock until tender and sprinkled with red *pimentón*, like Mr Jones has told us about.

She pours more tea into the pot. The terrible, homely gurgle of tea pouring into china cups is like the sound of couch potatoes and overheated houses and 'pottering round gardens', a sound worse to me than the sound of brass bands on Sunday afternoons, worse than the Battenburg-heavy slabs of silence in the Lobster Pot or the seasick green wallpaper and the cold, religious light coming through the windows.

I get that Incredible Hulk feeling again, like I want to explode or turn the table upside down. I decide to smash the scone in front of me. I pull it to me, I scrape the butter from its face, I rip the sultanas from its entrails, I crush it till it bleeds. I don't want to play any more. I don't want to be in this moronic tea-room with my moronic parents and my moronic best friend. I look up at the pastel painting of horses galloping through sea spray hung on the wall and then, through the net curtains, I see an aeroplane etching a white scar into the blue sky as it flies off into the distance. Brenda says, 'More tea, dear?', the terrible pot cocked in her hand, and I just burst into flames.

I scream helplessly from the bottom of my lungs, 'I want to get out! I want to live! I want to eat something with tentacles on!'

When the kerfuffle dies down the only sound in the Lobster Pot is of Jack sniffing his fingers. 'Roast beef and Yorkshire pudding?' he smirks. 'Spotted dick and custard? Paella and chips?'

Chapter Three

Instead of presenting *truite à l'estragon* in the classic manner, we cooked and skinned our trout and then sank them in a tank filled with aspic shaded to the colouring of water on a sunny day when tree vegetation is reflected in it.

***Something's Burning*, an autobiography by Fanny Cradock**

I first met Jack when he arrived at St Dougal's just in time for domestic science. A couple of months ago, just after the Easter holidays, a gangly boy with blue eyebrows was brought into the domestic science lab by Mrs Ward, the headmistress. She announced that he'd come all the way from Barcelona to join our school and that we were all to help show him the ropes.

When Mrs Ward left the room, Chivers, the domestic

science teacher, who looks like a Russian shot-putter, beamed at Jack as if he was her gold medal in the Olympic decathlon finals. 'Welcome!' she said, clapping her hands together and sending ripples all down her body. (Her name is really Miss Norwood but we call her Chivers because she wobbles like a jelly.) 'Welcome to St Dougal's! We'll have you making paella, I expect, before the term's out!'

Her smile got bigger as she looked at the cloth-covered wicker basket he was holding in his hand.

'I imagine you're more used to the Catalan version of paella, though, aren't you? The *fideuà* – made,' and she turned to the class, 'made from miniature strips of fine pasta, fresh seafood and the king of spices, saffron.' Turning back to Jack, she confided that, 'One of my greatest memories as a young girl was my first taste of *zarzuela*, that most regal of fish stews, which – and I'd welcome your opinion on this, Jack – puts the *bouillabaisse* to shame.'

Jack said, 'I'm going to make blue peppermint creams with bubble-gum bits.'

'Oh?' Chivers hesitated, like they'd just told her it was the bronze medal and not the gold after all. 'Oh, well,' she smiled, 'I expect you're just finding your feet in our humble supermarkets after, what was it?, two years living in Barcelona?'

'I like blue things,' he said. 'Blue bubble gum, blue drinks. In Spain they have blue shark-flavoured ice lollies.'

Chivers' smile started to wobble. 'Really?' she said.

'Yes. Of course, they're not really shark-flavoured.' He smirked. 'They're only shark-shaped.'

When he started to tell Chivers how raspberry-flavoured Slush Puppy was the only blue thing he'd been able to track down in Mousehole, the class started to snigger and Chivers said brightly, 'Come along, then, dear, I think we'll pair you up with Rosa. She'll show you the ropes, won't you, Rosa?'

I was scowling when Jack smirked on to the stool next to mine. Miss Norwood seemed to be implying that there was some connection between his ramblings about blue ice lollies and my own interest in the art of cochineal usage. Even in domestic science I excel above the rest of the class so that while they all make recipes from the boring *Good Housekeeping* book, I am allowed to cook from my Fanny Cradock collection. Whatever task Chivers sets us – a family picnic on the beach, a romantic candle-lit dinner for two, a light snack for a patient recovering from open heart surgery – my dishes are always laden with cream, Cognac, wine, garlic and *duchesse* potato dyed a variety of colours and piped into shapes such as horses, boats and aeroplanes.

The day Jack Flowers arrived, my chosen menu for a retired couple celebrating their golden wedding anniversary began with angels and devils on horseback (prunes and oysters soaked in Armagnac and wrapped in bacon), followed by *tournedos Rossini* (a buttery croûton topped with fillet steak, *foie gras*, a black truffle sliver and Madeira sauce) and concluded with syllabub (sweet white wine, Cognac, lemon rind and double cream).

There was a small bottle of purple cochineal on my

work station. It was for the mauve *duchesse* potato I was going to pipe into the shape of a life raft.

'Hello,' Jack said, beaming at the bottle of cochineal. He turned to me and said, 'I like the look of you!'

I ignored him. He leaned over towards my pile of recipe books. 'Fanny!' he said, with a stupid giggle.

I ignored him.

'I'm going to do peppermint creams,' he said. 'Blue peppermint creams with bubble-gum bits.'

'How old are you?' I said, in a sarky voice.

He didn't get it. 'Thirteen years old!' he said. 'My birthday's on June the tenth. Pretty soon. How about you?'

'Fourteen,' I said, leaving a dramatic pause before adding, 'My birthday was in March.'

My allusion to age-related superiority went right over his head. He just blathered, 'I've got the recipe for the peppermint creams. Have a look if you want.'

He pulled back the cloth from his wicker basket and took out a big thin book. On the cover it said, *My Fun-to-Cook Book.* There was a drawing of a dog and a hamster standing before a table laden with buns and toast and hot dogs. Underneath them it said, 'Quick and easy recipes for young cooks'.

He looked at me, widening his green eyes as if he expected a round of applause. 'The hamster's called Sebastian and the dog's called Alex,' he said shyly. 'Got it a couple of years ago. Silly, isn't it?'

But obviously he didn't think it was silly at all for a thirteen-year-old to be using such a monstrosity because before I could snap at him to take his nasty book away he'd placed it in front of me on my work station and was flicking through the pages so that I could view the contents.

A blur of Corned-beef Burgers, Mixed Grill, Hot Dogs, Honeycomb Crisp, Toffee Apples and Sausage Popovers passed before my eyes. At the bottom of some pages there were printed comments like, 'Don't be in too much of a hurry to eat these – hot sugar can be very, very hot!' or, 'Eat Apple Snow immediately – before it melts!' or even the humiliating, 'Ask Mother to turn up the heat and to stay within reach until you have finished this part of the cooking.' On the first page of Jack's baby cookery book there was some grown up hand writing that said, 'Happy 11th birthday darling, lots of love from Mummy'.

Mummy! And what sort of mother wouldn't even notice that this was a book for seven-year-olds? The flicking pages sent up a wind of incense and smoky-bacon-flavoured cigarette ash.

'Look!' I shouted at him, pushing the book away. 'I couldn't care less about your stupid book. I've got work to do even if you haven't!'

An even bigger smile came over his face. 'Thought fat people were supposed to be nice,' he said. 'Thought only good people made cakes.'

I couldn't believe he'd dared to say this. Especially as that week I wasn't even using a coat-hanger to do up my jeans. The only thing I had time to snap back was, 'Good people make cakes. Bad people make Fanny Cradock!' and then Chivers tapped a piece of chalk on the blackboard and asked if anyone could name three functions of egg in a lemon meringue pie with rich shortcrust pastry.

For the O level Domestic Science syllabus it is compulsory to do half an hour of theory from the boring *Good Housekeeping* book before you can get down to the cooking part. So far we have learned about kitchen hygiene ('Use rubber gloves for washing the dishes so that the water can be hotter than the hands can bear') and produce selection ('It is important that the meat smells good. It should never be sticky as this indicates bacterial decomposition'). It is all a bit rich, if you ask me – especially in the light of the damp stains Chivers always has underneath the arms of her polyester smock. Good job the domestic science lab is usually filled with the smell of burning.

'Come on,' she said, 'thinking caps on, everyone.' She was looking over at me because I am the only one who ever answers her questions. I put up my hand and started to say, 'Protein emulsification, coagulation and . . .'

But I didn't finish because at that moment Jack slid his cookery book over to my work station. I looked down to see a cartoon he had drawn under the recipe for cheese straws. There was a short, squat woman with damp patches under her sports vest tossing a cheese-straw caber up through the roof of the domestic science lab. You couldn't deny it. It was very accurate. There was Chivers' trademark furry red face and her hair that looks like it's been plugged into an electric-light socket.

Before I knew it, an odd sound had come out of my mouth. I hoped it sounded like a polite sneeze but Chivers shot me a glance that said she knew very well it hadn't been a sneeze. She looked as if she was about to cry: her star pupil had betrayed her. She turned round to the blackboard again and began to write frantic notes about raising agents, the flesh on her upper right arm whirring round like a pneumatic drill.

Letting Chivers down wasn't the worst of it, though. The worst of it was when Fiona P tossed a paper note on to my work station shortly afterwards saying, 'Glad you're getting on so well with your new boyfriend!'

'I can't believe you just did that,' I hissed at Jack, as the sound of breaking eggs and clanking bowls started to fill the room again. 'You come here with your – your stupid blue eyebrows and your stupid recipe book for kids and – and you don't even know anything. You don't even know who I am. Who I'm going to be. I'm going to be in the diplomatic service ... international relations. And just cos you've lived in Spain – it doesn't mean anything. It doesn't mean you're smart. You don't even know who Fanny Cradock is! What am I preparing at this moment in domestic science class? Oh, I think you'll find it's not blue peppermint creams from a cookery book for retards. I think you'll find it's gherkin tassels for a garnish accompaniment to a meal you couldn't make in a million years. So don't you get any ideas about being my friend. Don't even talk to me! Don't even look at me!'

After I'd said it, I hoped he'd cry so that he'd learn

his lesson. But he didn't. He just beamed as if no one had ever shown him so much attention.

'You're really clever, too, aren't you?' he said, rubbing the back of his cochineal hands over his forehead, turning his right eyebrow blue-black. 'I bet that's why they put me with you. Thought you might bring me on a bit.' He hesitated. 'Go on. Come home and have tea with me. You can stay the night too. Mum thinks I need a bit of bringing on.' He shrugged. 'Dunno. Maybe it's all the different schools I've been to. Different countries and that. Never even really learned any of the lingo. Just the basics for the maid. "Can I have some milk?" "Can I have some bread?" "What time can I get up in the morning?"'

I couldn't believe he was still daring to talk to me – not just talking but boasting about living in foreign countries and having maids. As *if* I'd ever go home with him. I sliced into a gherkin.

'I usually cook for myself,' he said, making a pig's ear of cracking an egg and separating the white from the yolk. 'Mum has kidney problems. She has to lie down.' A huge cloud of icing sugar tumbled into the sieve. 'They have weird things in Barcelona,' he spluttered. 'Sheep's heads and rabbit. Rabbit with snails. Disgusting.'

I stormed over to the fridge and put two glasses in to chill for the syllabub. The fridge looked greasy and grimy, like the inside of a pensioner's house whose wife had just died and he'd let things go because he couldn't be bothered any more. Then I realised that it looked more like the inside of my house – except we haven't even got a fridge because of my mother's stomach-cancer obsession – and suddenly it all came home to me: how terrible my life was, how devoid of any kind of interesting experience. I sneaked a look at Jack, who was dabbing his index finger on his damp nostrils and licking off the icing sugar. I wondered what it must feel like to wake up every morning and be in another country. I wondered what the air tasted of, I wondered if people's sweat had a different smell, or if they would be in a good mood because they didn't have to put up with drizzle all day. Then I started thinking about Jack's house. About if there would be straw donkeys hanging from his bedroom ceiling or special Spanish memorabilia that I didn't know about or if he sometimes ate octopus with *pimentón* for his tea.

I decided to risk it. I decided to swallow my pride and talk to him, see what information I could get. I went back to the work station and mumbled, 'What did you eat in Spain, then?'

I'm not sure if he heard me because he said, 'Did you know that pigs' orgasms last for thirty minutes?' Then he chucked a handful of icing sugar over his face. 'Look,' he shouted, pouting his lips out, 'David Bowie!'

An orgasm is one of the words in my Big Words Book. (Other words include 'masturbate', 'faeces', 'marijuana', 'voluptuous', 'villa', '*dépaysé*', 'deracinated', and 'cerulean'.) *The Joy of Knowledge* says an orgasm is when human genitals get swollen with blood. I didn't see why anyone would want to take thirty minutes over it.

'Well, pigs are stupid, aren't they?' I snapped.

'They're very clever, actually.' He smirked, throwing a handful of pink pieces into the mixing bowl. 'Might be a bit exhausting, though, an orgasm that lasted for thirty minutes.' His eyes, like clear green marbles, began to sparkle as he added, 'David Bowie had to have his stomach pumped once because he sucked off so many men.'

I looked at him uneasily because I'd never heard anyone say 'suck off' before. I wondered why you'd have to have your stomach pumped just because you did thirty minutes' worth of sucking off. I suspected Jack knew things I didn't. But I just carried on cutting so he wouldn't know that I was impressed.

'I like pigs,' he went on. 'They're like toenails. Toenails are thicker than fingernails, aren't they? They've got crackling stuff underneath.'

I had to make a really big effort not to grate my lemon grater down his stupid face.

'Very funny,' I said, with a fake smile. 'So, what did you really eat?'

'Turds.'

I pummelled the lemon hard against the grater. I was stupid to have asked him anything in the first place. 'If you're going to lie,' I said coldly, 'you might at least make it believable.'

'It's true,' he said. But he couldn't keep a straight face. 'There's a man called Caga Tío. It means "Uncle Turd". He shits you presents at Christmas. They're like that in Catalonia.'

'Oh, yeah,' I said. 'Blue as well, is he?'

Jack's face became serious for a second. 'No. Well, I don't think so. I never saw him. I suppose he's brown.' The smirk reappeared. 'They eat turds in posh restaurants too. We went to this posh restaurant once – Mum and Dad and me – and we had snails. I've had them before when we lived in France – they're nutty, aren't they? Nutty-tasting, I mean. But they don't have poo in them in France.'

I knew he was lying. Fanny Cradock has done a special on Catalan cuisine. It is known as the most sophisticated of any in Spain. 'Shut up,' I said, turning on the electric mixer.

'It's true,' he said. 'You have to nip off the poo bag with your fingernail. I told Mum it was lucky she didn't bite her fingernails because otherwise it would mean she was eating snail big jobs.'

'Shut up.' I imagined his head whirring in the blades.

'But imagine if you did bite your nails when you'd had Spanish snails for lunch. You can just imagine what's churning round in your guts – not just snail poo but the poo of all the insects that the snail has eaten.' He broke off a big lump of icing dough and put it in his mouth. 'I don't know if snails eat other insects, do you? But, anyway, even if they don't eat meat then they definitely do eat things like lettuce, don't they? And lettuce could have fly poo on it, so really you're eating snail poo and fly poo on a plate in a really expensive restaurant. It's like one of those bags called . . .'

It might have been the egg white. There was a lot of it on the floor. Accidents like that happen all the time. He might easily have slipped on that. Only he didn't because I pushed him. I kicked one of the legs of his stool as he rocked it. I kicked it hard because he deserved it. Because I was fed up with hearing his nonsense, his disgusting nonsense about snails and turds and toenails. But mainly I was furious because the only thing I did believe out of all his twaddle was that he had eaten snails at some point in his life and I have never eaten snails – never eaten them anywhere and it just wasn't fair. It wasn't fair that this annoying boy had been abroad all this time and all he had come back with was a taste for blue eyebrows so he might as well have spent the time in Bournemouth for all the good it had done him. It was a huge volcano of anger and frustration that culminated in a kind of blackout. It felt like falling down a hot well with no bottom and no sides to grab hold of and it also felt as exhilarating (exciting) as jumping off the top of a high cliff in a dream.

But even in a dream, jumping off a cliff is only exhilarating for a couple of seconds. After that, the practicalities of the situation come flying at you pretty quickly. The current situation is that Jack is writhing around on the floor like an upside-down ladybird that can't right itself and I'm wondering if he's going to sneak on me and wondering also if I'm a bit mad maybe for doing such a mean thing to someone on their first day at a new school. Luckily, though, I haven't whipped the cream yet so I take the electric whisk in my hand and I start work on it, hoping the distraction will make my current predicament disappear and half hoping that the noise will drown out the sound of Jack choking to death on the floor.

But Chivers does hear the sound of Jack asphyxiating on a lump of blue peppermint cream. She comes wobbling up as fast as she can. She crouches down by his side and starts wittering on about food intolerance. She paraphrases chapter six of the *Good Housekeeping* book at him. 'Do you have allergies?' she's shouting, worried about losing her job probably. 'What is it? Shellfish? Have you eaten any strawberries? You wouldn't think that a strawberry could be hazardous but I've seen some cases in my time. Don't worry, dear, just keep calm. I'm trained in matters such as this.'

She starts fanning him with her hands. This sends stale polyester-smock fumes shooting up his nose, which seem to help burn through the piece of peppermint cream that's lodged in his throat. At last, the classroom hears an urgent little voice coming from the depths of his lungs. Chivers puts her ear nearer to Jack's mouth to try to hear what it is that Jack is trying to say. 'Insulin shots? Do you need an insulin shot, dear?'

And then it comes: 'Colos-colos-tomy . . . colostomy bag . . .' he says, breathing as if he's in pain. 'A colostomy bag, Rosa . . .'

If Chivers' hair could stand up any more on end it would. 'For goodness' sake,' she says, wrenching her head back a few feet as if she can smell something nasty already. 'I think I should have been told about this. I really do think this is beyond the call of duty.'

But then Jack starts wheezing again and Chivers obviously feels a bit bad about abandoning a skinny boy to die in the middle of her cookery class just because *Good Housekeeping* doesn't tell you what do to about a colostomy bag exploding within the vicinity of lemon meringue pie with rich shortcrust pastry. 'Are you leaking, Jack? Is that it?' she says, her nose wrinkling only slightly now.

'Col-colostomy bag,' Jack struggles.

'What is it, dear?'

Jack sits up and says helplessly, 'It's one of those bags old people do turds in.'

While Miss Norwood marches a droop-headed Jack over to the blackboard and gives him a scary, Russian shot-putter ticking-off – telling him that this isn't very impressive behaviour for his first day at St Dougal's and that he'd better hurry up and finish his meal because she'll be round to do testing in half an hour – I realise that I have overwhipped the cream. I won't just get a curdled-syllabub-slightly-docked mark. Now that I'm linked in Chivers' mind with Jack's fall from grace, I'll probably get nought out of ten. The only worse thing that could happen now is if Jack scores better than me.

Luckily, I am good at sliding out of trouble, coming up with an instant plan. I turn my back on the rest of the class, stick my index finger up my nose, stir it around a bit, plunge it back into Jack's blue dough, pour the whole bottle of peppermint essence into the hole, refill the bottle with water, knead some extra icing sugar into the dough – and throw in a couple of long red hairs for good measure.

Just before the bell goes, Chivers spits Jack's golden wedding anniversary meal for a retired couple on to the work top, exclaiming, 'Oh, for goodness' sake!' before giving me a very respectable seven out of ten, in spite of the accident with the cream.

[illegible] the [illegible] goes [illegible] got two [illegible] for [illegible] on [illegible] and [illegible]. [illegible] in [illegible]

[illegible]

[illegible]
[illegible] we [illegible]
[illegible] fish [illegible]
op the [illegible]
and [illegible] a [illegible]
Cook [illegible] our catch [illegible]
[illegible]

The Family and Friends Cookbook Cook
[illegible]

I went down to Jack's because [illegible] day is [illegible] cod in parsley sauce night at [illegible]'s house. When I [illegible] there I [illegible] that Jack didn't just live in [illegible] as opposed to a flat [illegible] shops [illegible] in a [illegible] that looked as if it [illegible] of ginger [illegible]

Chapter Four

A Moroccan couscous eaten in a tent in the Sahara dessert at 110 degrees F in the shade can be a perfect meal. So can a Provençal octopus stew for which you have fished the baby octopus from the wavelets on the sands on a moonlit night in a hot August and built a fire a little further up the sands for cooking your catch *in situ* with pimentos, saffron and oil.

***The Fanny and Johnnie Cradock Cookery Programme* magazine. No. 54**

I went for tea at Jack's because Wednesday is boil-in-the-bag cod in parsley sauce night at Brenda's house. When I got there it turned out that Jack didn't just live in a real house, as opposed to a flat above a pasty shop, he lived in a cottage that looked as if it was made of gingerbread.

The roof was thatched and the walls were candy-floss pink with green angelica leaves criss-crossing down the front like a laced-up corset. Inside, the air smelt of joss-sticks and black coffee and smoky-bacon-flavoured ash and the rooms were filled with golden bees. There was a range of bees – gold-thread bees embossed on almond-coloured curtains like plump golden bows, and bumpy glass bees on the row of tumblers displayed in an array of black lacquered cabinets. The rooms were so large that walking across them felt like walking a tightrope and you felt you should hug close to the walls in case you fell over.

There were statues of kneeling women with Oriental faces and silver bangles round their upper arms. They bowed their heads and held offerings in their hands. There were mirrors large as ponds hanging over white marble fireplaces chiselled with flowers and grapes and trumpets. There were lamps made of long-bodied, small-breasted girls stretching and wriggling like fish, and there were polished wooden floors covered with dazzling rugs woven like colour TV sets gone wrong.

Jack gave me a running commentary like an overexcited estate agent as he led me from room to room. The house was from Mr Flowers' side of the family, apparently, but it was Mrs Flowers who had taken charge of all the decoration, or 'décor', as Jack called it.

'Bees were a décor motif favoured during the reign of Napoleon, the French general,' he announced, as I reflected how the only décor motif in our house was *Steptoe and Son*. He went on again about how the house belonged to his father's family but that the things in it were all down to his mother. 'Those teacups with the square handles in the cabinet are called art deco. I have my coffee in them sometimes for breakfast. The wooden floors are called *parquet,* which is a French word,' he said. 'The rugs are Turkish and each rug has an imperfection woven into it because in Turkey they say that nothing is perfect, only God.' I started to feel all sulky because it was so unfair that I'd never been abroad but Jack had. I wouldn't have been too scared to eat rabbit or snails in Spain like the typical stupid English person that Jack was. I could feel myself going red as I thought how I wasn't allowed to have coffee for breakfast and how I had only ever slept in two different beds in my life – my bunk bed and the camp bed in Bournemouth – even though I had sneaked into one of the cabins the time I took the Portsmouth–Le Havre ferry with Brenda. (While everyone else was getting off except me and Brenda, I lay in the top bunk, bobbing gently up and down on sheets as crisp as linen napkins, pretending to be Tom the cabin-boy awaiting court-martial.)

And then I saw the Venetian Room and I forgot about everything.

I could tell immediately that the Venetian Room was a special place. Here, the bee curtains were made of heavy crimson velvet and tied back with cords like gold rigging that bloomed into tassels thick as hula skirts. There was a white *chaise-longue*, a large dining-table covered with a white tablecloth as crisp as linen napkins – 'from one of Mum's Spanish friends,' Jack said, in a hushed voice – a white piano and a small table that looked as if it was made from stiff yellow lace until Jack told you that it was made from elephant's tusks.

But apart from the drowsy heat, the main feature of the room was that it looked as if you could eat it. It was hexagon-shaped and all the windows were made of coloured glass. Coloured glass filled the room too. There were shelves and shelves of drinking glasses, standing to attention like boiled sweet soldiers. It was all antique, hand-blown glass from Venice, Jack said. There were fragile goblets of swirling green with curly stems thin as spaghetti standing next to glasses thin as lightbulbs with seahorse stems that shimmered in a kaleidoscope of pale pink and blue when you touched them. There were glasses like wafer-thin butterscotch or satin cushions, held up with barley-sugar twists and lemon-sherbet snake coils. There were decanters too: blue and green striped with silver threads; wine purple and peach Melba orange, spiralling up to tops like flames or mosque roofs or Ali Baba shoes or toadstools. There were decanters that made your eyes go funny if you looked at them for too long. There were ones like cremation urns or tears or upside-down bells, there were transparent ones with tiny pinprick bubbles, swarming with more dancing bees, all flecked with gold and crimson, all jostling for position on the black lacquer cabinets, all filled with liquids dappled elaborate colours of the rainbow. You just knew that none of them had Harvey's Bristol Cream inside.

But the thing that really made my heart race was an immense stained-glass window showing a naked, muscly boy spearing a human bull rearing up on its hind legs. At least five feet high it must have been. The figures flickered into life as the wind blew the branches of the tree in the garden outside and the evening sun rained in through the glass. A surging mass of splurging crimson and scarlet and peach Melba smeared the monster's body and red jammy lumps of blood dripped from the boy's spear. Shortly after you noticed that both the boy and the bull had naked penises showing – like little glass eyebrows edged in black – you noticed a glass scrawl above them both. Ominous words in bold, skinny letters, warned: '*Mais ne regarde jamais le monstre dans les yeux.*'

A stained-glass window with two penises on. Not Jesus ascending into heaven or Mary at the foot of the cross, like at school, but Theseus with a much better body than Jesus and not even wearing a loincloth. Plus, 'Never Look the Monster in the Eyes' is a much better inscription than INRI which stands for 'This is the King of the Jews'.

Then the smell started to hit me. Lulled by the flickering waves of red and orange and gold glass, it took a while to register that, steeped within the sleepy perfume of a trapped spring day, was the smell of rotting flesh. I breathed deeper. Yes, it was definitely there, a scent of bad meat or unwashed body. Jack saw me sniffing the air and rushed over to the dining table where a porcelain vase filled with browning daffodils stood. He wrinkled his nose and pulled the flowers out of the vase. 'Forgot about these,' he said. 'Mum's favourite flowers. Smell horrible when they're dying.' A sticky string of green and brown slime dribbled on to the white tablecloth and Jack looked terrified. He stuffed the stems back in the vase and rushed both daffodils and vase out of the room in search of a cloth.

It was strange to be left alone in that mysterious hot room. My legs melted and I sat down on the white carpet – like a white woolly lawn that needed a trim. I gazed at the enormous stained-glass window as I stroked the carpet; I thought it would be nice to take off all my clothes and lie down flat and stare at the window for a very long time.

Suddenly, the house didn't smell of smoky-bacon fag ash and joss-sticks any more. It smelt of voluptuous black masses and witches' cloaks and ritual sacrifice of human flesh. And a woman who dared have a pagan stained-glass window as the heart of her house – when God might exist after all and then she would burn in hell for ever. 'Remember what it feels like when you burn your little finger on a pan of toffee,' Sister Celestine says at school. 'Just imagine then what hell must feel like. Your whole body burning up and never enough water to cool it down.'

Mrs Flowers should have candles lit, I thought. Candles flickering among the coloured glasses to splash light against the crimson curtains like a big flickering bruise or people burning in eternal orange damnation.

Then Jack came back and mopped up the tablecloth as best he could. He seemed anxious to leave the Venetian Room, promising me that there were even better things to see. Just before we left, he pointed out a couple of features – a brown lamp on a plastic coily lead like on a telephone that you can pull down over the table, and a machine called a quadrophonic sound system with plastic things as big as books that you inserted into it. Then he took me back to the sitting room next door and showed me the other modern features of the house, like dimmer switches and a huge TV with teak shutters that close over the front if you want ('Mum says teak's good taste'), and a video-recorder which means you can record things off TV and watch films without going to the cinema. A friend of Mrs Flowers' from London sent it. There was something comforting about the sitting room when you looked at it more closely. As well as the marble fireplaces and the mirrors large as ponds there was something slightly grubby and down-at-heel about it. As if it could have done with a good clean. There was a battered old green settee in velvety material with fringing round the bottom and dimples with buttons in on the back, there was a scratched old record-player with smoky glass doors and a compartment holding a collection of records. 'Mum's,' Jack said, smirking.

There were names on the sleeves like Helen Reddy, Astrid Gilberto, Sacha Distel, Shirley Bassey, Juliette Gréco and Charles Aznavour. There was a picture of a woman with blonde hair and a short skirt on a motorbike that said, 'Brigitte Bardot *et* Serge Gainsbourg'. There were Spanish words on sleeves too, words more advanced than *Modern Day Spanish.* There were bookshelves holding books with names of authors I had never heard of – Jean Cocteau, Jean Genet – next to trashy-looking paperbacks called *Once Is Not Enough* by Jacqueline Susann and *The Carpet Baggers* by Harold Robbins, with a picture of a lipstick kiss on the front cover partly covered by a real-life red-wine stain. On the marble hearth there was a discarded scarf with a leopard pattern, a bottle opener, a pile of *She* magazines, a pot of nail varnish and a small ball of cotton wool with a dirty red damp patch.

Jack tutted as he scooped up the soiled cotton wool ball. But as he droned on about how they didn't have a maid any more, how his mother wasn't very good at cleaning and how he had his work cut out for himself, I kept thinking back to the Venetian Room. He started talking about how his father sold yachts now, although he hadn't sold any yet. But it was Mrs Flowers I was interested in. I pulled up a red-velvet-upholstered chair that crunched like straw when I sat on it. It was spindly as a pin with legs like shapely Parisian ladies in books and a carved back that dug into your bra strap like a blade. I liked it, though: it worked like a flying carpet. You sat on it and you were another person; it took you to another country, another time. You expected that any minute now a man with a powdered wig and breeches was going to walk into the room.

A man with a powdered wig and breeches did not walk into the room but when we walked into the kitchen a skinny man was standing by the table hitting a row of tortoiseshell brandy glasses with a steak tenderiser. He wasn't going at them like a madman. Each glass was getting a careful inspection. Each was held up to the light then aimed in the direction of an overhead cupboard as if the man was an artist getting his perspective right. The hammer blow that followed was light and mathematical.

He looked younger than my father. He had a shock of greying black hair that fell boyishly into his sea-green eyes. He might have been handsome if he'd wiped the worried frown off his face and if his skin hadn't been quite so grey-looking. He grunted a hello to Jack without looking at him. When Jack told him who I was, he just mumbled, 'Pleased to meet you, Rosa,' as if he was shy. He tapped the rim of a glass with the tenderiser and watched a jagged shard fall on to the table.

I liked him being shy with me. It gave me courage to say, 'Actually, I think that if the liquidiser had fallen from the top of the cupboard on to that glass, it would have smashed it to smithereens.'

I could see he was about to say something like 'I don't know what you mean.' But in the end he just narrowed his eyes and looked up at the liquidiser. 'You think so?' He frowned deeper.

'Trigonometry, Mr Flowers,' I said.

'Yes. Yes, of course.' He looked at me nervously.

He needn't have been nervous about me telling on him, even though I understood immediately what he was doing. I had imagined doing something similar myself, although unfortunately my parents have nothing worth insuring in their house.

'You can't leave these things up to chance, Mr Flowers,' I said. 'You have to imagine what story you'll have ready for when the insurance man comes round. You have to be able to look him in the eye and say, "Yes, it's terrible. They were an heirloom of great sentimental value. I knew I should have checked that the liquidiser had been put back properly." And then you have to lower your eyes to the table because you are so sad about the destruction of your heirloom.'

I felt extremely pleased with myself when I'd given Mr Flowers this advice. He squinted as he looked at me, as if he couldn't quite get me into focus. 'Maybe you're right,' he mumbled. He looked up again to the top of the cupboard and then Jack grabbed hold of my sleeve and took me upstairs, telling me on the way that his dad was always doing funny things and he didn't get it at all.

He led me to a room with a poster on the door advertising a bull fight. '*Corrida – Señor Jack Flowers – Barcelona,*' it said, and there was a photo of Jack's head in the body of a matador. On the walls inside the room there were posters of Carly Simon, Boney M, Elkie Brooks and Abba pulled from issues of *Smash Hits* and *Look In* and a print of a dancing girl with some French writing on it: '*Le*

Frou-Frou.' Jack's bed was covered with a white mosquito net like a see-through tent – or a princess's bed, as Jack explained – and stuck to one side of it was a bold felt-tip drawing of a woman with a kiss curl on her forehead like a huge black question mark.

On a wooden ledge above a granite fireplace there was a collection of fake rubber objects – a fake beans on toast, fake spaghetti bolognese, fake sick. At the very end of the ledge there was a yellow cassette-recorder. Jack went to turn it on and it began to crank out 'Brown Girl In The Ring' by Boney M. I hadn't seen a cassette-recorder close up before. Especially not a yellow one. But when I picked it up to have a closer look, Jack dashed over and took it from me, cradling it in his arms as if it was his pet rabbit. 'My tape-recorder,' he said quietly. 'You press play and record at the same time. You can record songs from the radio. Or your own voice you can record.'

'Brown Girl In The Ring' droned on. I tried not to look too impressed.

'Mum gave it to me,' Jack said. 'She remembered for once! For my twelfth birthday. My eleventh and twelfth birthdays are the only ones she's remembered. Forget her own head if it wasn't screwed on!' He looked awkward. 'She gave me a present when I was eleven,' he said. 'My cookbook, remember?' He saw me glance back at the fake rubber collection. 'I did have a fake fried egg too,' he said quickly, 'but I lost it. The sick's got bits of egg in, though. You can see them, look.' But I just turned away and sighed a deeply bored sigh, which he must have noticed because, in the nick of time, he drew back the flap of the mosquito net and trilled, 'Tea-time!'

I was about to tell him that there was no way I was getting into a mosquito-net bed with him when I saw the display of Wagon Wheels, chocolate marshmallows, Iced Gems, cheese balls, Penguins, Mr Kipling Caramel Slices and Mr Kipling Raspberry Sundaes sprawling all over the bed and I couldn't help smiling. They weren't your run-of-the-frangipane-mill, dead-old-lady-type cakes. This was what you ate when you got invited to a children's party. When I was six or seven, Brenda had organised parties in our flat. We ate jellies and cheese balls and chocolate marshmallows, and then we did the usual games – musical statues, pass the parcel, hunt the thimble – and I'd always end up bossing everyone around. The children who were frightened of bursting balloons – I pushed them on to the balloons and made them cry. And then I'd eat their cake. And afterwards, the pins that were meant for bursting the balloons, I'd get hold of them and stand behind the best players of musical statues and stick the pins in them so they'd move and I'd win the prize. There's something exciting about cheating and being spiteful, even through afterwards you feel a bit sick like you do when you've eaten too much party food.

I climbed into the mosquito net, I grabbed the Raspberry Sundae box from Jack's hands and ripped it with my teeth. Jack followed suit. Scarlet corrugated cardboard was pulled from containers, orange cheese balls flew through the air, wrappers were tossed, plastic packets crumpled. We ate with our mouths open, we were a chimps' tea party. We stuck out tongues laden with chocolate and peanut butter mulch, we dipped Twiglets in pots of chocolate spread, we pushed fondant fancies through our teeth like we were being sick, we dunked whole sugar lumps in cups of Coke, we giggled like seven-year-olds.

I think it must have been the sugar – the thrill of the sugar shooting through my bloodstream like a spear. I never eat like this at home. My father is under doctor's orders to use Sweet 'n' Lo in his tea and Brenda occasionally tries to bribe us with a piece of barley sugar – hoping that a half-hearted sugar rush is going to get us interested in the Common Man.

I couldn't sit still. I thought of all the glass downstairs and I felt like smashing something up myself. Suddenly it was jigging time, roaring time, tornado time, whizzing-round-the-room-with-arms-out-like-a-sycamore-helicopter time, going, 'WAAAAAAAAA!', knocking-fake-beans-and-sick-to-the-floor-with-my-wings time. It was like going on the scenic railway in Bournemouth – which they call a roller-coaster in America – and getting to the top and it saying, 'Gates of Heaven,' then just plunging down like jumping off the top of a high cliff in a dream.

'WAAAAAAAAAAAAAAAAA!' I yelled some more, adding, 'This is probably what it feels like when you're about to take off in a plane,' until I remembered that Jack had already taken off in a plane, loads of times. But he just started jumping around going 'Brown Girl In The

Ring! Brown Girl In The Ring!' as the disco beat cranked out from the crackly yellow rabbit.

I swirled round some more in time to the music and came to a halt in front of a large snowstorm collection. A dozen or so blue plastic bubbles holding a series of boats and lighthouses, cathedrals and dragons, cancan girls, water-lilies, flamenco dancers, dolphins. White flakes lay in drifts around tiny plaques that said, St Tropez, Bangkok, Col des Aravis, Barcelona, Sitges, Sevilla, Le Havre.

He saw me looking and said merrily, 'Snowstorms! That's what it's all about!' I started throwing Barcelona up and down in my hand like a ball. 'Raspberry Sundaes, more like!'

'My friend in Spain,' he gasped for air, 'his mother used to give us raspberry milkshake for tea.'

'Liar! Bet you didn't have any friends.'

'Didn't have any foam on, though. You could tell it wasn't raspberry milkshake. It used to make you do big explosions in the toilet afterwards.'

'You're disgusting!'

'It was because of the cats he had.'

'Jack's a brown girl in a ring!'

'It was threadworm powders!'

'Jack looks like a sugar in a plum!'

'I saw the worms once.'

'Plum! Plum!'

'They were all swishing about in the toilet, like minestrone soup.'

'Plum!' I said. '*That*'s your name!'

'No, it isn't, it's your name,' he shouted, cramming another marshmallow into his smirking mouth.

'Plum . . .' I said dancing round the bed. 'Nancy . . . Nancy Plum.'

'Fanny!'

'All right, then, Fanny Nancy Plum. And Caramel, after Mr Kipling. Repeat after me: My name is Fanny Nancy Plum Caramel . . .'

It was just like the Bournemouth water-slide. It was like your body hurtling down the plastic chute like fizz shooting through a spiral see-through straw – like you were flying through the gullet of a whale. A shark more like.

'What's my surname?' he said.

'Norwood!' I said.

We snorted with laughter and gagged down another handful of Iced Gems. But when I grabbed hold of the yellow tape-recorder from the shelf and waved it above my head, Jack went pale like he was going to be sick. Boney M wailed on about water running dry and having nowhere to wash their clothes as Jack whined, 'Don't!' and jumped up from the bed to try to snatch it back from me. 'Be careful, won't you, Rosa?' he pleaded. 'Rosa!'

That was the worst thing to say to say to me. I carried on jumping up and down like a maniac, enjoying the feeling of having all the power in the world towering above my head in a little yellow oblong.

'"It is something, in whatever place, in whatever corner, to have become lord and master even of one single lizard."

Juvenal, Satire III,' I shouted at Jack, thinking that Brenda did have her uses sometimes.

My throat burped up a puddle of Twiglet acid into my mouth and my neck felt like someone had tied a red garrotte lightly round it, pulling tighter and tighter. I was looking at the St Tropez snowstorm at the time. The cathedral with the clock tower vanished to be replaced with a hazy Twiglet, monstrous in size, dripping with chocolate spread. I knew it would be unwise to jump any more but I wasn't going to give in now. So I kept my body still and I just started throwing the yellow box higher and higher in the air while he kept pleading, 'Please! Please!' as if I had his life in my hands.

'Please!' he squealed, when it hit the ceiling.

But I didn't stop, I kept going until finally he said it.

'Fanny,' he went quietly, screwing up his eyes. 'My name is Fanny Nancy Plum Caramel Norwood.'

'Can't hear you,' I said, clutching the yellow plastic so hard that I could feel the 'Brown Girl' throbbing in my sweaty palms. Even my palms felt excited, like when I go on the monkey bars in the backyard at home and, to be extra hard with myself, I put the pig-bins underneath so that if I drop off I will fall into rusty cans of turnip and skirt gristle (and also gherkin tassels and syllabub because that is how much interest for Fanny Cradock there is in my house). But I never do fall down. I swing along until my hands bleed.

I gripped the cassette-recorder even harder and ordered him to say his name.

'My name is Fanny Nancy Plum Caramel Norwood!' He was panting as if the words were painful to get out.

And then, all of a sudden, I fell silent. He was thrown off his guard. He opened one of his eyes a tiny crack to see where the tremendous bird was going to attack him next but all he saw when he looked up was the beaming face of Rosa from school. Then he didn't know where he was. He looked puzzled, he gazed into my eyes, searching for the truth. He wasn't sure where he was any more. This is an alternative to being mean. This is called manipulation.

'Very good!' I said, and counted in my head the time it would take for him to come back to me again, to love me again. But by the time I got to five I couldn't be bothered any more. I tossed the yellow rabbit on top of the mosquito net. It came untied from the wall and both Boney M and it flopped down on to the litter-strewn bed. Jack rushed over to inspect his precious possession for damage and I felt sad. Inexplicably sad. A feeling that jumped between sadness and boredom. The desperate irritability you feel when you've spent the whole of a sunny day watching television. Suddenly it felt weird to be in this room – a room that smelt of hot socks and still echoed with the sad, pathetic tale about a mother who obviously couldn't care less about him. I watched him as he checked the rabbit for broken bones and I almost felt sorry for him. And then, at the last minute, I didn't. I didn't see why I should feel sorry for him. He had a better life than I had and, anyway, I hardly knew him. He hardly knew me. Or maybe he did now. That was the worst of it. The peanut butter and Wagon Wheel sandwich gave me a big kick in the gut.

Jack put the silent rabbit back carefully on the shelf.

'I knew you'd be fun,' he said shyly, not meeting my eye. 'Mum'd like you.'

Really fun, I thought. Inviting a bully back to your house. Being humiliated in your own bedroom. 'Where is she, then?' I snapped. 'You're always talking about her.'

'I didn't definitely say she'd be here,' he mumbled. 'She's probably lying down. She gets ill.'

The throat garrotte squeezed again. 'I'm going to be sick,' I groaned.

'Wonder what colour it'll be,' he said, brightening up.

Chapter Five

> The dreary business of dressing crab is just about as twitch-making as boning quail.
>
> *The Cook Hostess' Book* **by Fanny and Johnnie Cradock**

I think of splashing some cold water on my face to make myself feel better. But then I don't need any water because when I walk into the bathroom there is a huge crab walking around in the bottom of the bath. A live crab in the bath – like a black water-lily or a black witch turned into a crab the size of my school hat. It is skulking around in the bottom of the bath in five centimetres of water. Its huge front pincers remind me of Brenda's big, beefy claws when she's folding her arms, giving Brydie and Mary stern advice.

The crab is trying to scramble up the sides of the bath but it can't because the sides are too slippery. Its eyes are stuck on the end of stalks. When my shadow passes over them they whir round. It's panicking. You can't blame it. It must have realised by now that its escape plan isn't going to work. I wonder if it will get me if I put my finger near its body. It is truly horrible, this thing skulking around in the shallow water. I want to get nearer. I sit on the edge of the bath and dangle my finger down in front of its crab face – whipping it out of the way when its front claws rise up in the air and start snapping like a pair of nasty nutcrackers. My father says you should pick crabs up from behind because there are no legs or claws in the back and their joints are incapable of bending back to get your fingers. So I try to poke the crab's hind end, but it is too quick. It scuttles round quickly like an arthritic tarantula and I think it's going to reach me with its front claws to give me a hard nip. I'm ashamed of being so scared of a stupid crab. It doesn't even have a brain. I don't think it has a brain. It has four tiny tentacle things at the front, four short stumpy stalks flailing around like an itchy nose, and behind the nose is a cave with two doors and behind them you can see more stubby tentacles, thinner and more lively – like maggots or threadworms – swaying from one side to the next.

I lean further in, my hands supported on both sides of the bath, and I lower my face as close as I dare towards the heaving worm cave. I force myself. I can't help it. I am breathing quite quickly now. I make myself. I open my mouth, I look the bristly cavern full in the face and I hiss melodramatically, *'Mais ne regarde jamais le monstre dans les yeux!'*

'Oh, for Christ's sake!'

Shock buckles my elbows and I tumble down into the bath. I put my hands down to stop my fall but I can see, as if it's in slow motion, that I am heading straight for the black Cyclops – forty feet high with wet tentacles and muscular legs and crunching mandibles dripping with black slime – and I know it's going to kill me, eat me up, swallow me, and I'll have to live in the belly of the cold black witch for the rest of my life.

I make a low-pitched 'Uh!' sound, like I've been tapped on the back in the dark, and my hands land right next to the horrible thing. So I shut them, I screw up my face and shudder another 'Uh!' and wait for the embrace of the cold nutcrackers. Suddenly there is a loud clank, something sharp touches my right arm, and I shout, 'Uh!' again as I feel myself being yanked from the depths of the bath by claws that penetrate deep into my arm flesh and touch the bone. Then I feel springy lawn under my feet and the air smells spicy.

When I open my eyes there is a brown piece of chicken skin. Then there is vibration all around, the claws dig into me again and I am wrenched away from the crinkly warm chicken cleft, back into the world.

'Ker-rist! What the hell's he done now?' A woman with a deep brown tan is standing before me. She lets go of my shoulders and passes two pairs of red talons through her hair. 'Ker-rist,' she says again, collapsing on the edge of the bath and picking up a large tumbler decorated with bees from the window-sill. She takes a gulp of the clear liquid, replaces it on the sill with a clank and screws up her face like she's breathing out fire. 'Bloody skinflint!' Her words smell of syllabub. 'Another of his bloody bargains. At least the last one was dead.'

She looks like she has just got out of bed. She is wearing a black petticoat with a lace trim and a black bra that doesn't cover up much of her brown, freckly breasts. The freckles are quite interesting, but mainly my eyes keep going back to the chicken skin, the crêpy crack.

Her head drops towards the carpet. A big, lazy kiss curl hanging over her right eye swings back and forward like a pendulum. I look to the ground, too, and notice that it is covered with more of the white woolly lawn. The rest of the room is not white. It is avocado green. The wash-basin, the toilet, the bath and the bidet are all avocado green although the taps are gold – gold with dolphin heads on. The other unusual thing about the bathroom – apart from the fact that there is a bidet and a crab in the bath – is that there is a shower cabinet in one corner, just like they have in America. I am wondering what it feels like to have a shower and then what it feels like to have a shower with clothes on, when Mrs Flowers gets up from the bath edge, snatches up the tumbler and flops down on the bidet. She balances the tumbler on her lap and then she stretches a languid arm down behind the green stem of the bidet and pulls up a cardboard box of Ariel. She tips the box on its side and out of the opening comes a dusting of blue-green washing granules and a rattling cluster of miniature red-topped bottles. She takes out two of the bottles, replaces the Ariel box behind the bidet, untwists one of the red caps and pours the see-through liquid on to two olives that have come aground on the bottom of her glass.

She takes a big swig and the top of her body starts to sway. I wonder if she's poisoned herself. I wonder if she's forgotten that I am standing here. She hasn't asked me who I am yet. My yanked arm hurts.

Still swaying slightly, she lobs the empty bottle into the bath and leans over to tip the contents of the full one on to the crab's back.

'"If you can't stab him, make friends with him,"' she says. 'Maghreb saying.' She stops pouring. 'Bloody England. Bloody rain.' And then she does it. She does a Spanish J sound. She hacks up the sound from the depths of her smoky throat, she tears a live heart from a ribcage. '*Joder!*' she spits, like purring sandpaper. *Hod-air*, it sounds like, long and serrated, *hhhhhod-air, hhhhod-air*, slicing the infidel's head, twisting a neck, ripping a heart, tearing the sky. 'Fuck,' she is saying. I know the meaning of this from Nikki Kilroy, except that when she utters it the word sounds thrilling and light as air and it looks like a fine spray of syllabub perfume shooting up from a sparkling brown fountain.

She makes a slow, wriggly laugh. 'Know any Spanish, then, little girl?'

I start to gabble. 'We've just started,' I go. 'You could choose between German and Spanish but I chose Spanish because you have to go to the country some day and it rains in Germany – doesn't it? And – and there aren't any beaches

I don't think in Ger . . .' I peter out because I realise I must be sounding like a little girl and I want to prove to her that I'm not a little girl, that I'm fourteen years old, even though I only turned fourteen a couple of weeks back. So I add, 'I like the sound of Spanish. I think it sounds really . . . savage.'

I'm a bit worried that this is the wrong word to use but Mrs Flowers stands up and sways over to the mirrored medicine cabinet above the wash-basin. I step hastily out of her path but Mrs Flowers doesn't seem to notice me. She just stares at herself in the mirror, going, 'Yes, savage. Savage and aromatic. The smell of burning rosemary and scorched earth.'

She licks her finger and runs it round and round the rim of the tumbler like it's a crystal ball. She does it for so long that I wonder if she's forgotten I'm still there.

'We've got a rosemary tree in our backyard,' I say, in case she has forgotten about me. 'I haven't noticed that it smells of anything, though. It's usually all wet. Its leaves are soft like – like lychees.'

There's no response. I try saying it again, 'You know, the white things you get for dessert at Sun Doo City . . . you know the Chinese restaurant next door to Oggies. That's where I live . . .'

'The pain in Spain stays mainly on the plain.' She twists the tumbler into her hand like a glass screw, tighter and tighter into her palm. 'The pain on the plain,' she recites, through gritted teeth, 'the pain in Spain. A haemorrhage of perfume over the hills. An agony of scent.'

She stops suddenly and bangs down the glass on

the wash-basin. Now the bees are frosted with smeared fingerprints. They look like squashed flies now. You could scrape the flies and squeeze their blood into a cup to keep your strength up.

Outside in the hall the grandfather clock chimes six o'clock. Brenda and my father will be eating boil-in-the-bag cod with parsley sauce at this moment but I am learning about life. Mrs Flowers is experienced.

'I went to Le Havre once,' I blurt out. 'On the ferry. From Portsmouth. We didn't get off. My mother ... she hadn't got passports for us. Doesn't believe in abroad, my mother ...'

I'm not sure if Mrs Flowers is listening but I go on anyway. 'I saw it, though – the continent. I smelt it from the front of the ship. I leaned on the railings for three hours and breathed in all the smells. Sort of salty and oily it smells. I looked out over the docks and I watched all the other passengers driving off the boat to buy up lots of beer from a big supermarket called a *hypermarché*.'

Then I realise that what I have just said must sound really boring for someone as cosmopolitan as Mrs Flowers. But she doesn't seem to mind because she just looks back into the mirror and carries on talking. 'Very noisy, Spain,' she says. 'Place we lived, there was always some dog barking, some woman screeching in the street.'

'Did you wear earplugs?' I ask her.

'No,' she says. 'I had a lot of affairs and I got very high.'

The slow, wriggly laugh comes again.

I feel my face go red. Mrs Flowers said 'affair' and 'high'. Fiona P says that 'high' means you are a drug addict but when Mrs Flowers says it, it reminds me of *Alice in Wonderland* and Alice's neck stretching up high in the sky when she ate too much of the 'Eat Me' cake. Or it sounds like a beanstalk – climbing right up to the top of a beanstalk, passing through the clouds and looking down on everybody else. It sounds like an adult version of the monkey bars and the roller-coaster.

I wonder if Mrs Flowers had the dirty kind of sex in her affairs. There are two kinds of sex, according to Fiona P. The clean one is when the man kisses you all over but never goes lower than your tummy button. The dirty kind is when the man goes below that line. In my *Joy of Knowledge* it says, 'The act can take anything from a few minutes to a few hours.' I'm not sure why you have to wait several hours for it to happen. Probably Mrs Flowers is very good at it and she only has to wait for a few minutes, like she probably doesn't have to wait very long in shops to get served because everyone must be a bit afraid of her.

Mrs Flowers isn't so different from the crab. Black and scary and exciting. Her smell makes me feel awake. I want her to say something else that I don't fully understand. I want her to take me again to the chicken cleft.

I realise that now is the time for me to say something cosmopolitan – to keep her interest going. I think that oysters are what is called for. In her *Cookery Course* Oyster Special Fanny Cradock writes about when she and her brother were very small and their parents spent winters in the South of France and they bought Portuguese oysters for six old pence per dozen because they were never ones for jelly babies or toffee apples. From Fanny Cradock. I know that the French think oysters to be more beautiful than any religion. 'Oysters are more beautiful than any religion, Mrs Flowers,' I say.

In the mirror I see Mrs Flowers' eyebrows arch upwards. I know from looking at pictures in magazines that she has plucked them. They are thin as a line of ants. She turns round and stares me in the eyes for what seems like ages and I think my stomach might blow up like a Hoover bag stuffed with butterflies. And then the beginning of a smile – I think – twitches in one corner of her mouth. 'Yes,' she says, in a more cheerful voice. 'And you can feed them to your lover with your toes.'

I can't quite believe Mrs Flowers has said this to me. Me! Who didn't even get off the boat at Le Havre!

'Mind you,' she adds, looking over at the crab again, 'I do rather like shellfish. Anything you can crunch and suck and rip apart with your fingers can't be all bad.'

She takes another swig of the drink and lowers herself back down on the bidet. 'You must be Rosa. Rosa the egg-head. I've heard all about *you*.' She pronounces 'you' softly, like she's flirting or something. 'Call me Penelope,' she says.

'Penelope,' I say quickly, thinking, She is smiling at me! I want to do everything I can to make her smile at me like that again.

I ask her if she's travelled a lot. She takes another

swig from her glass and says that, yes, she has travelled a lot.

'First time I went abroad was on my honeymoon,' she says, in a bored-sounding voice. 'Ended up cutting it short by three days. All my so-called millionaire husband wanted to do was drive round the Mediterranean in a Mini. The map was bigger than the car.'

'Did you have nice food?'

'We ate crap. He kept taking me to what he called "offbeat" restaurants. He had no idea. They were just crappy bars down back alleys.'

My insides jump a little bit when she says 'crappy'. It is another word to add to my Big Words Book. I ask her if she stayed in a hotel. In Bournemouth we always stay in a self-catering apartment. 'Bloody hotels.' She sighs. 'Couldn't work out how to use the hairdryer. Nobody told me about adapter plugs. "Do Not Distrub" they had on a sign you put on the door. It was too late. I already was disturbed.' She stands up, concluding that the final leg of the horrible honeymoon was in Rome.

'Rome?' I say. And then I feel that I should add, 'Apparently there's a big staircase in Rome called the Spanish Steps.'

'Is there, chicken?' she breezes. 'I came on in Rome.'

The wiggling laugh comes like a snake that goes on and on like it's never going to stop and it makes me a bit afraid. And when she comes towards me – the warm spicy laugh nearer and nearer to my face – I can feel myself blushing again because she's said 'chicken'. I look in at the crêpy cleft and I think of the window in the Venetian Room again. '*Ne regarde jamais le monstre dans les yeux.*' Then she puts her nails, red as fly blood, on my shoulder and it makes all the hairs on the back of my neck stand up and my whole body starts tingling. I don't fully understand what she is talking about or what exactly it is I am feeling but I know that I have to see Mrs Flowers again.

'Now, if you'll excuse me,' she says, tripping over her words, 'I think you'll agree that it's *l'heure de l'apéritif*.'

But I can't let her go like this. I stammer, 'I can cook. I can cook for you if you want. I mean, if you needed any help . . .' And then I fold my arms over my chest because I am horrified by what's happening to her.

Some sort of Incredible Hulk thing is happening to her. Her chest is swelling up and her lips are getting pinched and her eyes have shattered to smashed mirrors. She grabs hold of my arms again and starts shaking me. 'What *are* you talking about?' she bellows furiously, sending a furnace blast of syllabub into my face. 'Are you trying to insinuate that I'm an unfit mother? Little girl! Little English girl! What do you know about anything?'

'Oh! I didn't mean to be rude,' I stammer. 'No! I really didn't. It's just that Jack said—'

'My son! What did he say!'

The springy white lawn beneath my feet feels squelchy.

'He said – he said that you had kidney problems!'

'What?'

The springy white lawn beneath my feet is going to eat me all up.

'He said that you had kidney problems and that you couldn't always make him food.'

Mrs Flowers stops still. 'That's what he said, was it?' A small smile leaks on to her lips. 'Not the brightest of sparks, is he?'

A wave of relief mixed with pleasure comes over me because Mrs Flowers is implying that I am a bright spark.

'Well,' I shrug, smirking, 'it takes all sorts.'

Mrs Flowers starts to smooth her breasts with her hands and I watch. She looks up while she is doing this, catching my eyes in hers, and it feels amazing and a bit like I've bitten on a piece of silver foil with a filling. She says, 'I think my son has what they term a "crush" on you.'

I don't like to tell her that I think he has a crush on Mr Jones and Nikki Kilroy more like. And, anyway, it doesn't matter. The important thing is that she thinks someone is capable of having a crush on me, Rosa Barge, the girl who has red hair and not the five holes and who is sometimes fat and sometimes thin. I feel a swell in my own breast. I decide that I have to get in even more with Jack, just so that I can escape from our horrible, pasty-fumed flat and spend more time in the gingerbread cottage where Penelope, my sophisticated new friend, will tell me about Spain and rosemary and having affairs. And it must be my lucky day because she asks me to get in more with Jack too. 'I would appreciate it if you could take him under your wing a little,' she says, in her flirty voice. 'I'd really appreciate it. Make my life a bit easier, if you follow my drift,' and she gives my cheek a pinch. 'You're going to be my saviour, aren't you, Rosa?' She pushes her breasts up and says, 'Enough to eat for you, is there?'

'Yes,' I stammer.

'Jolly good,' she slurs. She turns and starts to walk out of the bathroom.

I follow her and blurt out, 'If you ever need me to cook something special one day, I could make something for you . . . Penelope?' But Mrs Flowers is on her way down the hall, rushing off to catch *l'heure de l'apéritif*. I run after her and gabble, 'I can bone a bird and roll it back over its carcass as if – as if it were a silk stocking,' because this is the sort of thing that Fanny Cradock would say. I have to admit, though, that it sounds a bit, well, silly, when I say it here in the hallway.

But strangely enough it makes Mrs Flowers stop in her tracks. She stops still, turns round and puts a steadying hand out to the wicker chair that rests against the wall by the grandfather clock. I can't tell if she intended to lower herself on to the chair or if she's just lost her balance. She lowers herself gently down into the chair and starts stroking her black petticoat like she's in a trance. 'Stockings, eh?' she says, stroking and stroking. 'Not just stockings but *silk* stockings. Good God, the girl has taste.' She does her wriggly chuckle and reaches out a hand to pick up a cigarette from a packet that seems to be wedged down the side of the chair.

She lights it, closes her eyes and sucks in deeply. With her eyes still closed she lifts her black petticoat up over her knees, over her thighs, until I can see the tops of her stockings. At a quick guess I would say that Mrs Flowers definitely has the five holes and it's number five that I'm interested in. My eyes keep darting to the strips of naked thigh between the tops of the stockings and the end of the rolled-up petticoat.

She blows out a plume of smoke, starts to stroke her legs and then adds, 'The important thing in love is always to have someone in reserve. A back boiler. Two or three, if you can get them.' She closes her eyes and mutters, 'None at all if you've got the guts.'

And all the while I am looking at the brown strips between her stockings and the rolled-up petticoat. They are covered in downy blonde hairs, which are even finer than any cilia I have ever seen. They told us in biology lessons that there are cilia up your nose. Their purpose is to catch pieces of dust. But the tiny blonde wisps on Penelope's legs are much nicer then nose hairs: they are like the soft down on ear-lobes and they garnish legs the same colour as the chicken cleft. Beautiful brown chicken skin. Brown as golden roast chicken, *poulet* basted in honey and spice. *Poulet forestière, poulet Véronique, poulet Normande. Suprême de volaille*. There seems more experience and knowledge in these strips of skin than in all the foreign recipes in my scrapbook. I know that Mrs Flowers is giving me too much knowledge. Maybe it's to do with her kidney problem but if it is then I'm glad she has one.

'Do you like silk stockings?' she says, still stroking her legs. 'A naughty little present from a rather persistent admirer.'

'They're very nice,' I say, feasting my eyes on her lap.

Mrs Flowers looks at me in her witchy way and I start to feel the same feeling I felt in the Venetian Room. I say to her, 'I could start with a dessert maybe. I can do choux pastry. Do you like *gâteau St Honoré*? That's St Honoré like a saint. But you pronounce it "sant". That's the correct way to say it . . . in French.'

My voice fades a bit when I say this. It is probably because Mrs Flowers is pulling the petticoat back down over the strips. She looks at me as if she's suddenly very bored. She slurs, 'I suppose it would be good to have more than coffee and nail varnish in the fridge.'

She heaves herself up, leaving the empty bee glass on the table next to the wicker chair. 'I can't make pudding to save my life,' she says. 'In fact, there's something quite unpleasant about my cakes.'

I nod rapidly.

'Next week then!' she snaps. 'Bloody dinner party. Patrick's idea. Still, Mr Silk Stockings is coming.'

She wriggles her cleavage into position again, saying, 'Remuneration will naturally be in order.'

I think that remuneration means money but then she strokes my cheek again and the day freezes into just silence and breathing, a ticking clock and smells of spice and syllabub. There is a black witch's cloak wrapped around us.

Chapter Six

> Unless you know or can see the oyster service in any establishment, say this when you order, 'I will have mine on the flat shell, if you please, unbearded, without ice and please do no detach them' ... If you want a bit of first-class one-upmanship, you just murmur to your companions, 'I do so agree with the great André L. Simon who once said, "Even a drop of lemon juice is the thin edge of the wedge of heresy."'
>
> ***Sociable Cook's Book*** **by Fanny Cradock**

This is my secret: I am afraid of the night. In the night, a witch comes and gets me. She won't leave me alone. My eiderdown is my only protection. If I don't have it pulled tight over me I know that she's going to come into my room and the horrible tickling is going to start all over again. Often, even the eiderdown is a useless shield against the witch. She can easily get through it. Even if I can't see her face I can tell she's there because of the tickling in my tummy, but I won't turn to look at her because I know her eyes will dig into me like a big, sharp dagger trying to force open a mussel that's closed. Fanny Cradock says you shouldn't force open shellfish that don't want to be opened because they will be bad inside. You should leave them alone.

The black hag is the only person who knows me in the whole world. She usually comes like a horrible guest appearance in the middle of a dream. Most people probably wouldn't be scared of her at all. She looks like a silly cartoon witch with her warty face and her black pointy hat and floating robes. She even has a broomstick.

Sometimes she looks at me and there is silence, but sometimes she laughs and then she pokes me in the ribs with her long bony fingers and it tickles me so much, it's like going over a bridge very fast. It's a tickling pain that's nice as well as horrible but if you let yourself stay in her spell for too long, the tickle goes deeper and deeper in, it pushes down on you and crushes your bones until you can't take it any more. All the tiny bits and pieces that my body is made up of – called atoms – jump out of me like excited pins and needles when she comes. They get mischievous. My atoms skedaddle in different directions and I can't hold them together. I literally come apart. Sometimes, while this horrible dream is still going on, I know it is a dream and I know that I just have to open my eyes to escape from the frightening black witch. If I can prise open my eyes I can kill her. But sometimes her tickling holds me back. The more she tickles, the harder it is to open my eyes and escape back to the real world. I am on the edge of despair, I think I will never be able to make it back. And then, finally, I find the energy to tear my eyes open and I find myself back in my dark bedroom with its twisted eiderdown and the sound of my own hot breath. But my eyes get so heavy, so tired and heavy, and before I know it they droop closed and I am pulled back into her bony breast, her spiky quail bosom, and I have to escape all over again.

Sometimes my dream will be that I am in my bedroom, in my top bunk, awake. All will be quiet and then I turn to the door and she will be there, in the crack between the edge of the door and the wall. Her black arm, her hat, her thin, wasted body, her broom, maybe – they'll all be there and she will be cackling again, sending ants all over my body to gnaw me and plague me and tickle my ribs. And sometimes, when I yank open my gluey eyes to escape her clutches, I still see her. She is still there, even with my eyes wide open and me looking down and seeing myself in my bed, she is still there, cackling. I can't escape from her land into my own and this sends me into an even greater panic. Maybe there's no return, I think. Maybe I am going to be clawed at by her for the rest of my life – and then I shake my head and heave open my eyes like I'm going to burst a blood vessel and finally, finally, I wake up in my real bunk bed, in my own pitch black room with the catering packs of baked beans and the ever-present smell of extractor fumes and I have to make sure to keep the light on and my eyes pinned open or it'll be in-out-in-out of witch country all night long.

Jack tells me that he's not scared of witches. He thinks it's silly to be frightened of them. It's ghosts you have to watch out for, he says. Ghosts aren't just clowns draped in white sheets like in *Rent-a-Ghost,* he says. They're like silk scarves. They can glide though a space the size of a ring, a crack the size of a hairline fracture. They can come in the day, too. They can make you do things.

This is why he is taking precautions. Precautions against the ghosts, he says. He papers over the keyhole in his bedroom door with a revolving selection of pages from *Smash Hits* and the *TV Times*. He also puts posters over the crack between the bottom of the door and the carpet.

I don't scoff too much about all this. I think of my dream. I have only told Jack a bit about the witch and in a way it reassures me to know that he has even worse tormentors than me – that his dreams last even into the day. Sometimes I can't tell what he means about his ghosts, if he's being serious about them or not. For instance, on the hinges of his chest of drawers he has recently stuck two posters of Olivia Newton-John. 'Better safe than sorry, Rosa,' he says.

The thing he seems most afraid of, though, is Mrs Flowers. At the same time he is desperately eager to please her and this, of course, is fighting a losing battle. Mine, on the other hand, is not a losing battle. I am going to keep my promise to Mrs Flowers. I will entertain Jack. I will become his friend and her saviour. I will do anything to see Mrs Flowers again.

I start to do things with him. I take an interest in him. I talk to him at lunch-break, I invite him to my house, I use him as my personal secretary. I get him to copy out letters from the letters page of *My Guy* and *Oh Boy* (I get back issues free from Fiona P in exchange for doing her French homework). I get him to resend them – often to the same magazine – in slightly altered form and signed by different names. Sally Kettle from Scarborough in Yorkshire writes:

Dear My Guy,

I went to my best friend's house last weekend and I was helping her mother put the washing in the airing cupboard when I saw some clay pots on a shelf. 'These are nice pots,' I said. 'Pots!' she said, horrified. 'They're not pots. They're meringues I made for your tea!' How we laughed afterwards – after I'd made a full apology, that is!!

And I dictate to Jack:

Dear Oh Boy,

A really funny thing happened to me at my boyfriend's house the other week! We were looking for a bottle opener to open a bottle of cider when I suddenly found some beer mats in the drawer. 'These are nice beer mats!' I said. 'They're not beer mats,' he said, horrified. 'It's my mother's shortbread. You're chucked!!' He later admitted that he was only kidding – about the being chucked bit!!

You get two pounds for each letter published and five pounds if they make it letter of the week. The secret is to use lots of exclamation marks, to pretend you are younger than you really are and to seal the letter in an envelope made from a colourful advertisement page of the *TV Times* like they suggested on *Why Don't You Just Switch Off Your Television Set and Go and Do Something Less Boring Instead?*.

One day, almost three weeks since my first meeting with Mrs Flowers, Jack and I are leaning out of my bedroom window on the day of the Mousehole Carnival. The smell of pasty meat and Mr Whippy ice cream mingles with something that smells like frying bacon, singed hair and cold PG Tips. This is because I am burning a clump of red ants on my window-sill with the help of an impressively hot May sun and a large magnifying-glass while Jack is throwing a stream of wet teabags at the float carrying the Carnival Queen and her retinue of nymphs – a group of five- and six-year-olds done up in white tutus and tiaras. The teabags were meant for the Jolly Roger float and any baddy floats in general but Jack, as usual, has seen fit to do something entirely inappropriate. Even when the little girls start crying and the Carnival Queen's father starts jumping up and down, shaking his fist at my bedroom window and threatening to tan Jack's ass, Jack still keeps on hurling out more teabags until finally I have to shout, 'Duck,' grab hold of him and pull him down out of sight. I glare at him and hiss, 'Idiot,' although secretly I am quite impressed, especially as the Carnival Queen this year is Fiona P.

I feel really irritable because after all this time and after all this babysitting there has still been no cake order from Mrs Flowers. I have hardly seen her – even though I've been to Jack's house on several occasions. Usually she has been sleeping off her kidney problem, although once we glimpsed her accelerating off down the drive in her white Mini van – on her way to a sun ray lamp appointment at the hairdresser's probably, Jack said.

Jack gets up from under the window-sill, goes to sit on top of a catering pack of beans and starts eating a packet of Monster Munch. I don't want to let on to him about how desperate I am. I don't think he's noticed. He seems too happy that someone is taking an interest in him at last. He loves coming to my house. He even seems to like the tangerine flock and the wood-effect wallpaper that cover the inside of much of the flat. He likes the thornless roses and the vulva lip petals that sprawl over each non-matching acrylic armchair. One of his favourite things is to press his ear to the worn lino floor and listen to the chatter going on in the shop downstairs. He enjoys listening to the older women talking about their annual trips to Blackpool – the making of the apple-pie beds, the hiding of whoopee cushions, the clockwork walking willies, the red rubber balls which, when pressed, inflate red-tipped tubes, which are willies too. Sometimes Jack brings round his dirty lighter and his dirty mug collection to show them. He likes walking through the shop in his 'Open Your Gob and Gobble My Knob' T-shirt and eyeing the boys with their white nylon overalls open at the chest. I'm nervous of the boys. They remind me of the sign at the swimming-pool –

the one alongside 'no running', 'no splashing' and 'no eating' that says 'no petting' and is illustrated by a drawing of a man with his arm around a woman with big breasts. Sometimes the boys shout questions at me as I walk past, like what car will I have when I am older, and when I mumble, 'A Ferrari' they all laugh at me and tell me to get off my high horse. I kissed one of them once. He had a smear of baked beans on his lips – sticky, I imagined, as the red-tipped inflatable thing in his trousers.

Jack seems fearless, though. 'I do like a bit of meat,' he says to the boys, in his Dick Emery voice, and some of them make wolf whistles and say, 'You are awful, but I like you!' because presumably taking notice of Jack is more interesting than cutting up skirt and slicing potatoes and turnip.

Jack looks so content up there on the baked-beans raft, swinging his legs from side to side, scoffing his Monster Munch without even getting fat, that it irritates me even more. Everything that isn't Mrs Flowers irritates me.

It's not as if I haven't tried to get to her. I do things so that Jack will be told off by Mrs Flowers and I will learn what she said and how she said it and how her face moved and how her eyes flashed. Last week I dyed Jack's hair with blue cochineal and I made sure we did it on the white carpet in the Venetian Room. When there was a blue stain the size of a saucer on the white shag pile carpet I suggested to Jack that he cleaned it off with Domestos and when it got all matted and stained yellow I suggested waking Mrs Flowers up to see what suggestions she might have for stain removers. But the only person in the house was Mr Flowers and all that happened was that he sent Jack to his bedroom and I had to go home early. I have been back to the Ariel box behind the bidet – to make contact at least with her that way. Several times I have been back to inspect it, but when I tip the box only blue-green granules come out – there is no sign of any bottles.

Sometimes I wonder if I imagined everything, not just the bottles but Mrs Flowers too. Mostly, though, I know that it was all real. I might have met her briefly but her presence still lingers, indelible as a nightmare, irresistible as a dream. I can't work, I can't sleep and I eat too much. I push food into me because she is absent. Ever since the day I met her I have been playing back in my mind the events of that evening from different angles: the way she looked at me, the foreign words she used, the brown strips, the shivers that went down the back of my neck. 'Call me Penelope,' she said. 'Call me Penelope.'

The cake is very important. I like to think that when she puts the delicate, light pastry in her mouth she will not only think of me: it will make her see who I really am. She will realise that I am just like her, that I can help her, that I think England is pathetic, too. If only I can get us alone a bit more I know she will like me.

When I persist in asking Jack when the day will be for me to make the cake, Jack just smirks and mumbles in his uniquely annoying way, 'Good people make cakes. Bad people make Fanny Cradock.'

Finally, I have to say it, even at the risk of humiliating myself: I turn to Jack, still swinging his legs on the baked-beans raft, and I say casually, 'Jack, is there anything I can do to make your mother have her dinner party?'

Jack smirks. 'Maybe you need to get a tapeworm.'

I can't believe what he's just said.

'You know,' he goes on, 'models have them. They come out of your nose. They smell the meat and they come up for lunch.'

I stiffen. I know exactly what Jack is digging at. He is saying that I am fat. The elasticated waist of my Laura Ashley skirt suddenly bites teeth into my waist.

'Mostly they just live in your guts, though. Suck up your food. Make you skinny.'

I am furious, and at the same time I know that Jack is right. It is the fault of pasties that I am fat. I have developed a taste for piecrust and even the air in Mousehole is thick, like breathing clotted cream.

I am furious also because he is only here by the grace of Mrs Flowers. I pull him down off the baked-beans cans and push him on the floor. I get a roll of rope out from under my bed, sit on his arms and consult my new book on knots. There is something satisfying about yanking his hands behind his back and pulling the rope tight into his hands so it makes red marks on his wrists. When he starts to laugh I put Sellotape over his mouth. I go from clove hitch to reef knot to hangman's noose so that soon he is trussed up like a skinny chicken. When I get bored of practising knots, I drag him to my wardrobe and throw him inside. I slam the door shut, slam him deep into the darkness for as long as I wish, and then I remember that he's not scared of the dark. I can hear him giggling, even through the Sellotape. I wish he wasn't made of rubber, that he didn't bounce back from everything I do or say to him. I wish he was made of china so that I could watch him break. I hurl my knot book out of the window but my dramatic scream is muffled by a loud rendition of 'The Floral Dance' by the Mousehole Lifeboat Young Men's Choir.

And then, on Monday, Jack comes to school and announces that Mrs Flowers needs the cake for Wednesday. Wednesday is to be the day of the dinner party. My heart starts galloping wildly in my throat.

On Tuesday afternoon, in domestic science class, I make *gâteau St Honoré* as part of a 'hasty supper cooked by a working mother of three'. To tell the truth, I have never made choux pastry before but luckily it turns out to be easy for someone with my experience. What you do is put butter, milk and sugar into a pan and wait until the milk comes to the boil. Then you toss in the flour, take it from the heat and beat thoroughly. You add the egg then beat some more until the mixture is as thick as cement. You leave it until it is absolutely cold, then pipe and bake it in whatever manner is required.

For *gâteau St Honoré* you need one dinner-plate-sized ring and twelve walnut-sized balls. When cooked and cool, you cut the base in half and fill it with *crème Chantilly* and sandwich together. For the topping you tip two cups of granulated sugar into a very thick-based saucepan. You place on a low heat until the sugar has turned brown in the middle of the pan. You remove it from the heat then shake gently until the whole mass has turned to a golden brown caramel. Cover the choux circle with the caramel, pipe *crème Chantilly* into the small choux balls, place them on top of the cake and drizzle with the remaining melted sugar.

Ever since I have been going round with Jack, Chivers has been giving me lower marks. When she comes up to mark our things at the end of the day, she asks me what the cake is and I tell her. 'Sant Honoré, you pronounce it in French. It means "saint". It's for Jack's mother's dinner party.' A big, fat grin comes over my face because I am talking about Mrs Flowers and me in the same breath.

All Chivers does is comment that choux pastry is hardly suitable as a hasty meal for a working mother of three then turn to Jack and give him better marks for his plate of hot dogs. And the funny thing is that I don't care. As I watch her furry red cheeks churn round with Tesco baps and tinned frankfurter sausages, all I can see is Mrs Flowers digging her squashed-fly nails into my neck and saying, 'Call me Penelope, call me Penelope.'

On the evening of the *gâteau St Honoré* dinner party, Jack and I are sitting inside the mosquito net. Jack is sticking a complete *Smash Hits* Abba pull-out on the inside of one of the gauze flaps. At first he says he's doing it because he likes Abba (he does like Abba) but then he lets slip that the poster serves a double purpose. 'You can't be too sure,' he says quickly, clambering over the bed with pieces of Sellotape stuck in his mouth. 'It might look like a cotton wall but there are holes in it. Might keep a mosquito out but there's things smaller than—' And then he stops talking and there is a loud 'Ow!' because I have just shoved his skinny body on to the floor. He falls off the bed, through the bottom of the mosquito net, taking the Sellotape and the Abba poster with him.

'You're so clumsy,' I shout from the bed, cupping my arms protectively round the Quality Street tin that holds the *gâteau St Honoré.* One of the choux pastry balls on top of the cake has been nudged from its place by Jack's frantic movements. I climb out carefully through the opening of the mosquito net and put the damaged cake on the desk. I carefully lever the ball back with the aid of a ruler and an extra blob of *crème Chantilly* liberated from the middle of the cake while I get Jack to repeat his latest name to me. So far, his name is Fanny Nancy Plum Caramel Dolores Ramona Shirley Norwood. (Dolores is one of the cousins of Señora Sanchez from *Modern Day Spanish* and Ramona is an American name from a book by Saul Bellow on Mrs Flowers' bookshelf.) He forgets about Ramona so I hurl the ruler in the direction of his head. There is another 'Ow!'

He doesn't seem too upset about the drops of blood seeping from his left eye. He dips his index finger into the wound and inspects what he finds there. 'Blood's a nice colour, isn't it?' he says.

'What?'

'It'd be good if blood was made of paint.'

'What?'

'Everyone would have a different colour.'

'What?'

'Wars would be pretty, wouldn't they?'

For a few seconds I can't think what to say and this irritates me even more. I look at the liver-red smear on his face. Behind it is purple shading, which comes from the big bruise that has been there for a few days now. It came from Fiona P's boyfriend, Nikki Kilroy. Apparently, Jack put his hands down Nikki's trunks in swimming class. This is a typical idiotic thing that Jack would do. It's obvious that Nikki Kilroy is not going to want Jack's advances and that he's going to beat him up for it. Jack sees me looking at his black eye. He smirks as he traces its shape with a blood-crusty index finger.

I start pacing up and down the room. It's so frustrating waiting for Mrs Flowers to come and say hello to me and take the cake and thank me. Then I have a bright idea. 'Look, Jack,' I say softly, 'why don't we go and record your mother's voice? It'd be nice, wouldn't it?'

Jack stops fiddling with his eye.

'You could listen to it when you wanted then, couldn't you? Even when she's ill with her kidneys.'

'Record Mum's voice?' He sits up. 'With my tape-recorder?'

'Yes, with your tape-recorder.' I try to sound calm. This idea has actually been brewing in my mind for several days now. I'm going to need Jack's co-operation, though.

'We wouldn't damage it, would we?' he says, lines of worry coming into his forehead.

'Of course we wouldn't. Don't worry.'

'Well, we could go down, couldn't we?' he says slowly, looking at me with his green glass marble eyes. 'Mum said she'd call us when she's ready but we could go down and see if she's ready, couldn't we?'

I bite my tongue. I nod.

We creep downstairs and when we get near the kitchen my heart starts to beat faster because I can hear her voice.

It is the first time I have heard the deep, husky voice in more than three weeks. She is on the phone. Through the crack in the door I can just see a dark blue satin arm and a brown hand with nails painted squashed-fly red. The middle and the index finger hold a thin pink cigarette with a lipstick-stained gold filter. I stick my nose up to the crack and breathe in fumes of cigarette smoke and black instant coffee. I think I might burst. I jump when Jack taps me on the shoulder and signals for me to put the recorder as near as I can get it to the door. The smirk is back.

'Yes, well, we all know it doesn't take much to get you going,' the raspy voice is saying. Some puffs of smoke cloud over the hand. I press 'play' and 'record'.

'Fernando . . . you know I miss you.' There is a glug and then a bang as a chunky glass hits the table.

'Mmmm, yes, hit the very spot.' There is another long, deep chuckle. 'Look Fernando, *guapo,*' the voice carries on like granulated sugar melting in a thick-based pan, 'you know I have to be careful about Patrick . . . Yes, but we don't want the kibosh on us just yet . . . Him finding out . . . I know, but you always did talk better than me . . . All right, my darling, I must go . . . Of course I loved the last package . . . when's my next one coming?' Long snaky laughter. 'Until later then, *guapo*. Big kiss.'

The phone goes back on the receiver. Now there are just clouds of smoke through the crack punctuated by the occasional sound of a tumbler hitting the table with a bang. I press 'stop' and my heart begins to race.

Chapter Seven

Sex and beauty are one thing like flame and fire – if you hate sex you hate beauty. 'The greatest tragedy of our generation is the morbid hatred of sex,' I scrawled on the walls of my hotel bedroom which set poor father back a pretty penny for the repapering of the walls.

***Something's Burning*, an autobiography**
by Fanny Cradock

Mrs Flowers has a Spanish lover called Fernando who brings her silk stockings. The fact of her having a love affair makes her even more appealing. At least, I try to convince myself of this back in Jack's bedroom, frantically rewinding the tape, listening for clues, wondering if the fact of her speaking to him a bit in Spanish makes it any better. Five or six times I listen to it. I know it off by heart. The end of it goes, 'Until later then, *guapo*. Big kiss,' followed by a chopped-up line from 'Brown Girl In The Ring'.

I try to look on the bright side. At last I might get to meet a real Spanish person. And just because she is having an affair it doesn't necessarily mean that she might not be interested in someone else – like me. The very fact that she has strayed from Mr Flowers must surely mean that she could stray with lots of different people. She is used to having affairs. Although how can I compete with a man who brings her silk stockings? Is choux pastry as good as silk stockings?

Jack seems more concerned that I've recorded over his Boney M tape than he is about the shocking news on his mother. This makes me feel even more anxious for some reason. I throw the tape-recorder on the bed, announcing, 'Jack, your mother is having a love affair!' and he just goes red and clutches his long pipe-cleaner arms around the yellow rabbit.

'She is not,' he mumbles. 'She's not having a love affair.'

'Nothing wrong with it,' I say, fishing to see what he does know. 'Could be romantic.'

Then he flares up. 'She's not having an affair,' he says, his face twisting with anger. His face looks so unusual that I can't help laughing.

'Stop laughing,' he shouts. 'Don't say things like that about my mother or I'll – I'll—' He gets off the bed and stomps over to the snowstorm shelf. For a second I think he might turn the *gâteau St Honoré* upside down on the floor.

'It's just her friend,' he's muttering. 'She's always on the phone to her friends.'

'So why does she speak in that lovey-dovey voice, then, if he's just a friend?'

Jack's shoulders flinch. ''S not a lovey-dovey voice. Mum's got lots of friends.'

I sigh a big, bored sigh. I'm bored now. Bored of this game, bored of being in this room with this unappreciated cake and this tiresome mummy's boy. But then the red nails come back to me and I know that I have to try to make it better. Jack's eyes are clouding. I can see that he's starting to believe me and I realise that this is the wrong tack. Mrs Flowers must never be found out. If she is found out, she will leave and that will be terrible.

'Look, Jack,' I say, in a making-up voice, 'I didn't mean to be nasty about your mum, you know I like her.'

Slowly, he turns round. 'She said, "Fernando," didn't she?' He's smirking now. 'Like in Abba.'

'That's right.'

He starts to hum 'Fernando' as he scrabbles around on his tape shelf. 'I'll find it,' he says, excitedly.

'Even if she was having an affair,' I carry on, as he searches his tape collection, 'even if she was, there's nothing wrong with passion. French people have passion. They say "*volupté*". It's a nice word, isn't it? Reminds me of "soup". Baudelaire says that "The supreme *volupté* of love lies in the certitude of doing harm."'

But I've said something wrong. He stops riffling and starts screaming, 'Don't you say bad things about my mother!' like he's going to raise the roof. 'Don't you say bad things, Rosa, or I'll—'

But once again he doesn't say what he'll do because at that moment the door bursts open. Mrs Flowers stands on the threshold, her kiss curl swinging like a noose from side to side. 'What on earth is going on, Jack?' she explodes. I'm glad I'm not Jack.

Jack shuffles back and forth on the piece of carpet he is standing on. He looks down at his feet and mumbles, with a smirk in his voice, 'Be good if you could lick your own eyebrow, wouldn't it, Mum?'

I can't believe he's said this. I nearly laugh. It feels as if Sensurround sound is shaking the room, like the vibrations that went on in the cinema in *Earthquake* – only Mrs Flowers isn't like a character in *Earthquake,* she's scary as the Cybermen in *Doctor Who.* She advances closer and closer to Jack with metal flesh and a steel mask for a face.

'What on earth is going on, Jack?' she demands again, her eyes ablaze with paraffin.

'We – we were just talking about the cake, Mum,' Jack says, eyes still down, retreating towards the snowstorms.

'What cake?' Mrs Flowers snaps.

'You know, the *gâteau Sant . . . gâteau . . .* What's it called again, Rosa?'

When I say, '*Gâteau St Honoré,*' Mrs Flowers turns to me. I've been hoping that she might notice my new hairstyle. I washed my hair last night and stayed up really late trying to get a kiss curl in the front of it using a hairdryer and a toilet-roll holder. It hasn't worked very well. Mrs Flowers just stares at me and says, 'Who the hell are you?'

It's like she's slugged me in the stomach with a big boxer's fist. I can't believe she's forgotten who I am. I have been thinking of Mrs Flowers non-stop for the past three weeks – having imaginary conversations with her in my head, seeing her smile at me when I say something funny, confiding pieces of information to me that I only half understand but which make me a bit short of breath. Last weekend at the cinema, when I looked up at the projector and saw tiny particles of dust floating around in the lemon white light, I thought of the cilia, the strips and the cilia. I want her to meet me in the eye again, like she did before, like she did when she knew I'd been looking at the chicken skin between her breasts.

I know that my voice is going to sound a bit quavery but I open my mouth and speak anyway. 'You . . . you asked me to make you a cake – for your dinner party . . . You're having a dinner party tonight and you said that I could make a cake.'

Mrs Flowers looks at me like I'm someone she maybe remembers from a former life. Jack says, 'Mum, you know! This is Rosa, Rosa, my friend from school.'

'Cake?' she slurs, like it's a new word. 'Cake?'

Then she makes a brief shriek, as if she's just seen a mouse on the floor. But it's not a mouse on the floor, it's Jack's fake sick. When he goes to pick it up, to show her that it's nothing to be afraid of, she flinches from him. 'It's not real but it has got cracks in it,' Jack says, in a quiet, blank voice. 'There are a lot of things with cracks in, aren't there, Mum?'

Mrs Flowers has composed herself now. She looks at Jack as if she doesn't even want to waste her time looking at him. 'Bloody childish,' she snaps. 'Can't leave you five minutes. Got called up by the school because of your ridiculous behaviour, Jack. Got to stop.'

I can't help but feel a bit sorry for Jack. It's not very good payment for all the nice things he's always saying about her. It's not that I'm saving Jack exactly but I do think that now is the right moment to dash over and pick up the *gâteau St Honoré* from the snowstorm shelf. Only when I have it in my hands I'm too scared even to look at her face. I just push it forward slightly, obediently. I close my eyes and say, 'It'll look better out of the Quality Street tin.'

I can feel Mrs Flowers' shadow pass over me and then the next thing I know, a hurricane of cinnamon blows over me and a prickle comes over the back of my neck. 'Ah! Of course! The little crab girl!'

I think I prefer 'little English girl' to this but I breathe a sigh of relief anyway. At least she's remembered me. 'The little crab girl has made me some real choux pastry!' The green light has gone on. Now is my chance. I might not know about affairs and getting high and eating oysters with toes but I bet Mrs Flowers knows little about the development of world cuisine from Brillat-Savarin to Fanny Cradock.

'It's a recipe from Fanny Cradock, which I imagine was influenced by her hero, the great nineteenth-century chef, Marie-Antonin Carême. He was called "the architect of French cuisine". He invented the *pièce montée,* which is a huge centrepiece made of pastry and shaped into replicas of buildings and statues and temples and—'

'Statues and temples?'

'Yes, he trained with the master of choux pastry at the time, Jean Avrice, who is also credited with the creation of the Madeleine . . .'

Part of me is floating above myself, cringing at the nervous gabble I'm coming out with. But this same part of me knows that the other half can't help it. That the other half has to fill up three weeks of absence from Mrs Flowers in whatever way it can.

'Carême was the sixteenth child of twenty-five. At the age of eleven his father took him to the edge of town where he fed him a final meal then sent him out into the world on his own.'

'You hear that, Jack?' Mrs Flowers says, without looking at him. Jack makes a weird grin. Mrs Flowers carries on staring at the cake, which, now I let myself think about it, does look quite impressive.

'Such a good idea!' she slurs. 'And when Carême's own children were of the age to abandon at the edge of the forest they probably stuffed their pockets with choux-pastry crumbs instead of breadcrumbs! Both useless in the end, of course.'

I feel a bit clammy in my stomach because I wonder if she means that the *gâteau St Honoré* is a waste of space, too, but I can't worry about this for too long because the next thing I know, there is a deep, throaty laugh, a gas cloud of musky perfume and a pair of sharp red nails digging into my arm (I have only just got rid of the bruises from the last time). There is her saying, 'Come for your reward, little crab girl,' and there is Jack's fading voice in the background, going, 'I made hot dogs, Mum . . .'

I smile to myself as she whisks me off down the stairs because I know she can have no use for hot dogs. I try to keep the Quality Street tin steady in my hands as my heart pumps in my throat and she drags me down the helter-skelter stairway into the marble sitting room, her dark blue dressing-gown flying up in the air as she goes.

She finally releases me in the kitchen. I put the tin down on the worktop and watch her going to open the kitchen door. I am firming down a couple of choux balls that have come loose in the journey when a fiery petrol breeze comes to my face and says, 'Are you ready?' The next thing I know, my arm has been grabbed again and I am pulled out into the frosty night air.

A woman in a dark blue négligé and the voice of a wolf is pulling me into the sharp night air and the next thing I know there is the smell of orange. We are sitting on the red seats of a white Mini van parked in a clearing at the back of the cottage surrounded by a partial ring of thick conifer trees. Mrs Flowers is in the driver's seat and I am next to her in the passenger seat. The orange smell comes from a black card hanging on a gold chain from the choke knob. It looks like a traffic light: red spot on top, liquid-filled orange bump in the middle and green spot on the bottom.

You pierce the back with a pin and the smell comes out. I know this because Mrs Flowers sees me looking at it and she takes it off the choke knob to show me how it works.

Her hands are cold. She shakes them around to try to warm them up, and as she does this, her dark blue négligé comes open at the top and her breasts shake up and down. The movement blows up a storm of sweet orange and cigarette ash and Mr Sheen furniture polish. She stops to light a cigarette and I turn round and look at the back of the van, which is fitted out with a blue carpet, blue embroidered cushions and *Smash Hits* posters all over the walls. She sees me looking. 'Jack's work,' she says, with a hard smile. I can tell that Mrs Flowers wishes Jack was one of those adolescent sons who walked ten paces in front of her in the street pretending he had nothing to do with her and referring to her as 'my old lady'. 'Like my little run-around, do you?' she says.

The freezing night has made her sharp again. I can tell by the tone of her voice that she doesn't like the van at all. She is being sarcastic. 'Fact of the matter is,' she says, jerking open the glove compartment, 'we're bloody skint. When I met Patrick he told me he had twelve months to live.' She snorts. 'Heart problem, he said. I thought it sounded perfect. Thought I could put up with him for twelve months.'

She starts rummaging around in the glove compartment until she locates a mini-bottle of yellow brown liquid saying 'Jack Daniel's' on the label. She unscrews the lid. 'Twelve months married to a so-called millionaire seemed a perfect prospect.'

I am quite surprised that Mrs Flowers is telling me all this. It sounds like past-my-bedtime TV. I wonder if I will ever become as clever as Mrs Flowers. She wipes her mouth with the back of her hand and screws the lid back on the bottle.

'Bloody liar. The only thing that vanished in twelve months was his money. Burned his way through the family fortune. Well, actually, I burned our way through the family fortune. Only thing right as rain was his health. Still is.'

She starts taking out handfuls of things from the glove compartment. I rub a pair of soft beige gloves against my cheek.

'It wasn't all bad, though.' She sighs. 'Not at the beginning. He was pretty good in the sack and . . . I don't know . . . he was sweet. And it was nice having someone to look after, in a way. Made me feel like a good person sometimes – because, believe me, I'm *not* a good person.'

I try to interrupt her to say that I bet she is a good person really, but she won't let me speak. 'Resourceful, too, I'll give him that,' she barks. 'We moved to Spain when the money went and he got a job with a TV company. Foreign rights. It was a good life. Always new people to meet who wanted to try their English out on me. Wanted to try *it* out on me – let alone their English. I wasn't averse either. Something they liked about me, the Spanish. Always bade a cheery *hola* by the supposedly ferocious doorman whenever I went to pick Patrick up from the office. Always lighting up the face of the waiter from the local restaurant. Always being given that little bit extra meat by the butcher.'

She tosses a series of objects on to my lap as she digs around even harder in the glove compartment. 'Bloody butchers,' she mutters, under her breath. The tip of her cigarette smoulders in the dark. 'Now, then,' she says, delving back into the compartment, 'I have it stashed back here somewhere. My own little bottom drawer.'

It looks like five or six handbags have all been emptied on to my lap at once. It makes me feel warm looking at it. Tissues with lipstick on them, packets of pills, pens, photographs, things in foil wrappers that I think might have something to do with sex, boxes with rings in, bracelets, necklaces. She starts poking round in my lapful of treasures. 'This is my particular favourite,' she says, picking up a silver necklace with a turquoise stone in. 'Present from a friend in Spain.'

I grip tighter on to the soft gloves. I am shut inside a Mini van with Mrs Flowers rummaging around in a secret treasure trove in my lap.

'Yes, those are nice too, aren't they?' she says. 'Spanish leather. Calfskin.'

She stops rummaging and looks at me. 'The bloody heart thing cropped up again, of course, and he had to stop the job. My Mother Teresa complex stopped round about then too.'

At first her eyes are cold as they stare at me. Then they relax – as if they've just sighed or let out the belt a few inches. 'Hence here we are, back in England, penniless, living in his father's pile with Patrick trying to sell something about which he knows precisely nothing.' She shrugs.

There is silence all around us apart from the sizzling of her cigarette tip as she sucks on it.

I say, 'Do you love Mr Flowers?'

Mrs Flowers almost chokes on the smoke. 'Love?' she says, as if she is reading some extra difficult word from my Big Words Book. She takes the cigarette from her mouth and waves it round slowly like she's making strokes with a paint brush.

'*Estoy enamorada,*' she says. 'I am in love. Didn't learn much Spanish while I was there but the two verbs "to be" I did find quite interesting.'

'*Ser* and *estar,*' I say quickly.

'Exactly,' she drawls.

'*Ser* is the permanent one,' I carry on, enthusiastic now we are on common ground. 'Like, "I am a woman", or "I am intelligent", or "I am English".'

'Exactly.' She gazes into space. 'Then there is *estar,* non-committal *estar*. The temporary sort of "to be". "I am hot." "I am happy." "I am in love."' She lets out a long sigh. '*Estar enamorada,* to be in love. *Estoy enamorada,* I am in love. For a short while. No *ser* in sight. Not for ever, you see.' Her stare gets hotter. 'Some would say that's a good thing: passionate love, then death. To be dead. *Estar muerto.* Also a temporary form of being. Not dead. Just sleeping. Optimistic lot, the Spanish.'

Mrs Flowers is starting to get a bit out of my depth again. I'm pretty shaky when it comes to knowing what love is, in spite of my Baudelaire quote. I used to think that if you loved someone it meant you would eat their snot and their turds and their toenail clippings. I would definitely eat Mrs Flowers' nail clippings, even with red nail varnish on. I am thinking about the snot and the turds when she says briskly, 'Patrick will do anything for me. Unfortunately.' She stops and lights another cigarette. 'We once moved from a beautiful house a stone's throw from the Mediterranean because the sea was bad for my hair. Sea makes my hair flat.'

She pulls down on her kiss curl. 'Shame, really,' she reflects. 'There was a good veranda there. Sun all day long. Nobody could see you. You could have a wank, switch off, go to sleep.'

Her shoulders drop and she turns slowly towards me. I am blushing because she said 'wank'. Then I get another little peek of her bra through the blue dressing-gown and I go even redder. I can feel it. She sees me looking. She smiles and touches my arm. 'It's nice to have a bit of extra attention.' Then she says something that sounds like, 'You only have to think about it for half an hour anyway, then it's over,' followed by – in a louder voice, 'You'll understand that when you get older.'

It annoys me a bit when she says this. As if she's calling me 'little English girl' again. As if she thinks I'm a kid. I feel like reminding her that I've just turned fourteen and telling her that I know she's having a lot of extra attention. That I have proof of it. But maybe she sees my face clouding over because then she starts giving me some attention and I like it. 'I'm glad I met you, Rosa,' she says, with a smile on one side of her mouth. 'I never really had anyone to talk to in

Spain. You should have seen some of the grisly people I got involved with when all I really wanted was a chat. Now, what will you be? My daughter? I always wanted a girl. So much more fun than boys.'

Then her face hardens again. 'Oh, I know I'm a bad mother.' She sighs, slamming herself back in the driving seat. 'For God's sake. Look what I've done to him.' She wipes her hand over her forehead. 'I can't deny it, though. I can't bloody deny it. I wish he was . . . well, you know . . . normal.'

Then she's tipping the Jack Daniel's into her mouth as if she's forgotten I'm here again. Now it's just the glove compartment and her. And Jack. And the whisky. Fanny Nancy Plum Caramel Dolores Ramona Shirley Whisky Norwood. At least she's saying bad things about him. But I want to be more than a daughter.

'I'd like to be your friend,' I say quietly.

Her anty eyebrows rise up. 'Would you now?' she says, with a rich chuckle.

'Yes,' I say, staring at the sizzling amber tip.

'Well, Rosa,' she says, screwing the top back on the bottle, 'if you are going to be my friend then you must help me with Jack. You know that, don't you?'

The hand goes back on my arm. She squeezes my arm with her cold fingers, like she is the Hansel and Gretel witch checking to see if I am fattened up enough for the fire yet. Of course I will help her. I already am. I would do anything for her.

'I think if I'd been an animal I'd have eaten my young.'

She sighs again. 'All right for animals. Get a bit peckish and that's that. Can't be helped.'

She smiles to herself and I feel electric. I imagine her tearing away at me in a nest, clawing and scratching, and then, at the last moment, deciding not to eat me at all, just covering me in Baby Oil and thrashing me with some twigs that happened to be growing in a tree nearby.

'Now, then,' she says, putting sudden authority into her voice and pushing her kiss curl back behind her ear, 'I'm sure I've told you far too much. Bloody drink. Patrick's right, I should cut back a bit. It's got me into a spot of bother over the years, but that would really be telling.'

And then she finally finds the thing she was looking for at the very bottom of the glove compartment. A black purse.

She opens it and hands me five pounds. Five pounds! More than a month's pocket money! 'Righty-ho.' She looks into the rear-view mirror and slaps herself lightly on the cheeks. 'Better go inside and attend to the old parchment.' She turns to me and puts a cold finger and thumb around the bottom of my jaw. She squeezes tight. 'Remember the importance of secrets, little friend,' she says. She squeezes very tight indeed.

Chapter Eight

On one fog-bound European expedition our flight was held up in Munich. A bland young jack-booted Hun accoutred with guns suddenly put his booted foot on one of my cases. All my revulsion was concentrated in this ill-mannered gesture. I snapped in German, 'Take your boot off my case, young man, and behave properly.'

He looked up, amazed. 'What have you got in this bag?' he countered.

'Stand up straight,' said I furiously, 'salute me respectfully, address me as madam, remember to say please and I may consider replying.'

***Something's Burning*, an autobiography**
by Fanny Cradock

The door bursts opens and a new smell enters the house: overcooked broccoli, sweet talcum powder and sour male sweat. Four adults sway like puppets as they exit the kitchen and veer across the *parquet*, drinks held high in the air. They look like four swollen heads from the special Spanish fiesta Mr Jones told us about: one red papier-mâché face with stiff egg whites for hair and eyes like black slits cut into a hollow pumpkin; one thin stick in black-rimmed glasses and a smile welded to a pair of pink lips; one gold witch with a curly black curtain swinging past her eyes; one man with a frown on his forehead big as an upside-down seagull. They all come rolling in from the kitchen like swirling mists bobbing on rough seas until, with one loud whoop, they reach the Venetian Room and in one big gulp the solid black rumble is gone, vanished, swallowed up in a big glass belly.

Jack and I are in the sitting room. We are lying in a hot triangular tent formed by the back of the green settee and a radiator against the wall. We are spying. I am waiting for it to be *gâteau St Honoré* time. I want to know the noises everyone will make when Mrs Flowers brings my cake into the Venetian Room. I wonder how she will tell them about me. 'Friend of Jack's made this wonderful thing. Rosa, she's called. She's his age but somehow there's something more mature about her. She's very clever. Very pretty too, in an original way. We've become very good friends.'

But it's still *apéritif* time so, for the moment, I have to make do with crouching squashed up behind the radiator with an overexcited Jack. The view we have is of four pairs of legs sitting round the elephant-tusk table and, sometimes, hands reaching down to pick up glass tumblers studded with bees. Next to Mrs Flowers sits a pair of trousers – two pinstriped bags overstuffed with *duchesse* mashed potato. The bags move slightly when a northern voice says, 'Nice outfit, Pen, love,' and you can tell that they are attached to the same stumpy sausage hand that pats Mrs Flowers' legs from time to time.

She does look amazing tonight. It's the first time I have seen her wear proper clothes. Not that they are that proper. Her outfit is made from squares of gold-coloured metal linked together into a mini-dress. She literally sparkles. Her hair is smoothed down close to her head so the only bit that moves is the swinging kiss curl at the front. I can only imagine her smell of lipstick and foundation. She's being more lively than I've ever seen her tonight, like an actress in the first few seconds after curtain-up.

'Well spotted, Jerry,' she says. 'An old Paco Rabanne, actually. Latest in Patrick's line of chastity belts.'

Mr Flowers starts to scratch his ankle as if he's got fleas while a dirty laugh gurgles from Jerry and the fat chipolatas clamp on to Mrs Flowers' thigh. They only let go when the red, banana-shaped shoe belonging to the stick woman kicks the pinstriped trousers on the shin.

I didn't know you were allowed to call Mrs Flowers 'Pen'. Even Mr Flowers doesn't call his wife 'Pen'.

I keep waiting for Fernando to turn up. I can't believe that Jerry is the man who bought the silk stockings. He looks more like Mr Sow's Ear than Mr Silk Stockings. I can't believe that Mrs Flowers would want to have an affair with him.

'I hate him,' I whisper. 'Sausage and mash.'

'Sausage and mash.' Jack nods.

'Come on, Jerry love,' a female voice attached to the red boots says. 'Don't start getting tricky with Penelope.'

The mashed potato bags sag out even wider and one of them glues itself to Mrs Flowers' leg. 'Nonsense, I'm sure our Pen has known trickier men than me in her time. What say you, Patrick?'

Mr Flowers' fleas seem to be getting worse. 'Um, thanks ever so much for the joint,' he says to Jerry, still rubbing at his ankle. 'Very kind of you.'

'Oh, Jerry knows a thing or two about meat, don't you, Jerry?' Mrs Flowers purrs. She holds out her hand so that the chipolatas can top her up again. More greasy chuckling comes from Jerry and Mrs Flowers, upon which Mr Flowers tries to change the subject by enquiring, in a nervous voice, if Sal and Jerry enjoyed their recent trip abroad.

'Oh, it was stunning,' Sal barges in. 'Stunning. Wasn't it, Jerry?'

'Bloody good trip,' Jerry grunts, sinking deeper into the settee as if it's a bed, the mash spreading ever wider as he goes. 'Course, we had the usual pool problems.'

'Yes, Jerry likes a pool, don't you, love?'

'Pool!' Mrs Flowers' voice scoffs, her brown legs clamping together like a mouse-trap. 'What on earth was wrong with the sea?' She makes the word 'earth' last for ever.

Mr Flowers starts scratching his ankle even more frantically as Jerry protests, 'Sea! Not going in the bloody sea! Bloody things in the bloody sea!'

Sal wriggles in her seat. 'Funny thing was, when we finally found a decent pool, the attendant fell in love with me. Didn't he, Jerry? Said he thought I was stunning.'

'Stunning! Brown as a fish supper my Sal was by the end of the fortnight.'

'It's funny,' Sal shrugs, 'whoever we meet, people always love me. They want to know all about me. We talk about books and that. I love the classics.'

'That's my Sal!' Jerry eases off his right shoe with the toe of his left and puts a damp beige sock on the bit of ankle showing between Sal's long skirt and her red banana boot. He rubs it up and down.

'She's really ugly,' I say.

'She looks like Olive from *On the Buses*,' Jack says.

'Bet she eats pickled onions in bed.'

'Bet she wears a face pack like in *George and Mildred*.'

'Mildred!' I say. We catch each other's eye and start to giggle.

'You're not so bad yourself, *guapo*,' Mrs Flowers is saying to Jerry. 'Look at this mop of curls.' She called him *guapo*, just like in the phone conversation. Maybe Jerry's pet name is Fernando. When you have a lover you have a pet name for them but you can't always say it in public because you have to double bluff, like you do in the escape films. She must be stroking his hair quite hard because Jerry's whole body starts to shake and he makes a dirty laugh like he's a dirty old octopus with one tentacle on Mrs Flowers' knee, one on his glass and one on his wife's ankle.

'You'll have to come with us next time, Pen love,' Jerry says. 'Bet you wouldn't have minded a bit of skinny-dipping, am I right? Bet she likes a bit of that, eh, Pat?'

'Now, don't start on that one again, Jerry,' Sal snaps. Her body turns towards Mrs Flowers. 'Pool attendant said I looked stunning. Most people I meet think I'm brilliant! Don't know what it is! Must be something special about me!' The banana boot starts twitching again. 'Course, Jerry said how could I know anything when I don't speak a word of Spanish. But we know these things, us women, don't we? We know these things.'

'Absolutely right we do, chicken,' Mrs Flowers exclaims, pushing Jerry's hand off her knee. 'I don't speak any Spanish myself. Just a few words. I know *vale*, for instance. It means OK. You pronounce it "Bally". Like the shoes. Not that old Scrooge over there ever takes the hint.'

Mr Flowers starts his scratching again but Mrs Flowers carries on, 'Whenever we go to the South of France he's always dragging me away from the shops, into some God-awful French film. Why *are* French films all about tedious love triangles taking place in bourgeois Parisian flats?'

'Rather romantic, I thought.' Mr Flowers blushes.

'Romance!' Mrs Flowers groans as if she's going to be sick. 'As you know, darling, I'm much more of the Pasolini school. Doing it down a back alley, humping on a rubbish tip. That sort of thing.'

There is a guffaw and Jerry's tentacle unsticks from Sal's ankle as he moves his body even closer to Mrs Flowers'. 'Get a load of this one,' he booms to Patrick. 'No wonder she didn't want to come back to this country. Mind, you've got your mucky windows to cheer you up, eh, Pen?'

He points to Theseus and the Minotaur. 'Which one's you, Pat? The knackered-up old cow or the pretty boy with the blond hair? Either way, wouldn't like to be standing next to you in the showers! Eh?'

'So, what exactly is the problem with your yacht, Jerry?' Mr Flowers says hurriedly.

'Eh?' Jerry grunts. 'Yachts! Bloody hell, you like to get down to business, you!'

'I haven't noticed that to be one of my husband's chief characteristics,' Mrs Flowers slurs, and starts one of her slow, snaky laughs. When Jerry realises what she has said he is off too.

Sal tries to break it up. 'Well, Pat love, I suppose we're just a bit bored with the whole yacht thing. No, I tell a lie. It's not so much we're bored of the whole yacht thing . . . well, we're not sure if we want to do yachts or cruises, basically.'

'Aye,' Jerry says, forcing himself to keep a straight face. 'Being on a yacht parked in Marbella with your wife and a couple of cabin-boys all day. Well, no offence, Pat, lad, but it's a bit bloody boring.'

'Boring?' Mr Flowers sounds nervous. 'But with all your

experience . . . Maybe you could do with something bigger. More of a challenge. Now, funnily enough I can get my hands on a very good—'

Jerry ignores him. 'If it weren't for the sun and the mixed saunas,' he drones, 'I'd wonder if it were worth going abroad at all.'

Sal flinches when he mentions the saunas. She says pensively, 'Food was a bit funny too, wasn't it? We thought we'd hit rock bottom when we had the pheasant, didn't we, Jerry?'

'Aye, but then we had the bloody goat stew in Portugal. Bloody goat stew. Tasted like bloody dirty knickers more like!'

'What a charming revelation, Jerry,' Mrs Flowers says, smoothing down her cleavage. 'I've never eaten goat stew, but if I don't make it to Portugal, I'll know whose linen basket to come to.'

Jerry erupts into laughter and the sausages appear on her leg again. 'Bloody cheeky monkey, aren't you? Bad as that son of yours. Had his hand down our lad's swimming trunks this week. You want to bloody get him seen to.'

I look at Jack to find out what's happening. 'Is that Nikki Kilroy's dad, then?' I ask him. But Jack's head is turned towards the wall. I can't see what he's thinking.

'You never normally notice them, do you?' he whispers. 'The cracks, I mean.'

'What?'

'The Devil wouldn't come to Cornwall, would he, Rosa?'

'What?'

'Your dad says he wouldn't because the Cornish people would put him in a pasty.'

'Stop being stupid, Jack.'

'Jerry's pants taste of goat's meat.'

And, like in Miss Norwood's class, I can't help but laugh at Jack's stupid joke.

Luckily nobody hears me because suddenly Jerry starts to choke. A stream of gin shoots out of his mouth and dribbles down his tie. You can tell that this is the build-up to a really bad joke. And it is. 'Eh!' he says, turning to Mrs Flowers. 'I hope it doesn't run in the family. I mean, you're not going to put *your* hands down my Sal's knickers, are you?' There is another explosion. He's got both hands on both knees and he's tipping his face down towards the carpet. Liquid is coming out of his nose with the hilarity of it all. Sal's feet look really embarrassed. They're grinding into the carpet as if they're trying to put out a very stubborn cigarette end. Then there's her voice, all flustered, going, 'Disgusting! Disgusting. Jerry . . . honestly . . . trust you . . . disgusting . . .'

There is a splinter of laughter from Mrs Flowers while Mr Flowers' hand just scratches his ankle harder and harder. Now that the room is full of liquid snot and vibrating bellies and Sal's grinding banana boots and her parrot mouth going, 'Disgusting, disgusting,' his itch seems to have got really deep. Matters take a turn for the worse when Jerry blurts out, 'What say you, Patrick? Bet you wouldn't mind having a bit of a watch of that, eh, lad? *Frottage*, eh? Now, there's a foreign word for you, Penelope my lovely . . .' Mrs Flowers can't hold back a laugh – a deep, burnt-sugar laugh that starts deep down in her belly and makes the back of my neck prickle.

The idea of Mrs Flowers touching the fifth hole of another woman makes me prickle all over with pain and pleasure. I can't remember what the French verb *frotter* means but I have an idea. I imagine Mrs Flowers pushing me into the front seat of the white Mini van and strapping me in with the black seat-belt and not letting me get away and me just sitting there in the dark – just me and her and smells of Mr Sheen leather and orange air-freshener and smoky-bacon ash. And then she'd drive us away, me not wearing anything apart from a layer of Johnson's baby oil – squirming around like a handful of choux-pastry batter – and her wearing the gold metal dress, all hitched up because of the seat. Just me and Mrs Flowers. We'd drive off into the horizon and you could see the golden hairs on the inside of her thighs when she changed gear.

Jack looks back from the wall. He says, 'Yuk, Sal would probably smell of pickles down there,' and we both start giggling.

Jerry is wiping tears from his eyes. 'Sorry, Pat, lad, no, no,' he's saying. 'I don't want to bring the tone of the evening down.' You can't tell what Mr Flowers really thinks because he suddenly announces that it's time to eat.

By this time there have been a lot of top-ups and the others seem to think it's hilarious that Mr Flowers has made such a suggestion. Mrs Flowers heaves herself up from her seat with the help of the elephant-tusk table and announces that she's going to help her husband bring in the avocado prawns. Jack and I watch their shoes leaving the Venetian Room and Jack whispers that his mother always does avocado prawns and topside of beef and overcooked vegetables for every dinner party. 'It's the only thing she knows how to cook,' he says. 'She does it really well.'

You can hear the jingling of a metal dress and suddenly Mr and Mrs Flowers are standing right by the green settee. There are wedge heels and brown toes and some splashes of drink fall on the *parquet*. The wedges totter a bit and Mrs Flowers collapses into the green settee. Hoots of laughter spring from the Venetian room. 'Spiked your drink, have they?' Jerry guffaws, and Sal is laughing too.

Mr Flowers lowers himself gently onto the green settee next to Mrs Flowers. 'Do you have to be quite so friendly with him?' he says, in a low voice.

'Bloody rich!' she hoots, as he hisses, 'Keep your voice down!'

Mrs Flowers makes a low moaning noise and says, softly this time, 'For God's sake, Patrick, here we are, heading rapidly for the bankruptcy courts, and you're worried that I'm getting on too well with the millionaire who's thinking of buying a boat from you.'

'I'm just saying there's friendly and there's friendly.' His voice softens. 'Darling, what's happening to us? You know I love you.'

Jack nudges me. The smirk has reappeared on his face.

But Mrs Flowers is having none of it. 'Oh, here we bloody go again.' She takes a swig of the drink. 'It'll be the heart-condition story next.'

'Don't bring that into it.'

'Why not? You always are! And what about you, anyway? You should try spending a little less time watching me and a little more time chatting up Nana Mouskouri. She's the one who wears the trousers.'

'Keep your voice down!' he says, through gritted teeth.

'Shan't!' she says, giggling like a little girl.

'Don't give me that cutesy stuff, you bloody floozy,' Mr Flowers hisses. 'Don't forget, this is your last chance.'

'God,' she says, firing up again. 'You really are low, aren't you? Do you seriously believe I fancy that fat northern pig? Good God, Patrick, you're pathetic.' The wedges grip on to the parquet and Mrs Flowers is off again, veering towards the kitchen.

'Penelope . . .' he calls after her, as if he's really sorry she's gone. 'Penelope . . !' he shouts, as if he's really sorry he accused her of anything bad.

When he rushes off after her, Jack says, 'What does floozy mean?' His eyes look at me as if he wants some reassurance. But I can't give him any. Well, I could, but the thing is, there's this feeling rising up in me like the sickly, flabby steam that comes when you fork off a layer of compost heap. It's quite nasty and dirty, but if you let yourself you can get into it. Now I know that Mr Flowers doesn't understand at all about how Mrs Flowers needs her little things. I know that they are unbalanced – that Mrs

Flowers is at the top of the see-saw, having fun, laughing into the bright blue sky, while Mr Flowers is at the bottom, on the ground, wishing he could get some springiness about him and catch up with his wife. But he never will catch up with her. She is restless. She does whatever she wants.

Jack is in a panic now. 'What's a floozy?' he says again, like he's about to burst out crying. He wants to know and I have the answers. It's like burning red ants under the magnifying-glass – only with red ants you can't see what their faces are like when they're frying. With Jack you can, though. His burning up doesn't involve him turning red. His skin just turns paler and paler and his eyes go all watery. And then I have to do something because he starts making a moaning noise. I lunge to put my hand over his mouth and tell him to shut up. Now that I am really close to him I look into his suffering eyes again and the nasty excitement feeling wells up in me again. Jack doesn't look so rubbery now. Now he's pure china. I could smash him easily if I wanted to. I'm not sure what floozy means but I can guess. I also know that there is some connection between the meaning of *frottage* and Mrs Flowers' snaky, burnt-sugar belly laugh. In the end I just say, 'It's not as if it's a secret, is it?'

'What isn't a secret?'

'It's not a secret that your mum doesn't love your dad any more.'

And then I realise I've gone too far because Jack starts moaning, in a really loud voice. 'Stop saying that!' he goes. 'You're just like one of them. The ghosts! There's nothing wrong. It's all right, it is!' and he pushes past me and wriggles off down the green triangle, coming out at the other end, running past the Venetian Room and then up the stairs like a bat out of hell.

I am stunned that he's blown our cover like this. I pull the settee back as quickly as I can and then I just squeeze my eyes shut and wait for the uproar. But none comes. All I hear is Sal saying, 'Was that the boy?' and Jerry grunting, 'What?' He can't have seen anything.

'Their son, that Jack,' Sal insists. 'The one who was fiddling about with our Nikki.'

Jerry sounds weary, as if he's really uninterested. 'I don't bloody know. They want to get him seen to. Probably her and her bloody ways.'

'What do you mean her ways?'

'You know,' he mumbles, 'unstable mother, poof son.'

'You don't seem to mind her instability!'

'Come off it, Sal, love. She's just flirting with me. Thinks I'm going to buy a yacht from old Misery Guts.'

'He's quite sexy, actually. Would be if he took that frown off his face. You should see the way he's been looking at me. Can't keep his eyes off me.'

Time is passing too slowly now. The radiator is too hot. I'm getting sleepy. I just want them to hurry up and eat the avocado prawns and the rare beef. I want this bit to be over. I want it to be time for the *gâteau St Honoré* but there are still starters and main course to get through. Nothing much is happening. Mrs Flowers wiggles her wrist from time to time as a signal for Jerry to top her up, while Sal regales the room with her and Jerry's experiences of abroad.

The cockroach on the toilet bowl, the sand in the bed, the deadly waitress, the runs, the rip-offs, the Bavarian drinking party on the terrace opposite the villa, the coral wound, the baby in the hotel dining room who looked like a slug, the irritating cough of a man on the towel next to them on the private beach, the hair in the green curry. You wonder why they bothered. Why they didn't just stay at home in their horrible beige socks and their stupid red banana boots.

'Course, you have to hand it to abroad for sunsets,' Jerry says, suddenly. 'Got some smashing photos of sunsets, haven't we, Sal?'

'Oh, lovely pictures, Patrick. Stunning sunsets. I can show you the latest ones, actually.' A hand comes down and grabs a handbag. 'Thing about a sunset is that it's really . . . stunning. Isn't it? Lots of yellow and purple—'

'Pink as well,' Jerry chips in. 'Pink's very nice – not that I'm bloody that way or anything!' He gives a little chuckle. 'Bloody cracker, though, weren't it, Sal? That one in Jamaica.'

'Oh, that sunset, Patrick. Here it is, look. Have a butcher's at that, as we say in the trade.' Titters from Jerry and Sal, and sounds of photographs being taken from packets. 'We've seen some good ones in Europe, haven't we, Jerry? But that one in Jamaica was top notch.'

'Top notch it were, Pen love. Should have seen that sunset. You'd have peed in your pants.'

I am woken by a body hurtling into the green settee. It is Mrs Flowers. There is the din of metal dress hitting radiator and then of Mrs Flowers cursing. 'Bugger bollocks,' she says, as I watch two choux balls rolling across the parquet. Then she's back on course, tottering towards the Venetian Room with a plate of *gâteau St Honoré* in her hand. I really hope she's not going to drop it on the ground. I want everyone to see how perfect it is. I want to hear her say my name. I want to hear the sounds of excited interest when she tells them the story of how the dessert came into being.

When she arrives in the doorway of the Venetian Room she makes a hiccup and announces to the gathered assembly, '*Pièce de résistance*.' She staggers into the room and bangs the gâteau down on the table. Sal says, 'Stunning,' and even Jerry takes a look at the impressive piece of architecture and says, 'Not bloody bad, Pen, love.'

Mr Flowers has a smile in his voice as he whispers, 'Darling, I really am most impressed.'

The thing is, though, Mrs Flowers doesn't say how mature I am, how clever or what understated beauty I possess. She doesn't even mention my name. She passes off the *gâteau St Honoré* as her own. For a split second I am angry and then I realise that she must think it's really good and that is why she is claiming to have made it herself. I beam and it gets even hotter in the green tent.

The four adults are enthusiastic at first. You can feel Jerry looking hungrily at Mrs Flowers as he eats with his mouth open. Maybe he's wondering what present he's going to give her next, what he's going to say in his next phone conversation with her. Then, after a few mouthfuls he slows down. Finally, he lets his spoon fall into the plate and says to Mr Flowers, 'All right, then, Patrick, lad. Let's talk business.'

On hearing this, Sal lifts her chair up and takes it over to Patrick's side of the table. 'Yes, let's,' she says, nuzzling down next to him.

'Might as well, chaps,' Mrs Flowers hiccups as she stands up, 'before we get too bleary. Show you the drawings if you want, Jerry. Patrick makes me study them morning, noon and night. I told you he's a slave driver.'

Mr Flowers sounds worried again. 'I really think it's better if I show you, Jerry. Penelope's *au fait* but . . .'

'Nonsense, Pat,' Sal says, rubbing Mr Flowers' forearm. 'I think it's about time you and I discussed figures.'

And then there is just a slurry of voices and hot radiator and heavy eyes. Some time seems to pass before I see her – she comes round the corner of the settee with her knife eyes and her cold cloak. Like a cold breeze coming nearer and nearer, her dagger eyes break up into tiny dots, swooping down on me like a swarm of bees: buzzing, burrowing, burning to a rage of tickling. The black laugh gets louder and louder. I'm trying to wrench my eyes open because I think I know this is only a dream and the witch can only get me in a dream, but then all I can see is her sharp, wrinkled face and she does something she has never done before – she lifts up her cloak and underneath I see that her legs are orange crab claws, attached to her body, but they are not big, bent, beefy front claws, they're slender side legs and they wiggle round like they're worms in high heels. The legs walk closer to me with a tip-tap, tip-tap – the nail at the end of each is as thin as the nib of a black felt pen. The slender legs are going to straddle me. They step over my head and spread and I see a gusset of orange shell with grey cilia sewn around the edges – except they're not cilia. The legs squat closer into my face and I see that they are maggots. I look up for mercy to the witch's warty face but she just throws her cloak over me and I'm wrapped up in a cold wall of that laughter, that hateful, cackling laughter that runs through me like a cold tickling blade.

Then comes blackness and a jolt. The pain in the ribs changes to a trickle – the trickle of liquid on the back of a crab. There is still cackling laughter but there is no pain. I can see a long, bent pincer but it isn't orange: it is white and plump. I look at it so long that I finally see it is part of me: my arm, just my arm, just a skin pillow bent and numb with imprints of my hair. I can hear the echo of the witch's laugh: a rich fruit cake doused in brandy. The green settee jolts again and there is another metal jangle and another fruity chortle. I hear Jerry's stupid laughing-box laugh and Mrs Flowers going, 'Ssssh! Patrick will hear us!'

Then Jerry says, 'Patty! Little Patty Pants!' and the green settee lightens up as I hear a dress jangling towards the kitchen followed by a dirty laugh coming from Mr Silk Stockings gradually fading into the distance.

I've no idea what time it is. It must be quite late. I drop off to sleep again but wake up what feels like a few seconds later. The radiator is stifling me. I need some air. There is silence in the house. I creep out of the green tent and walk to the kitchen. The back door is open. The cold air wakes me up and I walk towards the ring of black conifers to get the witch out of my system. I decide to be brave, to bury myself in the middle of the trees and just stand there waiting for a cold bony finger to prod me. Feathery leaves brush my face, then whip me as I go deeper in, right into the prickly bosom of the black trees. I am going to wait there for the count of thirty to prove to myself that there are no things that go bump in the night, that no finger will come to prod me, that there are, in fact, no bony fingers in a whole world of cold dark nights. Then, as I bury myself further in the branches, I catch sight of the white Mini van parked in the small clearing in the middle of the trees. The wind doesn't feel that strong but it seems to be moving the van from side to side. And there are voices. The night fills with the sound of Mrs Flowers laughing her burnt-sugar laugh – a bored, sad laugh. It makes me hear the blood in my ears, feel the heat in my cheeks. It sounds cruel, like the witch is in there instead of out here with me. They are having bad sex, not the kissing-you-on-your-shoulder type at all. This is wrong, this is the dirty way. This is Jerry taking advantage of Mrs Flowers' kidney problem.

'Tickler . . . feel that tickler . . . big hairy seahorse.'

'Put it in!'

'Big fat dolphin, rubbing against little prawn.'

'Put it in!'

'Hungry little prawn likes a bit of rough.'

'For fuck's sake, put it in!'

'Ouch!' The van jumps in a spasm. 'Bloody dress! Bloody nicked me on the leg.'

'Fuck me, you useless bastard!'

Mrs Flowers explodes with fury until a pound of sausages gives a big slap to what sounds like a prime rump and the hullabaloo dies down. There is a sound of brandy bleeding from a cake, moaning from the cake, and then the van is still.

I am frightened. I don't fully understand. I can just about see the shape of things but nothing is clear. I think of the sausage hands and the gold cilia and the sharp spikes of gold metal stabbing into Jerry's mashed-potato piping bags. I wonder if it will take two hours.

My throat gets thicker and thicker, it's bulging out like a big toad's – bulging out with tears, as if it may explode at any moment. Jerry is a toad. Why is she having an affair with him when she could be spending time with me? Talking to me, telling me things. I would listen, I would. I could advise her. I am clever. I have read books. I fight free from the clutch of the conifer trees, I walk back quickly to the kitchen door, not quite running in case I panic myself, and not turning round in case I see a bony finger. But then I have to turn round because I think I deserve to be punished and eaten up by the mouths of slavering wolves, or something. But all that I see are the conifer trees, waving their black skinny arms in the air like they're jeering at me. And then I stumble on a piece of gravel and I turn back towards the kitchen door, running as fast as I can – even though it feels like I'm running in dream treacle. I'm breathing hard. I know someone is staring into my back, that any minute now someone will jump out from the blackness and come and tickle me or throw a net over me and capture me and a witch is worse than a giant coming down a beanstalk because with a giant you can chop down the beanstalk and that will kill him and put an end to him. But there is never any end to the witch.

And then I am inside the house. I slam the kitchen door shut and try to pretend that none of this is happening. But soon, when my breathing has calmed down, I start to notice voices coming from the top of the stairs. Mr Flowers and Sal. Mr Flowers is trying to console Sal. 'No, no, they're lovely,' he's saying.

'They're bloody stunning, that's what they are,' Sal says, sounding upset.

'I don't want to be rude, Sal, but I did think you wanted to talk to me about figures.' Mr Flowers sounds like he's blushing.

'Oh, you did think, did you? All right, then, Pat, let's talk figures. How old do you think I am? Go on, guess how old.'

Mr Flowers sounds like he really doesn't want to guess how old Sal is. 'Well,' he says like he's in pain, 'I – I don't—'

'Thirty-five!'

'Really?' he says weakly. 'I thought it was around that.'

'You think I *look* thirty-five? Most people put me in my mid-twenties.'

'Well, I—'

'You're a bloody bastard, that's what you are. Leading me on all night. There's others would have leaped at the chance – leaped at it.'

I wonder if Mr Flowers is going to have an affair with Sal. But then he says, 'Look,' like on TV when they try to talk a suicidal person down from the rooftop, 'look, just put your top back on, Sal, my darling,' he says gently. 'You've really caught me at a bad moment.'

'And what about Jerry? I bet he hasn't caught Penelope at a bad moment. Penelope showing Jerry her etchings, is she?' Her voice is a big blustery gale.

'She's just gone to show him the yacht plans in the office,' he says, with a smile in his voice. 'Don't you worry about her. She's all talk, is Penelope.'

It's pathetic. I don't even care if anyone sees me now. It's all pathetic. Everyone's lying to everyone and there isn't even any good-looking Spanish lover, there's only disgusting Jerry Kilroy and his horrible, pathetic dolphin and Mrs Flowers who puts herself through all this for a pair of calfskin gloves.

I walk through the sitting room into the Venetian Room. It looks like a bomb has hit it. So does the *gâteau St Honoré*. The cake sits in the middle of the table, drenched, slumped and defaced. The choux pastry is not just soggy, it's waterlogged with sticky brown liquid. An upturned bottle that lies on the table next to the cake says, 'Courvoisier, Le Cognac de Napoléon', and when I dip my finger into the moat of tea-coloured liquid that has seeped through the pastry circle up to the edge of the plate, it matches the fiery petrol smell in the mouth of the bottle. An avalanche of cream has fallen into the fiery moat and curdled to white frogspawn.

Less than a third of the cake has been eaten and what remains is pitted with After Eight wrappers and cigarette stubs. Like Cinderella's hair the morning after her big night out, everything has drooped. The air in the room is filled with the ghosts of cigar smoke, cigarette smoke, overcooked broccoli and old breath. Littering the table are screwed-up red paper napkins, compacted bread balls, overloaded ashtrays, a few wet grapes, a blotch of pink beef juice, smeared bee glasses.

I sit in Mrs Flowers' chair and touch the big glass bell that has her fingerprints still on its sides and her lipstick marks on its rim. It has some of the tea-brown liquid in the bottom and I pick it up and whirl it around, cupping it underneath in the palm of my hand like I've seen her do.

I look up at Theseus and the Minotaur but when I dip my nose into the brandy glass and breathe deep, it's not Mrs Flowers I see. It's Jack. Jack and his blue peppermint creams and his green marble eyes.

Chapter Nine

> The true gastronome is a fastidious beast . . . He will rate an epic meal less highly than it deserves if the company is ill-chosen, brash, strident, carping or fatuous. The epigram is both a cut of meat and a verbal enhancement to dining.
>
> ***Something's Burning*, an autobiography**
> **by Fanny Cradock**

La Familia Sanchez is dead and buried. No more Señor Pérez's dog, no more *familia* Rodríguez *de vacaciones en Granada,* no more Pedro Ramón and his *novia* Conchita going to the bullfight and sitting next to people who smell of *ajo* and *vino,* no more predictable tales with expanded vocab columns about *el contrabandista* at *el aeropuerto,* no more dull humour about Enrique Muñoz being accidentally locked out of his house when he was having a shower, no more *episodio en la playa* where two silly girls in bikinis get their boat lost at sea and have to be rescued.

The time is getting nearer.

Fanny Cradock believes that any competent cook should have a fully stocked store-cupboard. It is all very well, she says, to start out with the basics – garlic, sugar, salt (*gros sel* or Maldon), cochineal, cooking chocolate, rice (Patna and risotto), rose-water, rennet and Worcestershire sauce (only Lea and Perrins) – but before long they must be supplemented with greater things. These include almond *dragées,* asparagus spears, Bath Oliver biscuits, hundreds and thousands, lychees, okra, chestnut purée, orange juice (unsweetened), ratafias, red kidney beans, sago, silver and gold balls for garnish, and smoked oysters.

At the age of seventeen and after four years of study, my basic store-cupboard of Spanish grammar and syntax is bulging at the seams. I have ten sterling O levels under my belt, including an A in Spanish. All the basic workings of the language are at my fingertips: the tenses – present, future, past historic, imperfect and subjunctive – the radical changing verbs, the irregular past participles, the gerunds, the passive voice, masculine and feminine endings, numbers, the verbs to be (*ser,* pemanent; *estar,* temporary) and the false friends (*procurar* meaning 'to try' rather than 'to procure', *quieto* meaning 'still' rather than 'quiet'). I have memorised idiomatic phrases reflecting the history and culture of Spain: there are Moors on the coast ('watch out'), the tortilla was flipped ('the tables were turned'), I cut the cod ('I am in charge'), Turk's Head ('scapegoat').

Now that A levels (and possible travel to Spain) are on the horizon I want to go for the de-luxe version of the country. I have borrowed advanced audio cassettes from the local library, which teach me how life really works at street level. I have learned what Spaniards have for breakfast: *churros con chocolate* (doughnuts with hot chocolate) and orange juice made from real oranges squeezed freshly in front of your eyes called *zumo de naranja*. I know what different types of coffee they drink: *machado* (mostly milk), *marisol* (half milk, half coffee), *cortado* (a splash of milk), and *café sólo* (black). I know that they eat sunflower seeds in the street and spit out the husks on the pavement. I know that on trains it is polite to offer people some of your food (*tortilla* or *chorizo* sandwiches usually), but that on no account must the traveller accept. The traveller just has to reply to the person offering, 'May it do you good' or *que aproveche*, an expression corresponding more or less to the French *bon appétit*. I know that when you visit a Spaniard in his home he welcomes the visitor with 'You have taken possession of your house' and you have to reply, 'Many thanks.' And when the visitor leaves, the owner of the house says, 'Depart with God,' and you have to answer, 'Remain with God.'

I know that when you are in a restaurant you will be asked if you want water *con gas* or *sin gas* – meaning 'fizzy' or 'still'. I know that the Spanish eat *chumbos*, which are edible red fruits that grow on cactuses, that lots of girls are called Adoración, Encarnación, Asunción, Inmaculada

Concepción, Gloria, Dolores and Angustias after the Virgin Mary, that they smoke black tobacco from blue packets called Ducados, that most Spanish men are known as *machista,* which means 'male chauvinist pig', that when you see someone in the street you have to say '*hola, guapo*' if they are male and '*hola, guapa*' if they are female (and also when you are having an affair with one of them it helps to say this, if Mrs Flowers is anything to go by). That they are very fond of ham, or *jamón* (or *hhhhhhhh-amon*). That the best type is *jamón de beyota,* which comes from pigs in the north of Spain that have been fed solely on acorns. It is soft and sweet and melts in the mouth. (I wonder what Cornish pigs that have been fed on syllabub and gherkin tassels from the Oggies pig-bins taste like. Thanks to Fanny Cradock, I bet it's the first time they've ever eaten truffles in their lives.) Now that my Spanish O level is well under my belt I am free to concentrate on the chestnut purée and the Bath Olivers of the language. This is where Federico García Lorca comes in. He is much deeper than Albert Camus, one of the writers we are studying for A level French. 'Meaningless and incoherent universe' has become a buzz phrase in the sixth form common room but I know that they only like *L'Étranger* because it's written in easy language.

Lorca is not easy at all. Sometimes he writes really odd things about death laying eggs in wounds and then he'll write really good lines about sky floating on the air like a giant lotus flower and it'll make you look up from the page and gaze out of the window and think of the Theseus and the Minotaur window. He's at his best, though, when he feels frustrated with life and just sees violence all around – the hysterical moon with streaming wild hair; the crocodile having its eyes scooped out of its sockets like spoonfuls of mousse; the mad fat woman turning octopuses inside out in an apocalyptic New York where blood and vomit run through the street.

Fiona P and Nikki Kilroy are in the Spanish A level class too – only because Nikki wants to put off the time when he has to take up the reins of the knackers' empire and Fiona P will still do anything that Nikki does. They left their store-cupboard pretty much empty from week one. All they have inside is scraps like 'to make', 'to be', 'to have', 'hot', 'cold', 'good', 'bad', 'beautiful', and a lot of vague hand gestures. Sometimes Mr Jones will ask them some easy role-play games like to go into a baker's shop and buy a loaf of bread. Nikki Kilroy will lie back in his seat, tap his fingers on the desk and, after a while, might say, *'Pan,'* in a loud, confident voice, as if he's just written a poem as good as Federico García Lorca's. Mr Jones will look encouragingly at him and nod helpfully but he really knows that *'pan'* is all he's going to get. Nikki doesn't care. He's going to inherit Jerry Kilroy's knackers' yard. Nikki, who has naturally been to New York, says that Federico García Lorca should have gone to a few 'downtown' parties and he might have loosened up a bit.

If ever Mr Jones asks Fiona P a question, she just flicks her hair and pretends she's not there. At the moment she does that a lot. According to Jack, she recently gave herself an abortion. Nikki Kilroy said he couldn't get her the money together for a proper one because his dad would find out. So when the fair came to Mousehole she went on the waltzers with Sally and Christine. They all stayed on for seven goes and in the evening she went to the loo and there was a lamb chop in her pants.

Not that you can believe too much of what Jack says these days. An alien has come to live in his body. It has sucked all the colour from his face, deposited fuzzy hair on his upper lip and given him an expression that wavers between gormless and evil.

Jack is rarely at school, these days, and when he does come, Mr Jones treats him with kid gloves. If he is looking spectacularly pale Mr Jones will ask him if he feels all right and Jack will blurt out, 'Gary Numan!' while boring holes through Mr Jones with his weird new laser eyes. But still Mr Jones persists in trying to get to the bottom of the new, troubled Jack. He even expresses an interest in the explicit gallery of naked *familia* Sanchez members that Jack insists on scrawling all over the cover of his Spanish homework book. Sometimes it seems as if Mr Jones is on the verge of including Jack in the lesson by asking him his opinion of how to ask for a stick of bread in a Spanish baker's shop. But as Jack is getting less and less verbal, he finally realises that it is a waste of time and his eyes will come to rest on me with what I know is a look of relief on his face.

Whatever I say is always near-perfect: '*Hola, quisiera un pan, por favor,*' I'll say. Then, as an extra touch for the class, maybe I'll add something like, '"*Quisiera*" is the conditional of the verb "*querer*". *Querer* means "to like".' And then I'll fold my arms and look over at Fiona P and Nikki K before adding grandly, 'It also means "to love".'

Now that I am seventeen I do know what love is. It means that when I leave Mrs Flowers I am going to feel pain. I know that Mrs Flowers feels pain and I secretly hope that some of it is over me. There is a depth of knowledge in her eyes that makes me never able to let go. Her eyes are enigmatic, which means they go down and down like deep wells with no end.

I have known Mrs Flowers for three years now. I see her three or four times a week – and more when I go round to create dinner parties for her. I am successful. My savings grow by the week. Following several dinner parties cooked by me, Jerry Kilroy eventually bought the yacht Mr Flowers had been trying to sell him. After that I was given free rein to create other dishes for more dinner parties for other potential clients. The yacht-selling started to take off. Mr Flowers said he was indebted to my specialities – my *boeuf Beaujolais*, my French Yorkshire Pudding (*gougère*, usually coloured mauve and shaped into a catamaran), my butter pagoda with ten tiers of petals, my creamed carrots in pastry boats (*barquettes Crécy*), my twisted cucumber slices, my tomato water-lilies, my lettuce leaves cut with pinking shears and my spring onions carved into chrysanthemum heads.

I have made myself indispensable to the Flowers' household. Even when there are no guests around I still come and cook for them. Mrs Flowers says that money is no object – although I am not to tell Mr Flowers this – and she encourages me to experiment with wines and liqueurs. Her favourite dishes are *escalopes de veau en papillote au vermouth* followed by *poires au Curaçao* (pear crescents arranged in cartwheels on plates and centred with a single pink azalea in a puddle of orange liquor).

During the time of the Kilroy yacht sale Mr and Mrs Flowers seemed happy too. There was talk of getting rid of the white Mini van and buying a proper car for Mrs Flowers. Sometimes, in the kitchen, Mrs Flowers would go up to Mr Flowers and kiss the back of his neck before handing him an evening drink she had made him. You could tell that Mr Flowers really liked the kiss because he would smile and his frown would lift as he shouted after her, 'Don't you think the menu is slightly alcohol-heavy, darling?' And she, in her deep, crumbly voice, would shout back in a fake French accent, 'Darlink, a little wine in moderation irons out life's creases!' He would fold his arms and make a secret smile and only then would he remember what it was he came into the kitchen to fetch in the first place.

Brenda soon started to accuse me of 'swanning round with that woman' and I congratulated her and told her that it was an appropriate idiom. I told Brenda that she was a seagull and Mrs Flowers was a swan. Mrs Flowers knows instinctively which clothes will set off her hair and her figure to their best advantage, at which angle she has to raise her thinly plucked eyebrow for maximum charm, how to cross her legs in a way to make the room stop speaking, how to stub out her cigarette in the ashtray as if she is painting a picture, how to shake the curl from her eye as if it is a personal kiss for you.

Mrs Flowers is a real woman. There is a dressing-table in her bedroom where there are china pots of powder, and jars of cream, and perfume bottles (Joy, Rive Gauche by Yves Saint Laurent, L'Air du Temps by Nina Ricci). She has proper lingerie drawers too, I have checked. There is silk and lace and satin in cream and pink and peach that make my hands feel as if they are being dipped in cold water on a hot day.

If you put your ear to her bedroom door or your eye to the keyhole you can sometimes hear chinking bottles and jangling bracelets and watch her patching up the 'old parchment' and preparing herself for the world. Sometimes she sings an anthem to rouse herself from her bed – an ad-lib version of 'I Am Woman' by Helen Reddy – and this will infuse her with the will-power to totter over to the dressing-table and begin the day's work with her makeup bag. Staring into the mirror, she belts out semi-incoherent phrases about being strong and invincible. Occasionally she bangs a powder compact or a perfume pot on the table for extra-assertive woman effect or she stops impatiently for a few seconds to curse a problem that's cropped up with her false eyelashes. Sometimes she just mouths the anthem silently from tight lips, giving herself a quick wink as she applies her lipstick.

I especially like her dirty clothes. Her dirty clothes are better than holiday snaps. My favourite time to rummage around in her room is when she has just returned from one of her foreign holidays. She didn't give me the stripy Brigitte Bardot top, for instance. I went into her room when she and Mr Flowers had just come back from Nice and I stole it. I licked it and it tasted sour. On licking it you could taste the smell also. The smell of France – a creamy, lemony, greasy smell. It smelt of the sea gone stale – shut up in a suitcase for a long trip home – and it smelt of sun that had been and gone, floated up and gone away leaving a damp, spicy whiff as an absence. It hangs now by the side of my bunk bed. It stands stiffly to attention like corrugated cardboard. It is a meeting of abroad and Mrs Flowers. By the pockets on the front there are smudged traces of expensive white sun cream – a heavy, perfumed scent, the deep-down fermenting scent I imagine to be between a woman's breasts in St Tropez on a hot day. The pockets are slightly frayed, thanks to incessant in-out hand movement to release maybe loose change or shells or cigarette packets and satisfy discreet itches. There is a non-specific ox-bloodish stain on the top of the right arm and down both sides are ridges of sand-coloured dirt and icy salt stains.

Thanks to keyholes and half-closed doors and sneaky strategies, I know more than I should about Mrs Flowers. There are more than a hundred tapes of Mrs Flowers in Jack's bedroom. I must have made a few hundred over the years but I record over a lot of them rather than buying more cassettes. Jack makes my borrowing the yellow rabbit conditional on leaving all the tapes in his room. He doesn't seem to take any notice of the contents. He doesn't even seem to like listening to them much, but he demands that I carry on recording. 'Good to have Mum in my room,' he says, in his weird new monotone. 'She can make them all go away, can't she?' I can't really be bothered to get involved in all his nonsense so I just nod and go off with the rabbit.

Jack asking me to make the recordings is good news. It seems to suggest that I have not become totally obsessed with Mrs Flowers (although I have). The other good news is that somebody called Fernando actually exists. I have worked it out. At first I thought that some days she was being romantic with Jerry Kilroy and sometimes she wasn't – that she just wanted to talk dirty to him. (I actually quite like the dirty days. Thanks to Jerry Kilroy and a book called *The Joy of Sex* that I found at the bottom of Mrs Flowers' lingerie drawer my Big Words Book is filling up nicely.) By now I have worked out that Jerry is the one she is dirty with while the tall dark Spanish stranger is the one she has the tender voice for. When she uses her few words of Spanish with Fernando – like *guapo* and *te quiero* (which means, I love you) – it's like she's pulled the curtains and let sun into the house, not the watery old English sun but the bold, hot Spanish sun. It is for this reason that I find it hard to understand why she would want to have anything to do with disgusting Jerry Kilroy – who looks worse than the hairy ape in *The Joy of Sex* – even if he does give her presents.

She doesn't even seem to like him very much. Sometimes on the phone she sounds irritable, as if the conversation with him is a chore and she can't wait till it's over. (I think she talks dirty to him just to speed up the conversation.) When he comes round to the house pretending he's lost his yacht contract or that he needs to know something about knots or sails or nautical charts, when he knows very well that Mr Flowers isn't there, she seems to laugh at him as he hangs around in the kitchen getting in her way. I like it best when he leaves. Then Mrs Flowers will talk to me as if I'm her confidante. She'll say things like 'Give a dog a bone,' and it will give me hope that she doesn't really want men at all.

She teaches me things, too, on her good days. She'll grab hold of the wine bottle I am using to make a casserole for her dinner, tell me that it's far too good for a casserole and pour it into a kind of a Spanish glass decanter with a long spout called a *porrón*. You fill it with wine, hold it at arm's length and pour the wine into your mouth in a big loop of liquid. The tricky bit is to make sure you swallow it in time so that your mouth doesn't fill up and you dribble all down your chin.

I am quite good at the *porrón* now because Mrs Flowers has given me lessons. I do it with water, though, because I don't really like the taste of red wine. It's like bitter oak trees and dries my tongue up. Mrs Flowers says it's a good thing I don't drink wine although I think it's only because she wants it all for herself.

When she holds the *porrón* high in the air and throws her head back, glugging wine into her throat, I want to go over and kiss her rippling gullet but I can't. I'm frozen to the spot. I am mesmerised by the grotesque sight of red wine tears dripping slowly from the side of her mouth like she's a vampire. Even crunching my knife through pigeon bones or slicing raw steak into strips only satisfies part of my desire.

When she's finished, she'll bang down the *porrón* on the table and tell me about how a meal without wine is 'like a day without sun', about how you must never fill a wine-glass more than two-thirds full as one of the joys of drinking wine is to swirl it gently round the glass to bring out the bouquet (smell), about how wine's best friend is cheese ('always served before dessert so that the last glass of good red wine makes its happiest marriage with its best table companion'). How dessert can bring along even happier marriages: apple and calvados, apricot and apricot brandy, blackberry and kirsch, cherry and kirsch, peach and peach brandy, strawberry and kirsch.

Then she'll pull me into the sitting room and put the record-player on with some of her Spanish records that sound like Spanish Shirley Bassey music. It's music with sleazy trumpets and sleepy strings and throbbing drums, sung by women with cigarette husky voices who go on endlessly about *dolor, tristeza, sufrimiento, angustia* and *crueldad* punctuated with the exclamation 'ay!' pronounced like 'eye' in a dramatic meeting of great pain and great beauty.

She'll pull me up from the green settee, put her slinky arms around my waist and we will sway together to the soothing clip-clop rhythm of her tragic music. Her head flops over my shoulder and she hisses a rough translation of the words in my ear:

'Remember me when you suffer,
When you cry, remember me,
Kill me this instant if you wish.
For my soul is in torment if you go away.'

My ear gets all wet and I pretend she is singing the words to me, although really I know she isn't. I suspect she is with Fernando in the Catalan mountains in the burning scrub with the smell of scorching rosemary bleeding into the air.

Sometimes I pretend it is me who makes her suffer. I imagine us both in Barcelona, both of us dancing together in a bar filled with smoke and hot breath and hotter bodies and women with dangling earrings and black hair thick as horsetails swaying to the clip-clop rhythm of the music. I know that I am more attractive than I used to be now that I am seventeen. My brace has come off and I'm using the coat-hanger for the zip of my jeans at the moment.

But sometimes I break off from her. I can't help it. She'll be dancing with a Cheshire cat grin on her face and she'll have drunk so much from the *porrón* that she'll step on my toes or stumble over the settee or fall over on to the floor and lie in a heap, laughing like she's crying, talking to herself like it doesn't matter if I'm there or not. I'll look up at Theseus wielding his bloody spear over the Minotaur and I'll remember how much there is I want to discover about life. I'll get frustrated, as if I've been sitting in the same position for days, for years on end, and I'll want to get out and run, run along a dusty hillside with scorching rosemary and explore things for myself, not just hear about them second-hand from someone who is using me because she doesn't like cooking and she doesn't like her son. On days like these the thought that Mrs Flowers might be using me creeps into my mind.

But then something will happen, and Mrs Flowers will draw me back into her crêpy crack. Maybe she senses that I'm moving away from her, and to stop me leaving her she'll tell me something intimate about herself that feels like she's never told anyone else before. 'Travel's a curse, Rosa,' she whispers to me, one *porrón* day, as she's singing along to Spanish Shirley Bassey. 'You go away, you discover somewhere new, then you have pangs for the old place. So you return to the old place and immediately you miss where you've just come from ... "Remember me when you suffer ..."'

She has spent almost an hour talking about the beautiful, perfect *guapo* Fernando. I have stopped dancing and slumped down on the green settee as a protest.

'Travelling is like having a string of lovers while you're still married,' she says, more gently, dancing over to where I am sitting and slinking her hips in time to the music – especially for me, maybe. 'You can never be truly satisfied ... "When you cry, remember me, kill me this instant if you wish ..." Most people are cowards and end up going back to their husbands anyway. Oh, they might still do a bit of travelling. Scrag-end travel, though. Nothing as spectacular as the journeys they made in their youth ... "My soul is in torment if you go away ..."'

It's all very well for Mrs Flowers to say this: she has

already been lucky enough to go places. Suddenly I blurt out, 'Is Jerry Kilroy your scrag-end travel, then, Penelope?' and immediately I am shocked that I have dared to ask this question and even more scared that I have dared to use Mrs Flowers' first name. She stops lip-synching to the music and glares at me. I can meet her gaze for only a second because her eyes are alight with a mass of tiny flames. It feels like she's the magnifying-glass and I'm the red ants. I lower my head to the parquet but the next thing I know a pair of calfskin gloves is pressed into my hand. When I look at her again the flames have turned to glowing embers. 'Take these, Rosa,' she says, with a strange expression on her face. 'Have them. Our little secret. They've been everywhere with me. Seen a lot of life. They run a brothel, speak eight languages and smoke with a cigarette-holder by now.'

I stare at them and I can't help but feel thrilled. I start to look slowly up towards her face when I see a scar zigzagging along the underneath of her arm. A white flash of lightning on a golden brown plain. She must see me looking at it because she flops down on the green settee and sighs quietly. 'Really catching me out today, aren't we?'

'Did you get into a fight?' I stammer.

'Only with myself,' she says. 'The only way to stop the pain sometimes. Like putting a burned finger under cold water. A pleasure of sorts.'

She strokes the scar with her fingertips. 'Like pricking sausages,' she says, a light smile on her lips. 'Like making slits in a piecrust. Has to be done or things get even messier.'

And immediately I love her again because I only half

understand what she is talking about and she sounds a bit like Sylvia Plath, whom we are also studying for A level. I scrunch the calfskin gloves in my fist. Mrs Flowers' scar is as glamorous and as horrifying as stained-glass windows and red wine and the death rattle of Spanish Js. 'Always liked the idea of drama,' she drawls. 'Dramatic deaths. Did you know that Gaudi was run over by a tram?'

'Who?'

'Catalan architect. Built lots of Hansel and Gretely houses in Barcelona. Bloody run over in his lunch-break.'

'I see.'

'Yes. Dull, happy-go-lucky deaths. Like dying in your sleep or choking on a fishbone in your throat.' She pulls the sleeve of her négligé over the white line on her arm. 'Mind you,' she says, 'I'm a fine one to talk. I'm hopeless at death. Not for lack of trying. I've come to the conclusion that I'm going to have to suffer along with everyone else.'

Suddenly, she jerks herself up from the settee and, with a flourish, raises the *porrón* high in the air like a salute. 'Here's to death,' she says, starting to pour, 'geath gy growning . . .'

She wasn't suffering like I was, though. I was babysitting beyond the call of duty. Jack was in a bad way.

Things started going downhill last year. I was asleep one night in the spare room when I felt a prod. I woke up to see a face as pale as a ghost and a pair of bulging eyes. I jumped as if I'd had an electric shock. It was Jack.

It was like everything inside him had been sucked out and his eyes were the last things resisting.

I disguised my shock as irritation. I snapped, 'Jack! What are you doing! Get back to bed this minute!'

But he didn't move. He didn't budge an inch. There wasn't even a trace of a smile on his lips. His eyes just bulged as if he'd gone mad and he said urgently, 'What about the blue thing? Rosa, what do I do about the blue thing?'

For about five ticks of the bedside clock I wasn't sure what to do. But by the sixth tick I didn't care any more. I didn't have the energy to deal with Jack and a nightmare. I said sternly, 'Look, get back to bed or I'll tell your mother,' and I lay down and pulled up the covers over my head.

I was even more shocked when he defied my authority and just didn't move. I could sense that he was still there. I ripped the covers off me, sat up again and spat, 'Get back to bed or I'll get your mum!' wondering how I'd go about getting her. And still he didn't move. It was as if another Jack had come to live in his body. He just stared at me like some person in a trance. As if there was something he didn't understand. I couldn't tell if he was about to cry or get very angry. And then suddenly he changed. He sighed and looked at the ground and said, 'Dunno. Just some stupid dream. Useless.' And off he wandered. I know he didn't go to back to his bedroom, though. I could hear him moving around the house. Doors shutting softly, floorboards creaking. There's no lock on the door of the spare room and it was a strange feeling, Jack making me uneasy.

I tried to tell Mrs Flowers about it but it was one of her days when she was wandering damp-eyed around the house in her dark blue négligé, slopping black coffee into saucers. She came into the kitchen, banged the cup down on the worktop, raised her hand to her forehead and shouted at me, 'Bloody noise. Stop that bloody chopping, for Christ's sake.'

When I hinted that something was up with Jack, she just told me not to worry. 'Adolescence or something,' she said, rattling round in one of the cupboards. 'Just trying to get attention. Now, where the hell are the bloody aspirins?'

I tried to put that night out of my mind but you couldn't help noticing that Jack had changed. Sometimes when I tried to put him through his Fanny-Nancy-Plum paces he wouldn't play the game. Sometimes I'd burst into his room as usual, except that unlike as usual he'd turn his back on me, make his mouth into a tight, knotty grimace and begin hammering yet another poster on to the wall with the palm of his hand, going, 'There are war planes coming, Rosa, war planes,' and the only noise in his room would be the buzz coming from a crackly tape on his cassette-recorder.

His bedroom began to change. Soon it wasn't only the keyhole, the walls, the wardrobe hinges, the space under the door and the cracks in the desk top that were covered with *Smash Hits* centrefolds. Soon he started to block out the windows too. There were a few posters of Adam and the Ants and some photos of Prince Charles and Lady Diana Spencer's wedding cut from the *TV Times,* but mainly the windows were covered with pages and pages of pictures from

Fanny Cradock's Cookery Course. He'd come across a bundle of old Cradock magazines in the Oxfam shop. It didn't help that the pictures were at the more frightening end of Fanny's repertoire – the ones that look like they've come from *Barbarella* or from a painting by Salvador Dalí. The whole place looked like a sinister papier-mâché bat cave. In the centre of the window was *omelette Villervillaise* – a block of wet omelette floating in a brown crabmeat cream sauce, garnished with pink hairy crab claws sticking out from the spongy sides. Another picture came from issue fifty-four of *The Fanny and Johnnie Cradock Cookery Programme* magazine: *Cooking with Game.* It was captioned '*Suprêmes de Pigeons en Croûte*' and showed four puff-pastry parcels on a plate dotted with baby Brussels sprouts and a rosette of *duchesse* potato rising up like a twirl of bird dropping in front of two raw pigeon wings – complete with feathers. The wings stood to attention in the mash like a pair of bushy grey eyebrows. If I commented on this odd décor scheme, Jack would reply in a robotic monotone something like 'Think you can get away, don't you? but there's always someone watching.'

And then, one day, it was the beginning of the end. We'd just finished doing another recording of Mrs Flowers and Mr Silk Stockings. Jack had had this pale, serious face on all day at school and he was even more passive than usual, following me around like a skinny shadow. I took the tape-recorder and held it up to the crack in the kitchen door. From the terrified look on his face you'd have thought we were peeking at a ten-headed wildebeest dripping with green slime. She breathed deep down the phone and spoke in an extra husky voice, 'Make me wet, oh, you make me wet . . .' but I could tell her heart wasn't really in it.

When we went back into Jack's bedroom I took the cassette out of the recorder, ripped the tape from the plastic casing and threw it all into the bin. I started to tell Jack how it was all a bit pointless, that I was fed up doing the recordings, that it wasn't interesting any more, when I felt a piece of rubber hit the back of my head. I turned round and another spray of plastic objects came hurtling at me – beans, vomit, toast, followed by his hairbrush, his felt-tip pens, coins, his Silver Jubilee mug, a Don Quixote statue carved from wood. 'Don't kill Mum's voice,' he screamed. 'Stop letting the ghosts in! She's the only one who stops letting the ghosts in! Now they'll all come in! All the voices!'

I was stuck to the spot. I was just so impressed. I was really impressed that the worm had finally turned, that Jack finally hated me, that he was deciding to trim off the fat at last. The odd, smirking boy who liked to wibble on about blue peppermint creams had fallen away to reveal a new Jack with furious sparks of self-respect, a pure Jack, focused on himself.

When the corner of *The Guinness Book of Records* struck me hard on the right temple I came to my senses. I put up my hand to it, found some blood on my finger, and then I realised that Jack wasn't being impressive at all. There was no sense to this hysteria: he was flailing round the room, screaming about ghosts and voices and devils, about the orders he had to perform, about the blue vapour over his brain. I just squeezed my eyes tight shut and as his voice got louder and louder I became smaller and smaller and smaller.

I burst into tears. I ran down the hall shouting for Mrs Flowers. I must have sounded a bit mad and hysterical myself because when she saw my tearful face she pushed aside her gin and tonic, ran out of the kitchen and up the stairs. I had never seen her move so fast. She charged into his room, booming, 'Dare you!' She was so angry that the 'how' didn't come into it. 'How dare you!' would have taken too much time. I stood behind her as she began to lay into him and I watched him shrivel like a piece of plastic in front of the granite fireplace. 'Dare you!' she said again. 'Dare you! 'Dare you treat Rosa like this!'

And all the time I was secretly gloating because I wasn't the mad one. I was sane and clever and now that I was thin again I was attractive and I was about to go to university and the world was basically my oyster while Jack was just going down the pan. Although this all happened last year when Jack was sixteen, sixteen is still quite old. Youth could no longer be blamed for his silliness. Jack was a failure.

He just sat there, floppy, in a corner of the room, as if his bones had all dissolved. He flopped there, collapsed, stroking his fluffy moustache with his index finger. He stared at Mrs Flowers as if she was very bright sunlight shining into his eyes – although obviously no sun had been in Jack's bat cave for months. Then the smirk started to come back into his face as if the madness was thawing out, although you couldn't exactly say that normality was being restored. 'And look at me when I'm talking to you!' Mrs Flowers howled at him. But she didn't look at him. She put up her hand to her head and tottered over to slump down on the desk chair. 'Bloody migraine now,' she muttered, closing her eyes. She gave her forehead a massage while she rested the other hand on my back. 'Jack, for goodness' sake, what's got into you?'

She opened her eyes and looked round the room. She couldn't have been in it for a few months. Jack had forbidden anybody to come in. She saw the scary Fanny Cradock pictures for the first time. She saw anaemic body parts, old people's home slops, giblet swamps, aborted babies and post-mortems. Cold duck with black cherries that looked like cancer, *champignons sous cloche* that looked like brain tumours, *chou farci paysan* that could be mistaken for sick, and *porc Normande* like nose gristle. The special Irish stew looked like a lake of diarrhoea and the *rouleaux de boeuf au chou rouge* looked like a group of hippos rolling around in urine and fly droppings. She looked at the pop-star faces and eyes and lips and ears peeking out from just about every covered surface in the room. Then she looked at him. Her hand dropped from her forehead and her brow creased. She saw him collapsed in the corner of the room, stroking the golden cilia on his top lip with a shaking finger and saying, in a pitiful monotone, 'You have to crimp the pasties really tight, Mum. You have to make sure there are no chinks in them or else the devil gets in.'

Mrs Flowers stared at him and then she gulped. She took her hand off my back. She stood up like one of the lepers who suddenly gets the miracle cure. Her eyes had the post-miracle look of awe and love in them. She walked over to him, her eyes bewildered, her head shaking. The tone of her voice was almost gentle, pleading. 'Jack,' she said, in her best Fernando voice, 'Jack, this has to stop, doesn't it?' He seemed to screw a look of wisdom and pain into her face as she stroked the top of his head and stammered, 'Chicken, my little boy. You have to put all this away now. I want you to tell me everything.'

When she hugged him to her chest two giant granite boulders smashed together in my guts. A shudder ripped through me, a jealous earthquake shook the room.

Chapter Ten

> One of the most sordid little offerings is the ubiquitous prawn cocktail . . . A tired prawn drooping disconsolately over the edge of the glass like a débutante at the end of her first ball and its opposite number – a piece of lemon tasting of the knife – clutching the opposite side of the rim like a seasick passenger against a taffrail during a rough Channel crossing.
>
> ***Sociable Cook's Book*** **by Fanny Cradock**

Sitting in the kitchen at tea-time, Mrs Flowers announces that this year Jack is to have a proper party for his eighteenth birthday. 'Only a week to go,' she says anxiously, watching him squash a Mr Kipling Fondant Fancy to a mulch with his spoon. 'I'll even get you a present this time. Forget some years, don't I?' She lights a cigarette with a shaky hand. No response from Jack. Cake crumbs get mulched even harder. Mrs Flowers sucks deeply.

Too right she forgets some years about Jack's birthday. She has forgotten every year since I've known her. June 10 is usually a cue for her and Mr Flowers to take off on holiday abroad and leave it to me and Brenda to sort something out. Last year my mother announced that we'd all go to the cinema – 'all' meaning me, Jack, Mary, Brydie and Brenda. It wasn't even the cinema, it was the Mousehole Young Farmers Film Society and the film was *Battleship Potemkin*. Half-way through, Brydie stopped slurping her lemon bonbon, leaned over to Mary and said, in a loud whisper, 'Next time we'll check what's on before coming out, won't we?'

'Gave you that tape-recorder, didn't I, in Barcelona?' Mrs Flowers battles on, desperate for reaction. 'Yellow tape-recorders were pretty modern things in Spain, you know. Pretty hard to find.' Forced laughter. I hate to see her like this, kow-towing to Jack as Jack laps up the attention. 'Rosa is going to be doing the cooking, aren't you, Rosa?' She looks at me briskly.

Relations between me and Mrs Flowers have become strained. It seems that the nicer I am to her the meaner she is to me. I can't help but admire her because those are the very tactics I used to employ with Jack. The fact that Mrs Flowers and Jack are now ganging up against me is called irony.

After all these years, Mrs Flowers is trying to make friends with her son. As if she only has room for one of us and I am the one who must be pushed overboard. I am the new Turk's Head. Jack is being pretty clever for someone who is supposed to be so ill. He's not leaping for joy that his mother is finally showing him a bit of affection. He's stringing her along. He's being mean to her. He's spurning her, and the more he does that, the more she tries to win him back. It's obvious to me that she wants to win him back more through guilt than love for him and it's also obvious that Jack is putting most of it on. Sometimes I think there's hardly any difference between his old smirk and his new gargoyle grin.

Jack had been in and out of school for over two years. But just after mock A levels, they sent him home for good. He came back with a shell-shocked glaze on a death pale face, as if he didn't care that he'd been suspended. As if he didn't even know he'd been suspended. Mr Flowers went to rouse Mrs Flowers from her bad-kidney bed. The bedroom door was shut and voices were raised. This time, Jack didn't even want to come and listen at the crack. Jack wouldn't go near cracks then. He was terrified of them.

The day Jack was diagnosed schizophrenic was one of the best days of my life. It was emergency, euphoria and the Dunkirk spirit all rolled into one. Something was happening at last, something that was going to bring me and Mrs Flowers closer together. She would have been helpless without me.

Mr Flowers had been taken into hospital a few days earlier with his heart and Mrs Flowers was beginning to crack up under the strain. I'd become a fixture in the

Flowers' household by this point. Every time I went back 'home' to Brenda's house, the tangerine flock wallpaper, the grime-streaked lino and the nylon chairs would feel like ammunition that was trying to kill me with its ugliness. Being at Mrs Flowers' house made my daily moods a hundred times better – and also enabled me to notice that the past two years of a teetering Jack had taken their toll on both of his parents. I'd come in from school and Mrs Flowers would be wandering aimlessly from room to room, a smeared bee glass in her hand, avoiding Jack and mumbling to nobody in particular about what a bad mother she'd been. In the end she retreated to her bedroom because it was so hard to avoid Jack. Now that his bedroom had been redesigned to his own satisfaction, he took to patrolling the house like a sinister clockwork toy whose key would never run down.

After the mock As we rarely saw the peppermint-creams Jack again. The new Jack would go to the kitchen at three in the morning and make weird psycho cakes – pouring spaghetti and Ribena and lettuce and Vim and mulched Wagon Wheels into a big mixing bowl and stirring gravely like Father Time, before leaving ramekin dishes of blue-coloured lumpy pap in the fridge for me to discover during my early-morning checks of the house. Sometimes when I went down at six in the morning he'd still be on stage. The first time, he was in the Venetian Room. He'd turned all the glasses upside down and was crouching with his head on the carpet talking to Theseus in urgent monotones about Kenneth Williams stuffing his mouth with white chocolate on a beach of red poppies.

Then he decided to follow Mrs Flowers round the house like her shadow or her assassin. He'd burst into her bedroom at dead of night and prod her and ask her when they were going back to Spain, when the taxi was coming, when they could leave. And when she shouted at him to get back to bed, he sniggered, as if there was someone over her shoulder or behind her back, someone wearing a silly hat or pulling funny faces. She stopped shouting at him. She grew afraid of him then. She asked me to come and sleep with her in her bed at night. I couldn't believe my luck. Even though they were rocky hours – ventilated with flimsy gusts of stale négligé and electric twitches of anxious sleep – I would lie there wide awake, my skin tingling, my body hyper-sensitive, watching her toss and turn and mumble in her sleep. I willed her to wake up. I lay close to her and if by chance one of her flying hands happened to hit against my face or my arm I would let it lie there, on top of me – a heavy flesh brand, burning heat into my skin – and I would grin into the dark.

In the day I was a hero too. Mr Flowers called me from the hospital and asked me to take charge. He said he couldn't thank me enough. I told him not to worry and hoped he'd never come home.

I did take charge. It was me who called out the doctor, me who insisted on getting the social worker, me who insisted on Jack taking his pills. Mrs Flowers was lying down in bed when Carol the social worker came round to introduce herself.

'Of course, schizophrenia is rather an avant-garde word for Cornwall,' she'd said, hoping that I'd join her in a titter. 'If he lived in Northumberland, for instance, he might be schizophrenic!' She crossed one leg over the other. She was wearing thin white plimsolls called 'pumps' and neat Marks & Spencer's trousers called 'slacks'. She would drop in news about her 'pumps' and her 'slacks' between dubious information about mental illness, which she presented as an imaginative alternative to going to university. 'Super facilities they have there, up in Northumberland,' she said. She kept saying 'super'. 'Art therapy they have in Northumberland. Super opportunities.'

She had already learned that Jack liked to draw. That really excited her. Not just a nutter but an artistic nutter, she reckoned. Maybe not a nutter at all. Maybe a real artist. Same thing, really. She bought him a set of poster paints she believed might help him fight his way out of his personality disorder, as Cornwall County Council called it.

'I want to see what you're feeling, Jacky!' she said, like a horribly enthusiastic drama teacher. 'I want you to paint me what you're feeling.' Jack loved being called Jacky. A familiar flicker came into his eyes when she said it.

Then she apologised for having to run but she had her tennis-coaching class at seven. She climbed into her TR7 and shouted, 'Wish me luck!' as the gears crunched into reverse and she backed into the conifer trees. The flicker turned into a smirk.

That was the last time I saw it, though. The medication changed everything. After the medication, he began to act like a cartoon character who'd had a heavy object smashed over his head. It was as if there were birds tweeting and stars sparkling all the time. He had a dazed look on his face, as if he was about to pass out at any moment. Carol said it might be a while before they got the medication right. 'There might be hitches to start with,' she said, two days later, when I called her up at home to find her in the middle of her book-club evening.

'But he's made tinned tomato and soil and poster-paint stew and he's wiping it all over the walls,' I said.

'Listen, Rosa,' she said, in her stupid caring-sharing voice, probably aware that all her book-club guests were listening to her being a social worker, 'Jacky needs to feel that he's got love all around. Tell him you love him once in a while, you'll find it makes a remarkable difference.' She told me to call her if any emergencies cropped up and then she put the phone down.

I was getting bored of the whole business. I thought madness would at least be a bit exciting. Jack never even told me what the voices were saying – only once, one afternoon when I went into the Venetian Room to give him the pills. He turned round sharply from Theseus and the Minotaur.

'Jack! What are you doing?' I said, exasperated, as if I hadn't seen this a dozen times before.

Normally he didn't say anything. He wouldn't even

look at me. Most of the time he was totally impassive. Only occasionally did it look as if he might provide me with a bit of diversion – like lashing out at me or something. He never did, though. Not that it would have had much effect if he had. He hardly ate any more. He was getting thinner and thinner. 'They're talking to me,' he mumbled.

'What are they saying?'

He started to rub his foot into the carpet. 'Say I've got to walk slower,' he said, finally.

Is that all? I thought. What was the point of all this if the voices were only telling him pathetic things like that? What was the point in having a schizophrenic friend unless he wanted to murder the President or get abducted by aliens?

I knew that sometimes Jack tried to hide his pills under his tongue. I was gentle with him for the first week, coaxing him patiently – especially when Mrs Flowers was in the vicinity – using the yellow rabbit as a bargaining tool. But suddenly I realised I was being stupid. With him out of the house, I would have Mrs Flowers all to myself. I stopped his medication.

The weekend that Jack was admitted to the psychiatric wing of Plymouth County Hospital I became the world expert in madness. On the Monday morning, people like Fiona P and Nikki Kilroy gathered round me at break, going, 'What's happened? How is he?' their minds drooling with thoughts of whirring chairs, spinning beds, revolving cages, plunge baths and penny tours through the insane wards of Bedlam. I had already looked up schizophrenia in *The Joy of Knowledge.* I told them that he was suffering from it, that it was a behavioural disorder typified by a detachment from the external world and a disintegration of the internal one.

'Genetic factors may not be sufficient for the disease to appear,' I said calmly. 'Many cases are precipitated by emotional distress such as family disharmony.'

Their eyes grew wide and their mouths opened and Nikki Kilroy said, 'Poor you, Rosa. You must be really sad.'

But I wasn't sad. I was happy. I enjoyed telling them how odd it was seeing Jack in hospital. It got me my chance to use my new phrase, '*idiot savant*', which means someone who's mad but even in the midst of their madness says things that are clear. For instance, Jack was walking with me and Mrs Flowers in the hospital grounds one day when he stopped suddenly and picked up a husk from under a horse-chestnut tree. He turned to Mrs Flowers and said, blank-faced, 'Look, a nutcase.' For a few seconds I felt like Carol, like maybe we really did have a genius on our hands.

I looked at the faces gathered around me, all thirsty for fresh news. 'He's catatonic at the moment,' I said, with a convincing sigh. 'That means he's like a cabbage. A vegetable. He just sits there like a vegetable.'

In fact, Jack is a variety of vegetables. On his catatonic days he is an overboiled Brussels sprout, all pale and floppy. Other days he is silly and hyper like Fanny Cradock's *salade Windsor* – a hollowed-out white cabbage with vandyked edges spiked with green olives and maraschino cherries, stuffed with shredded cabbage and raw carrot strips.

'Recently, he's been hebephrenic.' I heaved a dramatic sigh. 'That means getting silly and hyper.'

'What's new?' Fiona P said, and I gave her my new martyred look. In class, if anyone refers to someone as a 'nutter' or 'bananas' or makes a joke about Benny from *Crossroads* I'll make a point of walking out of the room with my new martyred look slapped over my face as thick as Fiona P's foundation. Nikki just looked coldly at Fiona P and told her to shut up and have some respect. I could hardly believe my luck.

And then Mrs Flowers changed. I think it was partly the shock of seeing Jack in the grey Victorian mental hospital in Plymouth – a place filled with unused table-tennis tables and hollow-eyed people in bobbly, easy-release cotton clothing, chain smoking in front of TV sets.

Her phone conversations started to take a more practical turn. There were no more phone sex conversations, no more mushy noises or long snaky laughs into the receiver. She'd wail something like 'I can't . . . I can't' into the phone and there would be a long silence during which Mr Silk Stockings or Fernando would be telling her that she could, she could. Then she'd say something like 'But it's too late.' And there'd be another gap where they told her that, no, it wasn't too late at all.

When Jack was discharged from Plymouth, Mrs Flowers stopped drinking for two whole weeks. This put her on edge and it was only a matter of time before Carol the social worker triggered off a strange domino reaction that culminated in the birthday-party idea.

One day, I watched Mrs Flowers listening stony-faced as Carol talked about her mixed-doubles finals with the women from the Rotary Club, and how she and Jacky had had a lovely day sorting out her best eye-shadow colour in Dingles' makeup hall. Mrs Flowers was incensed. Her self came back. 'She's no social worker,' she growled afterwards, pouring herself a glass of tonic water. 'She's a bored housewife. Whatever she's giving Jack, I can give him just as much. Good God, I'm his mother.'

From then on, Jack became her new project. Her kidney problem miraculously disappeared overnight and she stopped wandering round the house in a négligé. When Mr Flowers came out of hospital he said he was proud of her.

And now it has come to this. Mrs Flowers with her arms round Jack's shoulders. The earthquake feeling won't go away. I try to calm myself down. I tell myself that his illness won't last too long. That either he'll snap out of it – one day he'll burst out laughing and own up that it's all been a trick – or Mrs Flowers will get bored of being the dutiful mother. She'll miss the closeness that she used to have with me. She'll take me in her Mini van for a drive to town. We'll go clothes-shopping and she'll laugh about Jack like she used to in the old days – about how 'If you're going to act like you've taken bad acid then you might at least have taken the acid in the first place!' And I'll laugh like I used to, even though I didn't really understand what she'd said. Or, better still, we'll do as we used to do – not even mention him. She'll shut him out again soon, I'm sure of it. I can't stand being shut out for much longer. It makes me feel small.

'It'll be a party to remember,' she says, hugging him even harder, trying to sound jovial. She is not really jovial. I know this. I know so much about Mrs Flowers. I know too much and it has landed me in trouble. There's something quicker about Mrs Flowers now that she doesn't drink. I still don't like to think about it, about how she caught me listening at the door only two days ago. This is called being caught *in flagrante delicto*, in blazing crime. I stood there in blazing crime in front of blazing Mrs Flowers, who flamed like a torched haystack.

'You were spying on my phone conversation, weren't you?' Her tone really frightened me. Maybe she'd twigged that I knew more than I ought. I could feel that my face had flushed and that it must look really unattractive.

I fumbled around. I mumbled, 'I was just looking for you, I . . .' I hoped she wouldn't look down into my opened briefcase and see the yellow rabbit there. Her eyes were bubbling like blisters.

'You like to play with fire, don't you, Rosa?' she hissed, finally. Her breath doesn't smell of syllabub any more. It smells of metal. Cold metal. 'Well, play all you like,' she said, as if she knew some secret that I didn't. 'Play all you like because one day you are going to get burned. Very badly burned.'

She sits at the kitchen table, flicking ash into an ash tray and trying to be jolly. 'Real birthday tea!' she exclaims. 'None of my usual attempts at juvenile nutrition!' Her nail varnish is chipped. Because of Jack she is letting herself go to rack and ruin.

'Haven't got any friends,' Jack blurts out, in a dull monotone. 'Nobody likes me. Fanny Nancy Plum Caramel Dolores Ramona Shirley Whisky Norwood,' and he pushes the cake plate away from him so hard that it crashes on to the floor.

Mrs Flowers rushes to pick up the pieces. 'You really must tell me who these girls are, chicken,' she says, diving under the table to retrieve the plate. 'We can invite them to the party.' The gargoyle rictus comes back on to Jack's face and I really hate the brat now. Recently he's been mentioning the Fanny-Nancy-Plum thing more and more. I know he wants to get me into trouble. But I don't want to be uncovered just yet so I try to distract Mrs Flowers by saying, 'So, Jack, what do you want to eat for your birthday party?'

He breathes deeply for what seems like ages and I can see Mrs Flowers looking desperate, desperately hoping he'll saying something that makes sense.

'Prawn ... prawn ... cocktail,' he says, as if he's forgotten how to speak properly. Someone should tell him off and get him to pull himself together. I'd do it myself if Mrs Flowers let me get near him. 'And ... and *crêpe Suzette.*'

He sits back in his seat looking pale and terrified, staring at the kitchen door as if his famous blue ghost is going to burst through and get him at any minute.

I can't believe that he's said this. I stop what I'm doing (making my own green vegetable colouring by wringing out cooked spinach in a treble fold of muslin, re-straining and then simmering the liquor in a pan) and stare at him in anger. He knows very well that prawn cocktail is one of the things that Fanny Cradock and I despise most in the world. He also knows very well that *crêpe Suzette* is reserved for Mrs Flowers' birthday. Only she is special enough for it. Jack and I have talked about this already. In fact, one of the last conversations we had before he went bananas was about *crêpe Suzette,* about how it is one of the few great culinary specialities I have yet to try. About how Mrs Flowers would love it for her birthday. I'm not having this.

I look out of the corner of my eye at Mrs Flowers as I exclaim, 'Prawn cocktail, Jack!' in my special scoffing voice.

I look over at Mrs Flowers, expecting her to return my grin. At least a grin. But she's just staring at me like I'm some horrible thing she's found on the bottom of her shoe. 'I think prawn cocktail is a very wise choice,' she says coldly. 'A tyrannical palate is a very ugly thing, Rosa.'

I can't believe Mrs Flowers has said this. I'm not even sure if she's referring to me or Fanny Cradock. Am I ugly? Does she hate me? Maybe I am just a fat old gingernut with blue veins on her breasts and stretchmarks on her hips even though she hasn't even had children yet. She's right, I'm still just a stupid little English girl with no experience of the world. I've read Sylvia Plath and D.H. Lawrence and I don't understand why she's so depressed all the time and why he thinks penises are shrouded in 'phallic mystery'. All my views on love, on the real world, on how characters in books should act, on the difference between a crush and love, between deep love and shallow love, are useless. I've never been anywhere or done anything. I don't even know anything about music. Apart from Dean Friedman, the only records I have are by Elton John and Gary Glitter that my father bought me from the cash-and-carry and I know that you're not supposed to have them. And I didn't even know what 'downtown' meant until I asked Mrs Flowers. Who am I kidding that life is getting better every day? What worth do I have when I don't understand people and why they feel or do things? What chance do I have of ever becoming sophisticated?

'You like prawns, don't you, Mum?' Jack blurts out, as if he's in pain.

'Of course I like prawns, darling,' she says, stroking his frowning brow. She pinches his cheeks and makes him smile. 'I like prawns and I like you even better.' That night when I go home, I take *A Star in Faded Jeans* and I throw it into the pig-bins alongside an abandoned batch of *escalopes de veau en papillote au vermouth.*

Chapter Eleven

> Let us return to the realms of practicality with How to Make a Classic French Omelette. When the Normans brought it over here, as they did everything that was worth eating when they invaded us in 1066, the Omelette was known as an 'amulet' and, just to show you how bad the 'good old days' were, omelette eggs were always beaten with a bunch of goose quills.
>
> ***The Fanny and Johnnie Cradock Cookery Programme*** **magazine. No. 7**

History will be made tonight. At nine thirty tonight, Fanny Cradock will make her TV come-back on a programme hosted by Esther Rantzen called *The Big Time*. She has been asked to act as cookery adviser to a farmer's wife called Gwen Troake whose dream it is to make a meal for former Prime Minister Edward Heath. In these slapdash days of

Wimpy hamburgers and Pot Noodles (and prawn cocktails) Fanny Cradock food will hit the nation like a breath of fresh air, like a pinky-hued rosette of *pomme de terre duchesse*. A mix of culinary rigour and exotic imagination will make people sit up and take notice and wonder how they ever let this woman disappear in the first place. I will bask in the glory of knowing that I got there first. I will be vindicated, which means being proved that I was right all along.

Her TV appearance is coming at just the right time. She is the life raft that has appeared miraculously at sea when Mrs Flowers was pretending she couldn't see me drowning. Fanny Cradock has given me renewed hope, renewed courage – not just to go through with the ridiculous *crêpe Suzette* birthday party but to treat it as a battle that I am going to win.

Fanny Cradock says that all dinner parties should be treated like warfare: the hostess should act like a great general who can see the outcome and the triumph. You must work back from your vision of success, she says, and pre-plan in such a way that your mind is clear and your spirits high when the combat commences.

This is my plan of action: prawn cocktail at 2000 hours: (mature but knowing looks to the rest of the guests). 2030 hours: *omelette Villervillaise*, as a way of showing off to my guests (plus, Mrs Flowers said that poking around with shellfish makes her feel sexy). 2100 hours: lights dimmed and awed murmurs as the *crêpe Suzette* is brought on. 2130 hours: reinforcements. I have installed the portable TV in the corner of the Venetian Room so that everyone can have a clear view of Fanny Cradock in her finest hour. 2200 hours: back-patting. 'Where would I be without you?' from Mrs Flowers, Jack all blue peppermint creams. Things back to normal.

I have filled the room with jugs of blooming daffodils, hung paper chains of bunting in blue crêpe paper all around the room and prepared a series of tapes ready for the quadrophonic sound system including Jack's current favourite, 'Cruel Summer' by Bananarama. Finally, on top of all these thoughtful plans, there is a special bonus Factor X. The bonus Factor X is that Mrs Flowers has started drinking again. (This will surely act in my favour.)

My one fear had been that of guest relations (i.e., Mrs Flowers finally getting to meet my extended family). But at 2000 hours everyone is sitting round the dining-table getting on perfectly well. Mrs Flowers actually seems to be enjoying herself. She looks radiant in a short-sleeved, powder pink jumpsuit. She has become the vaguely insane cousin of whoever is inhabiting Jack's body. She's acting a bit like a little girl, sitting with her hands under the table beneath her knees, nudging Brydie mischievously from time to time. Brydie is her new best friend and she is Brydie's. 'Say, we're getting on like a house on fire, aren't we, Mrs Flowers?' she keeps shouting.

'Indeed we are, Brydie, indeed we are.' Mrs Flowers chuckles, activating her new no-legs method of getting a top-up by kicking Mary under the table and winking until, finally, Mary realises it means she's to go into the kitchen and fetch some ice and tonic for the G-and-T refill.

'Ah, now, there's a decent bit of drink,' Brydie says, every time she gets a top-up. 'One of the fellas at my bridge evenings, he was telling me that he was – now what's that word that sounds like sodomy? Thingummy word, means staying somewhere. Tory, he is. We've had a few good rubbers.'

She ignores the icy stare coming from Brenda's chair and pulls on Jack's sleeve to tell him that 'Course, that's our generation: your father was a Tory, you were a Tory.'

'Sodomy,' Jack moans, ashen-faced. 'Jiggery-pokery. Pig in a pokery.'

In the past few weeks I have begun to understand that madness is not green vegetables at all. It is not even prawn cocktail in a cheap restaurant. It is slushy instant mashed potato with baked beans. Cheap baked beans with lots of orange-coloured juice running round the edges of the mashed potato like a disgusting gooey moat. Sometimes I could almost feel sorry for Jack if only he wasn't doing so much to ruin my life.

Brydie stops munching on her Marie-Rose-sauce-covered lettuce *chiffonade*. She squints at Jack and then says, 'Sure, you're right, of course, Jack. Isn't he right, Mrs Flowers? What he says. The modern generation, isn't it?'

Mrs Flowers is ecstatic. These are the first words Jack has uttered all day. She pours herself all over him, giving him a hard, gin-scented hug.

When she surfaces, she gushes to Brydie, 'He's very

modern, is our Jack. A rip-roaring extrovert, aren't you, Jack?' Jack has glazed over again but she just clinks her glass against Brydie's, saying brightly, 'Call me Penelope, please. Call me Penelope!'

My spoon flinches in its prawn-cocktail dish. Then, under the table, I sense Mary getting another kick from the foot of Mrs Flowers. She gets up and trots out to the kitchen for more provisions. While she is gone, Mrs Flowers, still in high spirits, takes a prawn from her dish and throws it high in the air. She watches it land in Jack's glass of orange squash. 'Ahoy, Cap'n,' she slurs, 'man overboard!'

Jack folds his arms tighter round his chest and burns holes in the Spanish tablecloth with his anxious eyes.

Brenda misses all of this. She is still gazing at the stained-glass window, a puzzled expression congealed on her face. At least it seems to be taking her mind off Margaret Thatcher's landslide victory at the polls yesterday – a second term in office! – and, even worse, the wanton waste of electricity that's going on in the Flowers house. 'Mrs Flowers,' she's been saying stiffly, from the minute she got here (she refuses to call her Penelope), 'Mrs Flowers, would you like me to go and turn the lights out in the hall? I think you might have left them on.' And Mrs Flowers just makes a snaky smile and booms out the opening couplets from 'O Caledonia!' by Sir Walter Scott while a low-voltage charge of electricity shoots through my mother's body. She's not sure what's going on. She only came here tonight to show her support for Jack. Ever since I told her about his decline she has channelled much of her energy into being concerned for him. Suddenly, from being Rosa's effeminate friend who was to be tolerated, Jack has become the quintessential Common Man in her eyes: a social renegade, questioning the very definition of so-called 'sanity', fighting against society by a demonstration of what the capitalist regime describes as 'madness'. Catullus supports her on this one: '"Now he goes along the darksome road, thither whence they say no one returns,"' she quotes in spooky tones, whenever I tell her the latest nutty thing that Jack's done.

'Like I was saying,' says Brydie, coming back to the fella at her bridge evening. 'Sounds like sodomy – though you'd never guess it was pronounced like that when you see the spelling. Means staying somewhere. Sodemy . . . soj . . .'

'Sojourn?' Mrs Flowers enquires, eyebrow raised.

'Sojourn! That's the nail on the head, Penelope love. One of those foreign words. So they say.'

'It's French, Brydie,' I say. 'Comes from the French *séjourner,* meaning "to stay".' I try to pretend that I can't feel the sneer on Mrs Flowers' face.

'There you go! French. Dirty buggers, aren't they?'

'The Frenchman,' says Brenda, taking her eyes off the window at last. 'It wasn't the Frenchman who wanted the Second World War. It was that damn fascist Churchill! Biggest bloody fascist of all. He was all right in his crêpe-de-Chine bunker. Him and the Queen Mother. She falls out of bed, there are two people come to pick her up. There's a doctor to come and see to her. Me, I'll be lying on the floor for days . . .'

'Sure but, Brenda, you said yourself you don't like the

French.' Brydie turns to Mary and says, 'Mary, didn't she always refuse to serve the French in the Corner House?'

'You did, Brenda,' Mary says timidly. 'Brydie and me used to say to you, "You can't have it both ways, you can't have French fancies and not the French."' Then she looks at Brenda's face and says quickly, 'J. Lyon and Co. – we couldn't have had a better employer, could we, Brenda?' But Brenda is still a huge grey wave on the verge of breaking. Mary pulls back her chair and hurries off into the kitchen, even though Mrs Flowers hasn't kicked her leg yet.

'Never mind about French fancies!' Mrs Flowers snorts. 'Where's Jack's birthday cake? Can't have a birthday without a birthday cake, can you, Jack?'

Jack stares into space.

'Sure, we'll be getting some of that later, won't we, Rosa?' Brydie says.

I stand up, mumbling something about how we'll have to wait and see. I start collecting the empty prawn-cocktail glasses from around the table, thinking about how far *crêpe Suzette* is from birthday cake. My stomach starts to churn even though I keep telling myself that I don't care, that they should be grateful I'm raising standards. Plus, if Jack dared ask for *crêpe Suzette* then I'm certainly not going to kill myself by making a birthday cake too. But when I come to Mrs Flowers' place she grabs hold of my wrist. 'Clever little thing, aren't we?' she says, under her breath, and I start to beam. But when I look at her I see that her eyes are narrowing and I kick myself for still believing in her, for believing that she might still have some fondness left for me. 'Who knows what other information you've got stored up there?' she says, banging her index finger against her right temple. 'Who knows quite how grubby things up there have become?'

I can feel a lump in my throat but I try to hold it back because you can't have a general start to snivel right at the beginning of a battle. I start to open my mouth to say something bold, to stand up for myself. But when I'm about to speak she lets go of my wrist and blows a mouthful of smoke in my face and I start to cough. I move away and my hip hits the side of the table. The flesh starts to judder and I feel fat and ginger. I don't know what's happening to me. The closeness between me and Mrs Flowers keeps dissolving like the ping of pricked bubbles. There seems to be no stopping it. Even if I put out my hand to do something, it just makes more bubbles burst more quickly. Every day more pricked bubbles come crashing on to my skin like showers of spit.

'You all right, Rosa love?' Brydie says. 'Is that a bit of a cough you've got? It's the damp, isn't it? Aren't I always saying, Brenda – about Cornwall – it's not good for the chest?'

Brenda says, 'If you don't mind me saying, Brydie, I think we'd all like you to get to your point.'

For a moment Brydie looks puzzled. Then she hits her head with the palm of her hand and says, 'My point! You're right, Brenda. Forget my own head one day, won't I?'

Jack makes a short snort of laughter and a sticky stream of grey snot runs down to his mouth, sending Mrs Flowers into ecstasies again. She clasps her hands together and exclaims, 'Jacky smiled! Our birthday boy smiled!' She puts her arm around his neck and her movements are clumsy. She pokes Jack in the ear with her fingers and then her bracelets get caught in his hair and she spills half her drink down his shoulder. She doesn't seem to notice, though. Nor does he. He's gone back to staring at his bread plate as if some terrible thing is happening on it. Mrs Flowers notices this because she says to Brydie, slightly impatiently, 'Come on, then, on with the story!' She looks at me sharply and says, 'Jack likes stories about Spain, don't you, Jack?'

Brydie bows her head apologetically in the direction of Brenda and then carries on. 'So, yes, this bridge chap – the Tory – the Tory chap says to me, he goes, "I sojourned in Salamanca with the university choir ten years ago." I remember the "Salamanca" cos it sounds like that salami stuff we used to buy in Soho from that Italian. D'you remember him, Brenda? Anway, the Tory chap. I thought he was talking about funny business with little boys. I've met a few of that type in my life but I'd never have put him down as one.'

'"A pretty fellow is a waste of space,"' Brenda growls. 'Martial, Epigrams III.'

'Homosexuals and lesbians, aren't they?' Brydie says, munching on her bridge roll. 'Homosexuals and lesbians and, you know ... what are they called, the other ones? Not terrorists ... you know ... thingummy ... the ones that take to the streets.'

'Rioters?' Mrs Flowers raises an eyebrow.

'Rioters! Homosexuals and lesbians and rioters. All those.'

'Degenerates!' Mrs Flowers exclaims merrily. She chinks her glass with Brydie's and makes a Nancy Reagan salute. '"Just say no to alcohol and drugs!"'

'Oh, that's that Nancy, isn't it, Penelope?' Brydie beams. 'I like her. She's got that nice red suit. And that Margaret Thatcher in her blue suit. They're good friends, aren't they? Them and that what's-his-name – thingummy, the actor . . .'

Brenda's eyes have become dark and stormy nights. The emotion in her elbow nudges a glass of orange squash off the table. There is a very loud 'Jam tarts!' followed by the sound of Mary scurrying off to the kitchen to look for the brush and dustpan as Mrs Flowers snorts into her gin and tonic and I escape to the tranquillity of the omelette pan.

I feel better in the kitchen, I can breathe again. There is order in the kitchen. My two bowls of sauces stand waiting for me on the worktop. One is filled with a mixture of brown crabmeat, white wine, butter, cream and lemon juice. The other is white crabmeat mixed with a spoon of the brown sauce for the filling.

When Mary has scampered back to the Venetian Room with the brush and dustpan and a sponge it is a relief to smash twenty eggs into a bowl. When I have cracked them all open – without breaking one single yolk – I pour the whisked mixture into the pan. I read from the recipe about how omelette eggs were always beaten with a bunch of goose quills in the olden days and then I think of being strapped up to the Mini-van seat, teasing myself with the wrong end of a goose feather and pretending it's Mrs Flowers' fingernail.

And all the time I hate it. I hate that Mrs Flowers is the most interesting person I have ever met in my life. I hate that I can't get away from her, that I don't want to get away from her. I can't even concentrate on the feather fantasy because I can't help listening to her voice next door. She has relaunched the homosexuals and lesbians and rioters conversation: 'Homosexual men make some splendid clothes,' she announces.

'They're good at the jokes, too, aren't they?' Brydie says. 'Not many duds in them fellas. They can show you a funny time, can't they, Brenda? My John used to say it was because of the fem-femin-'

'Feminity!' Brenda says, disgusted.

'Pus-y!' Brydie bursts out, like there's pus everywhere. 'You remember that, don't you, Brenda? "Stroke my pus-y." What's that programme?'

'The penniless man in the street! Where are the programmes about him?' Brenda's off now. 'Lloyd George called this a country fit for heroes. Fit for down-and-outs!' She buries her face in the new glass of orange squash Mary has handed her, muttering about sexual perverts.

All this, of course, is sad and funny at the same time. My palms are sweating as I whisk butter into the cooking egg. My armpits go wet and it's not from the heat of the hotplate. What am I supposed to say, 'The birthday boy is a big John Inman and I'm a big sexual pervert too because I've been in love with Mrs Flowers for the past four years'?

Then I hear Jack blurt out, '*Are You Being Served?*.'

Everyone stops what they are doing and claps their hands when he says this, as if he's just revealed the secret of the Dead Sea scrolls.

'*Are You Being Served?* – that's the one,' Brydie says. 'Funny, isn't it, Brenda? Have you seen it? And that chap – John Inman, is it?'

'Backs to the walls, boys! Backs to the walls!' Jack says, jigging up in his seat as if he's about to explode, like a bottle of Corona someone's just unscrewed after a very bumpy car ride.

Again, more exclamations and clapping.

'Backs to the wall, boys! Backs to the wall!' Mrs Flowers squeals, imitating Jack, as if he's suddenly become a model son.

'Mollie Sugden,' Mrs Flowers says, turning to Brenda. 'You know, "Where's my pussy?" she says. "Where's my pussy?"'

'Pus-y,' says Jack, glancing at Brydie. 'Where's my pus-y? Where's my pus-y? Where's my pus-y?' like he's saying, 'We're all going to die, we're all going to die, we're all going to die.' Except that Mrs Flowers thinks it's really good. They all think it's really good. Brydie is clapping her hands in time to the chant like Jack is Terry Wogan hour on Radio 2, Mary is twinkling round behind him, topping up his orange squash as a reward, Brenda is nodding gravely because apparently her bourgeois-conspiracy theory has come true just as she knew it would, and Mrs Flowers is slurring nineteen to the dozen about what a genius her son is. 'Well done, Jack!' she's saying, her kiss curl bouncing all over the shop. 'Look, everyone, Jack's come back to us! He's back to normal!'

But Jack hasn't gone back to normal at all because when I come in with the *omelette Villervillaise* he starts screaming like he's Damien from *The Omen* and I'm the priest with the sack of knives.

It doesn't look that bad, the *omelette Villervillaise*. Turning it out of the pan was a bit difficult with all the filling in, and I had to put extra sauce over the top to cover up the cracks and now it does look a bit like the bloated body of a shipwrecked sailor floating around in a pool of plasma but, even so, you wouldn't have thought it was anything to get upset about. In fact, it almost perfectly resembles the Fanny Cradock original even down to the hairy orange claws straddling out from the side and the two de-shelled front talons that sit perfectly out on the top like an orange moustache with a sprig of parsley in the centre.

Jack is screaming something about devils and ghosts and chinks and he's shaking his head around like there's a wasp caught in his hair. 'Don't want to talk to him any more!' he's screaming. 'Don't want to listen. Done it, I have, everything he's said . . .'

I am frozen to my spot in front of the dining-table with the cloven-hoofed omelette hovering in the air. Jack has his back flat against the chair, as if he thinks it's going to fly off the silver platter at any moment, attach itself to his face and suck the life out of him.

'Must be the window,' Brydie is saying, as if she's saying, 'Nice weather for the time of year.' 'That window's enough to give anyone the willies.'

'Course it's not the bloody window,' Mrs Flowers snaps, glaring straight at me. 'It's the bloody food. Bloody crab omelette. Disgusting. Enough to give anyone the frights.'

So I just stand there, frozen to the spot while Mrs Flowers insults me. In my heart I know that my *omelette Villervillaise* is not enough to give anyone the frights. Nobody else in the room is scared. They're all just having a fit because Jack is having a fit.

I can't believe that this is happening to me. I know that Jack has a picture of this very recipe stuck on his window so why is he getting so worked up about it now? I bet he's just having one of his tantrums so he gets noticed. I can't believe this is happening, my life being ruined by a stupid boy I didn't even want to be friends with in the first place. I'm furious. I'm about to throw lumps of the stupid *omelette Villervillaise* in Jack's face and, for the first time, I consider harming Mrs Flowers too – flicking crab sauce in her face and telling her and her stupid nutty son to go to hell – when suddenly, out of the blue, my reinforcements arrive. Just when it seems that things can get no worse, the music starts, the pictures flash and I look up and realise that my battle is running a bit late. It is nine thirty already. Fanny time. *The Big Time.*

* * *

I can see her over Jack's shoulder. She's sitting at a table with a dumpy woman who is presumably Gwen Troake, the farmer's wife. Gwen Troake will never make *The Big Time* – unlike Fanny, who towers above everybody else on the set, even though her face looks like the scary woman's in *Rosemary's Baby*. Poor her, having to deal with a limp, mousy farmer's wife.

'And what exactly are you intending to serve with the duck with cherries?' she demands of Gwen Troake, her lips puckering like a lipsticked anus. When Gwen Troake timidly tells her, coffee cream (a glorified Instant Whip whose ingredients include instant coffee and whose preparation time is a mere twenty minutes!), Fanny turns a bulgy eye to the camera. She makes a face like she's about to throw up. 'Horrors!' she barks. 'You're with the professionals now, you know!'

The dumpy farmer's wife looks as if she has just wet herself and only now realises it. The other chefs in the kitchen look a bit embarrassed at Fanny's boldness but I like it. I admire her. She sticks by her guns. She knows who she is. She announces to the dumpy farmer's wife that they can't possibly make coffee cream for the former Prime Minister of Great Britain. She announces that they are going to make boats with sails of spun sugar because Edward Heath has a yacht called *Morning Cloud*.

And it gives me strength. To hell with the *omelette Villervillaise*, I think. Pearls before swine, I think. I imagine the beautiful pastry yachts Fanny Cradock is going to make, the downy sails that will melt on the tongue like clouds, like threads of raw silk or gossamer hairs on golden thighs. A small voice tells me to forget the main course and go straight to the *pièce de résistance*.

I look around the room and see that the time is ripe. Jack has gone back to being a Brussels sprout. He is staring at a red, spiral-tipped decanter as if there's a re-run of *Are You Being Served?* going on inside it. The low murmur of Esther Rantzen's voice seems to have lulled the others into exhausted silence. They all jump when I lean over Mrs Flowers (unnecessarily close) and plonk a tiny gold stove in the middle of the table.

Fanny Cradock says that for best *crêpe Suzette* results you should bring the flame to the table but she doesn't say how. So I have used my ingenuity. I have bought a calor gas camping stove from the army and navy shop and covered it in gold wrapping paper so that it doesn't look like a camping stove at all.

The golden stove certainly gets their attention. When I light it and put the pan on top, laying the thin pancakes into the pungent orange-juice mixture, you can feel their senses prick to attention. There is a rapt silence in the room, broken only by the low drone of the TV and the sound of butter sizzling in a pan.

'Now, isn't that fancy?' Brydie says, after a while. Jack looks away from the red decanters and starts to stare into the flames – but, of course, the one who this is intended to impress just yawns and says, 'None for me, thank you. I don't like oranges.'

My hand wobbles on the pan handle. I wipe sweat from my forehead. That's a lie. Mrs Flowers does like oranges. She never turned down my pear crescents with Curaçao before. She said it was an excellent marriage.

'Hot round here, isn't it, Rosa, love?' Brydie says. 'Makes you thirsty, doesn't it?'

'Honours, please, Mary,' Mrs Flowers says, in a bored voice, taking Brydie's glass and handing it to Mary.

'Will you get on with the Spain story, Brydie?' Brenda snaps. Food with fire on is uncharted water for my mother. I can see that she's getting nervous.

'Well,' says Brydie, 'turns out that he wasn't one of them fellas. He was just on a, thingummy, singing tour of the Spanish cathedrals. In the evening they'd go to one of those bars, in the open air, the seats, you know, what are they called?'

'I'm sure Rosa could tell us that,' Mrs Flowers says, as if she's *really* bored now. She is dangerous when she sounds really bored. My right hand is trembling as I pour a stream of Cointreau into the ladle.

'Well, never mind, it was the G-and-Ts, really. Apparently you'd sit in the . . . in the outdoor bit . . . and it'd be really hot and they'd fill the tumblers half full of gin – chilled gin and just a dash of tonic. Makes you a bit giddy in that heat, I imagine. Nice, though.'

'Sounds divine,' Mrs Flowers coos.

'Bet they all thought they'd died and gone to heaven,'

Brydie says, chinking her now refilled glass with Mrs Flowers' and fanning her face from the heat of the flames in front of her.

Then Brenda pipes up in her doom-laden voice: 'Heaven's nothing to do with it, Brydie! Earth, that's where we're all going.' She nods towards the bowels of the earth lying under the white woolly lawn of Mrs Flowers' carpet.

'Sooner the bloody better if you ask me,' Mrs Flowers drawls, knocking back the gin and tonic.

'Damp down *there,*' Brenda hisses, in apocalyptic tones. A doomed silence spreads over the birthday party and a damp feeling fills the air, which only lifts when I accidentally set fire to the table.

It was the ladle of Cointreau. It was flambéing perfectly until I jogged it against the gold paper of the camping stove. Suddenly, Jack's birthday dessert was enveloped in a crawling carpet of blue flame.

Nobody moves at first. They can't really believe it's happening. Also, there's something rather attractive about the whole display. Lots of sharp blue and amber arrows darting round in the middle of the table like the beginning of *Tales of the Unexpected*. But then Brydie's eyes start watering and she whispers to Mary, 'Is this the birthday cake, then, do you suppose?'

Mary doesn't reply. She just gets up and scampers into the kitchen, returning with a series of useless things – a sponge, a mug of water, a tea-towel. Then, just as she is about to ask Brenda what she should do next, Jack stands up and starts taking his clothes off. He can't take his eyes off the blaze, like the fire is his new best friend. A smile wobbles on his lips. 'Light my fire,' he says, pulling off his jumper. 'Light my fire,' he howls, in a monstrous Shirley Bassey voice, unbuttoning his shirt and slipping off his trousers.

Mrs Flowers seems to be denying what's happening all around her. She just leans back in her chair and looks amused. 'That's the spirit, Jack,' she cackles, lighting a cigarette on the abandoned Cointreau ladle. 'One big house on fire!' she roars. 'One big house on fire! Enough light for you, Mrs Barge?'

Brenda has had enough. She throws herself up from the table, runs to the white *chaise-longue*, picks up a cushion and comes charging back to give the burning stove an almighty wallop. This has the unfortunate effect of knocking it over and setting the tablecloth alight.

Now that her precious Spanish tablecloth is in the danger zone, Mrs Flowers doesn't sound so amused. She starts screaming at Brenda to stop ruining her possessions of sentimental value and to Brydie to go and fetch the fire extinguisher from the cupboard under the kitchen sink. But mostly she just screams at me.

'Bloody useless girl!' she erupts, her lip curling ferociously. 'Fat, spiteful girl who—' and she only stops because the black smoke is making her choke. She can't even breathe in her precious tablecloth, she can't even get it back that way because it's become so black and defiled. And it's all my fault, she's right. Jack, wandering round the table in his birthday suit, that's all my fault too. And now something terrible is happening on the TV: a kerfuffle is raging, Fanny is shrinking. She's shrinking like she's been thrown into a vat of acid. Something bad has happened. The beautiful sails are dissolving, the heat of the kitchen is wreaking revenge. Fanny flounders, helpless against the flopped spun sugar that hangs heavy as beer guts, heavy as dead limbs. The ships are sinking! Melt down! Run aground! All hands on deck!

The laugh comes like a knife, cutting through the black smoke, hysterical. 'Serves her right, snobby cow!'

The laughter tickles my ribs like a knife, digging, bruising. We are both getting battered, Fanny and me. Words stick in my throat. I am going down, down – my failure smells like charred cloth, like the cold metal taste of human blood, the bitter taste of experience. My life has become naked Jack chanting, 'Fat, spiteful girl,' and Brydie hopping around pointing a black nozzle at the inferno, going, 'Thingummy,' as she sprays white foam over the mess I have made, turning it into a better birthday cake than I could ever hope to have created.

Chapter Twelve

> Regrettably, figs cannot be sucked either. Spear the base of a fig with your dessert fork so that the fig is held upright on the plate. Cut from stem to within quarter-inch of base. Repeat crosswise, so that the unskinned flesh falls into four neat petals. Cut the flesh from each in a whole section (halve if these are large) and eat with knife and fork.
>
> ***Sociable Cook's Book*** **by Fanny Cradock**

The buildings in Barcelona look like Hansel and Gretel houses – like everything has been piped on in orange and pink and blue and gold *crème Chantilly*. The walls are raspberry ripple, the roofs are honeycomb crisp, the chimneys are glacé cherries, the windows are barley sugar, the shutters are marzipan flowers, the doorways are decorated with silver balls and the façades are made of pink marble striped with crystal glints like coconut ice or some kind of old-fashioned North of England sweet that nobody eats any more.

It is six twenty-five in the morning. A taxi driver has just dropped me outside a large food market on a wide street called Las Ramblas where the air smells of high-tar cigarettes, orange-blossom aftershave, moped fumes, cold ham and recently deceased partying from the night before. I follow a trail of shiny red sequins scattered on the ground. They wind past cigarette stubs, blobs of spit, empty beer bottles, sunflower-seed husks and lead up to a woman wearing fishnet tights and a headdress made from ripe tomatoes. She is pulling red and blue feathers out of a dustbin as another woman in a yellow boa scolds her.

'Enough, *hija*!' Boa moans huskily, scratching her crotch. 'I need to get something to eat.'

'Holy bread!' Tomato exclaims. 'There's some good things in here!' Excitedly, she throws the dustbin lid aside and fishes out a limp, dead chicken still covered in feathers.

'*Ay*! You're so cheap!' Boa says in disgust.

'Nothing wrong with chicken feathers.' Tomato grins. 'Needs must!'

'*Hija!* Chicken feathers. I wouldn't be seen dead in chicken!'

'It's a cock anyway,' Tomato announces. 'They're as good as parrot.' She strokes the mangled bird as if it's the finest of calfskins.

'Killed in a black mass more like,' Boa snaps irritably. Still scratching her crotch, she transfers a lighted cigarette from her right hand to her lipstick-smudged mouth and pulls the scrawny bird from the other woman. She holds it high in the air by the feet and wobbles the slit neck triumphantly with long, red talons on a big, hairy hand.

'You see! Black-mass chicken!'

'Probably brings good luck.'

The Boa throws the chicken to the ground.

'Luck! I'm up to the vagina with your nonsense!' She burps and screws up her eyes as the smoke from the cigarette clenched between her teeth starts to pour into them.

'Well, I'm having them, anyway,' Tomato mumbles sulkily. She crouches on the pavement, retrieves the bird and starts ripping the feathers from the carcass with a pair of hands only slightly less hairy than those of her friend. She sticks them in her headdress – right into the tomatoes – which start dripping down her face like lumpy blood. The lumpy blood is less interesting than the stubble I've just noticed growing along her jawline. She sees me looking. 'What's up, *guapa*?' she snarls, her pupils rocking around in her eyes like ships at sea. 'Something wrong?'

'No ... no ... I was just thinking that ... that you look very nice.'

'*Guapa,*' she informs me, quick as a flash, 'it's not an accident.' She wipes a red, mushy hand down the side of her dress.

Both of the women stagger off to sit down at the long zinc counter of a bar just inside the entrance of the market called Bar Pinoxo. I follow a few paces behind. I imagine that Pinoxo must be the Catalan for Pinocchio because next to a poster showing a thigh of ham next to a pot of geraniums and the words 'Aromas of Catalonia' there is a plastic mask of a boy with a long nose.

The man behind the bar wears a blue stripy shirt and a black bow-tie, and his nose is a bit like a banana. He looks constantly startled, as if there are dozens of cameras wanting to take his picture and he is ready for all of them. He is a very good performer. There is something of the Fanny Cradocks at the Royal Albert Hall about him. Sometimes he speaks in a gluey voice, as if there's a rubber band tied around his tongue – this, I have noted, is the sound of Catalan – and other times he talks regular machine-gun Castilian.

He greets everyone who comes up to the counter with a cartoon grin, and to some people I hear him booming, '*Hola, te quiero!*' which means, 'Hello! I love you!' and '*Hola t'estimo!*' which must mean, 'Hello, I love you,' in Catalan. The Tomato and the Boa get a '*Te quiero!*' from him and a simple '*Hola*' from the woman working next to Pinocchio. She wears a spotless white coat and sensible glasses. She looks like someone who, if ever you were ill with flu, you would like to come round to your house and look after you.

But the main person I notice is a customer with a face like a pterodactyl and eyes that glitter like a magnet picking up a crate of pins. His hands and wrists move like those toy plastic snakes you hold by the tail – wiry and ghostly – as he conveys a small glass of black coffee from the counter to his lips. From some angles his face looks like a scrawny lamb chop but mainly I think that he looks like Don Quijote –

tall, thin, distinguished bone structure, with leathery skin pulled tight over his jutting bones.

Above the sound of scratchy flamenco coming from an ancient radio behind the bar and the shrill noise of boiling steam from the coffee machine, the Pterodactyl is having a conversation in Castilian with the nice woman in the white coat. His voice is gentle and sleepy. Occasionally I catch his eyes sliding over me – flip-flop, flip-flop – like a feather duster over a marble surface. I wish he would talk to me because I am starting to feel nervous. Pinocchio is so engrossed in a feather conversation with the women in the outfits that he doesn't seem to have noticed I am here. I'm not sure how to get his attention above the clatter.

I haven't been to a bar on my own yet. In fact, I haven't been completely alone since I left Mousehole. On the Portsmouth–Le Havre ferry I got chatting to a man called Alan, a twenty-four-year-old medical student from Leeds University with a moustache. He told me that last summer he went to Nicaragua to pick coffee for the Sandinistas. He said things like 'filthy brown liquid' when he meant 'beer' and he wore an Oxfam collarless dress shirt under a brown leather jacket that smelt to me of bandits and cattle-rustlers. He sniffed quite a lot, even though he didn't seem to have a cold, but it didn't matter because he said interesting things. Things like how travelling was good for you because it taught you about the University of Life.

Later, when Alan had finished telling me about the

University of Life, he fell asleep in his deck-chair and I pretended to go to sleep too. I rested my head on his leather jacket and got a crick in my neck but I didn't care because it was my way of getting to him. It worked. When he woke up he told me that he was driving to Málaga to visit his parents. Málaga has three thousand hours of sunshine a year, he said. He said that this was amazing because there were only four places in the world that had more than three thousand hours of sunshine. When he asked if I'd passed my driving test I said that I had and he invited me to join him on the trip in his 2CV. We drove off the ferry together and at the end of our first day in France we went to a camp-site where he bought some wine that came in a ribbed plastic bottle. It was disgusting but I drank all of my share because I knew of the work that lay ahead. The sky turned a vivid pink, as if it was the end of the world, and Alan said, 'Sex is really boring. Let me show you.' He did, and it was. In my diary the next day, I wrote, 'Glad to have got rid of the millstone but can't help but think that maybe I'm deformed internally. Have a better time masturbating.'

Things went downhill from then. On 26 June, round about Montpellier, I wrote:

Alan is obsessed with faeces. Calls it number two. Gets up at seven in the morning and if it's worked he comes back with a huge smile on his face and tells me that I've been eating too much chocolate and that's why I can't do it. Also he tells me I have to touch his balls cos it's bad for a man not to ejaculate. He is really worried about me getting pregnant. He has bought loads of packets of condoms and spermicide gel that comes in a tube like toothpaste but is clear and you inject it up you with a syringe. Afterwards, it drips down your legs in the night like cold jelly. Alan says not to throw away the Nutella jars because we can wash them out and use them as wine glasses. Evening: Knorr soup, tinned cassoulet, peaches, wine, bed, gel, préservatifs. A. ejac. Starving. What's the big deal with sex? Is it me?

Usually I'd wake up with spermicide dripping down my legs, ants crawling over my face and black rings under my eyes due to being so freezing cold in the night. (Alan refused to let me get into his sleeping-bag, telling me I should have brought my own.) There were consolations, though. Once we'd driven over the border into Spain I took to eating *churros con chocolate* for breakfast – just like *Modern Day Spanish* said you were supposed to in Spain. The chocolate is thick as blancmange and the *churros* are fresh as the doughnuts you get from fairgrounds only in sausage shapes. It wasn't long before Alan started making comments about how it would be best if I didn't have *churros con chocolate* every day because I was too chubby as it was. If he saw me eating my other favourite, peaches and Camembert and *cidre,* he'd try to ruin my enjoyment by saying that eating your own faeces tastes of ripe Camembert (or maybe he just thought this was an interesting thing to say). By this time I didn't think that he or his observations or his sniffing were the slightest bit interesting. Even though he was someone to go into a bar with, his company started to become a big chore. Wimbledon kicked off when we were still in France, and things became even more tedious. We'd go into some 'offbeat restaurant' (or some crappy bar down a back alley, as Mrs Flowers would have called it), and there'd be some rubbishy game show on the TV and Alan would make me ask the patron if it was OK to turn over and watch the tennis. But he was never satisfied. Sniffing levels would accelerate and before long he'd tell me to ask them about adjusting brightness levels or something. And then I'd go to the loo and when I came back, there'd be a programme on about otters. Three weeks into the Portsmouth–Málaga trip, my diary entry reads:

On a camp-site in Béziers we met three Irish girls who have already been travelling round France for four months. They can afford to do it because they only eat carrots and boiled potatoes every night. They are always drinking beer and talking about boys in their tent. Alan says they are typical Irish girls. His sniff is starting to get on my nerves. Catherine, one of them, told me in the shower that in France when your period comes you say, 'Les anglais sont débarqués,' which means, 'The English have landed.' She also told me about a book she is reading called 'Synchronicity or Meaningful Coincidence'. Would have liked to read it but Alan wanted to move on. Later that night he invited two Swedish girls over to the tent for some 'filthy brown liquid'. They thought that was really funny. Back on the road, I crashed the gears and nearly ran a man down. Alan nagged. Said he wished he'd known I haven't really passed my driving test. He said that when we get to Málaga he'd tell his parents that me and him was just a platonic relationship. His mother is rather staid, apparently. Told me how last year he went to Corfu with another girl.

Then, at six o'clock this morning, after nearly a month on the road, we finally reached Barcelona. Alan (who drove into a ditch two days ago) parked in a small side-street and we went into a bar. I had a *cortado* and a *zumo de naranja* while Alan ordered his customary *café con leche*. When he'd drunk it, the usual happened: he got up like his trousers were on fire, sniffed long and hard and announced, 'Back in two shakes, Rosa. Some of us have number two to attend to!' By then I knew I wasn't going to be making it to Málaga.

I got my stuff from the car, jumped into the nearest taxi and asked for Las Ramblas because Mrs Flowers said that was where she used to go to gather her thoughts in the early hours of the morning. But now, as I sit on the cold metal stool at the zinc counter of the Pinocchio bar with everyone ignoring me, a cold shadow of doubt is starting to sink into me. Maybe I should have stuck with Alan, I think. At least he was someone to sit with so I didn't feel like too much of an idiot. And maybe Barcelona is too close to home – Mrs Flowers' old home. Why am I still following her so slavishly anyway? And why is she still chasing me around in my head when I tried to leave her behind a month ago?

I take a deep breath and try to concentrate on where I am right now: in Barcelona, on a stool in the Pinocchio bar, sitting next to a human dinosaur with skin like a crumpled-up sheet of brown wrapping paper. I try to appear casual by turning round on my seat and looking at the butcher's stall opposite. There is a wall of sticky ham thighs hanging above a glass cabinet displaying two dead piglets lying on their tummies. They look like they're masturbating. Their hips are pressed into a tray garnished with tomato and lettuce leaves and their pert buttocks are squeezed to attention. When I look up, I see the Pterodactyl devouring the display too. He meets my eye and says softly, '*¡Qué maravilla!* What a marvel! How nice to find someone like *him* in the mountains, no?' He points a gnarled finger at the suckling pig on the left. 'Pink and plump and cooling his groin in a bed of fragrant lettuce.'

I'm trying to think what the right reply to this might be when the Pterodactyl turns to Pinocchio. With a twinkle in his glittering eyes, he says, 'What do you say? In an ideal world, everyone would only eat haunch of slightly overweight eighteen-year-old boy?'

Pinocchio weighs the matter up for a few seconds. 'Perhaps,' he says. 'You wouldn't want someone who did too much exercise. Too sinewy.'

'Someone who walked in the mountains,' the Pterodactyl suggests. 'Someone who was happy. You'd want to eat him.'

'The best beef in the world comes from Japan,' Pinocchio adds. 'Every day the cows are massaged and fed on high quality beer.'

The Pterodactyl sighs. '*¡Ay!* A life of being drunk and massaged. *¡Qué maravilla!*'

'Fear is bad for taste,' Pinocchio goes on, passing him another glass of the black coffee. 'Scared meat is tough. Dead bulls from the Plaza de Toros are only good for stews.'

'Tough as dead gladiator flesh,' the woman in the white coat grunts, as she hauls a consignment of prawns, crabs and some pinky-red things like crayfish over the counter. When Pinocchio has given their wet shells the once-over and nodded his approval, she takes a dozen of the crayfish and puts them, still writhing, in a bowl on top of a glass display cabinet. The rest she throws on top of the grill. They start squealing and it reminds me of the carp in Roman times who gave you sexual pleasure as you watched them die slowly. The ones squirming on the glass display cabinet are so fresh that their black peppercorn eyes are playful as puppies. You know that it's only a matter of time before they join their brothers and sisters on the grill where death will turn their eyes the dirty white of sucked gob-stoppers.

You have to stop yourself feeling sorry for them, though, because once you start to enjoy the spectacle of shrieking shellfish squirming in the final spasms of life, it does wonders for your courage. As I stare at the grill I start to feel powerful and this soon becomes a feeling of annoyance at still not having been served. So I stand up on the foot rests of my stool and I say to Pinocchio, in a clear, measured voice: 'Maybe if you died masturbating, your flesh would be as tough as if you'd died in fear.'

I say this in a mixture of formal Spanish and a smattering of the slang words I've noticed everyone else at the bar using. When the sentence finally emerges it rolls perfectly off my tongue and it makes everyone in the bar turn to look at me. It is one of those moments of might and I feel very fine indeed. Pinocchio hesitates. You can see I've thrown him off his guard. He throws a quick glance at Tomato and Boa, before venturing to claim that if you did just a little wank before death then your flesh would be bloodier and therefore tastier. But the Pterodactyl argues that the tastiness of the meat would be directly proportionate to how good the wank was and this immediately gets Pinocchio all hot and bothered. Tomato and Boa, now eating bowls of purple mini octopuses with white beans, join in the controversy. They waggle muscly arms above their heads and soon the whole bar is awash with a debate about sex and death and meat. And it's all down to me.

The Pterodactyl is looking at me. A wide smile has overtaken his big, bony mouth – as if he's secreting some prehistoric digestive juice and any minute now his mouth will shriek open and he will suck me in. He's lost interest in the argument going on at the bar. I have become his focal point. He wants to know who I am and what I am doing here. I say that I am English and that I am doing research into the University of Life. '*La Universidad de la Vida*' sounds pretty good in Spanish, I think. He seems to think so too because his heavy eyes look into mine and he says, '*¡Ay, sí!*', pronouncing the '*¡Ay!*' like 'eye' – just like in Mrs Flowers' Spanish Shirley Bassey records.

When he notices that I haven't been served, he clicks

his fingers at Pinocchio and orders me a glass of what he is drinking – an espresso with a shot of rum called a *carajillo*. A *cara-heeeeeeee-o*. It nearly blows your head off when you swallow it, although if you stir in two sachets of sugar it makes things much easier.

When he sees me choking, he starts saying, '*¡Ay!*' with passion in his voice, as if he is one of the crayfish being roasted alive on the grill. '*¡Qué maravilla!*' he goes. 'I was six when I tasted my first alcohol. Quina San Clemente, it was called. "Makes your child hungry!" the advert went. *¡Hombre!* Of course it made your child hungry. It was sweet white wine! Five per cent proof!'

He says that then he progressed on to a kind of Spanish cheese-on-toast idea. Except it had wine and sugar on top of the bread instead of cheese. Then, when he was nine, he started slipping under the dining-room table to drink red wine from the family *porrón* – without the addition of lemonade – and only occasionally would his mother lift up the tablecloth and exclaim, with good humour, 'Hey, not so much of that young man!'

The Pterodactyl puts on a geeky grin – one where his top and bottom lip meet in the middle like a little boy's grin, like the grin he must have put on when his mother caught him under the table with the *porrón*.

He puts his nose in his glass and snorts deeply. When he surfaces, he makes a nostalgic '*¡Ay!*' and introduces himself as Jesús – or *hhhhey-soos* as you pronounce it in Spanish. I tell him that he reminds me of Don Quijote and he smiles and says that, yes, he is a bit like Don Quijote – *noble y* *despistado*, noble and dippy. Or rather, he says wistfully, he is just dippy now – without the noble bit. His Galician father used to have a lot of money, 'but then he became ruined.' Jesús shrugs his coat-hanger shoulders. *Arruinarse* is the verb he uses and it sounds much more flamboyant than 'to go bankrupt'. 'My father became ruined.' He shrugs.

I can't believe my luck because now I have a Spanish friend called Jesús. And *hhhhey-soos*, my new Spanish friend with the death rattle J, is going to take me under his haggard, leathery wing, show me Spain and make me king of the castle. It will be much better than Alan and his Nutella jars or Nikki Kilroy and his package holidays to Marbella or Mrs Flowers and her pathetic memories.

I take some more gulps of my *carajillo* because I don't even want to think any more about Alan or Nikki Kilroy or Mrs Flowers. I want the real thing and being friends with a Spaniard in Spain is definitely the real thing. I have been working up to this moment for the past month. It wasn't that the beginning of my journey was insignificant. It's just that things have become clearer in the past four weeks, gradually coming into focus, becoming brighter, sharper, less wobbly round the edges, as if the horizon is finally in sight.

I left England four days after Jack's eighteenth birthday party. By the time the night was out, escape had gone from being a nice idea to being an urgent necessity. Then, as soon as I'd made the break I wished I'd done it sooner. Abroad has been exciting from the word go: ever since I stood on the deck of the Portsmouth–Le Havre ferry and licked my arms and they tasted of salty dock fumes. There was the waft of sweat, too – a new kind of sweat. You never smell sweat like that in Mousehole. You only have clean sweat in Mousehole or BO from too-tight Dingles' nylon sleeves or pasty-oven sweat. It was coming from an Englishman sitting down at one of the railings. He was talking to an American girl about smuggling condoms filled with marijuana out of Holland. He was telling her that he used to be in the Foreign Legion. His sweat was like diesel oil and dust, it was sweat that had seen the world – as if his clothes had joined up with the perspiration and now he had a new type of skin. I wanted sweat like that.

The American girl said 'sucky' a lot. I heard her saying that she was driving a car down to the South of France. I edged my way closer to them and said that Europeans used to drive on the left side of the road too but then Napoleon changed it all. I didn't get any response so I asked her what she did. She said she was a lion-tamer and they both started to laugh and then they turned their backs on me. The English boy started playing the Beatles song 'Michelle' on his guitar. He got the words all wrong and the American girl didn't even realise. She kept saying, 'Wow! You speak French! Such a beautiful language!' She was a real Fiona P type. I felt a bit fed up because I obviously spoke better French than probably most English people on the ferry. But nothing was going to dampen my spirits. By this time we were nearer to France than we were to England so I just got up, took my rucksack, put a look on my face like I was really bored, and wandered down to the lounge, which was filled with lots of French schoolchildren with colourful backpacks and sweatshirts with strange slogans like 'Baby Flipper Best of Union'.

In spite of drawbacks and in spite of Alan, my first taste of abroad was just as brilliant as I thought it would be. I wanted to suck everything up and take it away with me. By the time we got to Amiens I'd already snapped ten rolls of film. Alan had hardly driven the 2CV off the ferry before my pen was scribbling away in my dairy.

16 June 1983

Driving on the wrong side of the road is frightening and exciting. Being in a foreign country is like driving on the wrong side of the road. In France there is a bar of chocolate with a purple cow on the front called Milka. Also, they have yellow headlights and blue road signs saying things like 'tenez-vous à droit' and 'cédez le passage'. Centre Ville is a sign in all towns meaning 'Town Centre'. The Casino service station in Amiens was much better than Little Chef. They had melon and Parma ham, which is raw ham from Italy. Also in France they have water in a bottle with a pink label on called Evian. Even litter is interesting. And there are sugar-lump wrappers with a sun on saying, 'C'est la vie!' and discarded bread bags, shaped like baguettes ('la baguette de votre artisan du pain') and a cartoon of a baker with a curl of fringe like a swirl of duchesse potato. Puddles of sick seem significant too. We went to a camp-site.

I noticed a boy eating a blue ice lolly in the shape of a shark. Had soggy microwave pizza in the bar and a lemonade with mint syrup called a Diabolo Menthe. Borrowed matches from Spanish boy in next tent who looked like a horse. His girlfriend was there too. He said she was called Anna Karenina. She didn't talk. Him and Alan talked about unemployment in Spain, the Falklands, the Tower of Babel, how Christianity is like a crutch really and how the meaning of life is learning to cope with different situations. Also about foreign trees. About how almond trees have soft fur around the almonds and olive trees are silver and ugly at the same time, like they've got arthritis. Very interesting. They also talked about Bruce Springsteen and Paul someone. Tried to impress them by using A level phrases like: 'If we examine the question more closely we shall see the facts in a different light', and 'The following are the factors that have to be reckoned with'. Think they were quite impressed.

In the evening, we sat round the fire at the camp-site drinking wine with people of different nationalities. Alan brought over the Nutella jars but I preferred to take swigs from bottle tops belonging to unknown people. Lots of interesting conversations:

A: 'Opium tastes nice. It tastes of lime and bitter oranges.'

B. 'Cicadas only live for one day and then they get so bloated with blood they explode.'

C. '"Alstublieft" is the Dutch for "please".'

D. 'With stream of consciousness, you have to read it several times.'

19 June 1983

New camp-site. Had cold shower. Washed clothes. Borrowed a hammer from frogs. Knorr ham and pea soup and chorizo for tea. Lots of new experiences: blue, shark-shaped ice lolly in the bar followed by my first taste of rabbit. A Frenchman in next-door tent was cooking some. You can tell a rabbit leg from a chicken leg because rabbit legs are slimmer and more shapely than knobbly old chicken legs. Rabbit legs look like they are wearing high heels. Alan looked at the rabbit and shrugged at the Frenchman like an idiot, going, 'English! No rabbit for me!' But I tried some. 'Tastes like sweet chicken,' I said. 'Everyone says that everything tastes like chicken,' the Frenchman said. 'Rabbit tastes like chicken, locusts taste like chicken, alligator meat tastes like chicken. I bet if fish could smell dead human bodies they'd say they smelt of chicken.' I was too nervous to ask him what horse tasted like but I plan to try some very soon.

These innocent encounters are all in my past now. Now that I'm in Barcelona I've wised up to life outside England. I'm bored of the hippie tourist view of abroad. I've decided not to go to any more crappy bars and not to have any more stupid blue ice lollies because the first reminds me of Mrs Flowers and the second reminds me of kicking Jack off his stool in domestic-science class. Both Mrs Flowers and Jack make me feel bad inside and I don't want to feel bad inside. This is where I think Jesús might come in. I think that Jesús sounds full of wisdom. He makes me want to confess things to him. I think that maybe he can help me understand some things. I know that it's a bit forward of me, seeing as I only met him a few minutes ago, but I can't help it. There are matters on my mind.

I take a big gulp of my *carajillo* and I turn to him.

I tell him that I have been feeling sad recently, although I'm not sure if sad is the right word. Jesús closes his eyes, lifts his glass to his nose and inhales the last dregs of his rum-laced coffee. In a voice gentle as sleazy trumpets and sleepy strings he whispers, '*Hija, tenemos todos nuestos secretos,*' which means, 'Daughter, we all have our secrets.' And it works like magic. I start to feel a weight gradually lifting off my chest. He adds, with a sluggish smile, 'I used to be sad but now I've given it up.' And that really inspires me. I know he's saying that it doesn't matter that I've done what I've done, because now I'm in Spain and that cancels out any actions I might have carried out hundreds of miles away. Life is all about living in the here and now, is what he's saying, in this country, at this bar, at this minute, with this Pterodactyl. Everyone has their secrets, he's saying, and as long as you don't tell anyone about them it's OK. Anyway, even Brenda has given me her blessing. She said that in the circumstances it would be a good idea for me to go abroad. University can always wait, she said. There's something slightly annoying in having her sanction, but at least it leaves me free to get on finally with the job of escaping. I finish off the last of my fire coffee and feel pretty pleased with myself.

The good thing about drinking *carajillo* is that it makes you forget your worries and feel quite bold and it is so sweet that it doesn't make you feel sick at all. Jesús orders me another one and to show my gratitude for him being my new friend and to show him that I have a good grasp of Spanish food culture I decide to order something typically

Spanish. So I stand up in my stool again and I say to Pinocchio in a clear, measured voice: '*Quisiera un bocadillo de chorizo, por favor.*'

Pinocchio starts falling about with laughter and Jesús starts doing a wrist-flicking movement, which denotes incredulity (*Modern Day Spanish,* chapter three). He finally explains that nobody says 'I would like' in Spanish. They say 'give me' or 'I want'. And then Pinocchio starts going on about politeness and how the English are repressed because they never say what they mean.

Once the limelight is switched on Pinocchio it seems there is no stopping him. He goes into an animated routine complete with hand gestures about how a *chorizo* sandwich is not the sort of thing you order in his bar anyway. A *chorizo* sandwich, he says, is what people in Andalucía eat. It is, he says, the equivalent of fish and chips in England and he does an impersonation of what I suppose must be a fish. He makes a joke about how I'm probably going to ask him for a bag of sunflower seeds next and go round spitting the husks all over the floor just like they do in Andalucía. When I say that, no actually, I was going to ask for *churros con chocolate,* he turns round behind the bar, crouches down and starts doing an impression of someone laying a log – complete with sound effects. Tomato thinks this is hilarious too. Her wide open mouth is a black fish tank filled with mutilated purple mini octopuses and it roars, 'Caga Tío! Caga Tío! *¡Ay!*'

I feel red shoot through my cheeks. I feel angry because

Jack and his tales of Uncle Turd suddenly flash into my mind. I'm also fed up because everyone at the Pinocchio bar is laughing at me. I'm fed up that suddenly I have become representative of all the English people in England. I'm not having it. Besides, my second *carajillo* is making me brave. So I sit up again, I look Pinocchio in the eye and I bark, 'Give me a plate of that, handsome,' because everyone here really does finish off their sentences with *guapo,* if you are male, and *guapa,* if you are female. I point to the plate of white beans and mini octopuses that the two hairy women are eating and Jesús starts patting me on the back, saying, '*Muy bien, muy bien, hija,*' meaning, 'Very good, very good, daughter.' Pinocchio seems especially to like the bit where I call him *guapo.* The lady in the white coat smiles and puts a steaming bowl in front of me and I am glad to be sitting on a stool like a high chair at the counter of the Pinocchio bar with a woman in a white coat looking after me and my new friend the Pterodactyl, looking at me like I am some rare dinosaur egg he has just unearthed.

The octopuses are the colour of fresh bruises. When I inhale the steam, smells of the sea mix with the high-tar cigarettes, the orange-blossom aftershave, the moped fumes and the cold ham. '¡*Ay!*' I say, just like real Spanish people say, and everyone laughs and says, '*Muy bien,*' again. Then Jesús pulls over a pot of parsley standing on the bar, buries his nose in it and inhales deeply.

'¡*Ay!* The mountain!' he moans. 'Poppers!' he purrs. 'To bury my head in the universal, the total!' When he comes up for air, he scoffs, 'That yoga teacher didn't know the meaning of pleasure.'

'Yoga teacher this time was it, Jesús?' Pinocchio inquires.

Jesús nods. 'You'd have thought he'd have been good at sex, no? A yoga teacher?'

Pinocchio shrugs as if he's not interested but you can tell he is really.

'On the contrary,' Jesús says, 'he was very bad at sex. Claimed he was looking for *amistad*. Friendship!' Jesús spits the word out, adding that the yoga teacher pronounced it '*Amistath*', which made him even more cross. Pinocchio is outraged at this too. Apparently, pronouncing 'd' as 'th' is a typical affectation of people living in Castilla, the capital province of Spain. Spanish spoken in Castilla is supposed to be the proper Queen's English way to speak the language, which, according to Pinocchio, is ridiculous because Catalans make the most money of anyone in Spain.

'They might have royalty in Castilla but they have more banks in Barcelona!' Pinocchio snorts.

'Exactly!' Jesús scoffs, signalling for another *carajillo*. '*Amistath!*' He hits his head with his index finger. '*¡Era como una cabra!*' He was mad as a goat! '*¡Hombre!* Why do you go to the mountain at four in the morning looking for friendship? I said to him, "Fuck first, *amistath* later."' In a panicky gulp, Jesús downs half of the new *carajillo*. 'He didn't know how to enjoy life. He told me, "You must sin alone."' Jesús makes another wrist-shaking movement of incredulity. '*¡Hostia! Tío!*' he exclaims. 'Holy bread! Uncle!'

Again, he grasps hold of the pot of parsley on the counter and caresses it with his large, bony hand. 'Sin alone! Like the priests used to say! He couldn't even bring himself to say "masturbate"!'

He calms down at last. He takes a deep breath and shrugs his bony shoulders. '*¡Yo que sé!*' he huffs. 'What do I know?' He buries his nose in the parsley again. '*¡Ay!*' he sighs. '*¡El argentino! ¡El argentiiiino!* Such a smile! Like a fresh slice of pie!'

He doesn't elaborate on who *el argentino* is. He just looks deep into his glass. You can't tell if he's in the depths of despair or if he's just contemplating the bubbles on top of the coffee. Suddenly he puts his finger in the glass and splashes some drops of coffee to the ground among the toothpicks and the olive stones and the crumpled napkins. 'In homage to Dionysus,' he announces, adding that the god of debauchery needs to be appeased with alcohol spilt on the ground. 'To stave off the dangers of an over-rational life.'

He turns to me and breathes a deep sigh. 'I am like you,' he says softly. 'I like to travel. As the Arabs say, "Happiness is in the saddle."'

'Yes,' I reply, with an enthusiastic nod. 'I've learned lots since I left England. I've realised that life can be quite bewildering. I mean, you could get run over by a bus or there might be an olive stone in your salad and you might break one of your teeth . . .'

'Or the person you're talking to might think you like them, whereas in fact you're just being nice because someone has been unkind to you and you're in need of a friend.'

'Yes . . . and . . .' I stop and smile when I think of what Jesús has said. He seems to know me already. I look at his parchment skin and say hesitantly, 'Once . . . recently, when I was with a friend, I saw a pile of leaves blow past like they were walking briskly or dancing or something. I thought it would be nice to be one of them – one of the leaves travelling around a twisty road on a draught of air. Light as a leaf, nobody taking any notice of you unless they were happening to have a special moment too and noticed how you were tripping the light fantastic. My friend I was with at the time, she . . . she'd travelled a lot. She did this funny laugh – a laugh like a snake – and she said the leaf thing was what you'd feel like if you took acid and it worked well.'

I say this because I hope Jesús will be impressed with my knowledge of drugs, even though I haven't taken any yet, apart from a couple of puffs of a joint in a youth hostel in Girona. I also say it because I can't resist bringing Mrs Flowers back to life by talking about her. But when Jesús hears my story he just picks up on the acid reference. His skin pulls tight over his face bones and he does one of his little boy smiles. '*El ácido.*' He chuckles, shaking his wrist in the incredulity movement. 'What a marvel!' He sighs and adds, 'Alas, everything seems interesting on acid. And everyone. Under the influence of acid I gave the yoga teacher my phone number.' He picks a purple mini octopus from my plate. 'Still,' he grins, popping it into his mouth, 'if he comes round I might make him dinner. Only spaghetti or pizza, mind. For *el argentino* I made *gambas. Gambas al ajillo.* Garlic prawns.' He sighs again. A wave runs through his shoulders like a shiver.

I finish off the second *carajillo*. My insides are tingling as the hot rum and coffee starts to rush through my blood. I feel much better. Jesús makes me feel light. It feels as if he has done a quick spell on me and as I dip my nose into the empty glass and inhale I think that I knew it would be like this. I knew everything in Spain would be better than in England. In Spain they have men like Jesús who roam like wolves in the mountains looking for goats and they don't have prawn cocktail. They have *gambas* that sound like gambolling on a beach in the sun instead of repressed English 'prawns' that sound like they were brought up at Eton. They certainly don't eat them with Marie Rose sauce and orange squash, they have them with garlic and eat them with people they love.

And then Magalí walks in.

She has eyes like the people in the *Guernica* painting and eyebrows like an angry bull. When she arrives, the bar perks up and Pinocchio goes into 'I love you!' overdrive. She ignores him and saunters over to Jesús to plant a languid kiss on both cheeks. She doesn't tell him where she's come from or what she's doing here at this early hour. She just sits down on the stool next to him, steals some of his *carajillo* and throws me a glance. She has the most beautiful eyes I have ever seen. They are like gold and green-coloured aspic – like water on a sunny day when tree vegetation is reflected in it. She is tall and willowy and wears an orange top with pink clouds on it. It is made of a kind of fancy nylon material so you can't really be sure where the clouds end and her breasts begin.

Jesús must see me looking at her because he says, 'I present Magalí Sanchez. We call her *la bruja gitana*, the gipsy witch.' '*Bruhhhhhha hhhhhitana*', he pronounces it, like five hundred cats all spitting at once. Magalí ignores Jesús and orders a tall-stemmed glass of Catalan champagne called *cava*. As she takes her first sip, though, Jesús whispers something in her ear and she leans into him to listen. It is strange because I feel both jealousy and attraction at the same time. I don't want her to take Jesús away from me but also I want Jesús to disappear and leave just me and her together.

Still listening to what Jesús is telling her, she knocks back the liquid in her glass and starts laughing. Pinocchio leans over and joins in their whispering. Suddenly, they're all staring at me and laughing – Spanish laughing, like they're cannibals and they're sizing me up for putting me in a pot and turning me into a stew. Not even a safe English stew, a frightening Spanish broth with chick-peas and garlic and tentacle-y, floaty bits. And just as I feel as if I might be about to cry, Magalí leans over to me and whispers, 'You are so white. It is like you are black.'

Her voice is like warm rock pools and her neck smells of bitter oranges and limes and hairspray and cigarettes. And ever so faintly of Mrs Flowers. It is quite shocking to find this spicy smell so far away from Mousehole. But thankfully there are lots of things that are totally different from Mrs Flowers. She has black hair, which is harsh and stiff like horsehair or guitar strings – and she can dance really well. She gets up from the bar stool and starts swaying to a song on the radio and it's as if every cell of her body is made up of a thousand snake hips.

As she dances, she hooks me with her eyes and she tells me that I am so exotic my ancestors must have been Vikings. She tells me – on a foamy sea of rolling Rs and savage Js – that I come from a land of cold waters, that she sees me in a past life, dressed in thick furs and a horned hat, arriving on Mediterranean shores to bask in the sun, to weave tales and haunt the people with my beguiling smile.

It can safely be said that nobody has ever been so charming to me in my life. And the best thing is that Magalí doesn't stop there.

'I will take you to swim in warm seas,' she says. She drinks the whole of her glass of *cava* without taking her eyes off me, then leans in closer and says, '*Eres muy guapa.*' *Guapa,* she says. Beautiful. *Eres* from *ser.* To be. The permanent one. Not just a passing thing. I am beautiful. It is in my nature. She says so. She asks me what my name is. When I tell her she seems even more delighted. She vibrates, 'Rrrrrrosa,' into the morning air and it sends an earthquake of Rs and an orange breeze of Ss all over my face. She tells me that she has only ever met one girl with real red hair before and I immediately feel a twinge of jealousy and imagine a story about being the only person in the world who is universally loved.

I don't want her to talk about other girls any more. So I ask her if her name is Spanish because I haven't heard of it before. She smiles slowly and replies, 'I define myself by seas not by countries. I am of the Mediterranean Sea.'

I suddenly get a vivid image of Brenda's murky Scottish lochs and then I just think how lucky I am because nobody would ever say anything like that in Mousehole. If they did, it would sound really pretentious and Fiona P would probably say something like, 'You've got a mouth bigger than the river Tamar.'

Everything sounds so poetic here, everything is like a Lorca poem. Even when I look over and see Jesús indicating to Pinocchio the size of the yoga teacher's penis by doing an impersonation of sucking a piece of asparagus, it seems an elegant thing to do. Then Magalí orders another glass of *cava* and says, '*El vino da alegría,*' which means 'wine gives happiness' and the whole of the market seems to vibrate with the springy R of '*alegría*'.

Pinocchio puts down a plate of prawns proudly in front of her. I watch her crunching into them and it reminds me of Mrs Flowers saying, 'Anything you can crunch and suck and rip apart with your fingers can't be all bad.' Meanwhile, Jesús' homage to Dionysus seems to be paying off. The smell of Magalí sitting next to me and the two *carajillos* on a near-empty stomach are making me feel the savage end of restless. I watch her oily fingers tearing at a prawn, decapitating it, rushing the head to her mouth and sucking out the brains. Salty brown juice runs over her lips. I feel the warm sea on my face and it is her, saying, 'The most exquisite of all,' as she tosses the empty husk to the ground and pushes the plate towards me.

I see my father telling me that you can't eat shrimp heads and I see Jack smearing orange shrimp brain lipstick on to his mouth in the Lobster Pot. And then I see the gold aura round the pupils of her eyes, like a golden moon, and everything else gets shut out. I pick up a prawn from her plate, I crunch and I drink. I suck a goblet of prawn juice – thick, sweet, warm, yellow – from the depths of the pink, salty head. And if everything exotic is supposed to taste like chicken then the good news is that the sweet and flowing river doesn't taste like chicken at all. It tastes like chicken and rabbit and pork and lamb and beef and fish and spiders and tentacles and blood and pomegranates and blue cheese and driving on the wrong side of the road and falling off a cliff in a dream all mixed up together, all at once. It tastes like white flashes of lightning and dark secret places in velvety caverns at the bottom of the sea and there is grit and sand and a sticky, livery tang, which rise up at intervals to try to frighten me off. She is still looking at me, the warm sea is still on my face when I come up, gasping for air. And I want to go down again, to swallow more danger, to fall down again to the magical mystery place, to hover on the edge of disgust, to lose my direction, to cast off, to escape, to bite and suck and squirt beige juice all over my hand like blood from a severed artery.

And I know it's silly because they are only prawns and it is only a show-offy Spanish woman of more than average attraction levels and I'm sure it has something to do with the effects of the fiery black coffee. But even so, everything seems to be spinning. A revving-up feeling is coming. A revving-up feeling and butterflies, as if my trousers have suddenly fallen down in a public place, but I don't feel embarrassed by it. As if I have soaked up as much happiness as is possible and there is still an excess pouring out of me like the bubbling steam rising up from the pots and pans in the Pinocchio bar. The woman in the white coat stirs the pots, the radio croons, the puppies woof, the crayfish scream, the pigs pump, the prawns sing, the feathers sway, the strings of red peppers hanging on the stall behind Magalí's head dance, the octopuses swim in the white bean sea like a soup bowl full of Busby Berkeley can-can girls. And all the time there seems to be more and more and more of everything coming from every direction. Dancing, moving, revving, prancing. Oh, mystery, oh, excitement, oh, dark streets and smiling strangers!

Albert Camus calls it freedom, Jean Anouilh says it's the infernal machine of destiny, Luis Buñuel says you should lock yourself in a small room to look at pictures of the Eiffel Tower and sit round the dinner table to have a shit. R. D. Laing says there's no such thing as madness, Baudelaire says the supreme pleasure of love lies in the certitude of doing harm, Sylvia Plath says you might as well kill yourself, Lorca says you should look at the moon and turn octopuses inside out. Alan says, 'No, you can't have another ice cream'; the man at the camp-site says, 'You have to read stream of consciousness several times'; Fanny Cradock says, 'If you are faced with a whole pineapple your hostess should be shot'; Brenda says, 'Waste not, want not'; Mrs Flowers says, 'Fat, spiteful girl'; Jack says, 'Stop letting the ghosts in!'; Fiona P says, 'You've got a mouth bigger than the river Tamar, Rosa Barge.' I say: I don't need any of you. I say: Shut up all of you. I say: This is the end of my English life.

Magalí touches my arm and the happiness roars through me again. I jig on my stool, I want to eat the world. It's the sound of rushing sea, of plugging your ears with fingers and hearing another world speeding along, a distant echo of some happiness you once knew. Everything is intense, everything is in the present tense: the breadcrumbs on the metal counter, the sequins on the floor, the bubbles on the *carajillos*, Jesús lamenting *el argentino*, Magalí's *Guernica* eyes, the '*¡Ay! ¡Ay!*' of pain from the flamenco woman on the radio. All these things have their part to play, all are part of one vivid, fearless moment that makes me want to hop into a matchbox boat and shoot off to the horizon and not care about falling off the edge of the world because the moon is round and the sun is round so the chances are that the end of the world is at least curvyish. And who wants to stay on land, anyway, if you're going to spend your life studying and eating in tea-rooms and babysitting mad boys and ego-boosting drunken women and feeling guilty about things that aren't your fault?

She slams her empty *cava* glass down on the counter and reaches over to kiss me on the lips. When she pulls away I gasp, 'Oh, shit,' and clutch my stomach like I've been stabbed and the life is seeping out of me.

Chapter Thirteen

When Johnnie and I went back to the Balearics we had a wonderful time. Juan Gaspart bought us champagne in a very high-class brothel. Here, the ladies took me to their heart and taught me how to play the castanets. Madame beamed at us all and we listened to wonderful guitar music in a marble patio.

Something's Burning, an autobiography
by Fanny Cradock

The appearance of a lacklustre *crema catalana* – the Spanish take on the *crème brûlée* – can be improved drastically by the simple measure of placing it under a grill. Before long, the cap becomes a sheet of bubbling brown sugar and, as if by magic, the dessert suddenly looks good enough to eat again. In the same way, human skin can be made to look fresh and tasty by the simple act of toasting it in the sun.

From where I am lying, my hands cupped behind my head, I can see the corner of a tanned hip. My hip, apparently. The tiny hairs growing there have been bleached white by the sun, which makes a nice contrast to the golden-brown glow of the rest of my skin. It's funny how the sun becomes addictive. It's not that you stop thinking, although you can't see the point of big, complicated ideas. It's more that the element of worry creeps in less. You forget words. You look up and the day means green palm leaf and blue sky through palm-tree branches. And your body becomes more and more alien the browner it becomes. Lying on the beach you become so body-conscious that you almost cease to be body-conscious. All there is to do is lie there and witness yourself becoming beautiful as the sun does its work.

I think I like my body better now, although I sometimes worry, as I feel the sun burning into my forehead, whether all the extra wrinkles that are bound to come are going to be worth it. Magalí reassures me, though. She is a strong believer in making yourself as *guapa* as possible. 'For four days we live, five at the most,' she says, meaning that life has to be lived in the here and now.

Since I met Magalí I have become much more attractive. My belly wobbles less even though it gets stabbed at intervals throughout the day. Being with Magalí in Spain is like going to the horizon. Even better, it's about not quite reaching the horizon. It's like staring out at it from the front of a matchbox boat that is scudding towards the setting sun when the sky is pink and there are peach and blue and silver lights blowing on the water. Better than getting there, moving is the thing.

Waking up next to Magalí feels like being eight years old and waking up to snow. It feels like looking out of the window and feasting your eyes on a changed landscape and hundreds of possibilities flashing before your eyes.

Magalí is not like snow, of course. She is more like an orange tree. Or an orange grove. Even though I am in Spain, I am still astonished every time I see a tree with oranges growing on the end of it. It seems as surprising as a tree that grows hot buttered toast or strawberry ninety-nines. And then she wakes up and looks at me and she gives me eye-contact, which has the power to make me forget my immediate surroundings in a way that a good *crema catalana* does – although, of course, the good thing about searing eye-contact is that it takes your appetite right away.

The colour of love is orange, *naranja* in Spanish, with one of those pickaxe Js. When Magalí whispers, '*Naran-hhhhhhhhhhhh-a*,' in my ear it sounds as if she is writing 'I love you' on my body in blood with a flint-tipped spear. Every night she takes me to a place made of warm ice. Hot as an orange grove, blue as a glacier. Not hard, though: the place is soft as squid skin, deep as a crayfish head and good as a well-cooked paella (wet). And afterwards, when I have orgasms, I feel like a delighted child describing my birthday meal out. I tell Magalí, 'I had two . . . well . . . sort of two and a half orgasms. I had the second one and I knew there was still some left . . .' and Magalí laughs and pulls me closer to her. Now I laugh when I think of 'clean' sex and 'dirty' sex.

I think that the only sex should be like seafood. You should feel slightly sticky afterwards in the way you do when you have finished extracting various-coloured oozy flesh from various spiky shells. Shellfish and *cava* make me want to go to the mountains and act like a lizard. So Magalí takes me to the mountains and I crawl naked on my belly in the dirt among the burnt rosemary and the dust and the crumpled Ducados packets. She licks *cava* from the small of my back and I devour her flesh like meat at a Roman banquet. I suck her bones, I gasp for air, I nearly choke to death my mouth is so full. And it is harsh as murder and there are cicadas screeching and almonds growing and Magalí's funny Spanish canvas shoes that she's still wearing and her sunglasses that she hasn't had time to take off, and she moans, '*¡Ay, mi amor!*' just like Mrs Flowers used to say and I hug her, inhale her, I breathe in Spain.

During these times I feel daring and safe as Tom the cabin-boy, swimming in clothes in warm seas. I even float above Tom the cabin-boy, look down on him from above. Magalí makes me forget Mrs Flowers. Even better, she makes me hate Mrs Flowers. I feed from Magalí. Pleasure drips down my face and she licks it off. Everything seems wet. Even speaking Spanish is slippery as a fish. It's as if I am another person when I speak Spanish. It's perfect. I can say really embarrassing things and pretend it's not really me. It's like speaking pillow-talk all the time. It seems that nothing trivial can ever be said in Spanish and whatever Spanish people say always sounds majestic and grand. When Magalí says something like, '*Me has robado el corazón,*' which means, 'You have stolen my heart,' part of me feels like it's a jackpot grammar exercise from *Modern Day Spanish*. Part of me wonders what it would feel like if I really did put my hand into her chest and pull out her squishy heart and another part of me couldn't care less if she was speaking Russian or Mongolian or Martian because I am so obsessed with her.

And when, occasionally, Magalí has to go out I am irritated. Everything irritates me then: my clothes irritate me, the sea irritates me, prawn heads irritate me. I want to rip out everyone's liver and throw it on the pavement to fry. When Magalí is not there it feels like a dream where I am walking through treacle – only I'm not walking through treacle, I'm floating through a world of aspic dyed the colour of Magalí and her orange breasts. An aspic jellyfish has attached itself to my face – and in the middle of the jellyfish is a vision of the breasts of Magalí, small and dark and wrapped in transparent orange.

The whole day becomes the breasts of Magalí. I can see the real world, more or less. I see the old men chewing on soggy cigars, I see the *marroquí* boys at the end of the street sneaking packs of contraband cigarettes from behind the hub caps of car wheels, I take in the gingerbread houses, the Gothic alleyways, the dusty palm trees. It's just that everything – all of them – is seen through the orange aspic sea of Magalí's breasts. If she doesn't come back after a while I can't see anything. I sit around on my own in the apartment, my eyes glazed over, my mouth itching. My lips pucker and chew, the noise in the street irritates me.

Mrs Flowers was right about the noise in Spain. The Nou de la Rambla, Magalí's street, is one big echoing tunnel of bedlam. The Poble Sec was the sleazy Montmartre of the thirties and forties in Barcelona. The theatre troupes have gone now but the chaos has remained. Normally the racket doesn't bother me, but when Magalí is gone I notice everything: the caged birds squawking from balconies, the dogs yelping from open windows, the woman who is always shouting at her husband, *'Te denuncio a la policía!'* through the slats in the bathroom windows. (Everyone in Poble Sec is always threatening to denounce everyone to *la policía*.)

Without Magalí, the Poble Sec becomes one huge block of squabbling neighbours – north, south, east and west – who make sounds like exploding bombs morning, noon and night. '*¡Oye! ¡Oye!*' the skinny boys shout from the street as they play catch with some heads of garlic in a net bag. '*¡Y qué! ¡Y qué!*' the woman with a cabbage hairdo screeches from the flat opposite. '*¡Eh! ¡Eh!*' a woman with a mouth of metal filings hacks back from the balcony below, until a whole chunk of hot housing is awake with squabbles and squalls and barks and slams and cars trying to start up and the din of shoot-outs from dubbed American movies on TV sets with bad acoustics.

There are mopeds that ride up and down the street twenty-four hours of the day, each one sounding like a hundred chainsaws. Sometimes I'm woken from a nap and think I'm in a forest with trees being felled all around me. Sometimes I wake up and it sounds like I'm being hacked down myself – but in fact it is only the sound of Spanish spitting. *'Escupir'* is the Spanish verb meaning 'to spit' and it is a good one because it sounds as if you are scooping up lots of thick, creamy gob in your throat and spewing it all out. I hear the hacking scoop and then the final spit comes like 'pip', light as a feather. I am sensitive to everything: the bottle-bank lorry that arrives at four in the morning and sounds like all the crockery in Barcelona being hurled on a concrete floor all at once; the clanging knife-sharpener man, who turns up on his ancient moped with a mini-workshop strapped to the back; the calor-gas man with his cart of cooking-gas canisters that he bangs with a spanner to let the housewives know he is there – as if they couldn't guess; the reforming male drug addicts who turn up to the makeshift church above the discothèque to sing insipid modern Christian songs to the accompaniment of an acoustic guitar and a reedy female voice. And just as you are getting used to all that, there is is the gypsy man who comes with a barrelful of oranges and a deafening sales pitch of 'Women! Women! Oranges! Oranges!'

And then Magalí comes home and life is a flying carpet again. She closes the shutters and the house becomes a cool, calm cave. The only sounds are of me stroking her brown skin – a satiny rustle like putting a shell to your ear and hearing the whisper of the sea. The heat and the dark mean that we just stay undressed all the time; the only occasion we put on clothes is in the late afternoon when we have to leave the apartment because it's so hot. Having a siesta in the apartment is like drinking warm water on a scorching day so we go to our beach that Magalí calls Playa

Silicona, or Silicone Beach, because it's a favourite spot for transvestites. I know all about transvestites now. Tomato and Boa are regulars.

When we arrive, Jesús will already be there smoking *chocolate*, which in Spanish doesn't just mean the chocolate that you eat or drink with *churros* but also the stuff that you smoke to get high, which is also called 'hashish'. I know all about hashish and gay men now too. I first came across both when I was with Alan in a youth hostel in Girona. I met two boys from Nottingham University called Will and Barney, who looked like skinny vampires. They put white stuff on their faces, they wore a lot of black eyeliner and very tight black jeans and Barney wore a T-shirt that said 'Joy Division'. I had already decided to ditch Alan at this point and I really wanted to be friends with Will and Barney but I worried that they might test me out on who Joy Division were. Then, one night, I came across them stealing food from the fridge in the communal kitchen. Will looked a bit sheepish at first and then he said, 'It's all those shite conversations about the Tower of Babel and the meaning of life. Drives us to it.' We all grinned and Will told me that he and Barney normally go to Amsterdam for the summer vacation. They stay in a place called Bob's Youth Hostel where the sign is pink with purple mushrooms on it and nobody gets up till eleven in the morning and everyone has joints for breakfast.

Then Barney mumbled in a shy voice, 'You get fish cakes out of slot machines in the wall in Amsterdam.' I was about to say that '*alstublieft*' is Dutch for 'please', but Will was so glad Barney had spoken (Barney hardly ever spoke) that he kissed him on the lips and I felt a big a twitch in the core of my stomach and suddenly I wasn't the slightest bit interested in the Dutch for 'thank you'.

After that, I felt above everyone else in the youth hostel. As if I'd got a really impressive record collection suddenly. Later that night, as Will was sticking bits of thin paper called Rizlas together, I tried to impress him by saying that this was a joint, wasn't it?, and that it made you want to eat a lot. He looked a bit worried and said that he and Barney didn't raid fridges all the time. Sometimes at college they just lay on the settee and drank a cup of warm water with a squeeze of lemon in it. 'And that's all we have all day,' he said. They both looked at each other and did a secret smile.

I tried a couple of puffs of the joint but it just made me cough. Then they asked me if I was going to university and I said that I couldn't just yet. I told them about the *crêpe Suzette* party and the burnt tablecloth and they started giggling uncontrollably.

'What – you ran away because of a burnt tablecloth?' Will asked, as if I'd said something really hilarious. I surprised myself then because I nearly snapped at him. I nearly said, 'Of course it wasn't just about a burned tablecloth! It was worse than that! You've no idea! You've no idea how terrible it was!' But I held myself back. After all, Will hadn't meant to ask a stupid question and the set-up probably did sound funny to him. It was too complicated to go into detail but mainly I didn't tell them the truth because I knew they'd hate me afterwards and I can't take being hated any more.

Here in Spain my new friends can't get enough of me. Jesús sits languidly on Silicone Beach and passes the joint to Magalí. '*Hola, guapas,*' he'll say in sleepy tones. (When he smokes, his voice sounds even more slow and purry than ever.) And then he'll turn to me and go, '*Te has puesto muy guapa,*' which means, 'You've become very beautiful.' While Magalí performs the ceremony of the laying out of the cloth on the sand, I will feel pleased about his compliment and soak up the sound of gay men shrieking in sea spray, of beach boys selling drinks from coolers, going, '*¡Hay Coca-Cola! ¡Hay cerveza! ¡Hay agua!*' and of the gravelly voice of Jesús telling his latest mountain story.

'*¡Ay! ¡Un travesti!* The poor *cubano!*' he might wail. 'He had the entire operation. Penis chopped off. Everything.'

'Really?'

'Thought he could make more money that way.'

'What happened?'

'He arrived and found he was out of fashion.'

'Pardon?'

'*¡Ay, inglesita!* Most of the men in the mountain are repressed homosexuals. They want to be fucked up the ass by a big cock. They don't want another woman. *¡Ay!* The poor *cubano!*' A brief wrist-flicking movement of incredulity.

Jesús' favourite nationalities are Cuban and Argentinian.

Argentinians, he says, are the Parisians of South America and Cubans are always exclaiming, '*¡Ay, mi amor!*' which is wistful and passionate at the same time and most Catalans would never dare to say it in a million years. Also, *cubanos* know the most there is to know about '*la mala vida*', which means 'bad life' and refers to smoking and drinking and dancing and flirting and having sex in the open air. In other words, Jesús says, 'bad life' really means 'good life'.

I soak up buckets of knowledge by the day. I have even developed a new walk. I have termed it my Mediterranean stagger because here, in this heat, the only walk you can do is a staggering one. Your legs work slowly and you drag your heels along the ground in your beach flip-flops and your arms have no purpose – they are just there to be heavy and hot and irritating and they hang limply by your side.

As I Mediterranean stagger along the beach I can't help but feel a bit smug. You can spot the tourists or *guiris* a mile off. There's always the fat English girl in her mid-twenties with tight red saveloy-skin legs and varicose veins on the backs of her thighs and mosquito bites and stray dogs coming up to make friends with her. There's always the Englishman with a body like a wet-fish shop. He'll have chest and shoulder fur and his non-aired genitals will be vacuum-packed in a pair of clatty, overtight trunks, all damp and salty and rank. His pale knees will be flinching and his joints waggling as if the sun is a flock of flies. He's only suffering the sun because he wants to get off with the beautiful brown Spanish girl lying still and serene like a beautifully grilled sardine on a piece of golden cloth a couple of metres away from his green towel the size of a pile of swaddling clothes.

I laugh at the English because they don't know anything about what it is to be Spanish, about how to deal with the food and the heat and the sun. The tourists, for instance, don't know that you're only supposed to wait for de-luxe sun – that it is shameful and painful to expose yourself on the beach when the wind is up, even if there is a lot of sun. They don't know that on suitable days you are supposed to rotate like the hands of a clock in the direction of the sun in order to get maximum coverage. The land and the air and the sky don't belong to the tourists like they do to the Spaniards, but since I have been adopted by a group of natives all of these things pretty much belong to me. I feel qualified to laugh at other people now that Magalí has taught me the rules. The rules are:

1. You never take a towel to the beach, you take a piece of cotton fabric with an interesting pattern called a *trapo*.
2. You must never get a single grain of sand on the *trapo* or in the bed because sand is evil.
3. You must only ever eat paella at lunch-time – and lunch-time is at three o'clock – because only the *guiris* eat paella in the evening.
4. The ideal thing to eat is *fideuà* (thin strips of pasta instead of rice) and not paella because paella is from Valencia and *fideuà* is Catalan and Catalonia is the best and most modern place in Spain.

5. You must never go into common *tapas* bars. You can tell the common ones because they have blinding light fixtures and the *tapas* have monosodium glutamate orangy sheens and there will be a thigh of ham on the counter with its leg up in the air like a *puta*.
6. *Pan con tomate* (bread rubbed over with a squashed tomato and drizzled with olive oil and salt) is the pride of Catalonian cuisine and was invented in the eighteenth century by a painter who wanted to combine the colours of the sunset on an edible base.
7. You must know the difference between a *tapa* and a *ración* – a *tapa* is nibbly food served in a dish the size of an ashtray while a *ración* is the same nibbly food in a small plate.
8. You must choose the shape of the glass you want to have your beer in. The best is a *tubo* (a beer in a tall lemonade glass), followed by *una caña* (in a wine-glass), and a *quinto* (a beer from a small bottle). On no account must you ever drink *sangría* from any kind of glass because *sangría* is just a vulgar *guiri* invention.
9. Remember that you never pay for beers as they come but always a few hours after you have drunk them. Usually the waiter will forget to charge you for a couple of them but it doesn't matter because they're only beers.
10. You must never eat *churros con chocolate* because people from Andalucía eat them. On special occasions, however, you are allowed to go into a *churrería* and order a plate

of freshly fried crisps, which may seem to you to be really oily and also the sort of things that people from Andalucía eat, but they are in fact a delicacy.

As an extra piece of advice thrown in for good measure, Magalí tells me to stop being so polite. It is hardly ever necessary to say 'please' or 'thank you' in Spain. It's just English hypocrisy. And I must stop saying, '*Estoy embarazada*.' Number one, the Spanish don't get embarrassed and number two, '*Estoy embarazada*' means 'I am pregnant'.

Magalí is like an arrogant horse and a headstrong bull rolled into one. I don't mind her taking charge of everything, though, because it makes my life a lot easier. At around seven o'clock Jesús and I follow her over to a beach bar that has red Coca-Cola advertising all over the chairs and tables. At the red bar we have our own personal puppet on a string who goes by the name of Chiqui, which you pronounce like 'Cheeky', and which means 'titchy one'.

Cheeky is a short man with black-rimmed glasses, a thatch of hair dyed an uncanny shade of black and a constant film of sweat over his face. Although Cheeky is a very amenable waiter, Jesús and Magalí treat him as if he is an annoying child. Cheeky seems to quite like it, though. When Jesús snaps his ghostly fingers, Cheeky does a little jump up from behind the bar and gives Jesús a salute like a sea hand to the captain of the ship. Every so often he dashes round from the other side of the bar to give Jesús a bird peck on the cheek, like a little boy or a mother hen, and to bring us free *tapas* and unasked-for beer.

He pecks me too sometimes. '*¡La inglesa! ¡La inglesa!*' he gabbles away, with his hands in the air, and he tries to make me eat a lot. He passes over a fried thing called a *croqueta,* which is like a small Findus crispy pancake with grey, ham-flavoured paste inside. Then he passes over a *tapa* made of dried cod (a very nice texture – soft and slippery) mixed with tomatoes, onion, black olives and olive oil. It is a Catalan speciality called *esqueixada* pronounced *es-kesh-ada*. This is followed by a *tapa* of Russian salad (peas and carrots and diced potato in mayonnaise) or maybe my favourite *tapa,* a piece of *morcilla* – squidgy black pudding oozing with more olive oil.

All my dreams are coming true at last and some things are happening that I never even dreamed of. Like how, when I eat all this rustic food, I suddenly become a real English rose – as if I have gold tissue paper for skin and my hands are made of rose petals. That is what my Spanish friends keep telling me anyway. I look so different from them that they seem to be under the impression that my ancestry goes back to one of the fairer queens of England. I have become some strange English person I have never yet met. Being English has suddenly become a trump card.

'*¡Mira!* The queen of *Inglaterra!*' Cheeky says, looking over at Magalí and Jesús for approval. And Magalí and Jesús will smile at me and maybe stroke me and I will laugh to myself about how I ever thought I needed the attention of Mrs Flowers and how I ever let her make me feel bad about myself.

Cheeky likes heavy-metal music, especially a Spanish band called Barón Rojo. Since I have been around, though, he has been partial to the B-sides of Queen, which he plays on the bar's sound system in my honour. He comes over to the table, mouthing the words to 'Fat Bottomed Girls' and I smile for politeness' sake. Magalí usually just waves an arm at him, irritated, and snaps, 'Bring some *jamón de beyota* for *la inglesita*,' because, she says, *jamón de beyota* is the best ham you can get. She says that it is made from pigs that have been fed only on acorns – just like Mr Jones told us. And soon, a shaking hand will put a *ración* of acorn ham in front of me, cut in see-through slices and laid out in fan formation. It is all just as it should be. Like when Jade from *A Star in Faded Jeans* was in Ibiza and she was 'presented with a huge pile of transparently thin dried ham which looked like a dish of autumn leaves'.

And the only thanks Cheeky ever gets from us is a row of contemptuous glances. I am being contemptuous too. I laugh at Cheeky with Magalí and Jesús, like I'm better than him – even though this is his country. I feel like the king of the castle on my red chair. And when we are all sitting round the red table, happily eating and talking, Cheeky will come up and furtively try to hand me some free ham to take home. His face will be like a colander – all the water that's coming out of it – and Jesús will protest that, no, we don't want any ham, as if Cheeky's being really tiresome. And Cheeky makes a *mou* like a naughty little boy, like he has been bad – not that he's given us a thousand pesetas' worth of food for free. We laugh at him again.

We eat like we live. First I put an olive in my mouth, then in goes a tug of bread followed by a slug from a bottle of San Miguel or a slurp from my *Cuba libre* – because *Cuba libre* sounds much better than rum and Coke. And then there is an oily kiss to be planted on Magalí's cheek before pulling out one of the *almejas* or clams from the paella dish and springing up from the red chair, still chewing, jumping down off the concrete terrace on to the sand and running into the sea. I stay in the water just long enough to wet my feet and then I race back to the red plastic table, wiping the sweat off my face with a sandy forearm before my hand makes its way to another tug of bread (which smells sweet as the head of a baby) and then to the paella dish again to rip off a prawn head or nibble the tentacle of some weird squiddy thing.

There is a whole range of variations on the theme of *calamar* or squid: tiny things with squiggly eyes and wiggly legs called *chipirrones*, others with a tangle of legs and feelers called *chopitos* and the tiny octopuses of Pinocchio's bar called *pulpitos*. The main rival to the squid is the *sepia* – which we call cuttlefish in English although, as I tell my Spanish friends, nobody ever eats it there. They just give its bone to budgerigars to sharpen their beaks on. They all think this is very funny.

When you have a *paella* it is hard to tell the difference between a squid and a *sepia*, although experts know that the *sepia* has a creamier, richer meat. When lying dead in the fish market, the *sepia* looks like a black brain. Inside, it looks like a baby's nappy that needs changing. Also, *sepia* has knobbly tentacles like old-age-pensioner callused feet. The squid is the cute little blue-eyed boy next to the *sepia*. It is an elegant purple colour with the smoothest of skins. When you rip the skin off a squid and stretch it over the back of your hand it feels softer than calfskin gloves.

In the sea it is the *sepia* that is the vicious one, Magalí tells me. It has a mouth like a parrot and it stings whereas the octopus just sucks. She knows these things because her father catches them and cooks them himself. She tells me proudly that during the Spanish civil war he was a cook in a concentration camp. I think of *Escape from Alcatraz* and wonder if I will get to meet him. Apparently he tells Magalí not to eat shellfish called *caracoles de mar*, or sea snails, because when dead bodies are found at sea they often have *caracoles de mar* sticking all over them. I imagine them sucking out human juice like I suck out *gamba* juice.

For Magalí and me, sucking prawns has become our way of being in love. When the euphoric, devil-may-care feeling hits me, the big things in life don't matter and the small things take on huge, non-specific significance. All I see of the world are the orange bubbles of oil glittering in the paella serving spoon, some stubs of rice on the tablecloth, a shard of wilted lettuce on my plate, the empty bottle of white Penedés, the shrivelled peppercorn eyes of the *gamba* heads, some burnt scraps on the bottom of the paella pan. The sky seems an astonishing blue, as if it's leaping in and out of the water like a slippery fish. As if it's more than it really is. At these times, Magalí and I, we look towards the sea and we talk about how the craving for security is silly.

Then comes dessert. Dessert is an essential component in *la mala vida*. Magalí and Jesús say that dessert is *de cojones* (with testicles on) and *de puta madre* (a whore's mother). Dessert, in other words, is very good indeed. It is not the run-of-the-mill Spanish dessert (which always consists of *flan,* crème caramel, *helado,* ice cream, *fruta,* fruit, and *crema Catalana* if you're lucky). If you are with Magalí, dessert means her tapping you on the arm and you chasing off behind her to the loos where you will kneel at the toilet with the lid down. She will lay out dessert on top of the seat, roll up a two-thousand-peseta bill, take a very big sniff of it up her nose then pass the money to you.

Dessert makes everything more interesting and more slippery. It makes my body and soul get wider – not fatter, just wider and deeper, like a big net bag that can hold tons and tons of red apples. It makes me able to do my sprints from the bar to the sea much quicker. It pushes everything out of my head that isn't to do with rushing to the sea. It also makes me lose my appetite so that afterwards I don't want any real dessert. Magalí says that I am a bit of a *tocinet,* which is Catalan for suckling pig, so I do my best to eat less than I did before.

When we come back from the loos after dessert, the red bar resembles a bucking ship filled with mutineers looking like Salvador Dalí and sounding like Captain Hook. Cheeky will be buzzing round like a fly and Jesús will roar, '*¡Ay! ¡La mala vida!*' his eyes bobbing round like a game of tennis as he watches different men in different swimming trunks parade around saying things like '*¡Ay!* His *polla* was so soft! With veins like fingers!' or '*¡Oye, mira!* These shells would make ashtrays with testicles on!'

Jesús will nudge me and do his asparagus impression. When he sees someone who interests him particularly, he puts his finger in his *carajillo* and flicks some drops to the ground in homage to Dionysus. Sometimes he does it randomly, in case it might bring him luck with one of the men in swimming trunks.

But all that usually happens is that a woman known as *La Cabra,* or the Goat, turns up. The Goat has thinning yellow hair scraped up on her head by a painful-looking gold comb. She always wears a lilac bikini, a tangle of stainless-steel virgins around her neck and gold rings studded all over her fingers. She is a bit like an over-topped-up bowl of *crema Catalana* that has had bright purple sugar reapplied to it again and again and someone has forgotten to take it out from under the grill.

In Spanish, if you are mad you are either a goat – *una cabra* – or *una chota,* a baby goat. This woman is too big to be a *chota*. She is definitely a *cabra*. Sometimes her eyes make her look like a village idiot. According to Magalí, she can't secrete endorphins and is therefore always in a state of depression. She lies compulsively but she is very entertaining.

'Magalí, *hija,*' she says one day, 'when I was in the mountain last week I got high on artichokes! It's true!' She makes a big snorting sound through her nose and grabs a plate of small yellow-coloured things from Cheeky that remind me of pasties. She removes the perforated beige plastic shoes she is wearing and eases her feet into a pair of tight black shoes with four-inch heels and gold curves at the back. 'I swear to God,' she says, as she tucks in, wiggling her toes in the peep-toe ends of the black shoes, 'if you have nothing else, artichokes are the whore's mother.'

She must see me watching her feet because she grabs hold of my thigh under the table. Then she snorts again and shouts to Cheeky in a voice that smells of vanilla essence and bad breath: '*Uncle!* Take that *mierda de* Freddie Mercury off and put on the gypsy prison music – the one about knives and shooting up heroin.' She is telling me how the only true flamenco is made by gypsies in prison when a blind man selling *lotería* tickets comes in. The Goat says that she will only buy one if she can touch his cock and the blind man says, '*¡qué no!*' as if he's been offered one of Cheeky's free *tapas* dishes and he's not hungry. When he approaches Magalí she says, 'I don't want to buy a ticket and I don't want to touch your dick either,' and the group of recently widowed ladies playing poker with oranges instead of money and drinking *carajillos* (which they call 'perfumed coffee') at the next table start cackling and going, '*¡Muy bien, hija!*' The blind man smiles and walks off as I'm wondering what is in the dessert that makes me want the Goat to keep her hand on my thigh. The hand makes me cocky. As I get used to it being there I want her to squeeze even harder.

Sometimes in the early evening we go to the cinema. We have seen films by an underground director called Pedro Almódovar who makes stuff about bisexual hookers and transsexuals and sex and drugs and gay Islamic terrorists. When the Goat sits next to me she'll put her hand on my thigh again and tell me that now is the time for freedom because Franco is out of the way. This freedom is called the *destape*, she says – literally, the 'uncovering' – and it means that now is a good time to be in Spain. When she squeezes my thigh too hard I giggle and Magalí asks me what's up and I say that I want to go now. It is a plausible request because usually we don't manage to sit through a whole film anyway. Dessert makes us so overexcited that we can't sit still in our seats for long.

At dessert time it is much better to be at Silicone Beach in the red bar. When new people come over to join us I shout, 'You have taken possession of your house.' And when they leave I say, 'Depart with God,' and everyone laughs even more and the hand clamps round my thigh even tighter because nobody really says these things in Spain in real life. I like my new job as exotic English entertainer to Magalí's friends. Magalí likes to show me off to her friends and naturally I want to make her happy. Her friends do seem amazingly impressed by me. When I leave the loo and come back to the table, fresh from my dessert helping, they all turn and chorus, '*¡Ay!* How *guapa* the *inglesita* is looking today!' This is nice, because *inglesita* is the diminutive form of *inglesa* and calling you 'little English girl' is an endearing thing to do in Spanish. It makes you feel even more *guapa*.

The drawback, of course, with the *guapa* system is that you get used to being flattered all the time so that you need the praise. When you don't get it you become obsessed with having it and you hate everyone else who you are told is *guapa*. Sometimes when I come back from the loo I feel a bit anxious because I think that one day someone more exotic than me will come along or that I will become too much like a suckling pig for Magalí to remain interested in me. Sometimes it feels as if I'm surrounded by a tanned group of small-time vampires who are desperate for their next slice of fresh pie. If I'm just *la inglesita* then maybe when they've sucked me dry or my blood has grown old they'll replace me with someone else.

Not at the moment, though. At the moment they think I'm perfect. Jesús says that I have a face of a good person and when I blush they all pipe up with a really loud '*¡Ay!*' like they've never seen anyone blush before. Magalí will grab my neck with her arm like a scythe – as if she is rounding me up – and she will announce to the gathered company, '*¡Mi inglesita más exótica!*' – my most exotic English girl – and all the gathered people will immediately be prompted to reply, '*¡Ay, sí! La inglesita* is looking like the whore's mother!'

If I start to feel anxious I just run down into the water. If it is one of those days when the Mediterranean is like green glass marble eyes and all the female swimmers seem to have crêpy cracks and chicken skin, then I just dive under the sea where the different currents swirl around like warm and cold raspberry ripple and where it sounds like the snap, crackle and pop of Rice Krispies. When I come up my head is refreshed. I check that I can see Magalí on the beach, and if I can then I will relax, lie back and let the sea buoy me up. Occasionally I will look down and admire my butter-brown knees piercing through the surface of the water. The sea peels down from them, making a map like a glazed pattern of the five continents.

Chapter Fourteen

> The cold platter is garnished with baby octopus, snails and *limace* – you can turn it up in the French dictionary if you like but it reads so nastily that we prefer not to print it!
>
> ***Sociable Cook's Book* by Fanny Cradock**

In October, Magalí takes me to her parents' house. We are greeted at the front door by a woman in her late sixties with a hand over her mouth, saying, 'Excuse my breath but I ate rabbit with aïoli last night.'

Funny she should mention rabbit because her skin is more the colour and texture of pigs' trotters, i.e., as if it's been shut up in a Quality Street tin for years on end.

'My mother doesn't get out much,' Magalí says, as she gives her mother a careless peck on the cheek. She stalks down the murky hall towards the living room, throwing behind her, '*Mamá* comes from a generation where women didn't even learn to swim.'

Señora Sanchez clasps her hands as she watches Magalí disappear into the darkness. Her eyes are sparkling – even the left one, which has a funny white blob in the corner the size and colour of a mini *sepia*. She turns back to Jesús and confides, 'In those days you weren't even allowed to make aïoli if it was your time of the month. Made the egg yolk curdle, so they said.'

Then a Jolly Roger voice pipes up from the end of the hall, 'No danger of that now!' followed by growling laughter, which makes Señora Sanchez jump up like toast popping out of the toaster. She scuttles off into the kitchen.

Jesús takes me down the hall and we emerge in a dimly lit, unventilated room. On the wall there is a wooden carving of four squat people holding hands and going round in a stiff circle doing what I think must be the traditional Catalan dance known as the *sardana*. There is also a picture of a naked young girl with a blonde bob and blue skin kneeling with her legs apart on a goat skin rug. Standing on one corner of the room is a man who doesn't look much like Clint Eastwood in *Escape from Alcatraz*. He looks more like a chicken.

Señor Sanchez has skinny stick legs and a huge barrel of a stomach. Stretched over it is an old grey sweatshirt with the word 'Virgin' bulging out in green letters. He is holding a *porrón* and when he sees me he lifts it to his mouth, revealing that the word on the sweatshirt is actually 'Virginia'. A thin trickle of red wine rains into his mouth. As his arm extends, the string of wine gets longer and longer.

His Adam's apple works faster and the wine hurtles into his mouth. After about thirty seconds, Señor Sanchez slams the empty *porrón* down on the table and starts panting as if he's just emerged from a long stint under water.

He wipes his matinée-idol moustache with the back of a hand, which he then runs through his hair – dyed so unnaturally black that a halo of red glows round the top of his head. '*Los ingleses* like to watch these things,' he pants. 'On the Costa Brava in the nineteen fifties, the *guiris* paid me good money to see that.' He looks over at Magalí with a twinkle in his eye and says, 'No?'

'The *guiris* loved my father.' Magalí smiles, filling the *porrón* again. She lifts it and gradually moves it to an angle of about ninety degrees above her mouth. I wonder if she's trying to impress me or Señor Sanchez. When the wine's all gone, she bangs down the *porrón,* sees that her father is looking at me and says, with nervous glee, 'You see, *papá,* you see what I brought you!' like the Artful Dodger to Fagin after a productive night out.

I can tell that she is tense. We are only here in the first place because it is snail season and it is traditional for Magalí and Jesús to come and celebrate the occasion at the Sanchez household. Of late, Magalí says she has found visiting her parents increasingly difficult, and it is for this reason that she has taken to bringing what she calls her little picnic bag whenever she comes. She hasn't had a chance to crack it open yet and you can tell.

'What do you think then, *papá*?' she snaps at her father. Señor Sanchez doesn't answer. He responds by doing a Clint

Eastwood swagger towards me. He thrusts the *porrón* into my hand with a sympathetic smile, as if he thinks I'm going to be really hopeless. I do a bit of a Steve McQueen swagger as I take the glass jug from his hand and move towards the window so there'll be enough light for everyone to see me at my best. I take a deep breath and think of snaky laughs and smoky-bacon-flavoured cigarette ash. I finish the *porrón* almost as quickly as Magalí and I'm not even out of breath.

Señor Sanchez starts clapping and going, '*¡Muy bien! ¡Muy bien!*' and I narrowly escape being press-ganged into a *porrón* contest with Magalí and her father by the appearance of Jesús in the murky sitting room carrying a wooden plate of what he announces to be *pulpo gallego* or octopus sprinkled with red *pimentón*.

Jesús nearly trips on a bit of loose carpet as he puts the platter down on the dining-room table. He saves himself, though, and does one of his pterodactyl grins, whereupon Señora Sanchez clasps her hands together and says, '*¡Ay!* My son! "A smile costs less than electricity but gives more light."'

When everyone has sat down at the table she leans over to Jesús and says, 'What was Sister Maria Teresa's other one this week?'

'Let's think,' Jesús says. '"Good example is like a perfume whose scent fills the whole house." I think.'

'*¡Ay, sí!*' Señora Sanchez exclaims with pleasure, pinching Jesús' cheek as if he really is her son.

I wish I hadn't been quite such a dab hand at the

porrón because Señor Sanchez has seated me next to him at the table and keeps poking me in the ribs at intervals throughout the meal.

His eyes watch me expectantly as I bite into my first slice of *pulpo*. I am quite expectant too, given the build-up I've had to eating the stuff. Unfortunately, I can't really register the taste because I'm quite drunk after downing the whole *porrón*. The white meat just feels soft and rich and vaguely comforting in the mouth.

But I don't have to say much because Magalí starts telling me about how her father cooked it, about how he used to cook in the concentration camp in France where he was sent during the Spanish civil war, about how he was a real red, her *papá*. There is something in her voice that is mocking, as if she has heard all the concentration-camp stories before and she can't be bothered, as if she's suddenly lost interest in her father. It makes me feel uncomfortable. Magalí has been making me feel uncomfortable for a while now. Her moods swing back and forth. When I told her I loved her this morning, she snapped back that it wasn't love I felt for her. That I was simply '*enchochada*' which means to be 'invagina-ed' with someone.

But the Spanish civil war is in the air now. Señora Sanchez mumbles something in Catalan to Magalí as Señor Sanchez takes up the *porrón* and starts to drink. '*¡Cabrones! ¡Los cabrones!*' he shouts at the top of his voice, meaning 'bastards!' or, literally, 'cuckolds!'.

Magalí makes a long-suffering sigh. She pushes her octopus round the plate, mumbling about how the smell of it is making her feel sick. Señora Sanchez heads off a row by quizzing Jesús about Sister Maria Teresa. Jesús is an editor at a celebrity gossip magazine called *Por Favor*. He edits the cookery page, which is written by a nun called Sister Maria Teresa, author of *Pasteles de las Monjas* or *Nuns' Buns*. As well as telling you things like how to cook *churros* and a thing called angel hair, which is made from quince plus tons of sugar then piped into a pastry horn, she also gives you tips about how to lead a good life. Or, rather, Jesús does. He makes up the quotes and pretends they're from her. Quotes like 'Loving is not only about wanting. It is also about respect and compassion', or 'If you want to be respected, make sure you respect yourself'. It is very different from Fanny Cradock.

'She's gone on to savouries now, hasn't she?' Señora Sanchez says timidly. 'Some sort of meat this week, wasn't it, Jesús?'

Jesús replies that, yes, it was and Señora Sanchez quotes, '"Don't forget about the small pleasures while you are waiting for the large ones to come along."'

'That'll be the one, Señora Sanchez.'

'Where was the meat from?'

Jesús squints and looks into the middle distance. He taps a skinny index finger against the side of his head just above his Spock ears. 'Comes from in here somewhere but I can't remember exactly what it's called when you buy it at the butcher's.'

'*¡Hhhod-air!*' Magalí is getting really agitated. She suddenly shoves her plate of octopus across the table. 'The stench!' she erupts. 'I can't stand it any more!' She scratches away at her arms as if she's got fleas. 'Sister Maria Teresa's an imbecile,' she roars, rubbing the backs of her hands. Señora Sanchez's shoulders hunch but Magalí doesn't leave it there. 'Everyone knows that nuns only like sugar because it's the nearest thing to drugs they can get.'

Señor Sanchez sees this as a cue to burst in with a lecture about how sugar is for *maricones*. When he has exhausted this topic, he proceeds to give the table a guide to the best way of catching an octopus. The best way, he says, is to get a piece of cloth, put a sardine inside it and leave it down by the rocks. The octopus climbs inside to eat the fish and you pull the cloth back up the rocks. The best way to kill an octopus is to bite its eye or, better still, to turn it inside out.

I am pretty impressed by this information and I want to try and make up for Magalí's bad manners so I accept another helping of *pulpo* to show my appreciation. Encouraged, Señor Sanchez starts telling a story of how, when he was ten, he caught an octopus with his bare hands. It wrapped itself around his arm – sucking his blood – and he had to hit it against a rock to get it off.

'My *maricón* of a friend, he'd come with all the right gear – diving mask, flippers, wet suit – and I just had my bare hands! *¡Maricón!*' He roars at the memory, wiping a dribble of peppery oil from his black moustache. 'He caught nothing! *¡Maricón!*' I am wondering what Jesús is making of all this talk of *maricones*. My Spanish dictionary defines the word as 'A pansy (derog.)' although I hear Jesús using it about himself and his friends all the time. I look over to him but he is just placidly chewing away at his octopus so I try to concentrate on mine as Señor Sanchez gets deeper into his sea hunting story. I am trying to work out why I'm not getting more interested in a tale like this – as I normally would – when I suddenly realise that I've bitten off more *pulpo* than I can chew. To my digestive system, octopus feels less like fish and more like a couple of hundred bags of chips bulging down in my stomach like an overweight trapeze artist in a safety-net. It feels as though octopus cholesterol is being piped though all my arteries and my liver has become a lump of bread buttered all around with goose fat then deep-fried in lard and served up with greasy pork scratchings.

Señora Sanchez sees me pushing the tentacles around on my plate. She asks me if something is wrong. When I reply that everything is fine, that the octopus is nice – that it feels comforting – she nods knowingly and replies, presumably in the words of Sister Maria Teresa, that '"The most comfortable pillow of all is a good conscience."'

This makes me drop my fork immediately because an entire octopus colony has now moved into my guts. It feels as if they're going to burst through my stomach at any minute and trumpet to the table about what a fraud I am. I wonder if Señora Sanchez knows that I haven't been sleeping properly, that I try all the time to forget about my conscience, but that it just rears up out of nowhere and gnaws away at me giving me worse indigestion than anything she could dish up in her kitchen.

Señor Sanchez pokes me in the ribs again and hisses, in

a saucy voice, '*¡Pulpo . . . afrodisiaco!*' But before Señora Sanchez heads off to the kitchen for the next course she reminds him that *pulpo* is also a good way to commit suicide. 'Remember the case of that man,' she says, in her dazed voice. 'He ate an octopus a metre long. He ate everything except the head. Nearly died of dyspepsia.'

Dampeners are put further on the occasion when Señora Sanchez returns from the kitchen brandishing a large dish of piping hot snails – with their full colons still attached. Fanny Cradock says the *escargot* is a wretch to eat because *escargot* scissors are difficult to open and close. She suggests substituting a Victorian ivory-handled tea fork for scissors. She never mentioned anything about shit bags.

There are no ivory forks at the Familia Sanchez house and definitely no *escargot* scissors. Just snail faeces, an old woman with a squid eye, a blue girl with her legs spread open and an old man digging me in the ribs to see if I'm ready for the oven.

Magalí calls me to attention and gives me a demonstration of pulling the snail out of its shell with her right hand, transferring it to her left, then nipping off the shit bag between her nails. I wonder what makes snail excrement palatable while octopus smell isn't. I wonder if I would eat snail shit if I really loved Magalí. I can't possibly eat snail shit so maybe it means I don't love her at all. And the more I think about this, the more my stomach turns into an underwater roller-coaster, as if it's crawling with live snails and octopus feelers and they are all interbreeding and laying logs on top of each other.

There is a growl of Jolly Roger laughter from Señor Sanchez and he starts talking about *maricones* again. The French are *maricones,* he says, because they remove the colons before bringing the snails to the table. 'They take out the shit and then they put the snails in plastic shells. *¡Maricones!* Petit bourgeois snails of a whore's mother!' He roars with laughter and from his snail shell he yanks off a membrane dripping with brown goo. He puts two index fingers (one brown-tipped) on top of his head and makes wiggly movements. This turns out not to be an impersonation of snail feelers but of the Frenchmen he has cuckolded in his life.

'Horns!' He chuckles. 'I've given those *cabrones* some horns in my time!'

Señora Sanchez notices that I'm sitting stiff in my chair as if my hands have been tied down to my sides. She says she supposes the English don't eat snails. 'I know England a little,' she says softly. 'I went there in nineteen seventy-one for an abortion. I'd had enough of falling downstairs and slamming myself in car doors. I noticed that the meat in the butchers' shops was cheaper than in Spain. I had difficulties finding a place to have coffee, though.'

I am just thinking of how to say, 'Excuse me, I must go and throw up now,' when I feel Magalí's arm on my shoulder. She is tossing her head back in that 'time for dessert' kind of way. And the next thing I know, she and I are in the bathroom with Magalí cracking open the picnic hamper and me staring at a picture of a waterfall crashing into a river in a green and woody glade. It is partly

Japanese in style, partly the sort of thing you might see in a porn magazine. When the two-thousand-peseta note finally gets handed to me I find myself swimming around in the waterfall, darting about with Magalí. It feels like I've grown about two feet in height and when Magalí pulls me to her and puts her tongue in my mouth it feels like a thigh of warm ham. The combination of these strange feelings takes my mind off the octopus legs and the snails messing around in my stomach. Suddenly I feel right as rain and when we return to the dining room everyone is happier. The snails have been cleared away, Señor Sanchez is bragging to Jesús about pouring champagne all over his wife's body for their first wedding anniversary and Señora Sanchez is daring to shout back, from the kitchen, that it was *cava* actually, not champagne. It feels like we are all slipping around on ice on a crisp blue day and it is just so funny and happy. And when Señora Sanchez brings out the cakes for the proper dessert we all clap. Jesús does a standing ovation before passing behind Magalí's back, lifting the picnic hamper from the back pocket of her jeans and proceeding to the bathroom.

Catalans pride themselves on their patisserie. Specialities include the *brazo de gitano*, or gypsy arm, which is a thick Swiss roll usually decorated as subtly as an infant-school painting class. The pride and joy of Catalan patisserie though is a *mille-feuille* made from pork fat called *coco de llardons* because pigs are so sacred here that they even have to make an appearance in the buns. On top of the oblong slab you get a crunchy coat of sugar and some pine nuts, which add fantasy overtones to the overall flavour of the *coco de llardons* which is basically, well, *mille-feuille* made from pork fat.

Señora Sanchez arranges two gypsy arms and a *coco de llardons* on the table. She is telling us that the *brazo de gitano* is from Sister Maria Teresa's own recipe when Jesús comes back from the bathroom. It is obvious that he has been taking quite a lot of dessert in there because when he sits back down at the table he wets a bony index finger and starts tickling the gypsy arm, which has been iced in a strange green and pink syphilitic effect. He croons in his oily asparagus voice, '*¡Ay!* Just like the arms of the *gitano portugués!*' The *gitano portugués* is Jesús' latest mountain story. Jesús met a Portuguese gipsy in the mountains and took him home. The Portuguese gypsy took off his clothes in front of Jesús, saying that it would be the equivalent of four hundred pounds if he wanted to have sex with him. Apparently Jesús was really insulted and sent him packing – although Magalí says that nearer to the truth would be that Jesús did it with him and gave him fifty pounds because he felt sorry for him.

Jesús tells Señora Sanchez fondly, 'There were tattoos and bottle-slash scars on his arms.' He does a vigorous wrist shake and makes an exaggerated frown. 'His hands, though!' he says, with the annoyance of a housewife whose family have just tramped all over the freshly washed floor. 'His hands! Nails chewed off to the quick and fingers like claws! Like talons!'

'Ay, sí, ay, sí,' Señora Sanchez nods sagely, adding, 'but,

Jesús, "The first step to unconditional love consists in accepting others as they are", no?'

A harrumph comes from Señor Sanchez's end of the table, which Jesús takes as a cue to grab the dessert bag and make for the bathroom once more.

There is a strained silence while I try and dig into my slice of gypsy arm. It looks like it wants to pick a fight with me so I start hammering pine-nut daggers into it with the back of my spoon. Señor Sanchez looks at my plate with a frown. 'Eat! Eat!' he's saying, which is a bit of an unfortunate command because with so much of Magalí's dessert inside me, eating is the last thing I want to do. By this time I'm not sure what I want to do. When Jesús comes back to the table his eyes are spinning away like fruit machines or gypsy arms come to life – reeling with cherries and oranges and lemons – and he is rabbiting away about cake, cake, how he loves cake.

'*¡Ay! El* cake, *qué maravilla el* cake!' His mouth goes mean and his jaw starts chewing. He turns to Señora Sanchez. 'Last night I made a cake. So much fruit. So many nuts. My cake was stuffed with everything! *¡Ay!* I was so impatient. I took the cake from the oven and put it on the balcony to cool. But I couldn't wait for it to cool. I took it back inside and ate it all up in ten minutes! How good the cake was!'

Then suddenly he's deflated. He looks down at his plate in front of him. He shrugs and admits that cake rush didn't last long. 'I need the throat of a long-necked bird,' he sighs. 'Think how long pleasure would last. Maybe then I wouldn't have had to finish the evening off in the mountain.'

He perks up at the memory, though: '*¡Ay!* Even better than cake – the sandwich!' He makes a pterodactyl lip-licking movement. 'The sandwich,' he says, in an indignant tone of voice that sounds like, 'How could you do this to me?' The wrist starts flicking again as he says slowly and emphatically, 'In the name of God – *qué mara-viiiiiiiilla!*' Señora Sanchez nods, unruffled, as if Jesús is Sister Maria Teresa giving her inside information on choux pastry.

Jesús' mountain sandwich was not, of course, like an English sandwich. It was not even the butch Spanish word for sandwich – a *bocadillo*, which literally means a 'mouth plug' – or even anything to do with a *bikini*, which is a toasted ham and cheese sandwich. Jesús informs us all that this kind of sandwich is the most tasty in the world because it involves you standing naked in the mountain – playing the part of sandwich filling – while two naked slices of bread rub themselves up and down over you on either side. He takes Señora Sanchez's hand as if he is inviting her for a dance. He pulls her to her feet and gives a quick demonstration of just how nice it is to be either bread or filling.

'In the words of Sister Maria Teresa,' he announces, '"When you have sex with a stranger, you know more about what they want than when you're fucking someone you love."' His hips start thrusting even harder into the back of Señora Sanchez's lacy apron. 'Don't talk to me of sugar and cakes, Señora Sanchez. I'm up to the vagina with sugar and cakes. I want sticks! Sticks and bones!'

'*¿Ay, sí?*' Señora Sanchez's pig's-trotter skin is really warming up now. But she doesn't get to hear any more apocryphal Sister Maria Teresa because suddenly there is the almighty crash of Señor Sanchez' fist crashing down on the table. The blow is so hard that it makes the pine kernels on the pork *mille-feuille* fly up in the air and twist around in triple salchows. Señor Sanchez stands up and starts yelling, 'Eat! Eat! Holy bread! Son of a prostitute! I shit in the milk!' He's whirring round at the head of the table like a liquidizer blade out of control. 'Eat! Eat! How dare you refuse to eat!'

I expect him to go into a rant about *maricones* but instead he starts shouting about biscuits. Biscuits for dogs. One dog biscuit in particular.

'A biscuit meant for dogs is all it was,' he roars again, stabbing the remains of the gypsy arm with the cake knife and flopping back in his seat. He pulls up his shirt and reveals a huge dent in the middle of his stomach.

'This is what they did to me,' he says, jabbing his finger into the scary *Jaws* hole. 'A biscuit meant for dogs stolen from the kitchens by a starving man. Beaten like a dog! Not even beaten by the French cuckolds. Beaten by the *cabrón* of a Gallego. A compatriot. A goat! A madman!' Señor Sanchez is trembling. 'He kicks me, he knifes me. He is mad with hunger, so he says. He says he wants to eat my flesh.'

Señor Sanchez grabs me by the arm and hisses through clenched teeth: 'I was sick at the time. I would have fought back. I was ill.' His eyes are pleading. 'A biscuit meant for dogs.' His voice cracks and his face disappears into his hands.

If octopus, snails and Magalí's dessert took the edge

off my appetite, then the sight of Señor Sanchez' mutilated stomach has taken away the rest of it. I look at the lard *mille-feuille* on my plate and I want to eat it to make him feel better. I want Magalí to stop chanting, 'A biscuit meant for dogs,' as if her father's telling a feeble joke instead of a sad and wretched civil war story. Jesús is making a vague effort to calm Señor Sanchez but Señor Sanchez doesn't seem to be aware of anything around him. His damp, ruddy face rises up from his hand. 'Slaves!' he explodes. 'We are all still slaves. *Cabrón de* Franco!' Another slammed fist. 'He died only eight years ago but already everyone wants to forget. When I was a child, my cousin was arrested in the baker's in this very street for asking for a loaf of bread in Catalan instead of Castilian. The daughter of a prostitute behind him in the queue denounced him to the police. You understand? You English and your happy tales of Dunkirk spirit in the Second World War. In the Spanish civil war we all hated each other. Mother denounced father, son denounced sister, your neighbour would smile at you in the morning, set the *cabrones de fascistas* on you in the afternoon. And that *cabrón de* Churchill who could have stopped everything if he'd wanted to except he was too busy smoking his cigars . . .'

Magalí is sniggering over at the door behind his back, waving the plastic bag of dessert around in the air, but I can't even get away. There is Señora Sanchez on my left, fixing me with her squid eye and telling me not to mind her husband because he gets like this when he drinks too much. There is Señor Sanchez on my right, squeezing my arm like an octopus sucking my blood, ranting about General Pinochet and severed body parts and cigarette burns in malnourished skin.

I want everyone to leave me alone. I want it to be like chapter one in *Modern Day Spanish.* I want Señor Sanchez to be painting a boat on the beach and Señora Sanchez to have prepared us soup, potatoes, tomatoes and fruit. But instead Señor Sanchez suddenly clutches his chest and starts making croaky '*¡Ay! ¡Ay!*' sounds. Señora Sanchez tries to make him sit down and scolds him by telling him that the young people of today aren't interested in what's dead and buried and Señor Sanchez tries to push her away, wheezing, 'Holy bread! Leave me alone, woman!' and it's all one big mess.

It doesn't even clear up when I run off to the bathroom again with Magalí and Jesús. I sniff up four long lines in one go because Magalí says it's a special Catalan tradition on snail day to have lots of dessert and I know she's lying to me. I know they're giggling and saying things among themselves and even the dessert doesn't make me feel any better. All that happens is that my heart starts pumping really hard and my eyes feel like they are being squeezed out of my head, like Jack's inflatable penis when you squeeze hard on the pump, and then I think I see a scarred penis in the waterfall and the room seems suddenly to shrink to the size of a matchbox and I can't breathe. I feel as if I am drowning in the waterfall and I just want to close my eyes and disappear, to find a pillow as soft and comfortable as a good conscience and I wonder if I'll ever have a clean conscience again.

And then Magalí snatches the two thousand pesetas

from me. She pinches my bum to get me out of the way so she can have her go and I laugh like I can't stop. And when we all stagger back into the dining room, the whole place seems to be fizzing like a wasp and everyone seems like a faraway character behind a TV screen. I look at Señora Sanchez and her cloudy eye chuckling about the high spirits of the young, and I wonder what would happen right now if she died, if she keeled over and died. She might be in my arms for her last seconds on earth. Would I try to give her the kiss of life (yuk), cradle her head in my arms, and stroke the skin of her face? Maybe I would come to love that lump of skin growing in her eye if I knew she was about to die. When she died, she would look down on me from above and she would be thankful. But she would also know what I was really like if she was dead because you can't hide secrets from the dead and I don't want her to know what I'm really like. The more I look at Señora Sanchez the more she becomes Brenda. Or is it Brydie? When they die it'll be even worse. And what about Mrs Flowers? What happens if she dies?

I don't like this TV channel any more so I turn over and see another screen showing Señor Sanchez hunched at the table. His outburst has made his moustache go all limp and the red halo of his bad black dye-job glows like a bloody crown of thorns. He looks like a very old man. His head is bent. He is pushing his mauled slice of syphilitic gypsy arm aimlessly round his plate. A slight glow appears in his eyes when he sees me looking at him. From a voice very far away in 1937, he starts telling me about the Spanish civil war again, about how he got injured in the leg and how they put him in an ambulance and the nurse in the back was very pretty – she had nice legs, he remembers that very clearly, oh, yes, indeed he does. And all the way to the makeshift hospital she sang him a song about the baby bull who fell in love with the moon one night. It was just a reflection of the moon in a river, you see, and even though there was a boy with a hole in his stomach in a stretcher above him and another who was screaming out for morphine, it was to him alone, to him – Señor Sanchez – that the nurse sang the song about the baby bull who fell in love with the moon.

His mouth is upturned in a pathetic attempt at a smile but I know the truth, the dessert is helping me know the real truth. I can see the pain burnt into his face. You can't pretend that pain like that will ever go away. You're dead meat after that kind of experience. Or like a potato that's been forgotten at the back of the kitchen cupboard. Even though pathetic pinky green shoots start to grow from its sides, like hope springing eternal, you know they're pretty pointless, you know the potato's destined for the bin anyway.

I can see his pain scorching through his concentration-camp skin, through the ruddy hues of his blacker-than-black hair. I can see everything and do everything. I can drink from a *porrón* and eat things with tentacles and inspire love, and go anywhere I want and do anything I want. There is the sound of a laugh. It is Magalí's laugh, a shrill scream that makes me think of robbing her raw heart through her ribcage. She is laughing with Jesús and they both sneak spying glances at me so I sneak a spying glance over at Señor Sanchez and I see that the suffering has dug even deeper into his face and it is horrifying – hilariously horrifying. I don't know what is funny any more – everything is funny – and I'm sure I can't stop myself laughing. Everything is funny, so amazingly funny, and before I know it, my mouth starts chanting, 'Dog biscuit! Dog biscuit!' while I look though the TV screen at the agony on Señor Sanchez's face, which is like slashed snail gut and ripped *sepia* innards, like an octopus turned inside out. But it is too funny to stop laughing now.

Chapter Fifteen

> There can be no mistake about one thing – there is witchcraft in the bubbling of pots, the bain-marie, the reduction of sauces, the composition of menus.
>
> ***Something's Burning*, an autobiography**
> **by Fanny Cradock**

The days of August feel like they've been winded. Like they've been punched in the stomach and left to flop. I feel winded too. The heat is so bad now that nobody's skin looks at all attractive by day. By day, tongues hang out, desperate for any last drop of moisture that might lie in the air, but there is only oven air and flabby breeze from electric fans. The heat turns human beings into wobbly, rippling shapes and makes everyone slouch with ennui. Old women whose nylon blouses sparkle under the blistering sun sit curled up over tables, hands over mouths as if in pain. The heat makes the noises louder and the children more irritating, and the Spanish language sound like smashing slates on concrete rocks and the only way to alleviate your frazzled spirits is to have an argument with someone you love over the pettiest thing in the world.

And even when you're not all sweaty your skin feels like soggy pork scratchings and your brain stops working very well and all you can think of are horrible drizzly days in Mousehole and freezing mornings when your hands are so cold that even a crisp packet in your pocket feels like a razor blade. You wouldn't mind that now, you think.

I have been in Barcelona for over a year but I don't feel like celebrating. Nights of non-stop dessert make everything feel clingy and viscous at the same time. The heat spends the day in Magalí's apartment like a smelly lodger. The coast's clear until 2 p.m. and then it comes and gets you. It fills the room with its fat belly, its breath makes you drowsy yet frazzled. Even my daily stint in the red bar does little to perk me up. I look down at the table and there it is again, 'that' salad. Wherever we go in Barcelona this salad turns up again and again. The Romaine lettuce leaves, the slices of onion that have been soaked in water to take the pep out of them, the slices of tomato, the sickly green strips of tinned asparagus that Magalí tells me are a speciality. And if they are feeling really adventurous they might put some grated carrot on top or scatter over a few wizened olives. 'Whatever happened to beetroot?' you want to scream at them. 'Or watercress, or whatever happened to that lettuce you get in England with the texture of damp green tissue paper?' You wouldn't say no to some of that right now.

Specimen two sits on my right hand side: a plate of *pan con tomate*. No, not a cheese soufflé or an *omelette Villervillaise* or even stupid boats with spun-sugar sails that don't work. Here, you see before you a couple of slices of bread rubbed with tomato, drizzled with olive oil and sprinkled with salt although you'd have thought that Auguste Escoffier and Marie-Antonin Carême had had a hand in it by the fuss Magalí makes about her region's national dish. I sniff the bread and think about decapitated babies' heads. The TV is extra loud because it is time for the afternoon Catalan soap opera, about a high class *cava*-owning family. When scary things happen scary music comes on and there is as much blood and guts as if someone is being chain-saw massacred. Sometimes people are chain-saw massacred. Sometimes the characters will be in a room alone saying soliloquies to themselves – as if they haven't realised they're not in the theatre and the script-writers can't work out a better way of informing the audience of the plot.

I pick at the plate of prawns in front of me while I look around for what I really want – a cool San Miguel – but all I see is a TV screen and a woman with big hammy tears, sobbing to camera, 'So! He was a diamond smuggler after all! I have been deceived!'

The panicky tone sets off some strange panic motor in my stomach. It requires that I have everything as soon as possible. But Cheeky is being surly and I know he wouldn't be like this if Jesús or Magalí were here. The beer 'might be here in a few short minutes,' he mumbles, bending over to wipe the next-door table. The sun shimmers on the bum of his black nylon trousers like a cheap silver mirage. The Romaine lettuce leaves stuff me up like straw and the prawns are too rich, like endless soft centres. I tussle around with them until a half-sucked head spikes my lip with one of its front feelers.

Then Jesús finally arrives. He chuckles and says that I've got a face like there are ants crawling all over me. I wish he'd shut up because ants remind me of Mrs Flowers' eyebrows and then the motor revs up again because I think that maybe Jesús doesn't think I'm *guapa* any more.

Cheeky tiptoes over to the table to plant a feeble peck on Jesús' cheek and bring him a San Miguel but, of course, not mine. Jesús didn't have to wait even five minutes for service. I feel like crying. I feel like the hammy actress in the soap opera.

A fly lands on the prawn head. Like a plump black bow, like Cheeky. I imagine Jack smacking his lips. 'Maybe their bottoms are in their heads,' he is saying, in a terrified voice. 'Stuff in there tastes disgusting.' His voice trembles. 'What do you think, Rosa? Rosa, what's going on?'

And suddenly my chest feels like it has been vacuum-packed, all the healthy air sucked out of it. My chest is as stiff as a board; my worry is located in my chest. It is as if an elastic band has been stretched overtight. My mind starts to rush: what is the point of *sepia* and *calamares* existing? What is the point of them both being there? How can I describe the sea in a perfect way? Why can't I do it? Are the waves like different kinds of orgasm? Is the sea laughing at me? Am I tanned enough? Does Jesús think I'm tanned enough? Is my beer coming? Is Magalí coming? Is dessert coming?

The elastic-band feeling doesn't feel like drowning, it feels more like floating up into the air, like setting fire to a piece of tissue paper and watching it flying unstoppably up into space. It feels like that baby feeling of needing something to suck on but this is a gap that not even Milka chocolate will fill and certainly not prawns. They just make it worse.

I try to concentrate on words to pin things down with. I think of the sea again. I don't want to go swimming today because the waves are messy, like Magalí. They are like people you thought were your friends but now they begin to smother you and then destroy you. They look so pretty and alluring even as they are pulling you down and you don't quite dare to look scared as it is happening.

Cheeky comes over again, still without my beer. He's asking Jesús when Magalí will be turning up. As if Jesús will know better than me, her own girlfriend. Supposedly. Jesús shoos him away then looks at me and frowns. He thinks I'm sad about Magalí. 'Magalí is very . . . difficult at the moment,' he says.

He has no need to tell me that. I also know that I'm not the only person she's difficult with. When we go out all together these days, Jesús and Magalí will start niggling at each other. She will call him a '*compulsivo*', which means a person with an addictive personality, and he will retaliate by calling her a '*maniática*', which means a control freak. To get her own back for this, she will make fun of his vanilla black magic devices to try and get the elusive *el argentino* to love him – like soaking his photograph in a glass of honey – while he will laugh at her love of 'freezing' people. It is strange what she does. She writes people's names on bits of paper and puts them on a succession of night-light candles, which she then covers in salt and stores in the ice box of the fridge. She says it is a way of protecting herself, a trick a fortune-teller told her once.

Yet still Jesús continues to be loyal to Magalí. He seems to have started working as her errand boy. 'She's always loved *la mala vida*.' He smiles indulgently. 'Besides, she's a good person to be around. People flock to you like flies.'

'But I don't want to be surrounded by flies,' I say, in petulant tones.

Jesús waves his ghostly wrists around dismissively. 'You must just think of new ways of charming her,' he says. 'There is a Spanish expression: "Patience and reshuffle."'

But I'm not in the mood today for his wisdom. 'That's not what Sister Maria Teresa thought this week, is it?' I snap, grabbing his bottle of beer and slugging it down my throat. '"He who has many vices has many owners."' I'm not actually sure what this means but I noticed it because it was on the same page as a particularly nasty-looking soup called *crema de San Valentin*, made from veal broth, semolina and curdled egg yolks.

'You're right, Rosa.' He grins. 'I think it's time we talked a bit more about me.'

He picks up the yellow-coloured pasty (called an *empanada*) that Cheeky has put down in front of him and sinks his teeth into it saying, '*Deliciosa*,' in his asparagus way – although I have already tasted them and they are not a patch on my father's pasties. I think of my mother's recent letter to me, about how my father has introduced vegetarian pasties to the shop and did I know that Pythagoras was a vegetarian and how the recent jumble sale put on by her and Mary and Brydie raised seventy-one pounds for the miners' strike. She signed off with 'NULLUS ADDICTUS JURARE IN VERBA MAGISTRI' – in underlined red capitals – which she translates as 'Bound To Swear To The Words Of No Master'. It made me smile and decide how much more interesting she was than Sister Maria stupid Teresa.

I think of Brenda increasingly as 'my mother' these days. I know it's corny and a cliché but absence does make the heart grow fonder. I know she is wondering when I'm coming back and I can tell – by her lack of reference to it – that she wonders if deferring my university place for two years isn't leaving it a bit late. But I can't help that. I turn away from the *empanada* pasties with a big sigh. Looking at them feels like looking into a snowstorm, like a snowstorm view of Mousehole and my former life: pretty and happy and ordered. I have to remind myself that it wasn't always like that and I know perfectly well from other things that Brenda hints at in her letters that much back there now is ugly and unhappy and very much out of order.

Jesús brings me back to the baking Spanish afternoon by musing on his ideal travel itinerary (Cuba, Argentina, Brazil) and his plans for getting a better job ('Paris, I should think, would be the place for me') and *el argentino* ('a drunkard who is wasting his life, *el pobre*'). And then it strikes me that Jesús never goes anywhere apart from the gay mountain and Magalí's house and the red bar and that he's as much of a drunkard and a life-waster as *el argentino* – if *el argentino* even exists. And when he strains his eyes to the far end of the beach and says, '*¡Ay! ¡Mi madre!* Look at that *guiri* girl. So white. So exotic,' it makes me feel more panicked. Have I become too brown to be truly *guapa*? Am I too old to be *guapa* now that I've turned nineteen? How dare he call another girl *guapa* when she is as white as a sheet and hasn't put in as much work as I have in the sun. I wonder how much time I have left. So I snap, 'Oh, Jesús, what do you know about people? You just drift in and out of life. You never put roots anywhere, you don't care if you see people again or not. You're just like a duck's back and people are the water.' Jesús stiffens and I think it might be because I got my Spanish wrong, but really I know it's because I'm being bitter and mean. And it's too late to tell Jesús that his drifting side is precisely what impresses me about him because he suddenly turns his back on me and invites a delighted Cheeky over for a puff of *chocolate*. My chest goes even tighter and I feel really bad now. I'm too scared to drink any more of his beer.

* * *

I'm not even sure why I'm so keen for Magalí to turn up. Things are getting worse between us. She's right about being like the Mediterranean Sea. Sometimes she's clear and bright and sparkling, and other times she's filled with old fag ends and litter and you don't want to go near her.

The orange grove is gone and stale cigarette smoke has come to take its place. These days, Magalí is hardly ever in the apartment. Sometimes she goes out for a whole day and other times she goes out late at night and comes back in the early hours. Sometimes when she returns she brings back a rabble of rowdy people. Their eyes are all like ships adrift at sea and I have to try and get to sleep to the soundtrack of insane *mala vida*.

Magalí's tongue is more and more like a thigh of warm ham these days. Only it isn't even warm, it's lazy and cold and furred up. The new, verbal nature of our infrequent sex life speaks a thousand words. 'No, not there – here,' we go. 'No, not here – there,' instead of the creeping shadow of desire that spread over us the first weeks we slept together when we tore at each other's bodies like unzipping flesh suits to get at what lay beneath. Even the times when she is interested in going to bed with me it's never just her that comes. She has to take dessert to do everything these days. Her eyes go like blind person's eyes and her hands become claws and her face looks at me so meanly that it seems to melt like rendering pork fat. I take dessert too sometimes and sometimes I say I'll take it – because I know she likes me to join in – and then when she's not looking I'll blow my portion on the floor. Sometimes I envy Magalí her spontaneity and I wish I wasn't so sensible but I can't help feeling that dessert has as many drawbacks as it has plus points. Even sex on dessert gets boring after a while. It makes it good to start with, the craven lust lizard thing happens for short stretches of time, but then it all turns strange. It feels like you're watching a TV show about you being a punch-bag and you want to be punched and you think there is nothing better in the whole world than to be punched – and then afterwards you think, What on earth was all that about?

Magalí won't tell me what her job is or why people are always giving her free drinks in the bars she takes me to. She just shrugs and says, '*¡Yo que sé!*' What do I know about anything? I have a pretty good idea what she does, though. I get hints of where she goes in the evenings from people like the Goat who fill me in on the gossip when she finds me on my own, yet again, in the red bar. The Goat seems to know everything about everyone. She talks about what a great night it was last night. About how hilarious it was when the son of the diplomat came into the bar selling some stolen records because he is hooked on dessert. And after he'd bought some dessert from Magalí how he went really *loco* and begged to lock himself in the toilet with her and lick her shoes. And how Magalí does love *la mala vida* after all . . . Then the Goat will stare at me some more, as if she's just waiting for me to say something bad about Magalí. The Goat is a big stirrer but she has a body like the women in porn magazines. Sometimes I want to throw her against the wall and tell her to shut up and other times I want her to throw me against the wall and do something to me. I want someone to take charge of me again even if they are mad as a goat.

Magalí has also become less generous with her money. Not that I didn't offer to pay before, but for the first year she used to forbid me to pay for anything. I think it made her proud to pay for me. She used to say, '*Me gusta presumir de ti,*' which means, 'I like to show you off.' She was always buying me presents, taking me to drink *cava* and suck prawns at Pinocchio's bar. But recently she's started saying how I must help to pay my way, which I wouldn't mind – except that Mrs Flowers' dinner-party money is starting to run out.

It's not only the money, though. Her mania about how she can't bear the smell of food in the house is getting worse. She snaps at me about how I have to cut down on the amount of sardines I fry in the kitchen because it's frankly not sensual and *la peste* is getting too much for her and I should know by now that she can't bear the smell of sardines in the house. I wonder if there's any point in me telling her how I'm fascinated by the Spanish cooking utensil that doubles as a toaster and a sardine frying pan. It's called a *parilla*. It is pan-shaped with metal ridges on the bottom. You put it over the hotplate and it works as a kind of upside-down grill. There's no time for me to tell her about it, anyway, because then she starts on about how I eat too much garlic. She says it is coming out of my pores as if I am a gypsy or from Andalucía. She says she can't stand it any more and she thought the English didn't like garlic anyway. She tells me I should eat more salad because my arms are getting like *chorizos* or like *morcilla,* which is a blood sausage from Murcia in the south where people are poor and fat, not rich and lean like the Catalans.

There are lots of things I could say to her. Like how I think it's strange that the ice box is getting more and more like a black mass every day. How it's filled up with so many candles holding the frozen names of so many of her enemies that there's no room for ice cubes, which is very unfair in this heat and how much protection from bad people does she need, for heaven's sake? I also want to ask her if she knows what happened to my calfskin gloves, which had been packed away safely in the side compartment of my rucksack for the past year and which now have mysteriously vanished. I hate to think that she might have taken them but, then, on my especially paranoid days I wonder if I put them there in the first place. Or I think that maybe the ghost of Mrs Flowers has vanished them back to the place where she is. And when I think about the place where she is it makes me feel very worried.

But all of this seems too complicated to explain to Magalí. In the end, I just try to explain that I feel upset about our situation. Except I can't think of the word for 'upset'. Something between angry and sad. '*Enfadado y triste,*' I tell her. But she just hisses in exasperation and makes a big Arab throat-slitting, ear-splitting '*joder*', which rips through the air like *hhhhhhhhhod-air* and I yearn for the fluency of English. I want to speak at a hundred miles per hour again.

And then, just when I think I can't bear it any more, Magalí's Mediterranean waters will become clear and enticing again. One day, she walked in at lunch-time after having been out all night. She was bright and cheerful and there was a new sparkle in her eye. She bounced into the bedroom and drew back the blinds. 'Come, *inglesa mía,*' she said. 'The *gambas* are on the horizon shouting, "Where is Rosa? Tell Rosa to come so she can suck our heads!"' She announced that she was inviting me to a classic Catalan restaurant that a new friend of hers called Pia had just told her about.

It felt just like the olden days when Magalí was full of energy and funny thoughts. I was so pleased that she seemed happy to see me that I didn't ask her where she'd been all night or who this Pia was that she is always talking about these days. I just jumped out of bed, showered and within half an hour I was sitting on the back of her moped, flying up the side of a mountain.

We stopped at a restaurant called El Jabalí – the Wild Boar – advertised with a picture of a chef holding a piglet by the back leg, and we laughed. We looked at the menu on the board outside the restaurant and the world seemed full of endless potential again just like it had in the old days when we looked at the midday menu and it felt as exciting as being invited to a birthday party. Going for the menu is always a bit of a surprise. We wondered what we'd get. What would the *esqueixada* be like? Would the lamb be too skinny? Would the chicken with *cava* really be as good as it sounded? Would the *crema Catalana* be the best you ever tasted? What kind of bread would it be?

But Magalí's energy seemed to run out by the time we got inside the restaurant – another of those hangar-sized Catalan places with pebbledash walls that are clammy in winter and stale in summer. The usual thoughtless music was coming out of the speakers – Elton John followed by some Spanish group singing 'sex, sun and sea' in English. And on the other side of the room were three balding men, with dark brown hair, and faces with that Catalan ugly look, as if they came from parents who never left the village for three hundred years, as if bits and bobs of five different faces had been stuck together with glue.

I sat glumly, reflecting how the Catalans are nothing to write home about. In Barcelona you don't walk down the street going, 'Phwoar!' like Mrs Flowers said you do in Italy. Barcelona seems to be filled with a mass of people wearing only brown, beige or olive green. The streets are filled with short, portly ladies with sensible haircuts – a sign of post-Franco liberation, according to Jesús – wearing peep-toed canvas shoes, huge blouses with loud patterns and carrying straw shopping baskets. The younger women look like sallow goldfish with bushy eyebrows, lots of mascara and black eye pencil, while the men are short with dark hair, pressed shirts, trousers with creases and sensible leather shoes.

In the restaurant we sat by the windows, but they felt like prison windows because they had bars over them and you had to stand up slightly and strain your neck to see out at the parched brown fields. Magalí was sullen too: she kept standing up and looking out as if she was searching for somebody, as if my company wasn't enough.

Even the waiter seemed more fascinating to her than me. He had two teeth missing in the front and the ones that remained were drain brown. His face was red and alcohol-ravaged and a mass of broken veins – like an overripe pomegranate that had been hacked open. Yet Magalí chattered away to him in Catalan, which she knows infuriates me because I can't understand it properly. All I could do was look at his clothes, which were disgusting: the zip slightly open at the top of his trousers, a stain down the zip line – slightly crusty, once white. And when he finally got round to bringing over our starters – ham and melon, the Spanish equivalent of prawn cocktail – the ham was as tough as windscreen wipers and the melon was warm, as if it had had some horrible connection with the inside of the waiter's trousers.

Our next course was *carne a la brasa* with white beans. A pile of meat arrived: a big dollop of aïoli and some greasy rabbit next to a piece of greyish pink meat, crusty on the outside, which might have been pork. The white beans smelt of steamed farts.

Half-way through, Magalí threw her knife and fork on to the plate and started on about how the whole restaurant stank of food. It was worse than that for me: my mouth was smelly with aïoli and my hands were sticky with oversalted rabbit thigh. My whole body felt as if it was wearing a damp suit of greasy membrane.

You could see that she was trying to pull herself

together, though, to make out that everything was fine. There were even some sparks of gold in her eyes and the space between them looked warm and helpless like an animal, a bull, maybe, who'd really rather not go into the Plaza de Toros this time. But after the meat had been cleared away she got up anyway and announced, 'Time for *postre!*' with a smile on her face – a rotten, tired old smile, like a huge old lock that's been cranked open with a rusty wrench. She knocked into the table as she went towards the *servicios*, mumbling 'I'll go first.'

I wish that love was like fat. I wish you could store it and see it and touch it if you want to. But you can't store it. You can only have a memory of it – like a nice sunset that you've seen but afterwards you can only recall that it was kind of pink and yellow and that it would have made you pee your pants if you'd been there. You can only talk about it afterwards and bore people. Love is like plastic melting in front of a fire. It's like Fanny's boats shrivelling in the heat.

My relationship with Magalí feels flat, like riding a bicycle with no tyres. There is no more air, nothing left bouncy between us. It is becoming painful. When I talk to her I look at her orange top and it just looks like an orange top, except that now I see faults in it. I think it is vulgar – it shows off too much flesh, for instance. I no longer desire to chatter on to her non-stop, there is no more sparkling, no more flashing silver lights. She seems to be very far away. She is no longer the sea, she is a beautiful shell that has been turned into an ashtray and when you hold it up to your ear you can't hear the whisper of the waves any more. Magalí is disappearing, and if I am honest I know that it is not only to do with her mood swings. It is not only to do with her. There is something else, someone else, seeping into me uncontrollably, gradually wiping out Magalí like invisible ink.

When Jesús has finished smoking the *chocolate* with Cheeky I try to win him back. To make amends for being mean to him, I pat his arm and say cheerfully, 'I'm not really sad, Jesús. I'm like you, I used to be sad but now I've given it up.' And when I hear myself say this, the stifling day seems a little cooler and the prawn heads seem a little friendlier.

But Jesús just turns his magnet eyes on me. 'You can't bury pain,' he says sharply. 'It might disappear for a while, but it's just spilled down into the soil. When it's passed through the soil it goes on to seep into the water and when you drink the water it poisons your blood.' He stops and lights a cigarette.

I can feel sweat forming on my top lip. Jesús isn't supposed to say things like this. He's supposed to be Sister Maria Teresa. He's supposed to say bland, happy things to make you think you're not such a bad person after all. I try to sound calm.

'But we all have our secrets, don't we, Jesús?' I say. 'You said so yourself – you said that we all have our own secrets.'

Jesús shrugs and swigs back his beer. 'Escape is just a

nice idea,' he declares, 'but the mess you leave in one town always turns up again in the next. The same boiled cabbage you didn't eat at lunch always gets served up again at tea. And it's worse the second time round.'

The sea hisses like a fuzzy TV out of control.

'Drinking, travelling, it's all the same thing.' His leathery forehead frowns as he stares into the horizon.

'How do you mean?'

He bangs the beer bottle down on the table. '*¡Hija!* Scars never heal. You might go to a hotter climate but the scars never tan over. Take my father. He turned his father's bakery into a chocolate company that ended up supplying the whole of Spain. A very ruthless man, my father. Our surname was Ajor but he chopped off the R because it wouldn't fit on the chocolate moulds.' Jesús shrugs. 'Then he got big-headed. He started investing in the stock market. In chocolate shares. *¡Hombre!* He didn't know anything about it! He started losing money so he began to drink. Drink and tranquillisers at the same time. Very bad. Turns your head mad. We were in a plane going from Kuwait to Egypt on a renewed chocolate-selling drive. By then he couldn't wait to get out of Spain, of course. We were about to land when the hostess came up to me to say that he'd had locked himself in the toilet and that he was threatening to commit suicide. He was shouting my name out of the door. "He wants me to kill myself! My own son wants me dead!" That was the first time. After that, the wounds would steam open every few months until the *cabrón* finally died of a rotten liver five years later.'

There is a slight pause. 'I suppose that people act the way they can at the time.' He shrugs. Then the geeky smile returns and the magnets come back into his eyes. He drags himself up from the chair. 'There are no new lands, no new seas.' He grins. 'Just sticks and bones.'

Everything is too strange. Everything is closing in on me. I have bad dreams and when I wake up I am sweating and the vacuum-packed feeling is in my chest again. I become ill. I am listless and short of breath and my throat feels tight as if, at varying times of the day, someone is trying to strangle me. I take to my bed. One afternoon, Jesús turns up at the apartment. He seems surprised to see me in bed. It's as if he's forgotten I exist. I feel sorry for myself because I have been all alone for two days and I start to cry. Jesús gives me a big hug that smells of stale bar smoke. He tells me he's sorry that he didn't come before and he's just here now because Magalí asked him to pass by and pick up some things. He would have come, he says, only Magalí didn't mention me and . . .

This makes me cry even harder so Jesús hugs me and tells me not to worry, that he'll be my nurse because he likes looking after people. So he goes round the apartment shutting all the windows because he says I might get a chill, and then he tucks in the corners of the sheets so the bed feels like a strait-jacket. He makes me some chicken broth with chick-peas because in Spain they give you chicken broth with chick-peas when you are ill, and I start crying even more because when you're ill you're supposed to have Ribena and Heinz tomato soup and jellies made in interesting shapes and afternoon TV by the bedside and the windows open and I'm fed up with being so cosmopolitan. I start to cry even more until Jesús gives me another smoky hug, crooning, '*¡Ay! Inglesita,*' saying that he has to go now but that he'll be back in a few hours. But he doesn't come back in a few hours at all.

Over the days my dreams get worse so I come up with the idea of starving myself. I think that maybe extreme hunger will flush simple thoughts forcibly into my mind when I am dropping off to sleep. No more horrible nightmares, just dreams of plain, uncomplicated food.

And, to start with, it works. I am ravenous by the time I go to bed. I don't count sheep, I doze off thinking of lamb chops with mint sauce. Real English lamb chops like plump girls curled up into a ball as opposed to skinny Spanish *chuletas de cordero,* which look more like mole chops. I think of Heinz tomato soup and Cheddar cheese sandwiches in white Mother's Pride bread, and cheese straws and hot dogs and Eccles cakes made with currants and Tate & Lyle's golden syrup.

I make basic Victoria sponge, like good people make. I drift off to the Land of Nod on a waft of sweet air as I cream butter into sugar with a wooden spoon, then beat in eggs, then gently fold in flour with a metal tablespoon. I divide the contents between two greased tins and I put the tins in the oven. I go back to the bowl and scoop raw cake mix into my mouth, and it tastes like paddling pools and grassy summer lawns and home-made pasties made on scrubbed wooden tables. I make pasties on scrubbed wooden tables: I chop up the fat and pour in the water, I cut up the skirt and slice the potatoes. I spoon the filling into a round of pastry, I gather the edges safely together, I seal and I egg and I crimp a soft seam like a properly made bed.

I fall asleep and I dream. I dream of perfect steaks – a perfect juicy rump of beef glistening on a hot plate – and then I cut into it. I cut. And I hack and I hack and I can't get it apart because there is a ridge of gristle across its length like the Great Wall of China. I dream of Heinz tomato soup. My mother brings it in on a tray to my bedroom. She hands it up to my bunk bed and her Loch Ness eyes are warm and speckled with gold and I thank her for the soup and I start to drink it from the spoon. But it isn't tomato soup at all, it's blood soup – sticky and thick and filled with clots – and when I look up to see why she's betrayed me, why she's done this horrible thing to me, I see that she's not my mother at all: she's Mrs Flowers and her eyes are black as squid ink. Her eyes are black and deadly and she's glaring at me as if she hates every fibre in my body.

Chapter Sixteen

When oysters went out of season Fanny's mother breakfasted off a cold bird, a peach and Champagne in a glass-bottomed, pewter tankard at eleven o'clock in the morning among the laces which covered her day pillow.

***The Fanny and Johnnie Cradock Cookery Programme* magazine. No. 54**

One night, Jesús offers to take me up to the mountain to cool me off and cheer me up. This seems like a good idea to start with but then nature starts to irritate me because it makes me feel so insignificant. Jesús, on the other hand, is a natural. When we arrive, he starts yelping on about the wolf's life, about chaos, about the vine and vital energy, about how he wants sticks and bones. He takes a deep swig from his bottle of Bacardi, breathes out like a dragon, smacks his lips, spits some beads of rummy saliva on the ground in homage to Dionysus and sets off into the trees, his eyes on fire.

The mountain is called Montjuic mountain. According to legend, Barcelona was founded by Hercules and populated by the crew of the ninth ship (*barca nona*) that went with him on his labours. It was on Montjuic that Hercules sat down to admire his creation. Tourist guides describe the place as a 'delightful place for a stroll' but they don't mention anything about how creepy it is at night. Jesús chooses to stroll in the zone where part of the 1929 Universal Exhibition took place. All that is left now is a series of crumbling columns and pillars and lumps of fallen frieze. That isn't what makes it feel sinister here, though. The worst thing is the moon. The frizzy old moon isn't like the sun. The sun, for all its faults, is pretty and biddable and does nice turns for the tourists, while the moon is big and bossy and hysterical. Here, on the mountain, it seems even closer to the earth, like a heavy white bubble about to burst. Its big white ego blanks out the stars and casts a frozen light over the silent ruins. Only sometimes do the clouds club together and pluck up courage to cover its face, turning it into a piece of membrane weak as rice paper.

Then I pull myself together. I tell myself that it's not scary up here, that the ruins aren't even that silent. There's a constant rustling in bushes and I keep spotting agitated men in leather jackets prowling around like they're searching for lost contact lenses. I tell myself to stop being so pathetic, to stop getting so bogged down in doom. I remind myself that there's nobody ordering me to sit here on these crumbling walls, waiting for Jesús to take me back to Poble Sec in his car when he's found what he wants. I decide to take control of things myself, to walk back to the apartment on my own.

The smug feeling of independence doesn't last long, though: as I walk down the hill, I start to feel nervous because there are only a few cars at this time of night. Occasionally, one rushes past with thumping music blaring out and boys shouting things from the window. I pretend I'm deaf and think that at least they're real people who exist and not the moon. The truth is that the moon is still making me feel uneasy, rushing around like a mad old woman. I don't really understand about nature. About why the moon jumps about in the sky without rhyme or reason, or why tonight it looms dangerously close to earth as if it's about to burst. I don't know why it doesn't stay still like the dopey old sun. The more I think of the moon, the faster I walk. I think of Federico García Lorca poems about the cruel moon but that just scares me so I try to think of domestic science class, about raising agents and aeration and foams: an example of a solid foam is meringue. The egg foam has been baked at a low temperature. The air inside the foam expands to increase the volume and the protein albumen coagulates to give a solid fine-mesh structure. But the egg just makes me think of *omelette Villervillaise* and I wonder if Jack felt as scared of the crab as I do of the moon. A twisted tree branch seems to be bent into a sort of P shape so I think of Mrs Flowers and then a yellow taxi screeches past advertising a crêpe restaurant on one of its doors and I think of Mrs Flowers and her crêpy crack. A squashed cat on the side of the road is the same colour as Mrs Flowers' calfskin gloves. In the distance I can see the rooftops and turrets of the gingerbread houses but they seem sticky and threatening, as if maybe children are trapped inside them.

There is definitely a smell of witch in the air. I feel as if I'm shrinking. I try to walk faster, but the faster I walk the smaller I become. In my chest there is a burning iron that makes me feel dizzy, like when you stand up too quickly. Maybe I'll never get home to Magalí's house, I think. And that's not even my home, anyway. And what about Brenda's house? Is my mother's house or the Lobster Pot any more my home? Breadcrumbs are useless. They don't lead you to where you need to be. They just lead you to where people have been eating. Maybe I should just get into a plane and go somewhere else. I could go to Peru or somewhere and at first it would be strange – for the first six months or so it would be strange – but then I'd get used to it and I could start a new life there. People here would forget about me and I could meet new people. But what if something happened to me? What if I got bitten by a scorpion or a spider and I got all infected? What if I didn't get bitten by a scorpion and the infection came through anyway? What if I met someone who looked like Magalí who looked like Mrs Flowers? And what would happen if the sun wasn't enough or if the food didn't take my mind off things either but just pulled me down and made me feel as if I was trapped in a cave with a ball and chain tied to my leg?

My panic grows. I stop on the road and wait to grow back to my proper size but it doesn't happen. I don't want to stand around any more on this silent bit of road in this strange white light because it feels like some witch with an ashen cobweb hand is going to come and tickle my back and the thought of this makes my heart start pounding in my throat, jumping around as if there's a frog in there.

So I start walking quickly again, walking briskly down the hill, along the narrow pavement, keeping my eyes fixed on the lines between the squares. When I notice that I am avoiding the lines it seems to bring me to my senses. I hear myself laugh out loud. I laugh because I know I'm being ridiculous. I am nineteen years old and I am afraid of being eaten by the bears!

I start getting cross with myself. I tell myself, I have just left my gayboy friend in the gay mountain scampering around being a so-called wolf and that is all. And now I am heading back to my girlfriend's apartment where she, no doubt, will roll in a few hours later smelling of alcohol and bar smoke and maybe it will be one of those nights when she is cuddly and wants me to tuck her in and protect her from the big bad world. And I will do this.

And just to prove that I am not afraid of the bears I turn round to face the moon full-on in the sky. And when I turn I see it there, all shiny and bossy and brazen. Only it *is* staring straight back at me. What's more, it's bathed in an orange light and I'm sure I can see pincers in it – pincers and eyes and bristly mandibles, opening and closing, like soft, wet flesh. It looks as if the moon is an egg – a big spider's egg – and the night is a crab, gripping the egg with its treacherous claws.

I jerk my head down from the sky and force my eyes to the bears because at least they're trapped between the lines of the pavement. I sound as if I'm out of breath, I can hear it. I force myself to look back up, just to be sure I'm not making this all up in my head. But the black-crab night is still there. The imprints of its legs are still straddled round the ashen white egg. Night, the crab, is laying eggs in the wound of the sky, filling it with hot worms for the day to come. I expect a cobweb net – like in the ghost train – to be flung over me at any minute, and when that happens I will be locked in a maze of never-ending crab chambers filled with cigarette ash and swarming flies feeding on diarrhoea-brown crabmeat.

I'm trapped in a crab chamber already. I gasp for air but there is only the rancid, sweaty air of August night. The sweat that has already started on my top lip starts seeping out through the palms of my hands. My pace quickens. My arms grow vigorous. I start to jog but I can't run because of the stupid flip-flops on my feet and, besides, running would be admitting that I've lost my head completely.

I need some electric light, some shops, another car of drunken boys, maybe, and then the fear will go away. Of late, when I have felt anxious, a quick trip to the shops seems to do the trick. The fake limb shop, for instance. It's called Ortopedia and it sells spare legs and wheelchairs and cushioned toilet seats. I speed-walk with cracked breath and I make myself list all of the different types of crutches:

the Tiny Tim crutches, the designer crutches with blue and turquoise tops, the crutches that look like walking-sticks, the two plastic legs in the window – cut off under the thigh – with blue and turquoise padded things around the knee, bending in alluring poses.

But amputated legs don't seem so alluring up here on the hill, so I make my head go into the corner shop, Alimentación Carmen. There she is, Carmen herself, sitting regally at her checkout like Gina Lollobrigida in her heyday. She is rabbiting away nineteen to the dozen about her son and taking ten hours to weigh me out a kilo of tomatoes for the – guess what – *pan con tomate*. She's going, 'Yes, yes, he lives in France now. Although, of course, he's lived in other places, like Sweden and Germany and Portugal, and he even speaks a little Arabic now. It's good for young people to travel, isn't it? Travel broadens the mind, so they say, although of course in my day we never travelled. Holy bread! The opportunities young people have nowadays . . .'

And then my head has to walk out of that shop without waiting for my tomatoes because I can't stand too much of Carmen right now. Suddenly it strikes me that she's not a naturally chatty type in the slightest. I think she must feel as I do about the moon. She has to talk compulsively to make out that everything is ship-shape and Bristol fashion, when of course it isn't like that at all.

And just as the burning iron threatens to take over the whole of my body, just as I think it's impossible for me to get any smaller, I realise that I've come to the bottom of the hill. I realise I can breathe. Everything is all right.

I have escaped from the mountain, from the moon. I am at the bottom of Montjuic and there is electric light, and parrots on balconies and a couple of *marroquís* lifting off a drain cover to sneak out packs of contraband cigarettes.

And then I see the car. A big red *Herbie Rides Again* banger. The sight of it is like turning out the light in a room full of thrashing moths: the bright light is switched off and suddenly the beating wings stop and you can pretend at least that they've all vanished into thin air.

The engines dies. I stop still by the car and look inside to see a woman with yellow hair in a lilac bikini. It's the Goat. I can't believe it. I feel like chuckling. I daren't open my mouth, though, because I suspect a bit of a deranged laugh will come out. I just feel so relieved, so glad to be back to normal again, so happy that I've bumped into a friendly face. Suddenly the night is calm and I am calm again. The left-over adrenaline from my moon fright is even making me feel bumptious, in the mood for a bit of an adventure.

So when the Goat finally opens the door and climbs out of the red car, I say something that I know charms Spanish people when an English girl with red hair says it. I say: *'Hola, guapa, tienes buena pinta,'* which means 'Hello, beautiful, you have a good paint job,' or 'You are looking very good.' Normally you use the expression in relation to the appearance of a paella but it seems apt to say it to the Goat because she has something edible about her – in a tacky Spanish bubble-and-squeak sort of way. I look at her from top to toe and it suddenly seems as if she's made up of lots of left-overs that you'd find in the fridge: a three-day-old piece of *tortilla de patatas*, some dog-eared slices of *chorizo* sausage, some cheap green olives floating around in a tin with grease on top of the water from various hands that have reached in to take one out. You might laugh at the contents in the smug light of day, but on a dark and stormy night when you can't get to sleep you wouldn't mind having a bit of a nibble.

She looks confused to start with, but then she recognises me and her face lights up. Her lipsticked mouth looks as if it was piped on with a wonky icing-bag and this makes her smile seem even friendlier. She hands me a cigarette she is smoking saying, 'Come, daughter. Take this.' I can tell by the smell that there is *chocolate* inside. I take it and I'm about to tell her that *chocolate* does nothing for me but when I take a puff it suddenly feels like I've been living in a cramped sardine tin and now I've been redirected to a much bigger and better tin where better lighting and better acoustics and better air are being pumped in like laughing gas. I start laughing, especially when she walks to the front of her car, grabs hold of the bumper and lifts the red vehicle ten inches or so off the ground with a, 'Look! Look at this, *inglesita*! Impressive, no?'

I cast a glance at the yellow hair, the lilac bikini, the clump of virgins around the neck, the perforated beige beach shoes and I don't want to go home. Maybe I want her to put her hand on my thigh again or maybe I just feel relieved because she looks even madder than the moon.

The only thing I am certain of is that I don't want

to go back to an empty apartment tonight. The idea of trying to get to sleep while I listen to the woman next door threaten to denounce her husband to the police for the millionth time is unthinkable tonight.

So when the Goat says, 'Come, *inglesita,* come to my house, we will talk business,' I follow her immediately because I think that maybe she won't be a compulsive liar tonight, and that maybe talking business means making money and that will make Magalí happy.

In a cloud of vanilla essence and with a choir of *chocolate* sardines blowing fanfares in my ear, I follow the Goat inside a building that smells of fried fish and lemon-scented cleaning products. The stairway echoes like a Victorian mental hospital, and on the second floor she lets me into an apartment smelling of dirty underwear – or maybe goat's meat.

Aside from the smell – the odour of lemon-scented cleaning products stops at her doorway – the visuals are quite interesting too. In the darkness of the entrance you can see some pots of plastic flowers, a framed photograph of a football team wearing white tops and black shorts, some plastic statues of the Virgin Mary and a Mickey Mouse clock. The Goat takes me into a living room lit with three red lamps. There is also a scratched coffee table – it looks like the one in the sixth-form common room at school – which holds a bowl of plastic apples. She tells me to sit down. She turns on the TV and the sound of a loud shoot-out fills the room.

All this is fine by me. I still have the *chocolate* cigarette in my hand as I sit down in a gooey armchair and just gaze at the yellow wallpaper to which years of cigarette smoke have added sticky, gravy-coloured dimensions. I find it all fascinating. It feels as if the sun has come out in the room and suddenly the wallpaper turns into Victorian girls on swings, flying to and fro with ribbons in their hair on a warm summer's day. I start to relax for what feels like the first time in an age. *Chocolate* is a different feeling from dessert. It feels like the tranquillity of sleep, except that I am awake. I start saying, 'Wow, your house is so beautiful. Your paint job is so fantastic,' because the Goat really does look like the days when she looked good in a lilac bikini and the dirty washing really does smell of pink apple blossom. She chuckles and tells me that I'm *una joya*, a jewel. She goes off to what I suppose is the kitchen, saying, 'Eat, we must eat!'

A lot of "holy breads" fly out from the kitchen and when at last she returns to the sitting room, she hands me a glass of sparkling wine and a sandwich. I presume that the wine is *cava* but when I drink it the taste is of fizzy sherry.

'Russian champagne,' she says, tapping her nose and winking.

I look at the sandwich and it consists of a chicken bone inside two pieces of bread waterlogged with olive oil. I don't look inside for too long because there is also a cat hair inside. The Goat slumps herself down next to me on the gooey chair, throwing up a puff of air smelling of musty cough sweets in cobwebby pockets. I clamp my sandwich back together.

'I like exotic fruit,' she announces.

I look at the bowl of plastic apples in the middle of the coffee table. 'What's your favourite exotic fruit?' I ask.

'Meat,' she replies.

The Victorian girls on their swings with ribbons in their hair screech to an emergency stop.

Before I can work out if the Goat has said something really mad or if it's just me and the joint, she grabs my thigh and says, 'You like *mi chocolate, inglesita*?' I make a guarded nod. She won't believe me when I tell her that it's never worked before. 'Come, daughter,' she says, 'you can be honest with me,' and she stares at me for what seems like the longest time.

'You like dessert, though, don't you?' she says finally. Her eyes don't so much sparkle as whisk round and round in her head in the village-idiot style. I get a sudden flashback to the psychiatric wing at the Plymouth County Hospital and the chicken-bone sandwich feels heavy on my lap. The laughing gas has stopped now. The new gas in the room is a dirty yellow fog.

'Magalí is a nice girl, *verdad*?' she says. 'Very generous, *no*?'

'Yes, she is nice.' The yellow fog is mustard gas.

'She must have her special place, *verdad*? Her special dessert cupboard?'

My body goes stiff. I know what special place she means. I'm not going to tell her about my riffling through the apartment, though. My fruitless riffling. Not looking for dessert, just any of Magalí's personal possessions – maybe my calfskin gloves.

'I don't think Magalí has any special places,' I say.

The Goat seems thrown. 'But you must have some with you, no?'

'Some what?'

'Some dessert. Daughter!'

'I . . . I . . .'

The yellow smog pumps into the room at a rate of knots.

She looks at me for another horribly long, intense moment until a barrage of *joder*s flies from her mouth and her eyes heave like maggots wriggling out of apples. She slams the arm of the sofa, sending up a mushroom cloud of dust.

'Hhhhhhhhod-air,' she screams. *'¡Hhhhhhod-air! ¡Hhhhhhod-air!'* as if her throat has become an endless tube of splinters. 'You have nothing with you? *¡Hhhhod-air!* Why do you insult me by accepting a meal in my house when you have nothing to offer me?' She heaves herself out of the goo of the sofa and staggers over to one of the lamps. She lifts it up and pulls out a plastic bag that has been tucked into its hollowed-out base. There is a sharp intake of breath and she starts shouting. *'¡Cabrón!'* she shouts, even louder than the TV shoot-out. *'¡Mi cabrón de hijo!* My cuckold son!' so that I soon get the general idea that her son must have stolen whatever used to be in the bag.

The smoke floods into my chest and starts to burn. The Victorian girls with ribbons in their hair are just burnt-out corpses now. The Goat's eyes are zipping round in her head faster than Scalextrix. She is pacing the room so fast it makes me dizzy to watch her. She drops the bag to the floor, rushes out of the room and returns with a vacuum-cleaner and a big green feather duster. She plugs in the vacuum-cleaner with a trembling hand and starts Hoovering the floor while, with the other hand, she thrashes the feather duster at various items of furniture, including my chicken-leg sandwich plate, which soon crashes to the ground. Then the duster knocks over the sixth-form coffee table and the bowl of plastic fruit goes flying. She throws herself down on the floor and tries to catch the spinning apples but she gets bored of that and decides instead to turn up the TV even louder, followed by the radio, and soon the room is filled with the sound of Hoover and gypsy prison music and police gunfire and the escalating racket coming from the street of young men throwing stones at tin cans.

'*¡Mira!*' she shouts suddenly, pointing at the fringe of the oozy sofa. 'Did you see the cockroach?'

I look down by my feet but I can't see any cockroach. I don't particularly want to see any cockroach but I half hope I will because then at least it might suggest that the Goat isn't so mad after all. I try to decide if it is better to be in a dirty old flat with a disgusting sandwich and a mad woman, or to be in a dirty old flat with a disgusting sandwich and a mad woman and cockroaches.

When I take another glug of fizzy sherry and another puff of joint I calm down a bit. I think that maybe the Russian champagne's not so bad after all. I think that maybe this is a funny experience. That maybe it'll make Magalí laugh.

I nod and say, 'Yes, there are many cockroaches in your house,' and smile. She shoots me a look like I'm the mad one so I decide I'd better try to get some of the disgusting sandwich down my neck so I won't offend her and she won't get out a gun and kill me.

The sandwich is horrible. A few greasy strands of meat. And a leg bone. I have never really thought about the idea of hygiene before. I wonder if there is a cat in the house, and if there is, if it ate all the chicken off the leg.

'*¡Mira!* Cockroaches!' She's off again, only it's really not funny any more. I stare down at the chicken-bone sandwich on my plate, the Spanish food on my plate – the plate I came to Spain for – and then, suddenly, the Goat disappears. The Goat disappears, all the noise around me disappears and for a moment I find myself in a brightly lit supermarket in Mousehole watching a woman in a pair of lumpy yellow leggings shouting to her husband in a dopey Cornish accent, 'See you in Chicken.' She's got a big round torso and a zit in the middle of her chin like a bullseye and she's saying, 'See you in Chicken.'

That was what did it. 'See you in Chicken.' As if that was the furthest she would ever go, this woman with a big round middle and the bullseye zit. She left her gormless husband in Coffee and Tea and dragged a snotty five-year-old towards the next aisle shouting, 'See you in Chicken, then, Clive.' Not even, 'See you in Wine' or 'See you in the Cheeses of Holland.' After the disaster of the *crêpe Suzette* party and *The Big Time*, 'See you in Chicken' was the last straw. The cheese straw. The burned boat.

In the end, Gwen Troake, the dumpy farmer's wife, got her revenge. In the final sequence of *The Big Time* she whispered to Edward Heath about her original coffee cream idea. Edward Heath said that, on the contrary, he loved the idea of instant coffee and cream and sponge fingers, and he would have loved to eat that.

Even though Gwen Troake popped her clogs a week after her humiliation at the hands of Fanny Cradock it was Fanny Cradock who suffered most of all. The papers were filled with the scandal of it all. It was as if Fanny was the dead one and Gwen Troake was still alive. Recipes for coffee cream were trumpeted all over the newspapers and it was Fanny Cradock who had to undergo the post-mortem. Fanny Cradock, whose only crime had been to speak her mind. Her career was over, they said. Washed-up, she was, they said. I had to leave home after that, although that wasn't the only reason.

The Goat jolts me back into Barcelona, into a dirty flat at the foot of a mountain at three in the morning. Now she seems to have decided that it's the cockroaches who have emptied her plastic bag. She's lying on her stomach with the green feather duster, poking under the fringe of the oozy sofa, shouting, 'Cuckolds!' at the invisible roaches while her lilac bottom rolls from side to side like the rump of a horse that's been out to grass for hundreds of years.

Suddenly there is a cool breeze. Not in the house – which is still stifling and smelly and possibly filled with cockroaches – it is a cool breeze in my stomach, much more dangerous than the burning feeling in my chest. Something inside me is cooling dangerously. I need to lie down, my head feels heavy and jumbled up. I feel sick. I start stammering to the Goat, apologising, saying that I think I might have to lie down here on the sofa but that I'll help her look for cockroaches when I wake up. And finally she seems to hear me. She stops whirling around with the feather duster and she looks at me. She looks at me for what seems like ages and then she smiles. Her face lights up and the maggots go away. '*La pobre inglesita,*' she coos. '*Sueño?*' she says. 'Tired?' I nod and try to smile. She says, 'My son will be home soon. You must meet my son. But tomorrow. Tonight you must sleep in the spare room.'

I manage to get up from the sofa and follow her down a long, narrow hall. We go past the kitchen, where I vaguely register a cat on the cooker licking a frying pan. But I don't take it in too much because the Goat is moving at a hundred miles an hour and all I can think of is sleep.

Inside the spare room there is a little rocking chair and a double bed with blue sheets and plumped-up pillows. On the floor are peach-coloured tiles run through with funny red threads like varicose veins. I sit on the bed and the Goat gives me a high-suction kiss on the forehead. She wishes me an agitated goodnight, then whirls round and leaves the room, slamming the door behind her. When I hear her feverish steps die away I dig into my pocket. I scan the room wearily before deciding on the floor. I take one of Magalí's tiny dessert bags from my pocket and kneel down on the peach tiles. I lay a line of dessert on the ground and sniff it up. For good measure, I tell myself. If people back in England are going to think me sneaky and not to be trusted then I will be sneaky and not to be trusted and it will all be their fault. Besides, if the Goat comes back to show me her porn-star body I'll be alert enough to decide what to do. I think of fooling around with the Goat's vertical hold and then I think of sniffing choux pastry up into my nostrils. Both things makes me chuckle. The floor, too, makes me chuckle. Peach is soft, peach is almost like orange, and now I feel alert, an alternative kind of alert, alert as someone tumbling on to a bed of soft, bouncy orange blossom. When I finally clamber back up into the bed it's just like in the best fairy stories – I fall asleep as soon as my head touches the pillow.

It feels like hours later when he comes in. A slamming door jerks me out of what feels like a very deep sleep. A young man – a thin version of Desperate Dan – walks over to the bed holding a plastic carrier-bag. Without looking at me, and as if we have been married for years, he takes off his clothes and climbs in. He sits there, next to me, rummaging in the plastic bag, which is filled with bananas. He peels and eats them – not as if he's hungry but as if he has to, as if this is some ritual, a preamble to something. I'm watching it all through slits in half-closed eyes, but he knows I'm awake.

After he's eaten two or three he pokes me in the arm with a banana saying, 'For you.' I open my eyes and say, '*No, gracias,*' thinking I'd better try to be a bit polite. He says he is the son of the Goat and jerks his head towards the door. I keep my eyes fixed on a cigarette burn in the blue nylon sheet. I say, '*Muy interesante,*' and then I say I'm tired and I'm going to go to sleep now and in seconds I flip over to face the wall. I don't understand why he is in my bed. I thought it was my bed. I thought the Goat was being a Good Samaritan. I keep seeing the way she smiled at me, such a kind smile – only now I see in flashback that maybe it was a fake smile, a bitter smile. My head aches from all the fizzy sherry I've drunk and my eyeballs feel a bit like they're attached to chewing-gum and they might suddenly tumble down out of my sockets and do a few yoyo turns before going back to their proper place.

I wonder if the Goat would do this to me, line me up knowingly to be raped by her son. Could anyone be like that? I don't want to think of the word 'rape' anyway. I haven't completely given up hope. I still think that maybe the boy is just being kind, that it is customary to keep guard over an English visitor to the country, to break bread with them, to share bananas with them. Any minute now he will finish eating his fruit, leap out of the bed and wish me a very good night.

The smell of banana lingers over the bed. A dingy smell of banana skin in a plastic bag in a hot, stuffy bedroom.

The bag is still on the bed and I am lying with my back turned to the boy. He is staring at me, I know it. I can feel his eyes burning into my back. He is staring at me like a boy peering into a hutch at his new pet rabbit, waiting for it to do something. I'm sure my pounding heart is making the mattress wobble like a water-bed.

If I move my leg I make the bag rustle. I try not to move. I want him to think I am asleep. It is still dark outside, cars are hooting, there are bluebottle whines of mopeds, the game of hitting the tin can with stones seems to have grown in size. There are gruff shouts of men going, 'I shit on your ancestors, I shit on your dead!' Probably it would be even more dangerous to try to make a run for it. I'm trapped. The hot air is stifling. The bananas are sickening. There is an air vent but it is furred up with a weave of grey dust. Even if there wasn't a naked man lying next to me in bed burning a hole into my back I wouldn't be able to sleep now. I wonder if he knows this. I wish my heart would be quieter. I wish I hadn't had dessert. I know I mustn't move. If I am still it will all not really be happening. And even if something does happen then at least I have all my clothes on. That's one good thing at least.

I don't know how long I have been lying on my right side, staring grimly at the chipped white paint on the wall. I am intimate by now with its scratches and its marks, with the green and red bogey smeared into a dent the size of a twenty-five-peseta coin. Then the light goes out.

I tell myself that the mattress is infested with bugs. I am sure it is infested with bugs. It seems to be packing itself around me, making me hotter than ever. Bugs like the heat. Cockroaches especially like heat. Oggies is filled with them. Everyone has their own cockroach story to tell at Oggies. And yes, I know that I am only thinking about cockroaches and pasties so I don't have to think about the naked boy lying next to me in the bed. He, too, is unnaturally still. Maybe he's fallen asleep. I wonder if he has.

Suddenly I can bear it no longer. I have to know. I turn my head slowly – wishing the bed wouldn't creak quite so much – I turn my head and I don't see a face. There is no face, just a pair of eyes, white and bulbous and red-veined, staring at me as if they're made of wax. As I nearly jump out of my skin he blurts out another offering of a banana. I refuse and jerk back to my original frozen position, staring at the chipped wall. I try to calm my heavy breathing but a shaky hand comes over my shoulder and I jump out of my skin again. The spasm seems to make him angry and he grabs hold of me hard by the arm. He lets go when I tug sharply too and jump up from the bed and skid to the other end of the room, pulling a sheet with me, wailing as I go.

'Daughter of a prostitute!' he yells, banging his hand on the bed, as if he does this all the time and sometimes he wins and sometimes he doesn't. '*¡Mira!* It's OK. I'm not going to touch you. *¡Hhhhhhod-air!* Be quiet, in the name of God!'

He yells and I whimper. I am scrunched up into a tiny ball, a hard little bread ball, whimpering at the opposite end of the room. He throws a pillow at me, saying, 'Shut up! I'm not going to touch you!'

When I don't stop crying, he starts shouting again about

how he's not going to touch me. He seems to think that if he shouts enough he'll calm me down – but he's just making me more hysterical and the more hysterical I get the more he shouts. He gets out of bed and comes towards me, closer and closer. I get frightened and make even more noise. I wonder what the Goat thinks of all this. She must be able to hear. Is this her way of getting revenge because I didn't give her any of my dessert? Because I lied to her about not having any? Is this my own fault because I was so sneaky? I pick up the pillow and hug it, like a shield in front of me or like a kidnapper holding a child with a gun to its head as the police come nearer. Eventually, the boy stops walking. He stays still for a few seconds, then makes an irritated sound and stomps back to the bed. He flops down in it and pulls the remaining sheet over his head as if I'm some tiresome child he's babysitting.

I drop my face into the soft pillow for some comfort. But it doesn't smell of anything I recognise. It smells of warm, damp cardboard. Where is Brenda's Sunday-night laundry wash? Where's her mangle for me to laugh at? Where is my smell? I bite my nails. The taste of cold fear is like bacon. The skin under my nails is smoky-bacon-flavoured, and even the rest of my skin doesn't smell like me any more. I smell of garlic and olive oil and my *chocho* tastes of crayfish. Just like Jack who, one day, tasted of shrimps down his trousers. I lie down on the pillow and put my hand under my left ear. I feel my ear-lobe, soft as a rabbit's ear, soft as the fluff on the back of Jack Flowers' neck. And then everything is suddenly colder. My fingers are cold, the temperature in the room feels cold, although I know it is still really hot and muggy. Most of all, the inside of my stomach is cold. A metal dustbin battered into the shape of a stomach, a metal shell, rusty and brown and hard as a crab, like a cold crab living inside me. That's all I am, a mean, creeping crab, a horrible hard thing that wants to destroy all that is soft like yellow rabbits. The crab is in me and I wonder how I will ever get it out. What way out is there? My body and mind feel like they are foam: they are floating around the room like meringue or Pavlova because there is nobody left they can trust and they will be safer that way, just coming apart, every man for himself. Any minute now I might look round and see a woman in a black cloak and that might be what is real. The witch would be a relief. But then I smell bananas and I feel sick. I go hard. I go harder and tighter, like a glazed pot, thin as an eggshell. And then the cracking comes. Hundreds of little fragments I become. I think of the look on his face. I see it. I can't deny the pain I feel, like the lump in your throat when you see a sad film. I think of the look on his face when he was making the peppermint creams, of him in the Plymouth County Hospital, standing at the door, shuffling in his pyjamas as Mrs Flowers and I went home. I think of his eyes like green glass marbles. Not a single fly in the ointment. The fine hairs on the back of his neck that make you think of someone coming along and bludgeoning him to death because nobody is allowed to be that unselfconscious. That simple and trusting.

* * *

Even as I did it, it was as if I'd done it already, and I knew I'd remember it for ever. I knew the granite corner of the hearth would always be there in my mind, and the radio itself would always be huge and yellow and bigger than the hearth, bigger than the room itself. And even when it started to melt in front of the fire it didn't get any smaller. It just got stickier and floppier like the sugar sails of the *Morning Cloud*. It stuck to the granite hearth of Jack's bedroom so that there was no chance of hiding it or covering it up and pretending it hadn't happened.

I was upstairs, on the chair in the hall under the grandfather clock. After the disaster of the *crêpe Suzette* birthday tea I had to escape from the Venetian Room. Jack appeared from nowhere. He didn't have to say anything. He was niggling me already. It was the look on his face. 'Good people make cakes. Bad people make Fanny Cradock,' he said. The smirk was back. My downfall had brought him back to life.

We went into his bedroom. I followed him. He said he'd come to stoke the fire. He'd wanted a fire in his room as part of his birthday treat, even though the June day was a scorcher. Mrs Flowers had let him have one as a reward for his being so good recently. Mrs Flowers would let him have anything now. He knelt down in front of the hearth and stared hungrily at the flames – as if he hadn't had enough of flames by now, what with the burning calor-gas stove and the inferno of the Spanish tablecloth. Then suddenly he turned to face me.

'Look at my bookmark,' he said. A trace of a knowing

smile passed over his lips. I told him to shut up. I paced the room, raging inside. 'Look at it,' he kept saying, and I finally looked and saw a thread of black cotton and then I looked closer and saw that it was a pubic hair, and that set me off. It lit me up like the touch-paper on dynamite. A shudder of anger passed into me. He might be able to fool everyone else but he couldn't fool me. In a red hot flash I thought that Jack was a waste of space on the earth, I wanted to break everything that was his, chuck everything dear to him out of the window, I wanted to hurl him to the bottom of the sea.

He took a packet of cigarettes from his pocket and lit one in the fire. 'Sobranie Filters,' he said, staring mesmerised again into the flames. 'Joan Collins smokes Sobranie Filters.'

There was little emotion in his voice, no fear. He kept on looking into the flames, as if he had more respect for them than he did for me, as if he didn't care if I was there or not. And when I said something sarcastic like, 'Enjoyed the prawn cocktail, then, did you?' it just went right over his head. As if he wasn't even scared of me any more. As if he was back to being made of rubber and he would always bounce back from anything I said or did. He flashed the garish packet in my face, saying, 'Mum bought them for me.' He blew a big fat smoke-ring in my face and added, 'Mum bought anything for you recently, then?'

It was that tone of voice. It was as if he wasn't ill at all. It was just his regular, irritating voice. It made me furious.

He knew it would make me furious. If he could speak like that then it meant he wasn't ill at all, maybe he'd never been ill. He was asking for it. I wanted to kick him into the fire and watch him burn. But that would be too easy. So I just stood behind him as he fiddled with the yellow tape-recorder, fast forwarding to Carly Simon. As a rich voice began to sing 'Nobody Does It Better', I looked at the nape of his neck, all downy and happy. I stood for a while, just watching the back of that neck, like people do in films just before they are going to murder someone. And then the idea came to me. Not so much an idea, more just a colour – yellow and red and then black. The rabbit. I reached over, I whipped it from his lap and I held Carly above my head, waving her to and fro.

> *'Nobody does it better*
> *Makes me feel sad for the rest . . .'*

That made him pay me some attention. He stiffened at once. He stood up. He looked like a sleepwalker starting to wake up. A tear oozed from the corner of his eye. Jack was upset. I had made him upset. My blood raced like the time I first saw Mrs Flowers' strips. I looked at his pain and I breathed it in as if it was fresh air.

> *'Nobody does it half as good as you*
> *Baby, you're the best . . .'*

I watched his eyes cloud over, then shut tight – as if

he thought he was going to make me go away like that – and it made the feeling of power even better. His pretty mouth started to tremble and I looked at the fine line of blond fur above his top lip. This was pleasure at last, as if I had climbed to the top of a hill and was looking down on everybody else. I flew off the hill, I flew down and I hovered above Jack's ear with the yellow rabbit hanging in my hands, hissing, 'Nancy. Nancy-boy. "Cry baby Bunting,"' as Carly Simon wavered on in Jack's defence.

> *'. . . And nobody does it better*
> *Though sometimes I wish someone could . . .'*

The tears turned into sobs and it was like being on a brilliant ride on a runaway train.

'My yellow tape-recorder, please.' He was whispering. 'Please don't hurt my yellow tape-recorder.'

Jack breathed as if his lungs were bruised lemons, as if he was slowly squeezing harder and harder and it was so hard. Soon he was just a resigned monotone, just a damp skin all out of juice.

> *'. . . Nobody does it quite the way you do*
> *Why'd you have to be so good?'*

'Please, Rosa. Please, Rosa,' he moaned. But there was no going back now. He looked up at me as if I was some terrifying word that spelled his final destruction and then I did destroy him. I did it. Right in front of his eyes.

It smashed like china. The yellow rabbit smashed to smithereens. There were plastic shards everywhere like smashed Honeycomb Crisp and two big pieces of silver metal stuff because they wouldn't break. Carly Simon wasn't singing any more and the only sound I could hear was of my heart booming in my throat.

And then, the minute I'd thrown it on the floor, the minute it was lying in hundreds of fragments on the hearth – some of them melting already like cheese on toast – at that very moment I regretted it because there was nothing left that he cared for now and I'd lost all my power over him. Only in a very tiny place was there elation that Jack's last hopes were now just as dashed as those of Fanny Cradock who also got too big for her boots. Mainly there was just reality flooding into my mind – like how much noise the yellow rabbit had made and how on earth I was going to explain to Mrs Flowers what had happened.

Jack's reaction was strange. He just stared at the yellow pieces of broken plastic. His mouth was open and he looked as if he might cry. Finally, he leaned forward and picked up one of the metal pieces. He felt it in his hand and then he put it down, quietly, on the floor. I was feeling panicked now. Would he tell Mrs Flowers? Would he go running to her, like I would? What was I going to say when he did? My fury was all vanished now and I just felt shock at what I had been capable of. I tried to concentrate on my breathing but then all I noticed was my breathing. I noticed how hard it was to breathe.

I'd never imagined being claustrophobic in my own

body but suddenly I was. Just as I am now, here in this vile house in Barcelona. I feel the same constriction in my lungs, as if my lungs are all bubbling brown meat – chambers of brown crabmeat trying to suck in more air but they can't. I am gasping, gasping, and then I become Jack, gasping and gasping on that terrible night – gasping so much until finally a huge howl spewed forth from his lungs, a gushing of pain and confusion into his mad bedroom, all papered over with Abba and Elkie Brooks and Fanny Cradock monstrosities.

It was a scream of ultimate desolation in a bedroom of snowstorms and plastic sick, and it becomes the same scream in a room with peach tiles and varicose veins. I jerk myself up from the floor and I don't even notice the stupid boy and his bag of bananas any more. It's like a dream where you've killed someone and then you wake up and it's OK because it was only a dream and you haven't really killed anyone at all. Only I have woken up and it wasn't just a dream. I have killed someone and I can never make it better.

The aroma of what I have done smothers the odour of rotting bananas and the sound of adolescent male yelling at me to shut up. Unfamiliar smells gas the room: the smell of the witch's cloak, the smell when the witch has passed, the smell of the walls caving in, the smell of the grandma stabbed to death, the smell of the man who died in agony. The smell of unknown herbs and children's homes.

I see a chuckling Jack with a pink Mr Kipling cake in his mouth and when I close my eyes all I can hear is the sound of under the water – the sound of madness. And I can't come round. I can't wake up. It isn't all right. It wasn't a dream. I have killed someone. I have killed Mrs Flowers.

Chapter Seventeen

> Either a *gourmet* or a *fine bouche* will stop eating whatever it is which is giving him the maximum pleasure long before he is replete. The *belle fourchette* – in literal translation 'one who wields a lusty fork' – will go on eating more than he should, and a *gourmande* is nothing but a disgusting guzzler.
>
> ***The Fanny and Johnnie Cradock Cookery Programme* magazine. No. 54**

What is the happiest meal you ever had in your life? What is the most frightening food? Do you wonder what the last thing you ever eat will be? On your deathbed will it be a morsel of overcooked cabbage? A grape? A sip of Ribena?

Maybe the Ribena will make you happy. It will remind you of your childhood. It will be the last thing you ever experience on earth – blackcurrant, sweet, purple – and then, bang, you're in the tunnel with the white light at the end and the feeling of overwhelming happiness.

But maybe it will make you sad, your last meal on earth. Maybe you will remember you weren't allowed Ribena when you were a child because it was too expensive and bad for your teeth, or you will recall that you were scouting out in a tree house from the top of a sycamore the last time you drank it. Or maybe your last meal will be cheap baked beans splurging from a well of instant mashed potato because you will be in the madhouse or it will be an irritating artichoke that you ate when you weren't really hungry, or a slice of Christmas cake that you never got to taste because you had a heart-attack as you were raising a cherry-filled chunk to your lips. Maybe a Scandinavian breakfast eaten with gusto on a holiday of a lifetime will be the thing to polish you off. Sticky black bread, Emmental cheese and coffee with evaporated milk will feel like shoes on the wrong feet as it lies mushed in your mouth and your last mortal thought will be of bacon and eggs. Will there be ketchup on your cheek as you collapse into the toilet with a hamburger in your hand? Will a well-seasoned salad be your final wish the night before the guillotine? Or a leg of mutton and a woman? Will you send out for a jar of Cooper's Oxford marmalade? Where will you be on the last mile? Bloated and cold with the remains of a dissolved Rennie on your lips? Combing the grass for the trail of breadcrumbs that were supposed to lead you home?

* * *

Some might call it bad luck. There certainly was bad luck involved. Downstairs, at the remains of Jack's birthday party, they wouldn't even have heard anything. The fire extinguisher grand finale had made them hysterical and thirstier than ever. I could hear Brydie ordering Mary into the kitchen for ice-cube reinforcements and Mrs Flowers was enjoying a Helen Reddy 'I Am Woman' interlude.

Everything would have been all right if Mr Flowers hadn't been right next door in the bedroom, getting changed after another unsuccessful day in the yacht-selling world. When he came into Jack's bedroom, his facial expression was an interesting mixture of anger and horror. It had to be said that Jack did look a pitiful sight. The ear-piercing wail had stopped and Jack seemed to have transformed into the rabbit himself. He was crouching in front of the fire, shoulders hunched, sniffling and picking up pieces of shattered radio cassette, which was already melting like chewing-gum. He was scraping them up as if it was his mother's body he was scraping off the road. In the goodie and the baddie stakes things weren't looking too good for me: one of us had big plump tears rolling out of green marble eyes while the other stood by the fireplace leaning on one leg and not knowing what to do with their hands.

So I did what I always do: I slithered out of trouble. Quickly, I shuffled my pack to see how my hand was looking. I went through all the things in my favour –

like how Mr Flowers hardly knew me, like how he only knew me as the girl who cooked dinner parties to impress his clients or how he knew me as Jack's best friend who cared for his sick son when Mrs Flowers was falling apart. I knew he had some respect for me. I saw it in his eyes the day I told him he wasn't smashing the crystal glasses properly. Then I remembered how inept he was at fending off Sal's flirtations and how ineffectual he was at getting Mrs Flowers to love him. How he didn't even know that his own wife was having an affair, while I did, I knew. And I remembered how he was giving her one last chance.

I saw my chance then. It was lying on the shelf underneath the snowstorms and the plastic vomit and the fake beans on toast. Dozens of different chances there were, all lined up in a neat row, all in chronological order, each in a box labelled 'Mummy one' to 'Mummy forty'. Trump cards they were.

I snatched a random one from the shelf. 'Look, Mr Flowers, I didn't want to tell you this, but I think the situation's getting out of hand.' I kind of panted as I spoke. I came up with just the right tone of drama. Jack was still speechless. It was perfect.

'It's Mrs Flowers, you see . . . It's not good for Jack. What I mean is that, well, he keeps playing them. Over and over again. It's not good for him. It makes him mad. The things she says. Look what he's done to the tape-recorder. And you know how much he loved that tape-recorder.'

Good move, Rosa. Just a little gentle stirring to begin with. Then lightly fold guilt into the confusion. Mr Flowers probably didn't even realise that Jack had a yellow tape-recorder, that it was his most precious possession given to him by his mother on his twelfth birthday.

'Um . . . What?' Spluttering is how you could describe his speech patterns. Then, 'Rosa, tell me. What's my wife done?'

Now a short silence. A pregnant pause they're called. And still Jack is silent. More than that, he has sagged and flopped, his face a giblet swamp covered in tears.

'Well . . . Mr Flowers,' it's obviously difficult for me to say this but . . . 'well, Mr Flowers, it's obviously difficult for me to say this but . . .' I'll give her 'fat, spiteful girl' '. . . but your wife . . . she's having an affair.'

It all flowed so naturally. I am tingling. I am more than tingling, I am flying down the water-slide on my tummy, quick and fast and slippery, up and down, side to side. I could write a manual about the art of lying: 'Get the big bit out of the way early thus distracting attention from smaller details,' I would say. If this had been Mrs Flowers, she would have noticed immediately that the cassette on the floor by the side of the dead rabbit said 'Carly Simon' on the label. She would have seen immediately that Jack hadn't smashed his yellow rabbit because he couldn't bear her adulterous rantings any more. Nothing gets past Mrs Flowers. But Mr Flowers isn't as smart as his wife and, anyway, by this time he'd got the drift.

While crows dig their claws into Mr Flowers' grey forehead, I hurtle down the Bournemouth water-slide. I see him as a blue steak in a pan of searing oil: hard on the outside but still very soft inside. He doesn't know what he's doing whereas I know exactly what I'm doing. I am charged, I am giddy, my body is shaking.

I have never gone this fast before and yet how easy it seems to go at full throttle. How exhilarating. I'm not sure when the scales are going to tip, when all the voices in his head assuring him this is not true finally shut up and let the evidence speak for itself. He doesn't want to believe that something so bad could have happened but I know that the wind will change, there is no way out. Now I see him as a tree, a tree marked out for felling but whose cut isn't quite deep enough yet for it to topple.

He is wavering, though. He is swaying. You can see his eyes darting. He looks at the melting yellow plastic and then he looks at Jack and then he looks at the cassette I am holding out to him in my hand. And then he looks at me. Bang! The scales fall and the mighty oak crashes to the ground. I've done it. I'm a genius. Treacherous as a leopard, David and Goliath rolled into one. The touch-paper takes, his eyes ignite and I don't have to explain any more. He grabs the tape from my hand and he rushes to the door. He hammers down the stairs and runs into the Venetian Room where the dregs of the eighteenth birthday party are still congregated.

I sneak in behind him and see that he doesn't even notice how the room is looking like a big baked Alaska, thanks to Brydie, whose use of the fire extinguisher has gone far beyond the call of duty. He just rushes over to the quadrophonic sound system, wrenches open the smoked-glass doors, yanks out 'Cruel Summer' by Bananarama and, with a trembling hand, slams my tape into the cassette deck.

'Oh, grand,' says Brydie, who is wiggling her index finger around at the bottom of a martini cocktail glass, trying to retrieve a green olive. 'Say, Penelope, d'you think we're going to have a bit of music? It'll be just like at bridge night.'

And then, like no bridge night ever before, the voice of Mrs Flowers comes slinking into the Venetian Room in full quadrophonic sound. Among the crackles and the buzzes of a very poor recording you can hear a wriggly laugh and heavy breathing: '... and then I put my finger in your asshole ... oh, Silky, my pointy finger in your asshole and I spank you hard, oh, oh, you're so swollen, so big, but I'm not going to let you come yet. I'm going to make you wait, Silky ... Oh ... Grind your face into my wetness ... mmm ... Grind your face into my wetness ... Grind ... Are you bloody deaf? I said, grind your face into my wetness ... No, no, I'm sorry ...'

The tape goes on. It's quite a recent one. You can tell by the extra irritation in Mrs Flowers' voice. The contents of this tape are quite good although my personal favourites are the one where she pretends to strip over the phone or the one where she sings the Spanish Shirley Bassey song or the one to Fernando where she says she's going to leave Mr Flowers.

It's a good thing that Brenda has had to make an emergency trip to the loo following the after-effects of a twenty-egg omelette with creamed crab filling on the digestion of a woman who is more used to ham salad and tinned pineapple chunks. She doesn't have to watch Mr Flowers' face turning an unhealthy shade of elephant while Brydie looks like she's won ten rubbers all at once. 'Say, Penelope, is that you on the, thingummy, gramophone?' she whispers, under her hand, like an excited spectator on a big night out at the Royal Albert Hall. 'You've got a lovely voice, so you have.'

Mrs Flowers' glass crashes on to the table before falling to the carpet with a dull thud. This sets Mary up on her feet, rushing to the kitchen for a cloth, only too glad to have an excuse to rush out of the room as fast as her legs will carry her. Martini drips slowly into Mrs Flowers' lap but she doesn't seem to have noticed until the tape gets to the bit when she starts calling him her frisky little dolphin. It's so cringy (although it's good, too, because her laugh is so dirty it sounds like she's just murdered a couple of babies) that she snaps back into life. She jumps up from the table and rushes over to the quadrophonic sound system where she rattles the smoked-glass doors, desperate to take the tape out of the machine. Only Mr Flowers won't let her. He grabs her arms and makes red marks around the tops of them as he struggles with her and fights her and she shouts, 'Bastard,' and he shouts, 'Bitch,' and Brydie can only sigh and say in a troubled voice, 'Oh, Lord,' as if the Royal Albert Hall is resurrecting memories of her heart-breaking time with the crêpe-de-Chine Englishman.

And then Mr and Mrs Flowers start rolling around in

the white fire extinguisher foam like it's part of a funny custard-pie routine only it isn't funny at all, it's making me feel sick. I want to tell them to stop it, I want the ride down the water-slide to stop. I want to tell Mrs Flowers that I never meant it to go this far, that I understand, really, that she needs her distractions, but the room is already filled with snatches of 'You promised me', and 'It meant nothing', and 'I swear to God', and 'I'll never forgive you' and 'But Rosa said ...' and this last bit makes me jump because I hadn't thought of that. Mr Flowers wasn't supposed to say that at all. My name isn't supposed to be in there among the custard-pie fighting because my thing has always been to rebel quietly with a smile on my face. And I can hardly bear it when I see Mrs Flowers flop. A spasm of shock runs through her and then she just flops to her knees, like all the life has gone from her, like something terribly wrong has happened and she can struggle no more. While she kneels there, stupefied, Mr Flowers tries to get to his feet but half-way up he just abandons the effort. He puts his arm on his knee and his face in his hand and he sobs like the worst thing in his life has just happened and there's not even any point in standing up ever again.

I have never heard a man cry before. It sounds quite high-pitched and it makes my mouth go dry and my insides feel like they've all been Hoovered out. And even when the sobbing stops there is still the terrible sight of his shoulders moving up and down, shaking and shaking like someone in a silent movie. I am glad when Mrs Flowers comes round a bit from her trance and puts her foamy arms around him and hugs him and says, 'Darling, please, my darling.' I'm not jealous because I don't want any harm to come to him, I don't want any harm to come to either of them, or anyone for that matter, I really don't. I want the birthday party to have been a huge success and I want Jack to stop being weird and Mr Flowers to stop crying and the yellow rabbit to be in one piece again and the stupid tapes never to have existed and Mrs Flowers to take me to her crêpy crack and tell me that it's all all right.

But then it's no good because Mr Flowers pushes her away from him saying, 'Get away from me, you fucking whore.' He's not really in control, though, because he flails around with his arms and then covers his head like the sky's going to fall down on top of him at any minute.

Mrs Flowers just stares at him with her trance eyes and then her nostrils flare. She takes in a huge deep breath and tries to stand up. She skids on the foam and falls on to the carpet, banging her knee, but this seems to bring her out of her daze. 'Bugger bollocks,' she hisses, rubbing her leg and heaving herself to her feet. She's panting heavily and when she's finally standing upright she closes her eyes and puts her hands over them and I wonder if she's going to tear them out or something from the stress of it all. Mr Flowers has started to weep again. Brydie has joined him, blubbering frantically, 'No! Oh, no! I don't like it at all!' and Brenda has marched back in from the toilet announcing to anyone who will listen that she's got stomach cancer for certain this time.

Mrs Flowers ignores everyone. She isn't going under

after all. The louder the noise gets, the deeper she breathes, the more she radiates calm. Finally, she uncovers her eyes and with trembling hands she smooths down the sides of her foam-smeared jumpsuit. She snatches up her car keys from the charred tablecloth and then, slowly, her eyes move around the room as deftly as crab eyes on sticks, as sharply as the wicked witch ordering Hansel to put his finger through the grate to feel if he's fat enough yet. She is not looking at Mr Flowers or Brydie or my mother, she is looking beyond them. There is something keen in her face as she surveys the broken room, a subtle twitching of her nostrils as if she's picked up the smell of smoke. Then she twigs where the smoke is coming from. She sniffs me out behind a swarm of golden bees. She walks to a corner of the room, she snatches the curtains back and I feel the roar of the oven flames.

I can't see her. I am blinded by hot light ricocheting on to a mass of sherbet lemon and barley-sugar goblets – glaring at me like a shock of searchlights – and there is a blaze of orange and crimson and scarlet as the last rays of the sun flood in through the bodies of Theseus and the Minotaur on the stained-glass window behind her.

But I know she's there because there's a smell of rotting flesh and a tickling in my tummy – the burning tickle from the bony finger that goes deeper and deeper until my whole body is burning up and I know there will never be enough water to cool it down. I know it's her because I can sense her mouth twisted into a horrible sneer, I can feel her eyes digging into me like a big, sharp dagger trying to jam open a mussel that's closed. And you shouldn't force open shellfish that are closed because they will be bad inside. Bad inside just like I am bad inside.

Mrs Flowers told me once that freezing to death is the best way to die. She said that it's a very peaceful way to go, that you just get more and more sleepy until finally you doze off for ever. I'd never thought about this before, although I did read once about how, in 1881, a French ship called *La Jeanette* became icebound on its way to the North Pole. The whole crew died of cold, apart from two sailors who managed to reach the Siberian coast. In memory of the expedition, Auguste Escoffier gave the name of the ship to one of his greatest chicken dishes, *les suprêmes de volailles Jeanette*. I said I thought this was a bit sick but Mrs Flowers insisted that, on the contrary, a tragedy of such classic dimensions was an excellent way of dressing up chicken. She said that Escoffier wouldn't have wanted to create a special dish in honour of someone who had taken a pills overdose. A pills overdose is very messy, she said. For a start pills are risky because unless you take enough of them you might wake up and be brain-damaged. Someone nearly always finds you, anyway, she said, and you get your stomach pumped and you come round with nasty black charcoal on your face because that's what they use to pump stomachs with and doctors get so fed up with people trying to take their own lives that they don't bother to wipe it off afterwards as a punishment.

Burning would be worst of all, though – almost as unthinkable as hacking your neck off with an electric chain-saw. Flesh melting like wax and a screeching of nerves, it would be. Mrs Flowers thought that drowning – although claustrophobic at first – would ultimately be the most romantic way to go out. She liked the idea of a lake. In Switzerland maybe, or Lake Como in northern Italy. She would push herself off from the shore in a wooden rowing-boat one misty summer dawn wearing a floaty Victorian white nightdress and suddenly the boat would roar up into flames. 'In that context, burning would be acceptable,' she said. 'Arthurian,' she said.

I agreed, although I added that I would prefer to drown in the sea. I would be in the sea and then, as the last inch of salt water came glugging in to fill up my lungs, I would hallucinate that Tom the cabin-boy was coming to take me home, home to the tunnel with the white light at the end and the feeling of overwhelming happiness. She agreed and said that, yes, that would be romantic too.

Of course, death by canal is not so romantic. Hurtling through the air in a rusty white Mini van then plunging into a murky green soup like the horrible green soup with beansprouts you get on the £3.99 menu at Sun Doo City was probably not the romantic trip that Mrs Flowers had in mind. When she finally roared out of the house that night – dripping in foam and shaking with anger – floating in a littery bilge of shopping trolleys and bicycle wheels and mannequin bits can hardly have been the end she saw for herself. Yet plunge to the bottom of a stinky green canal with a crab in her stomach – a crab pickled in a cocktail of Martini and gin and tonic – is just what Mrs Flowers did on the eve of her son's eighteenth birthday.

A dish created in honour of someone who had committed suicide would probably look like *omelette Villervillaise*. How I wish there'd been something happier in her belly than that. I wonder what she'd have chosen as her last meal. Not, surely, what I saw in her feed bag later that night in Intensive Care as she lay in a coma with punctured lungs and genuine kidney problems for the first time in her life. It looked like Ready Brek. On other days it looked like grated carrot or porridge or baby food. It glugged down a plastic tube the length of a gazelle's neck and ended up sticking into her stomach. There was a big machine panting away next to her too. It was trying to keep her cool but she was hot. Her skin was scorching, as if she was sunbathing under a very trying sun. As if she had the Ready Brek Central Heating For Kids. You could have fried an egg on her skin. Not that you would have wanted to fry an egg on her most precious skin.

In the beginning, when I believed she'd get better, I used to dream secretly of all the nice things I would feed her when she woke up. *Oeufs mollets à l'estragon*, spooned gently into fast-boiling, slightly salted water, cooked for exactly four minutes then shelled, slid into artichoke hearts and coated thickly with mayonnaise or *sauce Mornay*. Some oysters eased from deep shells and served with triangles of brown bread; a chocolate swan surrounded by a small flotilla of chocolate cygnets; an orange sculpted into a waterlily; a sea of aspic coloured like water on a sunny day when tree vegetation is reflected in it.

Chapter Eighteen

> We made a miniature *boucherie* display and set it under a triumphant arch of oxtails, sprigged with parsley and decorated with pork fat vegetation.
>
> ***Something's Burning*, an autobiography by Fanny Cradock**

There is an overexcited monotone going, 'Who wants to be buried? Who wants to be buried? Come on, there must be someone who wants to be buried!'

Jack is doing the ultimate thing of all the ultimate things you're not supposed to do in Spain. He has put on his swimming trunks, buttered himself all over with half a bottle of Ambre Solaire, dug himself a huge hole in the beach, and now he is holding forth from under his mound of Barcelona's special brand of gritty, cigarette-butty sand as if he is sitting in the world's most comfortable armchair.

He is going on in a very loud voice about a *Carry On* film whose name he can't remember. 'You know, the one where Sid James comes back home and he's turned into a werewolf and Joan Sims doesn't even notice . . .'

The Catalans, walking around in green anoraks and fur coats (because it is March and one of the rules is that even if it is hot, you are not allowed to show skin until at least May) are looking at him like he is something strange that has been washed up on the shore. Andalucian tourists up for the week are taking photos of him to feature alongside the other ones they have of the Ramblas, the Picasso Museum and the Sagrada Familia cathedral.

Jack suddenly bursts out of his tomb, springing up high into the sunny sky like a huge beanstalk coated in crispy breadcrumbs. Beaming from ear to ear and clutching a sandy electronic device in his hand, he waves to a Humpty Dumpty lookalike sporting a footman's jacket coloured Butlins-red. He gambols over to the bar to join us both.

'If you don't want to be buried, then I'll have to teach you to count,' he tells Humpty triumphantly. '*Uno, dos,* like does, *tres,* like ashtrays, *cuatro,* like Suzi Quatro, *cinco,* like sinks, *seis,* like sex, *siete,* like sex again, *ocho,* like octopus, *nueve* and *diez* – you just have to remember them. Got it? *Uno,* does, ashtrays, Suzi Quatro, sinks, sex, sex, octopus, *nueve, diez.*'

Humpty Dumpty tries it but gets lost after Suzi Quatro.

'I'm thinking in Spanish now,' Jack says proudly.

'That's good,' Humpty replies.

'Not if you don't understand Spanish, it isn't. You don't know what you're thinking about!' He smirks.

Humpty smacks Jack affectionately on the back of one of his plump hands as the other one shoots across the table to snatch up a fat garlic prawn.

'Soon be time now.' Jack grins at me, his mouth full. 'Five o'clock, remember?' Jack keeps going on about how it'll soon be time now. Despite his treacle-slow speech patterns, he's getting agitated about a date that he's set up for me. After the fizzling of me and Magalí I suppose that I should be pleased about it. I hardly know anyone in Barcelona any more and I'm not sure how to go about making friends. But I'm not happy about it. I feel even more agitated than Jack. I keep looking up to the sky, watching planes etch white scars into the blue.

The waiter thinks I'm a tourist. He keeps talking to me in English and he asks for money the moment he puts anything on the table. I feel humiliated. 'A thousand pesetas, please,' he says, as he dumps a plate of *jamón de beyota* on the table.

'Is this the posh ham you were telling us about, Rosa?' Jack says, stuffing his mouth afresh.

'That's the one.'

'How do they know the pigs only ate acorns?' he insists.

'Never really thought about it, Jack, but good question.'

'Maybe someone could have thrown a cake into their

field. How do they know that they didn't eat cakes as well?'

I am trying to be patient with Jack. I've just turned twenty and I like to think that I've learned something since I last saw him. Plus, I'm trying to make up for my sins. I take a big glug of drink from my glass and my crimson-stained mouth relaxes into a smile. 'I don't really care about ham any more, Jack,' I say.

That's true enough. These days, it gives me pleasure to wear T-shirts in March, to take sand into my bed, to devour *churros con chocolate* for breakfast (and bacon when I can get it), to eat paella in the evening, and to drink big jugs of sangria just like the *guiris.*

'Remember the pig-bins, Rosa?' says Jack, taking a stack of small boxes that Humpty is handing him across the table.

Jack keeps asking me to remember things and, to be honest, I don't really want to remember. He has just told me something about Fernando and his mother, for instance, that has knocked me for six. He doesn't seem to mind dredging up our past, though. Even though it feels as if I saw him yesterday instead of nearly two years ago, he seems to have forgotten the bad things. He's reverted back to rubber Jack. Or blubber Jack, as he now is.

'Mustn't forget to take my pills,' he announces.

He reels off the list of the pills he takes as if he's describing his career path over the past eighteen months. 'Largactyl, lithium, chlorpromazine and depixol,' he says, popping them from their foil packets on to the edge of the table. 'Lithium makes you hungry. Largactyl makes you tired in the day and it makes you sunburned, too, unless you put on lots of cream.' He sticks out his bottom lip and turns to Humpty Dumpty. 'Not sure what the other ones are for, though. What are the other ones for, d'you think?'

Humpty Dumpty scratches his head, making the line of medals pinned to his red footman's jacket start to chink. He sticks out his lower lip and says, 'D'you know what, Jackie? I'm not sure.' He pats Jack on the hand again and adds, 'Never mind. When we get back to the house we'll call my lawyers and ask them.'

He turns to me and gives me a conspiratorial 'it's all right, we're the sane ones' kind of wink.

I ask him if he's hot in his Butlins coat on this unseasonably warm day in March. He opens a mouth stuffed with half-chewed ham and says, 'Duties, Rosa. Duties.'

'Duties?' I say.

'Manners, Jack!' He smacks Jack playfully on the shoulder and pulls a shrimp head out of his hand. Jack has been dipping his tongue into its head and looking at me for a reaction.

'The Queen expects every good man to do his duty,' Humpty says, turning back to me.

'Pardon?'

'Oh, didn't Jackie tell you? The Norwegian side of my family has obligations to the Queen of England. Sometimes I'm called up to go and wait at Buckingham Palace.' I look at Jack but Jack is playing tiddlywinks with prawn heads.

'Yes,' Humpty Dumpty goes on. 'In the mornings you

wear a red jacket, at lunch time you wear a purple jacket and in the evenings you wear a blue jacket. Evening's for silver service. I'm not often called on to do that shift. Can do it, though, can't I, Jackie?'

'Yeah, you're always doing it to me, aren't you?' Jack says, in his Dick Emery sexual-innuendo voice. He glances at me to see if I've picked up on it.

'Gets you a reduction on the London Underground too,' Humpty says, pincering together a fork and a spoon and doing a pretty good job of lifting up a series of prawns and chunks of *pan con tomate*. In the end I'm not sure if he waits tables for the Queen of England or not.

I'm not sure what is true and what isn't any more. Turns out, for instance, that Nikki Kilroy and Jack really did have a thing for a while behind the rifle range at school. On the phone last week, Brenda told me that Nikki has gone to live in London with Mr Jones. 'In the same house,' Brenda said, with only a faint hint of the frozen Scottish lochs in her voice. Brenda has discovered homosexual liberation, as she calls it, ever since Jack went to live with her after the bad time.

Apparently, Mr Kilroy hasn't even disinherited Nikki. Mr Kilroy is very generous, these days. Only a week after Mrs Flowers' accident he bought one of Mr Flowers' fastest, most exclusive yachts which must have set him back a pretty penny and landed Mr Flowers with a huge commission. It was fortunate that Mr Flowers didn't know that Jerry Kilroy also went by the name of Silky but it was unfortunate that he had a weak heart because the following week Patrick Flowers died of a cardiac arrest. Not that this stopped Jerry Kilroy from getting the hell out of Mousehole. He and Sal fled to warmer climes and better sunsets.

'Very impressive,' I tell Humpty, of his silver-service display. Humpty takes this as a cue to get out his wallet and show me pictures of his family.

'He's got a very big family,' says Jack. 'Hundreds of them, he's got.'

'We come from a good lawyering family,' Humpty announces, wiping ham grease from his face with the back of his hand.

'Show him your pictures,' says Jack, jigging his legs under the table. More medals jingle as Humpty digs into the inner pocket of his footman's coat.

'Where did you two meet?' I ask Jack.

'Met him in Newquay outside Grab City. On a bench. It's nice there now. You can buy Bombay mix.'

'Really?'

'You can get a tan. On the benches and that.'

'Yes?'

'A DHSS tan.'

With a smirk, Jack puts a pair of headphones on his ears as Humpty pulls out a small black wallet. 'This is my elder brother,' he goes. 'I've got thirteen brothers and sisters. And this is Roger, the third youngest. He likes Bombay mix, doesn't he, Jack?'

But Jack is singing a version of 'Karma Chameleon' on his new portable radio-cassette-recorder called a Sony Walkman.

'And here's Herman.'

'Karma karma karma karma karma karma karma karma ... karma ... karma karma.'

'He's the business brains of the family. Can't fault him on that.'

'Think there's something wrong with my Walkman,' Jack suddenly shouts out in a very loud voice, nudging Humpty. 'Think it might be sand ...'

I make a point of ignoring this comment. It is still too early for me to be able to deal with Jack and electronic musical equipment.

'And here's Salvatore,' Humpty says. 'He's the beauty of the family – after me, of course! He looks like a young Rhett Butler, so they say.'

Humpty's family looks more like a selection of male models from the Freeman's catalogue. I wonder why all the photographs are on cheap magazine paper and why they all seem to be wearing brand-new suits and shirts and standing in poses like male models.

Jack tugs the earphones from his head and says, between gritted teeth, 'What about my Walkman? And what about the phone call?'

I pretend not to hear this. In spite of my reconstructed personality I still find it hard to hear him getting away with being such a brat.

'Nice,' I say to Humpty, handing back the picture of Salvatore and his 'free postage and packaging' smile.

Jack nudges Humpty again hard in the ribs. 'Shall we do the phone call now?' he insists.

Humpty pats Jack's hand. 'We could do,' Humpty says. 'Just to be safe. Let's wait till after tea, though.'

Jack starts jigging up and down in his seat. 'Cakes are important, you know, Rosa,' he says, with what I think is a significant smile. I flinch slightly. I suspect he's going to come out with his Fanny Cradock line. He doesn't, though. He seems to have moved on to Mr Kipling.

'I'm waiting for a letter from Mr Kipling,' he says. 'I know you might think it sounds stupid,' he says, lowering his voice, 'but I wrote to him about some ideas. Curried Bakewell Slices. French Fancies with chilli in.' He stares at me for a while then his mouth wobbles and he bursts out laughing. 'Garr! Not really!' he hoots. 'Fell for it, didn't you?' Both he and Humpty start giggling. Then he turns serious. 'There's a boy in art-therapy class who did a work placement at the factory. He's got the contacts. I told him all about Colonel Sanders.'

'Colonel Sanders?'

A frown creeps into Jack's face. 'It's not fair, is it?'

'What isn't fair?'

'Colonel Sanders is trying to look like Mr Kipling. And who got there first?'

'Who?'

'Mr Kipling, of course!'

The *sangría* is making my meeting with Jack and Humpty a lot easier. It deadens the flinch reaction that Jack still brings about in me all too easily.

'Well, I suppose they do look a bit similar,' I say, pouring myself another glass.

'Similar!' Jack explodes. '"Exceedingly Good" and "Finger-lickin' Good". That's pretty similar too! And what about Father Christmas?'

Jack sounds angry now, agitated. 'I don't know,' he says, 'I just want to find out what's going on.' He puts down his hand and drums it on the tablecloth. 'They're going to send me a letter in Mousehole. Brenda said she'd leave a message for us here if it came. I want to see what they've got to say for themselves.' Jack looks like he's going to burst out crying, and Humpty puts his hand on top of Jack's and squeezes it.

'Could be copyright problems,' Humpty says to me, with another of his 'it's OK' winks. 'My lawyers are going to look into the matter.'

He pulls a black plastic biro from his red top pocket. He licks the end of the pen, lowers his head to reveal some Robert Robinson strands of hair pulled over a bald, pink pate from a parting that starts above his right ear, and proceeds to scribble some notes on a piece of paper. It is then that I catch Jack's eye and we suddenly and vividly melt back into the past. There is a smirk on both our lips and something warm and round and slightly golden-syrupy swells large in my stomach. It's one of our gleeful, anti-Fiona P looks, a cheese-straw-up-Miss-Norwood's-bum look, a glance that says that we're not that different, Jack and me. This comes as a bit of a shock. It reminds me that reluctant complicity was one of the things I always had with Jack – sparks of carefree mischief that slotted alongside my desire to strangle him and my occasional longing to throw my arms around his gentle neck and weep and tell him that it was all right, that he didn't have to be scared, that I'd save him from the ghosts.

The day is starting to get a bit much for me. The thought of my date isn't making things any better either. We should be going now if we're going to be there on time and I just want it to be over – even though all I really want to do is run away from here and disappear into the sea.

But then, just as we're about to leave the bar, a woman in a bobbly pastel pink tracksuit with skin as red as a freshly cooked crayfish comes up to me and says, 'Excuse me, do you know of any Indians round here?'

She's puffing nervously on a cigarette. 'I'm looking for some normal food,' she says, with an awkward smile, introducing herself as Lee-Anne from Bradford. 'How many pesetoes do you reckon it'd be for, say, lamb tikka masala?' She offers me her pack of Super Kings as if that is supposed to make the question better.

I am still reflecting with a kind of awe on her ability to say 'pesetoes' like 'potatoes' without any sign of embarrassment when she puts in another request. She wonders if I know of any bingo halls – as if she seriously wants the answer. As if she has bitten off more than she can chew simply by being in Spain. When I tell her I don't know anything about bingo, she starts taking deeper drags on the cigarette and asks about the weather. 'When will it get really hot, then?'

I look at Jack. I know that both of us feel like bursting out laughing.

'Oh, I don't know.' I shrug, starting to walk across the beach so that she can't see my face properly. 'You get swimming weather in about April. May?'

She mumbles this to herself, repeating the words like she's trying to lip synch or memorise them. I could be telling her a load of old rubbish and she wouldn't even know. I can feel her eyes still burning into my back and then Jack, who must have read my mind, takes her off my hands for a while by blurting out, 'You had your legs amputated or something?'

'Sorry?' she goes.

'You're not very good at being abroad, are you?' he says, taking one of her Super Kings.

'Me and my friend are staying in the caravan park,' she tells him, tagging along. 'How about yourselves?'

'She lives here,' Jack says, pointing at me. 'Been here a year and a half.'

'Really?' she pants. 'My friend's on a two-week contract here tarmacking the roads. She loves it.'

'We're here for two weeks too,' Jack says. 'Staying with a relative.'

'That's nice.'

'Got a date in a restaurant now.'

'How romantic. Having a date on a beach in Spain.'

'It's Rosa's date.'

'Is that her name? She looks all right.'

'She is.'

'Pity she's spoken for.'

'D'you fancy her, then?'

'Never said that.'

I can hear all this going on behind me and I'm astonished. I'm a bit cross too if Lee-Anne is the only thing I can pick up after Magalí. She's not the slightest bit *guapa* in any shape or form. I wish she'd just take her horrible tracksuit and crayfish skin and go away. I've got enough worries with the date that's coming up right now.

'Do you wear men's clothes, then?' Jack says, with a smirk.

'Sorry?'

'You know, some of them dress like men.'

'Does Rosa like that, then?'

'Don't know what she likes.'

'I wear makeup sometimes. I wear cherry-coloured lipstick.'

'Do you like Boy George?'

'Prefer Dusty Springfield.'

'Dusty Fanny.'

'Sorry?'

'Do you like Mr Kipling cakes?'

'I do, actually. Can you buy them round here, then?'

But Lee-Anne suddenly loses interest in the availability of me and Mr Kipling because we have arrived at our destination. Her mouth drops open and her lighted cigarette falls into the sand. There is a sharp intake of breath and then, with horror in her voice, she whispers: 'What the bloody heck's that?'

There is a woman sitting on the terrace of the restaurant who looks like she has been dredged up from the bottom of a lake. She has a black tongue, black teeth and a mouth like the black hole of Calcutta. She has fly eyes and a head like a swarm of hungry tentacles. Thin as a stick insect yet bloated as a dead body, she makes watery sucking noises like a clump of cockroaches swarming at night in a damp cellar. A group of cats have gathered round as she idly throws discarded husks under the table with a skinny hand dripping black blood.

'Shangri-La!' the creature moans, long and blissfully, a mulch of black maggots squirming around in her mouth.

'Looks like you should get on a broomstick,' Jack tells her, before turning to me and saying, 'Remember the witch, Rosa?'

I knew this moment was going to happen but I wasn't sure how I'd react. Right now I am more than delighted that Lee-Anne is right here, gulping at my side. Lee-Anne doesn't know it but she is helping me keep it together. I can cope with all this, I think, just as long as she is here, asking her inane questions. '*Arroz negro* is a classic variation on the more conventional paella,' I inform her, directing my attention to what the date is eating rather than to the date herself. 'It's rice cooked in squid or usually *sepia* ink. Very black. It's quite popular.'

Lee-Anne's troubled gaze is still fixed on the pair of oily black lips glistening in the sunlight.

'They have funny food here, don't they?' she mutters, under her breath.

'How do you mean?' Please don't go now, please don't leave me here.

'Horses and sheep's head and that.'

'I like your tracksuit,' I gabble. 'It's a nice pink.'

She picks up her dropped cigarette and tries to light it, her eyes still mesmerised.

'My friend went to a buffet and they gave her pig's ear,' she says.

'Really? That's interesting. Did she like it?'

'No she didn't.'

'Did she eat it?'

'Yes, she did.'

'Why did she eat it?'

'Didn't know what it was till the end.'

'What did they tell her it was?'

'Told her it was chicken.'

It's too late, though. Lee-Anne's trembling hand has been unable to relight her cigarette and her eyes suggest that she's going to go directly back to her caravan and lock herself in there for the remainder of her two week holiday. She starts mumbling about how nice it was to meet me and then scoots off hurriedly in search of her Indian or whatever it was she was really looking for in the first place.

It's too late.

* * *

'Good afternoon, Rosa,' Mrs Flowers whispers, as she watches Lee-Anne's baggy pink form scampering across the sand. 'We meet at last.' She throws her fork on to her plate.

My tongue is paralysed, my heart is racing. She still frightens me but now she repulses me as well. The aroma on the terrace of sun-tan cream and hot, salty rice is powerless against the smell of steak and kidney pie.

The smell of steak and kidney pie was the smell of the hospital – right up to the doors of Intensive Care it went and only beyond them did it turn into the sickening stench of TCP.

Round about Christmas time, Brenda wrote to tell me that Mrs Flowers had come back to life after a year of unconsciousness. She spent time recuperating in a ward in the hospital and then, a month ago, she discharged herself. She's so thin, so pale. Her black bikini just emphasises how pale and baggy her skin has become. I don't notice any golden cilia. There is just a white ridge of gristle on her belly where the feeding pipe went. I can hardly bear to look at her, let alone touch her. If you touched her it looks like she'd cave in like an old mummy – an outer crust of sunbaked chalk all hollow inside. In the blink of an eye I wish that she was dead. If she was dead there would be no need for this gruesome unearthing of her grave. But I stop myself thinking this. I've done enough to hurt her as it is. I have to own up. I have come to take my punishment and then I want it to be over.

'Good choice of restaurant, Rosa,' she drawls softly.

'Surprised Fernando hasn't told me about it. Tell him about it when I get home. Have to come here more often.'

I feel dizzy. I'd forgotten about the Fernando twist to the tale. Barcelona was mine. I thought it was mine. I have given up the red bar because of Magalí and now I'll have to give up this restaurant. And maybe this country. Mrs Flowers has taken Barcelona as her own. She is with Fernando. She is the one it belongs to now.

'You've clammed up a bit, haven't you, Rosa?' Jack says, with a smirk. 'Like clams.'

'No need to be rude, my darling,' Mrs Flowers tells him gently. 'We haven't seen each other in a long time. Lot of catching up to do, haven't we, Rosa?'

I'm not used to this new, gentle Mrs Flowers. I wish she'd just scream at me now and get it over with. I wish she'd take off her windscreen-sized sunglasses so I can see what she is thinking. I wish my heart would calm down.

Jack announces that he and Humpty are going swimming. I watch them rush down to the sea as Mrs Flowers pushes away her plate and lights a cigarette.

'So, you're living here now apparently?' I ask feebly, sitting myself quietly in a seat next to her.

'Came over a couple of weeks ago.' She nods. 'Hospital said I should convalesce a bit longer. I laughed at them. I told them that if I can pull through a year on a life-support machine I can pull through a new life on the Costa Blanca.'

'I . . . I see.'

'Yes, and I promised the doctor I'd lay off the booze if ever I found myself in a rusty Mini van in the vicinity of a canal.'

'It must have been . . .'

'Bloody freezing in there!' she chuckles.

'And – and what are you doing now?'

'Living off my dead husband,' she barks. 'Why?'

My heart starts racing again and I look down at my feet, waiting for the swoop to come, for the big snappy mandibles to come and eat me up. But there is just a cough. A hacking cough. Mrs Flowers clutches her chest. She's forgotten that she's not her old self. She slugs back some *sangría.*

'I'm sorry,' I mumble.

'What?' She bangs her glass down on the table. 'Sorry for what?'

'I'm sorry for . . . for ruining your life.'

I look at myself squirming in her sunglasses. My shoulders are hunched. I look terrified. The wrath is imminent. She sighs and takes another drag on her cigarette. A plume of white smoke drifts gently up into the blue sky. 'My dear Rosa,' she purrs, 'I don't know what kind of drama you've been concocting in your head but as far as I'm concerned you did me an enormous favour. My son still seems to worship me, I have a free psychiatric nurse for him in the shape of your dear mother, and I've had a chance to come back to live in Spain with a man who adores me.' She makes a lopsided smile and dabs a dark red trickle from the corner of her mouth. 'A fairy-tale ending, I'd call it.'

She yawns and picks at the *arroz negro* pan with a flimsy hand.

'You shouldn't take life so seriously, Rosa,' she goes on, dabbing at her lips with a napkin but only making the mess worse. 'Lord knows, I take life with a ludicrously large pinch of salt. What's more, I intend to carry on having a good time. And that will be pretty much until I'm dead. There, that's my philosophy. And yours?'

The wiggling laugh comes like a snake that goes on and on like it's never going to stop. A mocking laugh that turns my mind, my body, the whole beach, the whole sky, into the screech of sucking cockroaches, the screech of air being sucked out of the day by Mrs Flowers' black mouth. She's telling me that she doesn't care, that there's no point in forgiveness because she doesn't care anyway. That she's never cared. About anything. She is just a leech – she sucks, she drains, she gets bored. She sucks and drains some more. Just like Magalí and all her friends who sucked and drained. I can't believe that she's being so casual while I've been burning up on hot coals for the past year. For nearly two years, ever since the night of Jack's birthday when I put her in Intensive Care – everyone said it wasn't my fault but I knew it was – ever since that night, I have been living in hell. I have tried everything to forget about her: shoving her to the back of my mind, forbidding Brenda to talk about her in her letters, pretending to be Spanish, snorting dessert, trying to bury my past entirely – there is nothing

I haven't tried. When, three months ago, Brenda decided it was time to tell me the truth, I considered finding my own canal to throw myself into. When I discovered that Mrs Flowers wasn't going to die after all, that she was off the life-support machine, getting better and coming to Barcelona at any minute, I couldn't believe it. I was terrified. I thought the haunting would never stop until I saw her again and she came to me in tongues of flame and torched me to dust.

And now it seems that all that worry has been a waste of time. That there was no point in only half enjoying Spain while the other half of me lived in a furnace with Mrs Flowers. Because she didn't give a hoot anyway. Even now I'm not significant to her. She's laughing at me. I start to tremble. I am pale, paler than she could ever be. I am about to detonate. I will erupt with more black bile than she could ever muster. I am the one who will explode into flames, I will fire all over her, spew a siphon of blazing squid ink all over her bloated stick body and puffy face.

I am about to yell at her exactly what my philosophy is – except that I am not really sure what my philosophy is any more, apart from the fact that the University of Life is a big swizz, that it's no guarantee against anything. I can see her trying to hold her mouth back from breaking into a smile. She hasn't lost her knack for making me feel foolish. I am fourteen years old all over again. I probably don't look like a scary squid fireball at all. How come she still has the power to frighten me, even with a face like a dirty old miner?

Then she stops laughing. Something else has caught her

attention. She creaks herself up from the chair and starts waving frantically in the direction of the bus stop. In the distance, an old man is emerging from a bus holding an enormous bonquet of white flowers. You can see that he has a large stomach, chicken legs and hair dyed so unnaturally black that a halo of red glows round the top of his head. 'Fernando!' she yells. 'Fernando, *guapo!*' as if Fernando is one of Humpty's male models from the Freeman's catalogue.

Then, suddenly, she stops waving. She removes her sunglasses and flops down in the chair. She exhales deeply. Her head drops forward onto her chest as if she is exhausted. All of a sudden she looks dead. She is nothing but stillness and the back of a neck. The gentle back of a neck. I was wrong. They are still there, the cilia – the kind of fine hairs that make you think of someone coming along and bludgeoning their owner to death. They are soft and innocent and still golden, they are downy and snug as the foamy mesh inside a broad-bean pod. Slowly, she opens her eyes and sits up straight. She glances at me with a sleepy gaze. Her eyes are no cauldron. There are no slimy feelers or swarming cockroaches. Just embers. There's no need to freeze her on a candle under salt in the ice box. Mrs Flowers is not only broomsticks and damp cellars. She is tinned steak and kidney pie. She is daffodils in spring. She is a messy eater.

'Look at Fernando,' she growls, with a smile. She turns back to me. 'Brings me bloody lilies. Makes you think, doesn't it?'

'Pardon?'

'About how God must be a schizophrenic. One day he's this man who creates daffodils and daisies and the next he turns into some awful fashion designer who goes overboard with the pinking shears and comes up with lilies and orchids.' She throws a black shawl round her shivering shoulders. 'Awful.' She chuckles. 'So blousey.'

'Smell a bit artificial,' I say.

'Smell like the grave,' she snaps, her eyes meeting mine at last. The wild light is back. It blazes like nails that dig in just in the nick of time as you were about to fall off the cliff.

'Still haven't managed to pull that one off, have I?' she says. Still staring at me, she pulls me into her eyes and I see that they look bewildered. 'Do you think I'm just going to have to give up and be happy after all?'

She hesitates momentarily and then her mouth breaks into a grin. A delicate bird's claw clasps my hand and pulls me up from the plastic chair while the other one tops up two very large glasses of *sangría*. We both walk away from the table clutching hands and glasses and when we reach the shore we sit on the sand. We look out at the sea and listen to the waves for a while. I'm glad the waves are there. Finally, I say, 'It's pretty brave of you to come back.'

'You think so?' She smiles, still looking out at the horizon. 'Life's all about making choices, isn't it?'

'I suppose so.' I think of the Tom, Dick and Harry tunnels in *The Great Escape*. I wonder which one I should go down now.

'Choices,' she says, with a tired sigh. 'And it's so hard to know what the right choice is.'

'Do you think you've made the right choice?'

'Not sure, Rosa. Maybe I'm just being bloody-minded. Have you ever noticed that the older people get the more cowardly they become? The more possibilities they have the less they do? Hate that.'

A grin creeps into her lips. It makes me relax at last. How can I not love being in the presence of Mrs Flowers? Just to listen to her. To her wisdom. 'You're like me,' I say, fixing my eyes on a lacy, lapping wave. 'You like escape.'

'Escape?' She turns and looks at me as if I've said something very strange indeed. 'I want roots,' she says urgently. 'Roots!' Her hands clasp tightly together over her knees. 'Sometimes you need to be adored more than other times, don't you find, Rosa? Adoration makes roots grow. And sometimes people need to take root so they can grow strong before becoming thistledown again.'

I can hear Fernando calling to her from the beach.

'He's safe and stable,' she says quietly. 'He's right at the moment.'

'I thought he'd be . . . well, different looking,' I mumble.

'You mean my new boyfriend's ugly?'

After a split second I realise that she's joking. 'Well . . .'

'Well, Rosa Barge, in my experience attractive people are never grateful enough. They're too busy loving themselves to love you as much as you need to be loved.'

I feel myself blush and I'm thinking of telling her that I

agree. That I have experience of this. I'm wondering if she'd like to hear about Magalí. But then she says something odd. She says, 'You're the brave one, Rosa Barge.'

'Me?'

'You're brave because you want to live like a ghost. You're always dreaming of escape, always dreaming of the taste of different air in different places but you're still plagued by doubts. And so you should be. I told you about the curse of travel.'

'And what about you?'

'Me? I'm just a bit mad.'

'But maybe putting down roots is good, though.' I'm confused now. 'You put down roots and then you get strong. That's what you said.'

She reflects for a while before snapping on her sunglasses once more.

'Rosa,' she says briskly, 'nothing in life is ever that certain. That's the point.'

'You're wise.' I shrug, keeping my eye on the sea.

'Wise!' she scoffs. 'Listen, Rosa, when I'm finally standing tall and strong I might do the thistledown thing but probably I'll just fuck up again.'

She heaves herself painfully to her feet and waves over at the beer belly sprouting a bouquet of waxy flowers that is walking slowly towards us.

'Maybe I'll just wake up one morning and look over at him and go, "What the hell is that?" And maybe I won't be able to leave because I'll have hit the bottle again and my roots will be well and truly pickled.' She chuckles.

'Never mind, I'll probably have died of boredom by then anyway.'

I want to ask her what she thinks I should do now, about if it's possible to be half roots and half tornado, about if she believes it's possible to join up your roots with someone else then fly up in the air in a tangled mesh of everlasting thistledown. But she just bids me a 'Happy trails,' and then she's gone, zigzagging over the sand towards the man with the flowers, closely followed by a procession of manky cats.

The sun is lowering in the sky. I squint back over the waves, looking for the edge of the world, but all I see are Jack and Humpty, wading around like they're treading on funny pins. It's like they never left Mousehole. They squeal, 'Ouch! Ouch!' every time a cold March wave crashes on to them above their swimming trunks, glazing their torsos like iced buns.

I put my nose into the glass of sweet red fire and I breathe in. I think of Tom, Dick and Harry. I think of rising high in the air like a kite even as my fingers are digging deep down into the sand like octopus tentacles. I start to drink and through the smeared glass I can see that the edge of the world is butterscotch Angel Delight and apocalyptic bubble-gum pink. On the edge of the world there is a line of living prawns in pink leotards and orange stockings, each with a dozen crunchy limbs sprinkled with golden cilia, each with a bristly headdress swaying in the breeze, all beaming, all tap-dancing in fluid motion. Led by Tom the cabin-boy cartwheeling through the waves in pink top hat and orange tails, they link legs and make high, bouncy kicks, calling out in a shimmy of words soft as squid skin, '*¡Que venga! Que venga Rosa al horizonte a chuparnos la cabeza!*' Come! Let Rosa come! Let Rosa come to the horizon and suck our heads!

There is a buzzing in the wind from the old ladies playing poker with oranges instead of money. 'You need to get good kitchen units,' one of them is saying. 'I'm going to get black marble worktops. Holy bread! You can only get the stuff in Norway.'

'*¿Ay, sí?*' the others go in wonderment.